THE TROUBLE WITH MAGIC AND FAERY CURSES

A CARY REDMOND NOVEL, BOOK 5

KAT SIMONS

*For my beloved family. We made it through a really bad year together.
And I'm so grateful for having you with me on this journey.
To better years ahead.*

*C*ary considered the little brownie chattering at her. She couldn't understand a word it was saying, but it sounded very urgent. The high pitched, rapid fire rolling…language? Yeah, the little guy was definitely talking and those were words he was speaking. Accompanying gestures too. But…

Nope. None of it made the first bit of sense to her.

Behind her, another flash of light from the attacking hobgoblins lit up the air. She could just see the sparks in her peripheral vision. It wasn't often she found herself protecting one member of the Fae realm from another. They tended to keep this kind of fighting to Faery and out of her world. Which was really handy because the Fae were powerful, overwhelming, and occasionally batshit crazy.

Her faery mentor, Jaxer, would not argue with this assessment.

"I'm sorry, little guy," she said to the brownie, "but whatever language you're speaking, I don't. I can't understand a word you're saying."

More rapid-fire chittering and frantic hand gestures. Cary frowned. This was really frustrating. She knew whatever he was trying to say was important. His thin little brown body vibrated with urgency. His brown hair, short and raged, waved around his head with every movement. His sharp, angular features tightened with his own frustration. His brown eyes were huge and round, staring into hers as he spoke as if trying to force her to understand by sheer will. And she just knew if she listened to him long enough, she'd figure this out.

Problem was, she didn't think they had that kind of time.

She glanced back at the three hobgoblins arrayed in a half-circle behind her. They were all standing inside a clump of trees just off the road leading up the hill to the Rose Garden. The air had that crisp, freshness of predawn to it, with a hint of the flowers from the nearby garden faintly perfuming the area. But she could already feel the heat just at the edges. The early summer in Portland had been warm and sunny so far, boding well for the rest of the season, but this week the temperature had climbed into the nineties and didn't seem inclined to drop. And it was actually more humid than they normally got this time of year. Nothing like that one, and *only*, time she'd visited her sister in New York City in August—that had been grossly humid and she refused to visit in the summers after that trip—but still, muggy for Portland in summertime. She really hated muggy.

At least this early in the morning, before the sun was up, the area was quiet and no errant humans were driving by to interfere and give her one more person to protect.

The hobgoblins were huge creatures, easily three or four times her width and about twice her height. Their gray skin covered thick muscles beneath rough leather pants and jerkins. That leather was gonna feel miserable in another few hours when the heat really got going.

The center hobgoblin, the one throwing jars of some sort of magical potion at her, had a long, hooked nose and shaggy greenish-brown hair. She kind of thought he might be the leader, but it was hard to tell. He was the one pulling magical Molotov cocktails out of the leather courier bag hanging at his hip. But none of them had said anything since she'd arrived, just started tossing those pretty green glass bottles at her and the brownie. So she couldn't be sure who was in charge.

The other two hobgoblins were not, outside of their size and being, you know, hobgoblins, particularly remarkable looking. They had some lumps and warts decorating their faces—typical species traits and given the arrangements could be considered handsome to other hobgoblins. She wasn't sure how to judge that, though. One was bald. The other had a long mane of black hair pulled back in a low tail. They both had muddy brown eyes. And at present, all they were doing was standing there staring at her and the brownie.

Hobgoblins, unlike their cousins the goblins, didn't tend to come into this realm much. According to Cary's reading, it was because they didn't like the smell. She'd also been under the impression they were supposed to be *smaller* than goblins on average. The one hobgoblin she'd encountered before this had been the same size as the brownie. Either she'd missed her guess on these guys and they were something different, or she just didn't know enough about hobgoblins.

Which, given the shear amount of stuff she'd been trying to learn over the last six and a half years, was entirely possible. There was a lot of stuff she didn't know nearly enough about.

She sighed and turned her back to them again to focus on the still frantically talking brownie.

Her bosses had sent her to intervene and save the little guy, waking her from a dead sleep to get her here in time. It was her job as a magical Protector to get between the good guys and the bad guys to keep the good guys safe. She even got paid for it. But typical of her bosses—who were also Fae, though members of a species native to North America—they hadn't explained *why* she needed to protect the brownie. Just that she was needed and needed fast.

She'd arrived just as the hobgoblins had stepped through a break in the fabric of reality that separated this realm from Faery and started throwing bottles. She'd skidded between them and the brownie just in time, only getting a little cut from the very first shattered glass. Her magic was purely defensive—and technically not even her own; she just channeled what her bosses had given her—so she couldn't really do anything to stop the hobgoblins from throwing the magic bottles. But she could stand in their way from now to the end of days and keep the brownie from getting hurt. A wonderful side effect of that was that she didn't get hurt either. At least, not much.

Okay, she couldn't be killed while she was protecting. She had actually racked up a substantial record of weird injuries over the years. But nothing deadly. Sometimes, especially when magic was involved, little things got through. And jumping in front of moving bullets was rarely fun. Still, she survived it all. She even had faster-than-normal healing thanks to her job, so the cut on her hand would be all better in another few minutes.

She could be killed, though. The trick for her was being in Protector mode, channeling that shielding magic that kept the good guys safe. If she was in the middle of doing her job as a walking, talking Kevlar vest, she could survive…well, just about anything as it turned out—though sometimes the worse for wear at the end. But when she wasn't in Protector mode, she was just an ordinary human, as vulnerable to bullets and magic potions as anyone.

She paused at that thought. Turns out she wasn't as ordinary as she'd previously thought. But that was an ongoing worry she didn't really have time to dwell on just then. The brownie's attempt at communicating had grown more frantic. There was something really important he needed to tell her.

"I am so sorry," she told him, raising her hands in a helpless shrug. "I just can't understand what you're saying."

Damn, she wished Jaxer could be here to help.

Jaxer was a faery—no subspecies, but one of the highborn Fae— and he'd definitely be able to speak brownie. But as her mentor, he wasn't supposed to help her with anything this year. She was smack in the middle of her seventh year as a Protector and the Seventh Year was a test year. If she managed to survive it, she apparently came into her full powers, whatever that meant. She was much more focused on the "surviving it" goal.

"Is it the hobgoblins?" she asked. Maybe if they were patient, she could work this out. The brownie seemed to understand what she was saying even if she couldn't understand him.

The brownie nodded, his little head bouncing up and down rapidly. The gesture made his short crop of brown hair ripple.

"Okay. So it's something to do with the attackers." Another bottle shattered against her shields, spraying orange sparkles and green glass. "You know you're safe right now, right? They can't get through me to get to you."

He nodded again. Then started talking fast.

"Wait." She held up her hands. "Are they after you for a specific reason?"

He nodded, making a gesture she didn't understand.

"So not just a random attack on a random brownie?"

He shook his head. Then stomped his foot and put his hands on his hips.

"Hey, I'm trying here. And this is more information than I've previously gotten from all your talk that I can't understand. Be patient. We have time."

The brownie made a very pointed look at the sky, which was growing lighter as they spoke.

She sighed. "Yes, yes, the sun is coming up soon. I know. But if you'll be a little patient, we do still have time." More glass shattered and scattered around her. This time the sparkles were a bright white. They must be changing up the potions. "So, they're after you specifically. Did you say something rude?"

Head shake.

"Did you attack someone?"

Irritated head shake and another foot stop.

"Did you steal something?"

He shook his head. Then paused and nodded.

"That's less helpful. But a hint. You didn't but you did steal something?"

He nodded, jumping around enthusiastically. He said something she still didn't understand, and gestured at the hobgoblins.

"You stole from them?"

Emphatic—and again, irritated—head shake no.

"You stole from…someone they work for? Are they, like, guards or something?"

The brownie nodded and made a continue gesture with his little hand.

"They're guards, you stole something they were supposed to be protecting…?"

He nodded.

"From their boss?"

A rapid and enthusiastic series of words in his language.

"An actual object?" Since he'd said he both did and didn't steal something… "Or is this more like…information or a secret or something?"

The brownie did a jig and patted her on the hand. Then did another little dance, spinning in circles.

Okay. She'd hit on something there. "So you stole a secret of some kind? The hobgoblins are here to bring you back?"

Head shake.

"Kill you?"

Head nod.

"Wow. That must be some secret."

Emphatic head nod.

More glass and sparkles burst behind her. She ignored the hobgoblins. "And you stole it from someone powerful?"

Another nod.

"On purpose?"

The brownie made a face and looked away.

"So, not on purpose. You accidentally stumbled on the secret and now they want to kill you for it. Do I have the gist?"

He nodded and held his hands out to the side in a little helpless gesture that made her want to hug him. Poor little guy.

"Well, don't worry. I'll keep you safe."

She looked around, considering how she could get them back to her house—where, hopefully, she'd find a book in her secret attic with a Rosetta stone for brownie to English translation; she didn't remember having one, but that didn't mean she hadn't picked one up over the years—without putting him into her car.

Almost all the denizens of Faery had an allergy to iron, to one degree or another. The severity of allergic reaction depended on the species. Goblins had the least trouble with it. In fact, they kind of liked the stuff even though it gave some of them a burn. She wasn't sure if the same went for hobgoblins. Though cousins, the two species had quite a lot of differences.

Jaxer could handle iron better than any highborn Cary had heard of, but he still didn't climb into cars if he could avoid it because steal had high enough iron content to irritate. Jaxer was counting down until humans had fully developed plastic cars with no actual steel and iron involved—Cary wasn't hopeful this would happen in her lifetime. He managed to navigate the human world without going into anaphylactic shock or burning up or breaking out in a constant rash. But he still didn't much *like* iron, especially pure iron that wasn't part of an alloy.

As far as Cary could remember, brownies were very very susceptible to the iron allergy. Which meant even her home would be an uncomfortable place for the little guy. But she had a backyard with trees so he could hang out there and be okay. The problem was getting through the city and back to her house. They weren't exactly an easy walking distance.

If Deacon had been in town, she could have called him and had him just run the brownie back to her place. As a leopard shifter, he was fast enough to get the brownie there in a few minutes, even in his human form, and at that speed, he blurred to human vision so no one would likely notice. But he was still in Eugene at a board meeting for the family business. And he wasn't due back until that afternoon.

That was another long and complicated bit of her life—having a leopard mate who hadn't been able to be away from her for very long until only just recently because otherwise he lost control of his leopard half, but who nonetheless had other things to do because he was on the board of directors of his family business which ran a bunch of animal rescue shelters around the country specializing in exotics. And she'd been really really upset that he couldn't work for so long because he *saved animals for a living.*

He'd finally been able to stay away from her for a few days at a time and not be super dangerous, so long as his mother was somewhere in the vicinity to help him control his leopard. He'd gone back to work full time last month, which she'd wanted to celebrate. He'd been pretty meh about the whole thing. And he definitely hadn't wanted to go away on this business trip. But she'd encouraged it. She loved having Deacon around and in her life, but frankly, the fact that she loved it so much scared the crap out of her. The fact that she felt his absence physically was equally disturbing. The mate business was new to her and because she wasn't a shifter it affected her differently than it did him, but she was still affected by it. In ways that made her distinctly uncomfortable sometimes.

Her reluctance to be away from him was one of the major "sometimes." Her inability to keep her hands off him…she minded that a lot less.

Without a handy shifter partner to do the running for her, though, she had to figure out a way to get the brownie away from the hobgoblins on her own, to somewhere safe, where she could translate his language. They needed to talk about this secret he'd discovered so she could figure out a way to keep him permanently safe. Which was the job she'd been sent to do. Without help from her mentor or the Nags— her maybe a little too on-the-nose nickname for her bosses.

If she was going to do her job, she needed to figure out what the brownie was trying to tell her.

More glass shattered around her as she considered the options. The number of bottles seemed to be increasing in frequency. Geez, how many magic potions did the hobgoblin have in that bag?

She glanced at him long enough to say, "You can stop now. You're wasting your magic."

The hobgoblin grunted and tossed another bottle at her.

She shook her head as it shattered a foot away, this time leaving a smear of rainbow color on the seemingly empty air where her shield resided. The color turned a deep purple black before sliding down to the ground where it sizzled in the dirt and grass like acid. That particular potion left a cloud of rotten eggs and piss stench in the air. Gross.

"Are you done yet?" she asked.

The hobgoblin with the bottles grunted something and turned to consult with his associates. She returned to her problem of where to take the brownie.

Her home was out of the question, at least in the immediate future. Too far and complicated. She needed to get somewhere nearby. Who did she know in this part of the city who might be able to translate brownie? Within walking distance? Who wouldn't be upset about her waking them up at this early hour?

She visualized where she was on her mental map of the city, and a perfect solution dropped onto that map like a little red flashing location pin.

The Bookstore!

2

The hobgoblins threw one last bottle of potion at them, this one not even pretending at sparkles and color. It just burst into a sickly green and black cloud of poison. There must have been a smell element to it, because suddenly Cary couldn't smell anything anymore. Just the small circle of grass and dirt and trees behind her shield.

She waited for the cloud to clear, then met the lead hobgoblin's eyes. He snarled at her, revealing some wickedly jagged green teeth and barked something in yet another language she didn't understand.

But in perfect, if guttural and accented English, he said, "This isn't done, human. We'll be back for the criminal. You have made an enemy in Faery."

"Why do bad guys always say 'this isn't done'?" she asked both the hobgoblins and the brownie. "I mean they *always* say something just like that. It gets really monotonous after hearing it for years."

"Bitch," the bald hobgoblin barked at her.

She grinned at him.

The hobgoblin with the long black hair dragged his sharp curved gray nail over the air and tore open a hole into Faery. All three leapt through, the bottle tossing leader the last to go. He held her gaze as he passed out of her realm and into his. The hole in reality separating them closed while he continued to stare at her.

"Well," she said with a little head shake to hide her discomfort. "That was interesting."

She faced the brownie again. "We need to get to a safer location where I can figure out what you're trying to tell me. My home is too far away but there's a super cool bookstore nearby, and I'm sure we can find help there. Is that okay? Will you stick with me for a bit longer?"

The brownie looked pointedly at the place where the hobgoblins had gone and then nodded emphatically.

She got the feeling there was some annoyance in that gesture, like she was being an idiot to assume he wouldn't stick with his source of safety.

"Hey, I don't want to assume," she said defensively. "Some people are in a hurry to walk into danger."

The brownie swept his thin arm out in an "after you" gesture, which made her snort in amusement. She turned toward the road, but stuck to the trees lining the roadside so the brownie could remain walking on dirt as long as possible. The more they could keep him in contact with soil and trees, the better he'd be.

The Bookstore was one of those places you had to know about in order to find. The first time she'd gone, Jaxer had given her directions, and she'd stood outside the door of a shop that looked boarded up and closed for a long time before finally pushing inside. Over the years since then, the "door" into the Bookstore had moved a few times. It wasn't a place confined to space. Or time for that matter. And entrances into the place popped up where they needed to be at any given point.

Most creatures from most of the realms were allowed into the Bookstore, so long as they minded their manners. There were a few spells on the place to help with that, too, ensuring natural enemies could coexist without, say, destroying the store and everyone inside. Only a very few realms were banned from accessing the Bookstore. Cary had never learned exactly what happened to initiate those bans, but since one of the realms was a particularly nasty demon realm, she had ideas.

The coolest thing about the Bookstore was that once you'd found it, it remembered your DNA—which apparently it scanned when you walked through the door. You always left into the same time and place from which you entered. A nice side effect of that was that the store couldn't be used as a passthrough to other realms or times. But mostly, she loved that she never had to worry about getting lost.

And when the Bookstore moved, she could always find it again.

Which was handy in her present circumstance, because it was actually closer to her current location than it had been the last time she'd gone.

At the base of the road, when they moved back onto sidewalk-lined city streets, she ended up having to carry the brownie. The minute he stepped too close to a car parked on the roadside, he started to shiver and whine in pain. The whole experience was going to be miserable for the poor guy. Cary just hoped he could go inside the Bookstore without issue. She couldn't recall having seen any brownies there, but she had seen a gnome once who hadn't seemed overly bothered by her surroundings, and gnomes had a pretty bad allergy, too.

"Almost there," she reassured the brownie as he wrapped his thin arms around her neck and buried his face against her shoulder.

She knew, in the logical part of her brain, that the brownie—being immortal and all—was likely older than her by several centuries. But in that moment and given his size in her arms, it was super hard not to think of him as a child in need. That just triggered her protective instincts even more and made her determined to get to the bottom of the threat against him so she could keep him safe.

The entrance to the Bookstore was located on a side street with limited traffic amidst a row of doors into small trendy coffee shops, restaurants, and clothing stores. The store next to the Bookstore had t-shirts in the window sporting funny sayings and pictures of the latest video game characters—most of which she didn't have the first clue about. She'd have to ask her niece who was the family gamer. The Bookstore's front windows looked empty and there were two boards across the larger of the two windows and a crack in the glass. Etched in white on the swinging glass front door were the words The Bookstore in a pretty, elegant script. But other than that signage, there was nothing indicating this particular shop was currently occupied.

The brownie chattered at her, making a gesture at the door.

She assumed he was asking the obvious question. "Yes, this is the right place. Trust me."

She pushed at the front door. There was a moment's pause, then a slight click, then the door swung opened.

A cool waft of air brushed her face as she stepped into the temperature-controlled interior. She wondered how it felt to those coming in from colder climates. Was it a warm burst of air as they stepped out of the snow? For her, it felt like the loveliest of air conditioners and she was grateful. The sun was up, the air already starting to warm. So far it was pleasant enough, but by the time she left the store, it was going to be hot.

And she'd left her car parked a few miles away.

Ah well. That's what taxis were for. Except, of course, she'd likely still have the little brownie with her.

One worry at a time. First, they had to figure out what was going on. If he'd fled Faery for her realm, he couldn't go back yet. That meant she had to keep him safe in her realm until he could.

The shelves and book-covered tables, the scent of paper and lemon-scented furniture polish, the soothing lighting and bright atmosphere always made Cary feel both overwhelmed and calm. She loved this place. Even the stack marked Demonology and Phylogeny seemed soothing. A place to find answers where no one would try to kill her.

Well, except for that one time. But literally that had been the *only* time anyone had tried to kill anyone while she'd been in the Bookstore.

There were only a few patrons circulating at that moment, which was kind of nice. It was usually pretty packed. Cary scanned the various creatures—a shifter in his human form (she could spot them by the way they moved), two vampires she didn't know (which was good as she'd had trouble with vampires a few months back and didn't need any right now) on opposite sides of the store, a creature with a tail and horns but who didn't seem particularly demonic hovered near the section on ancient religions, a being with three eyes and a squid-shaped body lounged at the back seeming to read three books at once, and a few more human-shaped people she couldn't identify as anything but human. That didn't mean they were human. They could just be very good at disguising their natures.

So long as they weren't the particular wizard—or wizards since Sheldon was still alive last she'd heard—trying to kill her, she didn't really care *what* they were.

Only the shifter and one of the vampires paid any attention to Cary and the brownie as they moved toward the central counter, and those were just passing glances. Everyone else was fully absorbed in their own business. Behind the u-shaped wooden desk that served as the checkout counter, the Bookstore's owner and proprietor stood smiling at her.

Renee had switched from a more seventies Earth era look to nineties grunge in the last month. Torn jeans and an oversized red flannel shirt suited her tall, thin frame. She'd kept her hair in an afro but had cut it a little tighter to her head. She wasn't wearing any jewelry, but then she rarely did. And her makeup was muted and complimented her dark skin nicely.

The only thing that marked Renee as being not quite human were her eyes—black with sparkles of white like stars in them. After all these years, Cary still wasn't entirely sure what Renee was. Jaxer had hinted that she might be a god of some sort even though Renee wouldn't call herself one. Sometimes Cary wondered if she was an alien—she did have green blood. Wasn't that supposed to be a sign of being an alien?

In the end, *what* Renee was didn't really matter. She kept the Bookstore going, ensured it was safe, and always had a friendly smile for her customers. Plus, she seemed to know everything. Which made her one of Cary's favorite people.

"I need some help," she said without preamble.

Renee glanced at the brownie still in Cary's arms and nodded. "Language problem?" she asked.

"How did you know?"

"Brownies are good at understanding other languages but their ability to speak them is notoriously bad." Renee switched to talking in a series of chattering high-pitched words that sounded a lot like the brownie's language from earlier, though with a different accent. The brownie jumped from Cary's arms to the counter and turned animated in his rapid-fire rush to explain what Cary hadn't been able to understand.

Well, that was easy, she thought, watching the conversation in bemusement.

"Ah," Renee said. Then went back to the brownie's language.

Cary tried to wait patiently. She wasn't a particularly patient person. But she did try.

After about ten minutes, she finally said, "So, what's happened? Did he explain why a bunch of hobgoblins chased him into this realm and tried to kill him?"

"He's getting to that part," Renee assured.

Just getting to it? What had they been talking about up to now?

Another ten minutes passed—or was it an eternity? Cary watched the conversation, tapping her toes inside her hiking boots and working hard not to rush them. Whatever the brownie was saying, it had creases forming on Renee's otherwise smooth forehead as she nodded.

"Okay, well." Renee looked up at Cary. "That's not good."

"What? What?"

"Seems he was tending to one of his trees in the royal palace..." She paused as the brownie said something else. Nodded. Then, "Sorry, yes, the English royal palace." Renee shrugged. "So many Faery courts. Have to specify or it gets confusing."

Cary nodded. That, at least, she remembered. But only because Jaxer was related to both the English court and the Irish court in ways he'd never explained to her. The added complexity of her boss's relationship to the rest of Faery only confused the matter. The North American Fae and the European Fae had some…issues apparently. But the source of those issues was complicated and not well examined in the literature. Cary suspected it had to do with the Europeans moving out to colonize other places and devastating the native peoples, but neither the Nags nor Jaxer would confirm that suspicion for her.

"He says he wasn't listening to the two highborns on purpose," Renee continued. "They were walking the gardens. He made an effort to blend into his surroundings so as not to disturb them. That's part of his job—to look after his particular section of the gardens and keep everything growing and healthy but without anyone noticing him." As an aside, Renee said, "Brownies are really good at tending formal gardens. Renowned for it even outside Faery."

"Cool," Cary said because it seemed like she should say something to that fact.

"Anyway, he overheard the highborn Fae talking and..." She paused to confer with the brownie again. "And Borir says they were discussing treason. Which, to be fair, isn't particularly unusual among the highborns at court either. Any of the courts. The English court seems to be the worst for it. Lots of plotting and potential coups in the works all the time. Tatiana and Oberon usually sort it all out without much trouble," Renee said this last as another aside.

The fact that the queen and king of the English court were still Tatiana and Oberon after all these centuries was pretty damned impressive, and proof they were good at stopping coup plots.

"Apparently," Renee continued, "something these particular Fae said struck Borir as being quite worrisome." She looked back to the brownie and asked another question. The brownie—Borir apparently—answered with a lot of hand gestures. "Yes, they were talking about a... spell or a weapon that could destroy Faery. Something that Borir, and most Fae, think is a myth. The word isn't translating well, so I can't be sure if it's an actual physical weapon, or a spell, or a bespelled weapon." She tried to clarify with Borir, but then shook her head. "No, the word in Brownie could mean any of those things. He doesn't know how to define it any better."

"But whatever it is, it could end Faery? That seems...kind of huge."

"Yes, it does," Renee agreed. "And not something I've heard of before."

"Which makes it a pretty serious secret whatever *it* is."

"Exactly."

"Does he know who the highborns were?" Cary asked, leaning in a little to rest her hands on the counter near Borir. She met his huge brown eyes. "Could you give us their names?"

He shook his head and said something that Renee translated as, "He doesn't get involved with the highborns because it's safer not to. Most of the brownies stick to themselves and only concern themselves with brownie politics, which is generally pretty straightforward. Not a lot of subterfuge and secret machinations. They don't like the deceptions inherent in highborn politics, so they just don't concern themselves with it. So long as the brownies can continue on about their business, they don't need to know who the highborns are."

"Damn." Cary rubbed a hand over her face. "But they must have thought you could identify them, or they wouldn't have sent someone after you to kill you."

"He'd know them again if he saw them," Renee said. "Brownies have excellent memories and can see through glamour magic—it helps them do their job tending to magical plants."

"Ah," Cary said. That was interesting, actually. Her mentor was known for his superb glamour skills. Borir would see through it, though, which meant putting Jaxer in the same room with Borir could be really interesting. For Cary anyway.

"Even without their names," Renee said, "Borir would eventually be able to point them out to the king and queen."

"So the conspirators decided to kill him," Cary said.

"They tried anyway. I suppose they weren't expecting him to find help." Renee smiled at Cary. They never really discussed it, but Renee was aware of Protectors and what they could and couldn't do. And that Cary was one.

"Why *did* you run away to this realm?" Cary asked Borir. "You couldn't have expected me either. And the hobgoblins were obviously able to follow."

Borir said something. Renee said something back, her eyebrows rising high over her star-filled eyes.

Then she said, "He's looking for…Jaxer." Renee met Cary's gaze. "He seems to think Jaxer can save him and all of Faery."

He came looking for Jaxer to be his savior? Jaxer who'd abandoned his position in Faery several centuries ago? Who had disavowed his links to two European courts so he could work with Cary's bosses training Protectors? Jaxer who didn't want anything to do with the Old World Fae anymore?

Borir expected *Jaxer* to save Faery?

Oh boy.

3

"Guess I have to go find Jaxer, then," Cary said with a sigh.

She hadn't seen him in at least two months. He wasn't supposed to be helping her with her test year. He wasn't supposed to interfere or aid her. Yet for the first few months, he'd been around a lot—and he'd helped her. But always with excuses. He'd been trying to track down the wizard out to kill her because the wizard's vendetta had started before the Seventh Year test began. He'd helped her—at the Nags' behest—with a dangerous magical weapon. And he'd helped her with some vampire troubles. All of which he had excuses her bosses couldn't gainsay.

He'd also told her he loved her.

She didn't share his feelings. Not romantically. She loved him as a friend and mentor, but not as anything more. And those conversations had been heartbreaking.

Since then, of course, things had been strange and not always comfortable, even though they'd been trying to get back to a place of friendship. He'd pulled back more and more, as he was supposed to during this year, so she couldn't be too upset by that. It was the distance in their friendship that made her sad. She supposed he had to put some space between them for his own sake. She couldn't blame him for that. Still, she missed her friend.

She had no idea what he'd been up to since the last time she'd seen him. For all she knew, he'd moved on to training another Protector. And she wasn't entirely sure how to find him. She had an idea where to start. She just wasn't sure it would work.

There was also the added difficulty of Borir and what to do with him while she went looking for Jaxer. She could hardly drag the poor brownie all around Portland, even if her end goal was a wild place. He'd had a hard enough time just getting here. She didn't want to go back to the spot the hobgoblins had attacked them—too easy for them to find him there again. She needed to get to a wooded area, but a place isolated enough to get Jaxer's attention was probably going to require a drive. And if she couldn't track down Jaxer directly, she was going to have to go through the Nags. That would also require a car trip back to her house.

She definitely couldn't put the brownie through all that.

She frowned at the little guy as he sat down on the counter, his shoulders slumped and the frantic chatter and gestures finally stilled. He looked exhausted.

"He can stay here," Renee said gently, resting a hand on the brownie's shoulder.

He leaned into her and closed his eyes.

"He'll be safe," Renee assured. "No one causes trouble in my store."

Cary smiled at that. Except for that one time, Renee was right. Cary was endlessly amazed at the different beings that frequented the Bookstore without starting wars with each other. She still couldn't get over the prey shifters and predator shifters co-existing in the same space, sometimes perusing shelves right next to each other, without any outward tensions. The Bookstore truly was amazing.

"Faery won't be a problem?" Cary asked.

"Not in my shop. Not if any of the Fae want to use the place ever again."

"Do you get a lot of the Fae here? I mean, with them being immortal, don't they…know most of this stuff already?"

Renee smiled. "You'd be surprised. Especially the highborns. So few ever leave Faery these days, there's a lot they don't know." She shrugged. "Probably for the best. Wouldn't want some of them to be too in touch with your modern world. Or some of the other worlds for that matter."

"Fair enough." Cary knew just enough about Faery and the highborn Fae to agree with Renee. "Thanks for letting him rest here." She nodded to Borir. "And for getting his name. I couldn't even understand that, but I felt bad just calling him 'the brownie' all the time."

"No problem." Renee looked fondly at Borir as he curled up into a little ball in the middle of her wooden counter, snoring quietly. The brownie blended in so seamlessly with the wood that Cary kept having to blink and concentrate on the spot she knew he was resting to actually see him.

"I'll be back soon," Cary said. "If I can't find Jaxer in the next hour, I'll see if my bosses can track him down. I'll probably need their permission to get his help anyway." She let out a long sigh and groaned.

"Yeah, the Seventh Year rules are complicated," Renee said. "I'm sure there's a book on them somewhere, but I've never seen it. Be worth a lot if I could get my hands on one, though." She wagged her slim eyebrows.

Cary chuckled, then turned to go, but Renee stopped her with a gentle word.

"I should warn you, that kid, the one whose teacher is trying to kill you? He was in here the other day."

"Sheldon?" Cary turned back to the counter.

Sheldon was the protégé of the wizard who'd been trying to kill Cary for months now. It was thanks to Sheldon—and Jaxer—that Cary had met Deacon. She'd had to rescue him from Sheldon, who, as far as Cary could judge from their brief interaction, was an evil little shit. She and Deacon had thought he'd killed himself when one of his spells had rebounded off

Cary's shields and back onto him. Turned out, Sheldon hadn't been killed. But—and Cary hadn't even known this was possible at the time—Cary had absorbed almost all of his powers during that attack.

Apparently, Sheldon was no longer able to do much in the way of wizardry, which was probably for the best since that whole evil-little-shit thing was going to cause trouble for the world at large if he could. But his teacher, his wizard master, hadn't taken well to his pupil becoming a useless and mostly ordinary teenager. The wizard had discovered Cary's secrets, both the secret of her ability to absorb magic —which she herself hadn't known until recently—and the fact that she was a Protector. Which meant he knew how to kill her and had spent months trying. Fortunately, he'd also spent months failing.

Unfortunately, the spiteful bastard had then gone and revealed her secrets to the Master vampire of Portland. Which had coincidentally revealed the secret she hadn't even known about herself to her. That part at least was…good? Probably good. Better to know than not. But she wasn't pleased all the local vampires knew. If not for the fact that the previous master was now dead and replaced by someone mostly willing to leave her alone and uphold the rules that kept her out of vampire business, she'd have been in real trouble there.

Since the whole vampire thing, though, she hadn't seen any signs of the wizard or Sheldon. To be fair, she hadn't actually *seen* Sheldon at all since last Halloween, except for that one time. But she'd been in the middle of trying to stop an army of supernatural bad guys so she'd been a little preoccupied and had assumed she'd imagined seeing him. She only knew for sure Sheldon was alive because the wizard had confirmed it. And Renee had described a young man coming to the Bookstore that they were all sure was Sheldon.

"What was he looking for?" she asked Renee. "What did he want?"

"He didn't ask to see the back room again," Renee said, referring the room full of special books that she couldn't sell for one reason or another—mostly because they were too magical or too powerful and couldn't be contained outside of the Bookstore. That was the room in which the book about Cary's powers could be found. It was a small book. Most people like Cary ended up dead very early in life. There wasn't a lot of information about them. "He stuck to the shelves on healing and witchcraft. Given he was a wizard before losing his powers, his looking around the witchcraft shelves struck me as…interesting."

"Yeah. Interesting."

Wizard magic and witch magic were two different things even though they tended to get conflated in pop culture. Wizards and witches could be male or female or anything in between. The words weren't gendered names for the same talents. They were both basically humans with powers, but their powers spanned different ranges and had different requirements.

Witches tended to use spells, potions, and earth-based magic. Their rituals to call power involved calling on the elements and spirits of the earth and nature. They used nature-based props like wood, candles, incense, and salt. If you came across a magical potion, it was more than a little likely that a witch had made it. Her friend Angie was a witch—also a psychic and she had some ties to the demon hunting world that she refused to talk about even to her best friends, but those skills were outside her natural witchy talents.

Wizard magic tapped more into the electro-magnetic field. They controlled things like fire and energy bolts, power they used as weapons. They used brute force and raw magic drawn from their internal stores rather than spells and powers outside themselves likes witches. Wizards did also use rituals, but theirs tended to involve blood (the good wizards just used a few drops of their own) and some sort of sacrifice (again, good wizards made personal sacrifices, like giving up something they loved—an object or a pursuit—in exchange for the successful completion of the ritual). And if there was a metal-based object infused with magic, you could pretty much guarantee a wizard was responsible for it.

Cary tended to think of wizards as more dangerous than witches, but that was only because one of her best friends was a witch with a lot of restraint. Angie had blocked and defeated a few wizards in her day, so underestimating witches was a bad idea. Something Angie regularly reminded Cary when she let her biases show.

One of the biggest differences between the two, though, was that having some sort of innate magic as part of your biology was *required* for a wizard. Witches could be perfectly ordinary humans who learned to use spells and potions to create magic—though some of them also had innate magic, like Angie; it just wasn't required. Wizards *had* to have an internal store of magic to be wizards. You couldn't be a wizard, couldn't command and control the elements of power that wizards controlled, without that core of magic. You couldn't do wizardy things without it.

Sheldon's magic had, apparently, been almost entirely drained off in his fight with Cary. He'd thrown so much out in his spell, there hadn't been very much left when he'd recovered. At least, that was what his teacher had implied, and what Renee had confirmed after she'd met Sheldon.

"You suppose he's looking for another way to access magic?" Cary asked. "That probably wouldn't be good, given what he tried to do with his magic when he had some."

"Got me," Renee said. "He didn't end up buying anything to do with witchcraft. He only got one book. A general education volume on the various kinds of magic healers."

Cary filed the information away. She should find out what Sheldon was up to, but first she had to help Borir. The brownie snuffled a little and curled into a tighter ball. The movement allowed her to see him easily for a few seconds before he blended back into the wooden countertop.

"Thanks for letting me know about Sheldon," Cary said. "I'll be back soon. You're sure it's okay for Borir to be here?"

"No problem." Renee smiled at the sleeping fae. "He has official sanctuary."

Cary blinked at the more formal statement but let it go.

She had to go find a faery.

4

By the time she'd walked back to her car and driven up high into Forest Park the day's heat was heavy and oppressive. Even the woods were overly warm, despite the green shade. The air was thick with the scents of cedar and maple and heated earth, which might have been nice if there'd been a breeze to cut the temperature.

After living in the Pacific Northwest for most of her life, she just wasn't used to these rare heatwaves. She fluttered her shirt, trying to cool some of the sweat as she wandered deeper into the trees along a narrow hiking path.

She'd never been able to get in touch with Jaxer directly, but up to a few months ago, she'd never needed to. He'd always just been around. Sometimes more than she liked. He just showed up. All the time. So it hadn't even occurred to her that she couldn't track *him* down if she needed him until right before the start of her Seventh Year trial.

Deacon had actually been the one to show her the trick of it. Go to a wild place and Jaxer would appear. Deacon had demonstrated this by walking her into a wooded area near his parents' house and Jaxer had just walked out from behind a tree.

She still had some hurt feelings over that, that Jaxer hadn't been the one to tell her. But at this stage, she was learning to let those feelings go. Things between her and Jaxer were just always going to be a little complicated.

"You're looking for me?" Jaxer said from behind her, sounding a little smug and also a little confused. "To what do I owe the pleasure?"

She faced him and made a show of scowling. Truthfully, she was glad to see him. Since meeting him, this was the longest they'd gone without contact. It felt incredibly weird not to have him in her life.

As usual, he was dressed in clothes that showed off his well-muscled physique. A shirt that gaped open at the neck, fitted pants, boots that were snug to his calves. His blond hair was longer than the last time she'd seen him and was pulled back into a low tail. She wasn't sure if his hair was really longer, though, or if that was just his glamour at work. He was as shockingly handsome as always, but he also looked a little tired, with a tightness around his green-blue eyes.

Maybe that was her imagination. Jaxer's greatest magic was glamour, the ability to make people see and experience exactly what he wanted them too. He showed her precisely what he wanted her to see, nothing more and nothing less. And because he was vain, he usually showed her an extremely handsome exterior with no discernable flaws.

She'd always suspected, though, that he tamped down on his actual beauty just to keep the humans in his life from being overwhelmed.

"You could have just stepped out in front of me," she said. "Sneaking up behind me is a little rude."

He grinned. "Sorry."

"You're not sorry even a little bit," she said, just to be grumpy about it. He chuckled, as she'd hoped he would.

The one thing he didn't do was step close and wrap an arm around her or kiss her cheek. That was a recent change. He'd always been touchy-feely with her, from the very first time they'd met. And for a long time, she'd just assumed that was the way Jaxer was so she'd let it go. Turned out, there was more to his physical affection than she'd guessed. Once she was aware of his feelings, she'd asked him to stop with all the hugging and kissing. And he'd honored her request. That went a long way toward her being able to maintain a friendship with him.

"What do you need?" he asked softly, his expression friendly but guarded.

"So, I had an interesting start to the day." She went on to tell him about Borir, the hobgoblins, and Renee's translation of the problem. Ending with the fact that Borir was here to find Jaxer for help.

"My help?" Jaxer frowned, his gaze moving inward as he settled his hands on his hips.

Cary couldn't read his expression, not well, but she got the distinct impression he was confused.

"I haven't been to the English court in centuries," he murmured. "I'm surprised a brownie would even know my name."

She wanted to say something but wasn't sure exactly what. Her curiosity urged her to question him about his history with the court. Part of her wanted to joke about his being a famous faery. Still another part was worried about him and what returning would mean for him. She settled on silence, in the end.

"Borir? Doesn't sound familiar," he murmured, talking mostly to himself. He finally met her gaze. "What the hell does he think I can do?"

"Got me." She lifted her hands in a shrug. "But Renee double checked. He is definitely here to find you." She pursed her lips as she considered him. "The Nags sent me to help Borir. Would they know he was here to find you? Is that something that...comes up in a premonition?"

"Not usually. Motivations are always fuzzier than actions."

Her bosses used premonitions, some magic they never discussed with her, and old-fashioned research in their efforts to direct the Protectors to likely places where they were needed. Obviously, the system wasn't perfect or there'd never be another horrendous crime in the world. There were only so many Protectors scattered across the country. And there was only so much that magic, premonitions, and research could do to find the people that needed Protector help.

The fact that the Nags tried, that they kept creating Protectors and training them and paying them to *try* and help as many people as possible, was one of the reasons Cary continued to do this job. They'd tricked her into it, she hadn't *intended* to become a Kevlar vest superhero—she'd intended to become a veterinary technician, although she'd been rethinking that when she got tricked into doing this—but because they tried to help, year in and year out, she continued to try as well.

"Since Borir is here looking for you, I'm allowed to talk with you. Right?" She was sure this was allowed. But a part of her worried she'd break the Seventh Year rules beyond repair and the Nags would leave her defenseless against the myriad enemies she'd managed to accumulate over the last six and a half years.

She had a real love-hate relationship with her bosses.

"We'll have to discuss it with them. I'd have to anyway. I can't disappear that deep into Faery without letting them know." His mouth tilted up at one side. "They're my bosses, too."

"Does this mean we have to go back to my house or can they just show up here and make our lives easier?" She said this up into the air in the hopes they'd hear her or know or whatever.

Jaxer wasn't the only one she couldn't contact at will.

The Nags showed up. Gave her a job. And then pretty much vanished until the job was done. Sometimes they continued to nag her. They'd followed her to Deacon's parents' house to give her a job back in January. She knew they didn't need to appear to her at her home because they'd shown up all over the place to give her jobs. But because they'd always showed up when they showed up—too often at weird or inopportune moments—she'd rarely needed to be in touch.

It struck her that maybe that was one of the things that might change after—if?—she survived this year. That her relationship to them might alter and her ability to contact...well, everyone might be one of the new "powers" she gained. She flattened her lips together, not sure that should count as a "power," but it would make times like this easier.

When the Nags didn't magically appear, and she didn't get that tingling down her spine that accompanied their appearance, she sighed. "I guess that means they're gonna wait until we go back to my house?"

"I'll find them," he said. "And don't worry, this isn't a violation of your test year rules."

She rolled her eyes. "This year is a real pain in my ass. On top of having to do my job, I have to rethink everything I do."

"It wouldn't be a test year if it was easy," he said.

To which she said something rude.

He grinned. "You're doing well, Cary. Don't worry. You'll survive."

"Ha!" She wasn't sure whether to be pleased or annoyed by his comment so she moved on. "Go find the Nags and tell them you have to go to Faery with Borir. He's got sanctuary at the Bookstore."

"Wait, Renee gave him sanctuary? Officially?"

"Yeah, kind of seemed official the way she said it. Why? Is that unusual?"

"The last being she gave sanctuary to was Pickles," he said.

"Pickles? My Pickles?"

Pickles was a foo lion who'd lost her mate and taken the shape of a basset hound to retire. According to the story Renee had told Cary, Pickles had appeared in the Bookstore in her basset form and then just stayed there. Until Pickles had decided to adopt Cary, that was. Now Pickles was part of Cary's little dog pack—which included a foo lion (she preferred that to foo dog), a demon dog (who hated being called hellhound), and a mundane terrier-collie mutt with enough energy to power Portland. Except for that one time at the Bookstore, Pickles conducted herself like an ordinary basset hound. Cary hadn't realized she'd had sanctuary at the store. She'd just assumed the basset had adopted the place the way she'd later adopted Cary.

"So, giving Borir sanctuary is a big deal, then?" she asked. "Not just a favor, or Renee being nice enough to keep him safe while I'm finding you? But, like, a big deal?"

"A big deal," Jaxer said softly. "If she gave him official sanctuary, not only is he safe, he's safe until he wants to leave. And no one, not even the Fae royal families, will be able to do anything about it."

"Wow." Cary raised her brows high and stared into the trees. "This day just keeps getting more and more interesting."

After a moment's silence, Jaxer cleared his throat. "I'm going to need a favor, if I have to go back to the English court."

"You believe Borir, then? That whatever this is, it's something you can stop?"

"I don't know. I'll talk with him. I need more information since I'm not sure what this spell or weapon is he's referring to."

"Renee had never heard of it either," Cary said.

"No matter what he's referring to…" Jaxer pressed his lips together before continuing. "The thing is, I can't just show up in England. Or Ireland for that matter. Not without running the risk of being executed."

"Holy hell. Why?"

"It's a long story."

"Which you aren't going to tell me." She made a face. She wasn't exactly surprised. Jaxer had always been pretty close-lipped about his links to the two courts and the real reason he'd cut all ties with them.

"Actually, I might have to tell you everything." He spread his hands, palms up.

She narrowed her eyes. "Why?"

"I'm going to need a Protector. I need you to come into Faery with me."

5

"**W**hoa, whoa, whoa." She held up a hand and took a step back from him. "You have told me repeatedly Faery is too dangerous for humans. Almost always. That I was to never get tricked into going there because I could lose my mind."

All her reading had backed up that warning as well. Faery wasn't a place for humans to tread. Most got lost there and never returned.

"I know it's a big ask," he admitted. "And I'm not even sure the Nags will allow it. But if Borir is right and these machinations are more serious than the usual Fae court infighting, if they can destroy Faery, then it's a problem for the Nags as well. A problem for a bunch of the realms that connect to Faery. Destroying the place wouldn't just destroy Faery. It could destroy worlds."

"Well shit." She put her hands on her hips. "No wonder Renee is taking Borir's safety so seriously."

"Her giving official sanctuary does more to convince me of the seriousness of all this than Borir's near death. That sort of thing happens. But the Bookstore getting involved… That's significant."

"Shit," she said again because it helped relieve some of the growing worry in her gut to curse a little. Actually, cursing a lot seemed like a good idea, so she released another few choice words before saying, "But still, I'm a human. I can't just…wander into Faery and do my Protector thing without risking my sanity." She paused. "Can I?"

He gave a shrug she wasn't sure how to interpret. "If you're in Protector mode—and you will have to be to keep me from getting killed—then you should be fine."

"Should be? Should be?" Her voice rose on the last word and she had to take a deep breath. "You want me to risk everything on a 'should be'?"

"More of a risk not to do it," he said quietly.

She growled and started to pace. The Nags would send her to do this. She was certain. Because the world was in danger and she had to prevent all hell from breaking loose. Again. It was her job. And she couldn't refuse them in her seventh year. Even if she wanted to.

Which, curse her stupid sense of right and wrong, she didn't want to. She felt the need to do this if it meant keeping everyone safe, even if it *risked* her life.

She snorted at herself. She'd been doing this job too long. She'd gotten brainwashed and now she couldn't seem to stop protecting people. Even stupid Fae who likely got themselves into this to begin with.

Jaxer's quiet voice stilled her restless movements. "You know how I feel about you," he said.

She tried not to wince at that, or react at all.

"I wouldn't ask this of you if I didn't think it was life or death," he said. "Not just mine. All the realms connected to Faery."

She sighed and hung her head. She wanted to curse again. Mostly to release the tension of knowing she was about to go into Faery.

And she might not come out.

"Track down the Nags," she said, straightening her shoulders. "I have to make some arrangements for the dogs while we're gone. And I need to call Deacon."

❧

"Not without me," was Deacon's response to hearing she had to go into Faery to protect Jaxer. "You're not taking that risk alone."

She smiled at her living room wall, the soft yellow color soothing at the moment. "I will have Jaxer there for backup," she pointed out, just to be irritating. She could hear the worry in Deacon's voice. He'd be less worried if he was annoyed.

"That doesn't help," he said. "I'll be back in less than an hour. Don't go before I get there."

"Deacon, you can't go into Faery. Shifters aren't any safer than humans." In fact, they might be in more danger. Faery had a weird effect on anyone not of Fae blood, and shifters were known to go feral, or have their animals…turn into things worse under the influence of the realm's wild magics. She didn't want them both risking their lives on this.

"You need more backup than an outcast faery," Deacon said. Then more quietly. "He's gonna need more backup, too."

Deacon and Jaxer had been friends at one time. Or at least close associates. Until Deacon had claimed her as mate, and Jaxer had declared he loved her. They hadn't been particularly close since then.

"I'm not going to argue that last point," she said. "I'm not going to do him much good in the weird world of Faery except to keep others from killing him." She paused. "Which I suppose *is* pretty helpful all told, but I mean, I can't do anything if there's an attack except stand there and try to keep him from getting dead. Despite all that, the extra backup can't be you. It's just not safe for a shifter."

"Have you considered," Deacon said, again quietly, "that going into Faery could be more than just normally dangerous for you?"

"Meaning?"

"The fact that you absorb magic. And Faery is made of it."

Oh yeah. She'd sort of forgotten that point. "But I only absorb what's thrown at me. I don't just pick up magic out of the ambient air." At least, she didn't think she did.

Frankly, she had no idea how her weird ability worked. No one did. Not in any detail. Because of that issue with people like her almost always dying young after their first contact with magic. The ones who survived... No one knew about them because they got through life managing to avoid magic and magical creatures. There were few records, less research, and a lot of half guesses and suppositions. There wasn't even a *name* for what she could do. And the book, the *one* book, with what little information there was on her ability was really really slim.

But maybe the worst part was the fact that this ability messed with her Protector shields. It was why she got hurt. Other Protectors didn't, at least not when they were protecting someone and their shields were up. Or so she understood. They might get hurt, or killed, when using their offensive abilities, but nothing got through their shields to hurt them once they were up.

Other Protectors always had some sort of skill when they came into this job—some magical talent or ability to do something besides just stand between bad guys and good guys. They had offensive skills.

Cary did not.

Oh, she was learning and practicing self defense skills a lot more with her friend Lucy who was a martial arts expert. And to be fair, since Lucy had forced her to up her training coming into the Seventh Year trial, Cary had gotten a lot better at hand-to-hand fighting. But none of it was instinctive yet. She still wouldn't give herself good odds in a fight with, say, a shifter.

Outside of that, though, she didn't bring offensive skills into her job. She was, in almost every way, a defensive weapon. Even the way she absorbed magic—just stood there and soaked it up—wasn't an offensive skill.

Until the magic exploded out of her, that was. But since she didn't control that, it was hard to count it. And also, every time it exploded out, she risked being killed in the process, so...yeah, there was that too.

She shook her head. "I'll be protecting Jaxer all the time. I'll be fine, even if I have to stand in the way of Fae magic. It'll be like with the baby god. I'll be invincible." She tried to smile, even though he couldn't see her, hoping the expression came through in her tone.

"Do I have to remind you that channeling baby god magic almost killed you?"

"Na. I just needed a nap afterward." She waved away his concern. Mostly because she was afraid to think about that too closely. Channeling god magic had been a new one for her and she still hadn't completely processed what had happened, even all these months later. She wasn't even sure she wanted to. "None of this diminishes the fact that Faery will be as dangerous for you as it is for me, if not more, and you can't go with us."

"You are my mate," he said. "And I love you. I'm not letting you wander into Faery alone."

She wanted to remind him she wouldn't be alone, but his declaration of love made her feel all soft and squishy. He said it more and more regularly, which was kind of thrilling because he'd never said it to a woman before her. The fact that she hadn't said the words aloud back yet was still a thing, but he didn't bring it up so they hadn't talked about it. She was still working out why she kept choking up on saying words out loud she was certain she felt.

"I won't be wandering," she said softly. "To be perfectly honest, I want you there. But you can't. I want you safe even more."

"I feel the same about you."

She sighed. "What a pair we make." She shook her head. Opened her mouth to say something nice and consoling.

And felt that damned tingling along her back and across her shoulders.

"Ah hell," she murmured. "I have to go. The Nags are here."

6

Cary set her cellphone aside and stood to face her bosses. They'd appeared near her little fireplace, opposite the couch, looking as cool, unique, and unaffected as always.

Liruk—all white and gold, with little golden horns peeking through her fall of pure white hair, her unreal green eyes sharp and narrowed—was the one boss that was typically most critical of Cary and her efforts. And so it was Liruk that Cary expected to tell her she'd somehow failed that morning. Even though Borir was safely ensconced in the Bookstore. And Jaxer had been made aware of his part in all this. Still, she couldn't help the kneejerk reaction and wanted to flinch a little under Liruk's silent stare.

Wisat was usual the "kinder" of the two bosses. His criticisms came in a softer tone, with a more chiding air. His red skin, long black hair, and black robes were very nearly a photo-negative contrast to Liruk. Where she had horns, he had a halo of red, velvet-covered antlers that circled his head. The only similarity were their eyes, bright bright green that fairly glowed even in her well-lit living room.

"So am I going into Faery or not?" she asked, her tone sharper than she'd meant.

She got edgy around her bosses under the best of circumstances, mostly because she felt inadequate to her job. But that defensiveness and irritation had gotten even worse this year because they'd basically blackmailed her into seeing this Seventh Year test through. They'd threatened to take the protective glamour off her home—the magic that made it impossible for people she didn't want to find her home from finding it. She had to give mental permission for someone to actually locate her house and that meant it was the one place in the entire world where she was always safe.

She'd made a lot of enemies in this city over the years. If she couldn't be safe even in her own home, she'd never be safe. The fact that they'd threatened to rob her of that, even though the fact that she had all these enemies was *their* fault to begin with since they'd tricked her into this job, meant she was carrying a lot of resentment. That resentment tended to pop out at inopportune times when she was dealing with them.

"We would prefer not to send you," Wisat said, his tone gentle and understanding.

"But you're still going to," she said. It wasn't a question.

"The European courts aren't within our usual interest," Liruk said, her tone even more sharp than normal.

Cary raised her brows, and Liruk's mouth pinched into an expression Cary couldn't quite read. But she suspected Liruk was more annoyed by having to deal with a situation in Faery than she was by anything that Cary had done wrong that morning. Which went a long way toward relaxing Cary's annoyance.

"I'd rather leave them to their own machinations, too," Cary admitted. "But if Borir is right and this, whatever it is, could end Faery, that affects us all." She paused. "Including your people."

They were Fae. And although the North American Fae were technically in a different part of Faery, it was still all the same realm.

She made a face. The way Faery was divided and sectioned off was a mystery to her. She had picked up enough to know that going in and out of Faery here in North America wasn't going into the same Faery you entered in, say, London. It was still all one place, but it didn't actually occupy physical spaces and interconnect in the ordinary human understanding of space and time. You could be in Faery here without being in Faery in Europe and the divide seemed to be an impassable one almost without exception, which meant you couldn't just enter here and wander into there, or fly or anything else. Except that, from what she understood, sometimes you could?

She rubbed her temples. Trying to wrap her mind around Faery always made her head hurt. The only thing she knew for sure was that you could always count on Faery being weird and defying logic.

"This could destroy your home," Cary said, "as well as damage my realm. If Jaxer can stop it, he has to go. And he's going to need protection."

"Yes," Liruk said, somewhat to Cary's surprise. "He will need protection. A Protector."

"But it will be more dangerous for you than for another Protector," Wisat said. "Now that we know…what we know about you."

His comment weirdly echoed Deacon's and sent a little shiver of unease down her spine. "Does that mean you'll send another Protector with him?"

The two beings exchanged a look before Wisat said, "We can't."

"Why?" Cary attempted to keep her tone level and reasonable.

"We aren't…" Liruk scowled at the wall, her gaze moving down and settling on Cary's little dog pack where they lay in their beds under her living room window. The window looked out into the backyard and spilled a lot of light onto the beds in the summer, making the dogs very happy to sleep there.

Fred, the mutt, was sound asleep—he might lift his head to look at the Nags, but he was used to them and they didn't bring food, so they were mostly uninteresting to him. Buck was watching them, his big Labrador head resting on his forepaws where they hung over the edge of his stuffed bed. Pickles, the foo lion-come basset hound, was paying particular attention to Liruk, her flop in the bed not as floppy as usual. Her jowls hadn't spread and she kept her nose on her short stubby legs. Her attention didn't waver from Liruk's gaze.

Liruk sighed, an unusual sign of non-annoyance emotion, and faced Cary again. "We are not allowed," she said. "If Jaxer brings you into

Faery, because you're his friend, it is not the same as *us* sending a Protector in officially. Our human guardians aren't welcome in the Fae realm. Not here or South America. Certainly not in any of the European courts. Not in the Asian courts. Not in the African courts."

"Nowhere in the Fae realm," Wisat said with a sigh of his own. "They came together when we first created the Protectors. It was one of the very few times the many and varied regions of our realm agreed on something."

"Okay," Cary said. That was…weird. And also illuminating. Although, exactly *what* it illuminated would take some more explanation. "Why not? What's wrong with Protectors in Faery?"

Wisat made a face, looking more annoyed than he usually did. "It is that you are all humans. And that we have…" He waved a hand. "The magic you channel is Fae magic. In a manner of speaking. What we give to humans to make them Protectors, that has always been forbidden. Fae, any species, anywhere, are allowed to help or hinder humans at their whim. If they care to pay attention to humans at all. Our tribe have always helped. There are tribes from this region who have…not. But it's been our calling to aid humans in any way we can."

"And when we conceived of Protectors," Liruk continued, "there were very heated arguments over allowing their creation. *Allowing*! As if it was anyone else's say what we chose to do with our own magic."

She made a gesture that Cary couldn't interpret.

"Selfish and narrow," Liruk grunted, and folded her hands together in front of her. She pulled in a breath. "You should not know of these things yet. The history of Protectors and their creation is given to those who pass their seventh year and choose—" She cut herself off, pressing her lips together. Then finished with a quiet, "And choose to learn that history."

Wisat's eyes narrowed. "We can't give you any more information at the moment. Not until you've officially passed this year. But it is important for you to know that if you *choose*—" he put a real emphasis on the word, holding her gaze to ensure she got the significance even if his tone hadn't conveyed it, "—to go into Faery, you go on your own. To help a friend. Not officially. Not as a Protector."

"Will my Protector shields even work in Faery?"

Wisat and Liruk exchanged another of those looks before Liruk said, "Your powers will be heightened. You will be close to the source of the magic that flows through you when actively doing your job. It will likely flow through you easier than usual. Maybe even constantly."

"You mean, I might be…indestructible?" She tried not to grin or look excited at the prospect. She knew her bosses weren't in the mood for humor. In fact, she got the feeling this was more warning of how the powers would work than meant to encourage her. But still… She liked the idea of being able to go into Faery with stronger shields against all that magic.

"So to speak," Liruk said, her brows raised. She didn't look as annoyed with Cary's humor as Cary would have expected. "But there is the complication of you absorbing magic. This might be more than your human body can take, even with the protections afforded you by channeling our magic."

"That's why we would encourage you not to go," Wisat said. "We don't know enough about how your unique biology interacts with our magic. The way you absorb and release magic while still channeling ours with no ill consequence."

"Well, I mean, I do end up unconscious for a day or two when the release happens," she pointed out.

Both beings ignored her comment.

"We can't predict what will happen to you in Faery," Liruk said. "We can't say how your Protector powers will work with any kind of certainty."

"And we're not getting any sort of premonitions to indicate if this is even something you should do," Wisat said. "We can't get even a hint."

"It is possible," Liruk said slowly, "this is all a trap for your mentor. The brownie, the hobgoblins, the supposed conspiracy, all of this might be something one of his enemies has arranged to lure him back into the part of Faery where he is not welcome."

"You can't tell?" Cary's voice rose to a squeak. She cleared her throat. "You don't have any hints one way or the other? Have you told Jaxer this?"

"It was part of the discussion," Wisat said. "He was not unaware of the possibility."

"Then he's not going and this isn't even a necessary discussion," Cary said more than asked. If Jaxer was convinced this was a trap, why the hell would he walk into it?

"He will go," Liruk said. "He's more afraid of what will happen if it's true, and all of Faery is in danger, than what would happen if it's a trap for him."

Wisat said, "He's decided that if it is a trap, having you with him in your Protector role will prevent disaster."

"But I can't be there officially as a Protector," she confirmed.

"No. But the magic of it can't be cut off," Liruk said. She straightened her shoulders and nodded her head.

Cary narrowed her eyes. That physical gesture looked like Liruk was trying to convince herself of this more than Cary.

"So you cannot stop being a Protector, even when you're helping a friend, and officially 'off duty'," Wisat finished. "As it were."

"And I should be a stronger Protector in Faery," Cary said.

They exchanged a look. "Should be," Liruk said.

"But of course, we can't be certain," Wisat said.

"You don't know whether this will work or not," Cary said with absolute certainty. "You don't actually *know* if my abilities as a Protector will function in Faery. Because of their ban. Because of my own…skill. Whatever you want to call it. There's been no premonitions, no signs, no indications. And because it's never been done, you simply don't know."

Liruk pressed her lips together, her golden skin a paler shade of gold than normal as she looked away from Cary.

Wisat let his shoulders relax slightly on a sigh, then lifted his hands, palms up. "Which is why we will not send you in officially, even if we could," he said quietly. "You must decide for yourself. Take the risk for yourself."

"And there isn't anything we can do for you, or to help you," Liruk said, finally looking back at Cary and meeting her gaze.

Typically, when Liruk said something like that to her, she was annoyed with Cary. The words were a rebuke of some kind. This time, Liruk sounded like she was warning her, encouraging her *not* to rush into this situation. Since they were usually responsible for pushing Cary into dangerous situations as part of her job, this was more than a little scary turn of events. She wasn't sure what to make of everything the Nags had said.

But one thing she did know. She didn't want to abandon her friend.

"You'll go," Wisat said quietly.

"I'll go," she said.

Liruk sighed. "The shifter will want to go with you."

Cary resisted the urge to roll her eyes. For some reason, Liruk refused to say Deacon's name. "Yes, Deacon has already asked me to wait for him. He was friends with Jaxer at one point, too."

"He goes for you, not your mentor," Liruk said.

"He shouldn't though," Cary said, more to herself. She had no idea how to keep Deacon out of Faery if she went in. She liked the idea of him at her back in a fight, but given this was *Faery* and not just any old realm, she didn't want to take the chance on what the place would do to him.

"We might be able to help Deacon," Wisat said, giving Liruk a look.

Liruk raised her brows, tilting her head to one side.

In the next moment, she'd vanished. A blink and only Wisat stood in Cary's living room. No tearing holes in the fabric of space-time for her bosses. Cary suppressed a sigh that might have contained a hint of admiration. Wouldn't do to have the Nags knowing she admired them.

"What can you do?" she asked Wisat.

Liruk reappeared before he could answer. "Have the shifter wear this."

She opened her hand, palm up, to reveal what looked like a Celtic brooch. A very old one. It filled Liruk's palm, circular in shape, with a mostly open center, a thicker base at the bottom of the circle, and an opening in the base. Celtic knots adorned the circle, and where the base opened, two carved animal heads faced each other. It was made of silver—at least she thought that was silver—and encrusted with red and blue gems that may or may not have been precious stones, but since Cary wasn't familiar with gems, she couldn't be sure of that either. Blue enamel inlaid some of the scrolling knot designs. A long, thick silver pin, sharpened to a point at one end, angled across the open face of the circle. It was fastened to the end opposite the thick base by a rounded fold of metal that was also decorated in beautiful scrollwork. The pin itself was covered in lines of lacing and what might have been runes.

Cary looked closer, putting her nose almost against the brooch. A faint blue glow seemed to swim over the surface of the silver, twisting around the knot designs and disappearing, only to reappear in the patterns along the pin. Liruk lifted her hand a little, and Cary took the brooch, fingering the design. A shiver of tingling energy vibrated faintly against the nerves of her fingertip.

"What is it?" she asked, her tone surprisingly quiet.

"A defense, forged by the ancient kings of Ireland," Liruk said. "This one was designed to be worn by the sons of minor kings—though it was actually the creation of a high king."

"A defense?" Cary asked.

"This particular brooch was infused with ancient spells to counter the effects of Faery. The high king who had it created intended it to protect his nephew, the son of a minor king, on a quest into Faery."

"Did it work?" Cary asked, still staring at the brooch.

"It did," Liruk said. "The prince survived the journey and didn't go insane. He also didn't lose control of his animal side."

Cary's gaze jumped up to Liruk. "The prince was a shifter?"

Liruk nodded. "A wolf shifter. His quest was to rescue the high king's son, who'd been taken hostage by a highborn faery woman with a grudge against the king for his refusal to marry her. She seduced his son into Faery with the intent of letting him waste away to nothing. The young man was the king's only offspring. His nephew volunteered to retrieve his cousin."

"Brave man," Cary said, looking back down at the brooch. "So, it will keep a shifter safe, then? That's what it's designed to do?"

"And because it was made for the son of a king," Wisat said, "it will convey the appropriate status to your shifter. Since he is the son of a queen and intended to be a king himself."

"Wow," Cary breathed. She tried not to think too closely about the fact that Deacon was going to be the leader of his people one day, that his mother was their current queen. The thought of it made her head spin and she had enough to worry about staying alive this year.

Liruk pulled a piece of purple wool cloth from thin air. Cary scowled at the needlessly dramatic and showy move. Liruk shook out the cloth and held it up so Cary could see it was a cloak of some kind. The material looked thick, the weave fine. It was long and plane with no adornments at all. Just a length of wool dyed a deep purple.

"The cloak of a king," Liruk said. "The color also indicates your shifter's status as royalty."

"The show will go over well in Faery," Wisat said. "Status is all important there. The son of a queen will be treated with more respect than the son of an ordinary shifter."

"Which should also help keep your shifter safer than he might otherwise be," Liruk said.

"For someone who can't bring herself to say his name, this is an amazingly generous bit of help," Cary said. "Thank you. Since he's going to come with us whether I want him to or not, having these to help him stay safe and sane is a real relief."

"We do this for you," Liruk said. "Not the shifter. You are ours. Losing the shifter to Faery would…cause you pain. We don't want that."

Cary blinked a few times, not sure what to say. How did you respond when you learned your bosses actually cared about you? She was a little afraid she might cry if she tried to say anything. Instead, she looked back at the brooch in her hand.

"Thank you," she said again. She had to clear her throat before continuing.

A brief silence fell before Wisat said, "I'm sorry we can't provide you with more, to help you."

"Keeping Deacon safe so he can have mine and Jaxer's backs is more than enough," she said. She straightened her shoulders. "Thank you for not preventing me from doing this. Especially since it might be a sort of world-ending incident."

Wisat's mouth twitched at one corner. Liruk pressed her lips together until they made a tight line.

"You still have months left on your test year," Liruk said after a moment. "Try not to die before you return."

Cary snorted. "I'll work on that." Before she could say more, the Nags disappeared. Leaving Cary to deal with the disconcerting realization that *both* her bosses actually liked her and wanted her to succeed.

Who knew?

7

*D*eacon arrived an hour later. He greeted her with a kiss that melted her bones the instant she opened the door. No words, no hellos, just pulled her into his arms and destroyed her ability to think for a few minutes.

"Hi," she said when he finally eased back from the kiss. She leaned heavily into him, but he was so lovely and strong he didn't seem to notice he was keeping her upright.

"Hi," he said. "I missed you. A lot."

"I missed you, too."

"How long do we have before Jaxer arrives?"

The heat in his golden eyes made her body tighten. She still had trouble believing this man was hers. He was stunningly gorgeous—black hair, golden eyes, lightly tanned skin, a body that any Greek god would envy. Sexy beyond words. With a deep voice that made her toes curl. And something about the way he smelled, like heat and musk and yummy male, just made her crave him. Worse than coffee and pizza. Worse than cookie dough ice cream or nachos. She could live on just the way Deacon smelled.

He'd pointed out before this was part of the "being mates" stuff. She couldn't say for sure because she didn't have his super shifter sense of smell, but she definitely couldn't get enough of his scent. Of him period.

"He's due soon," she warned of Jaxer's imminent arrival. "Renee was kind enough to call me about ten minutes ago to tell me he'd left the Bookstore. In fact, he should be here already given he doesn't travel by the usual means."

Deacon walked her farther inside and kicked her front door gently closed behind him. "I'll take whatever time alone with you I can get," he said and dropped his mouth to her neck, kissing his way over her throat to the sensitive area at the juncture of her shoulder.

She leaned her head back and moaned. "I love your mouth." She gasped when he lightly bit her.

"Dogs?" he asked as he moved back to her mouth. He caressed his fingers down her spine, curving over her ass and cupping her in his large, extremely capable hands.

"Backyard," she said, then gasped again when his hands tightened on her, pressing her hips against his. He was wonderfully hard and she wanted him naked more than she wanted her next cup of coffee.

He edged her into the living room, walking her backward toward the couch as he toed off his shoes. She tried stepping out of hers, stumbled with the effort, and laughed when he caught her so she didn't fall. The short journey into her living room was a hasty mix of stripping off whatever clothes they could get off and laughter when some poor piece of material got stuck. Her t-shirt didn't survive. Neither did his.

By the time he lowered her onto the couch, covering her with his big, warm body, she'd managed to get her jeans off, but he was still in his, and the rub of soft worn denim against her legs was so sexy she wanted to purr. In the back of her head, she knew time was ticking away, that they could be interrupted at any moment, and it only made her more frantic, kissing and petting and clutching him as he freed his erection.

She wrapped her legs around his waist, her hand around his cock, and guided him in. The slide and friction, the stretch of him lit her up inside. She dropped her head back against the couch, groaning as he filled her.

"I've missed you so much," he said into her hair as he wrapped her tight and moved into her hard.

His deep, hard, steady rhythm overwhelmed her ability to speak so she answered him with her mouth and hands, kissing him where ever she could reach, dragging her short nails over his back, across his shoulders, savoring his shudder and groan. Her orgasm built fast. Too fast. She wanted to savor it more, draw it out. But her body had other ideas. She raced to that peak and flew off the top in a burst of speed and heat and light that erupted through her, shattering her.

With her eyes closed, she felt his last pounding stroke, savored the sound of him crying out her name, the way his body shuddered and trembled, his muscle hard and still for one instant before he let go. She loved when he came, loved every minute of it.

When she could open her eyes, she looked up. He was still braced above her, his eyes also closed, his cheeks flushed and sweat beading his brow, his breath deep and heavy. She wrapped her arms around his neck, tangling her fingers in his hair, and brought him down to her for a kiss.

"I'm glad you're home," she said against his lips.

He nodded. "I'm very glad to be home."

Cary didn't often think about the fact that they both considered her little three-bedroom cottage their home, when he had a large penthouse in Nobhill—hell, practically an entire apartment building—that they rarely went to. Her home was safer for her, thanks to the Nags' glamour, but she hadn't told him about that yet. No one did but Cary, the Nags, and Jaxer knew about it. Not even her best friends. The fewer people who knew about it, the safer she was. So the glamour wasn't why they spent all their time here.

She did have the dogs to worry about. She didn't want to stay away from them overnight very often if she could help it—she couldn't always prevent it, and they were fine, but it was still a concern. Deacon knew, and completely understood, how she felt about her little pack, which was the reason he'd given once for spending all their time at her house.

But even then, there seemed to be more to it. They were both more comfortable here than at his big, echoing, spartan penthouse. The fact that *he* was more comfortable here than in his own home was something she probably should think about deeper.

Not right now, when she was still buzzing from the sex. But one of these days.

She hugged him close, reluctant to let him go and get dressed again. The sound of someone pressing her doorbell and not letting up broke the spell.

"That'll be Jaxer," she said with a sigh.

"I'll answer the door. You go get dressed."

He patted her hip as he rolled off her with a fluid cat's grace she always envied, then he cleaned up with his ruined t-shirt. She paused on her way to the bedroom long enough to watch him pull his jeans back into place, admiring his ass in denim—which was really a highlight of her life—then hurried to get cleaned up and dressed.

She was digging up a new t-shirt when her cellphone rang.

"Just got your message," Angie said without preamble. "I was with a client." Angie had a very successful psychic business she ran out of her house. Very successful mostly because Angie was a real psychic—although, she'd admitted to Cary that she didn't have to use her actual psychic skills all that often with her mundane clients. Mostly, they wanted a therapist. They just didn't know it.

"You'd get paid more if you just opened a regular therapist business," Cary said as she flipped open the t-shirt she'd pulled out—bright red with a superhero logo emblazoned on the front. She grinned. That would work for a trip into Faery. She put her cellphone on speaker so she could slip into the shirt.

"Too much hassle," Angie said. "Plus, I wouldn't get to wear the hippy-dippy clothes I do for clients now."

"You prefer business casual," Cary pointed out as she picked the phone back up.

"Yeah, but it's more fun to play the airy-fairy psychic with clients. If I opened an ordinary therapist business, I'd have to be the real me too much."

"Fair enough. Can you stop in and check on the dogs? I'm not sure how long I'll be gone."

"Of course. I love your pack. Where are you going?"

Cary had left that part out of the message because she didn't want Angie freaking out. "Uh, I have to go into Faery with Jaxer." She opened another dresser drawer, the one she'd given Deacon so he could leave some clothes at her place. It was full of t-shirts, jeans, boxer briefs, socks, and Deacon's scent. She dragged in that scent almost unconsciously as she lifted out one of his random white t-shirts.

"You're going into Faery?" Angie said. Very slowly. Very distinctly.

"Deacon's coming with us," she hurried to add. "And the Nags gave me something to help him keep control of his shifter while we're there."

"You. A human. Are going into Faery?"

"Yeah, yeah, I know. But hey, you've been there before."

"For about ten seconds. With my eyes closed."

"It was longer than ten seconds," Cary said. She'd been terrified for Angie, and trusting Jaxer to keep her safe because at that moment Cary had been busy protecting some people from a demon and she'd had her hands full.

"I was in and out," Angie said. "I didn't go in and just hang out for a few days. That place is dangerous. Especially for you now that we know you absorb magic."

"Yeah, that part keeps coming up. But I'll be in constant Protector mode keeping Jaxer safe. And probably Deacon. So I'll be fine. There's only so much magic that ever gets through the Protector shields. Otherwise, they work just fine."

"But we're talking about wild magic. And you with still no way of releasing the build-up consciously. Until we figure out how you can do that on purpose instead of on accident, being around Faery-level magic is dangerous."

She sat on the edge of her bed with Deacon's t-shirt in her lap. "I know. I've discussed all this with the Nags already. And Deacon. And I'm still going. The problem is serious and potentially world-ending."

Angie sighed. Cary could practically see her closing her eyes and taking deep breaths to steady herself.

"Angie, I have to do this."

"Not as a job?"

"The Nags aren't allowed." She straightened. "That's an interesting story. Did you know they'd parted ways with most of Faery over making Protectors?"

"No. What happened?"

"Longish story that I only know part of. I'll tell you what I know when I get back."

Angie let out another long, audible breath. "Okay, I'll keep an eye on your dogs while you're gone. But if you need me, do not hesitate to come get me. I will walk into Faery to guard your back."

Cary grinned and got misty-eyed at the same time. "I love you, too." She paused before saying, "Speaking of love, have you heard from Marianne?"

"Not since the text she sent us all after she landed in New York."

One of their other best friends, a magical weaver and the best seamstress Cary had ever met, had recently broken up with her long-time girlfriend. With all the memories here, Marianne had been considering moving back to New York City. She'd taken a trip there this month ostensibly to visit friends, but mainly to see if she wanted to go through with the move.

And while Cary supported Marianne in anything she wanted to do and would support her in the move if that was her decision, Cary would miss her friend if she did go.

"Well, if she does decide to move," Cary said with a sigh, "it's only a flight away. Not so bad really. My sister is there. I have to go occasionally."

"We could make it a regular thing," Angie said, trying to sound upbeat as well. "Like every few months we fly over for a girls' week instead of just a girls' night."

"Exactly," Cary said. "And there's always phone calls. And video chat."

"Right? That's why video chat was invented."

"We could make that a regular thing too."

"And texting. We can text every day just to say hi."

Cary nodded firmly, as if Angie could see the gesture and the forced determination behind it. "Right. It's not like she'll be on the opposite side of the world."

"Or in Faery," Angie said.

Cary winced. "Hey. I'm not moving to Faery."

"Yeah, sorry. That was a low shot. I'm worried about you."

"I appreciate the worry. I appreciate even more that you're looking after the pack while I'm gone." She paused. "Are you ever getting your own dog?"

Angie was a dog kind of witch, not a cat kind. And she'd been hemming and hawing over getting a dog for years.

"Maybe. We'll see."

Which was her usual answer. Cary didn't push. She'd left Jaxer and Deacon alone too long already. "Let Lucy know what's happening for me, will you? I don't want her to worry if she can't reach me. My cellphone isn't going to work where I'm going."

"Yeah, no video chat in Faery. Watch your back and take care. Don't stay there any longer than absolutely necessary. If possible, come out on a regular basis and spend as much time in our realm as you can. And tell Jaxer he'll have to answer to me if he lets you get hurt there."

Cary grinned. "I will. Thanks again."

"Also, try not to soak up so much magic you end up unconscious again."

"Okay. Okay. I get it, magical mother. Stop nagging. I'll be back before you know it."

Angie snorted at the "magical mother" comment. "Fine. See you soon."

"See you soon."

She gave the phone a little pat after she hung up, a sort of long-distance hug to her friend. Then she snatched up Deacon's spare shirt and hurried to the living room, hoping her mate and her friend had minded their manners while she was gone.

8

"Sorry to take so long," Cary said as she stepped into the living room. "Angie called."

Jaxer was leaning casually against her fireplace mantle, looking elegant and coolly amused. A mask he wore to irritate Deacon. Deacon was sitting...well, more sprawling on the couch, shirtless, the top button on his jeans still undone. He was glaring at Jaxer but also somehow managed to look smug.

She pressed her lips together in irritation. Gloating didn't become him—and since everything made Deacon look stunning, that was saying something.

"All right you two," she said, tossing Deacon his spare t-shirt. "Keep the male peacocking to a minimum. We have things to do."

She heard a deep woof from near the big window that looked out onto her backyard. Deacon had apparently let the dogs back in while she'd been on the phone. They were sitting in their beds under the window, watching the proceedings. Well, Buck and Pickles were watching. Fred was already asleep. The deep woof had come from Pickles. An affirmation that male posturing was tiresome no doubt. The girls in the house stuck together.

"He can't come into Faery," Jaxer said, pulling her back to the

53

issue at hand. Jaxer smiled but showed a lot of teeth in the effort. "Too dangerous for shifters."

"We've had this argument already," Cary said. She collected the cloak and brooch from where she'd left them on her coffee table. A move that also put her in between Jaxer and Deacon should they decide to let their animosity move into something less snarky-word and glary-stare based. "The Nags gave me something to help."

She handed them to Deacon. "The magic is in the brooch apparently. But the cloak and brooch together are supposed to convey you're the son of a queen so everyone has to be nicer to you."

Deacon's mouth flattened into an annoyed line at that. Jaxer snorted.

She ignored both reactions. "The Nags didn't show me how to pin the brooch on so I Googled it before you arrived."

Deacon waved that away. "I know how it works. My dad's mother is Scottish, and she showed me when I was young. Just to keep old traditions going. The Irish and Scottish versions of the penannular brooches work the same. Though this one is a lot more elaborate than anything my grandmother would have had."

That was more than she'd learned about his paternal family history in the entire time she'd known him. She knew his father was from Wales originally, and had a lovely sing-songy Welsh accent still. She'd had no idea his father's mother was Scottish, though. Unfortunately, she didn't have time to ask more questions.

"Both of you are going to need to wear something more…appropriate," Jaxer said. "The highborn faeries are snobs. The less cause we give them to make trouble for us, the better."

"I'm not wearing fancy clothes," Cary said. "If I have to do any kind of leaping or diving to keep you from getting killed, I don't want one of my nice outfits ruined. Marianne isn't here to fix them for me." And since Marianne was the one who'd made most of those outfits— and infused them with magic—Cary wasn't sure anyone else *could* fix them.

"How's Marianne doing?" Deacon asked. "You heard from her?"

"No," Cary said, flopping onto the couch next to him. "Neither has Angie."

"I'm sure she's doing well. She'll be back soon." He hugged Cary close.

"I hope so," she said. "But since that's not a problem I can sort out right now, let's focus on Faery." She narrowed her eyes at Jaxer. "Can't you just glamour us up, so to speak?"

He titled his head to one side. "I suppose I could. Only the brownies will see through my spells."

"You can fool Tatiana and Oberon?" Deacon asked.

Jaxer shrugged. "Yes. It's one of the reasons I'm not welcome in their court." His smile was smug.

Cary sighed. "You going to finally tell me what the issue is with you and the English and Irish courts? That might be important to know while we're there."

He considered her for a long moment. "I'm sure it won't come up. It's not…pertinent to the current trip."

"Right," she said, heavy on the sarcasm. He usually lied better than that.

"We'll be fine," Jaxer said, not sounding even a little sure of his statement.

"Except you need Cary there to make sure," Deacon said. "You wouldn't need her if you were safe there."

"It was all a long time ago," Jaxer said.

"And obviously still a thing," Cary pointed out. "Come on. Spill. If I'm going to stand between you and all the magic of Faery, I need to know what I'm getting into."

Jaxer sighed and looked toward the dogs, now all quietly sleeping in their beds under the big window. A patch of sun had crept over the area, and Pickles had pushed into Fred's bed to sleep more fully inside that warm spot.

"My mother was of the Irish court," Jaxer finally said quietly. "My father of the English. A bit of a Romeo and Juliet pairing. Neither side was happy. Lots of drama and angst."

He was trying for a casual air, like none of this was a big deal, like it didn't really touch him. He was a good enough liar it might have worked on someone else. Cary still saw the stiffness in his shoulders, the slight tightening of the skin around his green-blue eyes. He *sounded* unaffected. The look in his eyes said otherwise, even if those emotions didn't move into his facial expression in any other way.

"Did they have the same tragic end as Romeo and Juliet?" Cary asked quietly.

"They weren't killed and didn't kill themselves. But they were banned from Faery for a while."

"Which for a highborn Fae is practically a death sentence," Deacon said.

"They were more resourceful than most, my mom and da," Jaxer said, lifting his chin. "We were just fine. For a long time. Survived the human world like natives."

"Then what happened?" Cary asked.

"They were eventually called back to Faery. First by the English court. Then the Irish. More fighting over who had the rights to them. Which, I might add, really pissed off my mother. She was way ahead of the feminism movement and didn't think anyone had 'rights' to her." He grinned at Cary, and she smiled back because she knew he need that response. "Anyway, they decided to take care of their own courts —her the Irish, him the English. I went with her." He sighed. "That was a debate, too. I was grown by human standards by then. But with so few years under my belt, still a babe by Fae standards."

"Did they consider leaving you in the human world?" Deacon asked.

Cary realized he didn't know any of this either. Deacon had said once he didn't know Jaxer that well even though they'd been friends. She'd figured that was hyperbole. Now she realized it was truer than she'd guessed. No one seemed to know Jaxer that well.

Did the Nags even know all this?

"They considered it," Jaxer said. "But I was coming into my powers." He let out a soft chuff of a chuckle. "They didn't trust me not to glamour myself into trouble while they were gone. As I said, grown man by human standards—barely—just a babe among faeries." He shrugged.

"When was this?" Cary asked. She knew Jaxer was several centuries old. He'd been acting as a mentor for Protectors for nearly two centuries. For all she knew, he'd joined with the Nags from the very beginning. But how old he'd been before that… She'd just assumed he'd been around for a really long time because he was Fae. They were immortal. It hadn't occurred to her that his immortality had to *begin* at some point.

"Centuries," he said vaguely, avoiding a direct answer.

Cary scowled.

He ignored her scowl. "The meetings didn't go well," he said, continuing his story. "My mother, she was…" He pulled in a deep breath. "They claimed she'd been among the humans too long for a highborn. That she'd been *corrupted*—" he snarled the word "—by them."

That was both offensive and scary sounding.

"They wanted to banish her completely," Jaxer said. "Wanted to strip her of her…of her Fae-ness. Basically, condemn her to being human."

Cary ignored the implied insult in the word "condemn" to ask, "Could they do that?"

"Danu can do anything she wants with her subjects. And her courtiers were pushing her to punish my mother. There'd been dissent following her and my father's bonding and removal to the human world. Things were changing in Tirnanog, all over Faery really, and none of the old guard wanted that to happen." He shrugged. "The human world was encroaching as well, pushing against the borders of Faery, forcing them to retreat. The Iron Age had started that process. Humans spreading faster than any Fae could and bringing their gadgetry with them only made things worse." He snorted. "It was going to get a lot worse eventually, but none of us knew that at the time."

"Did Danu punish your mother in the end?"

His gaze darkened. "She stripped her of her magic. Of her

immortality."

Deacon cursed under his breath.

"But she wasn't banned from Faery," Jaxer said.

Cary's brows rose. "Why not?"

He spread his hands, palms up. "Me."

"You?"

"Both sides wanted me."

"Not to sound insulting or anything, but…why?"

Jaxer's mouth quirked at that. "I appreciate the admiration."

She made a face. "Ha. But seriously, why you in particular?"

He let out a long sigh and again glanced toward the window. "I was the first highborn faery child born in several centuries. We're not a very fecund race at the best of times. But that kind of a stretch of time with no children at all? It was unusual enough to seriously worry…everyone."

"Everyone?" Deacon asked.

"It's highborn faery magic that keeps Faery in existence," Jaxer said. "It's what keeps all the other species of Fae who live there safe from other realms. Some Fae couldn't survive outside of Faery for long —like brownies. For all their machinations and power games, the highborn faeries are vital to the survival of our realm."

"But since you are all immortal, what difference did no new children make, really?" Cary asked. "I mean, just keep the faeries you have alive and Faery remains intact, right?"

"Even immortality can't stave off eventual decay." Jaxer frowned slightly. "It's difficult to explain because it's more sense and intuition, but the…flow of magic, the life of it, needs renewal and replenishment. Like… Like food. Magic needs new flavors, new tastes or it gets…" He shrugged.

"Bored?" Cary suggested.

"In a way. It will start to fade without some new input of energy. Each new faery child born into the world provides that fresh energy, the necessary ingredient to keep the entire realm refreshed and vital. It doesn't take much, really. A new child every couple of centuries and Faery remains strong."

"Does it matter *where* the child is born?" Cary asked. "Since Faery is composed of different areas. Like if a child is born among the Fae here in North America—the Nags have a kid—does that benefit all Faery? Or does each area, each court need their own occasional child?"

"Well done. I knew you were learning more than the Nags thought." Jaxer smiled proudly, as if she were a puppy who'd just performed a particularly intelligent trick.

"Hey!" She had learned a lot over the years. She'd only had six years to learn a lifetimes worth of mystical *stuff*. The fact that she didn't know absolutely everything about everything wasn't *her* fault.

He ignored her righteous outrage and said, "Each part of Faery needs their own fresh blood, so to speak, but that infusion benefits all. It's a complicated balance. And both the English court and Tirnanog had gone so long without a new highborn faery at that stage, the entire realm was tipping out of alignment. The last child born in any part of Faery was in the Chinese court about a century before I was born. But most of the other areas had produced children recently enough to keep their magics refreshed."

"Not so in the English or Irish courts?" Deacon asked.

"Exactly," Jaxer said.

"Until you," Cary said as the realization dawned. "That's why both courts wanted you."

"And why my relationship to Faery is complicated," he said. "I belong to both courts and yet to neither. I both help the balance of magic and throw a spanner in the works by not being fully of either court."

"What happened when you moved to North America?" Cary asked. "Did that affect all this magic balance?"

He shook his head. "No. We can move around the entire realm, if we want—most highborns just prefer to remain in their own territories. For the magic balance, though, it's the claim of a court on a child that does the trick."

"And they both had a claim on you," Deacon said.

"It sort of…split the benefit," Jaxer said. "Both good and bad. A complication at the very least."

"What's happened since? What happened to your father?" Cary asked.

Jaxer pulled in a breath, then frowned. He tilted his head to one side and held up a finger. Cary felt the tell-tale sweep of sensation across her shoulders and sighed. Jaxer pointed to his left. Cary and Deacon turned at the same time to see the Nags standing there.

"We're sorry to interrupt," Liruk said, sounding surprisingly sincere.

"But you must go soon," Wisat said.

"What's happened?" Jaxer and Cary asked at the same time.

"Jinx," she said before he could. But only half-heartedly.

"We're feeling some…repercussions in our part of Faery. Already."

"Wait, what?" Cary sat up. "Somethings already happened?"

"No," Liruk said. Then frowned. "We're feeling the possibilities already."

"Our premonitions," Wisat said, as if that clarified everything.

"They can feel as if they are currently happening," Liruk said, which did clear things up a little bit. "When they come as feelings and sensations like this, through the very fabric of the Faery magic, they can be very strong and immediate."

Wisat looked at Jaxer. "I'm sorry we can't do more to help. I thank you for answering this call home."

Jaxer made a face at the word home, but nodded at Wisat's thanks. "It affects us all."

Wisat titled his head to one side in acknowledgment of that. "The brownie gave you more information?"

"Not much to go on. I don't really know if the curse the highborns were referencing could even be accessed by them." He glanced at Cary. "It's called the Lachlinain. It's an old story. A—" he grinned crookedly, "—fairy tale among our people. A spooky tale. The thing that scares the boogeyman into going to bed."

She raised her brows at that. "Why on earth does Borir think *you* can stop this thing that even scares the scariest monsters in Faery?"

Jaxer sighed, his shoulders slumping just a little. "That, I'm afraid, has to do with what happened to my father."

9

$\mathcal{C}$ary launched off the couch. "You said your history with the courts had nothing to do with this," she accused. "You just said the history with the courts wouldn't matter."

"It's complicated," Jaxer said.

"Everything to do with Faery is complicated," she spat. "Explain. Now."

"There isn't much time," Liruk said quietly. "If you delay going too long, things might move in ways that make stopping the catastrophe impossible."

"Premonition double speak," Cary said, snarling. "Give me a short explanation first or I'm not going."

"It's not a short story," Jaxer said. "If you want the highlights, my father wasn't stripped of his immortality, the way my mother was, but he was punished. The punishment…did things to him. Those things are the reason Borir thinks *I* can stop the Lachlinain being unleashed."

"That doesn't make any sense at all," Cary said, hands on hips.

"I told you it was a longer story. I can tell you more once we're there." Jaxer sighed. "It's complicated."

She groaned and jerked her hands into the air. "I hate *complicated*."

"Cary?" Deacon's quiet voice turned her around. "We won't go if you're having second thoughts."

"I'm not. I'm going. I'm just annoyed." She motioned him up. "Put on that cloak." She faced Jaxer. "Get to the glamouring if we need new outfits." She glared. "But don't think we're done with the storytelling here, buddy. I want answers and I want them sooner rather than later."

"Sooner is definitely going to happen when you meet my father," Jaxer said, and raised his hand toward her, palm facing her.

The idea that she was going to meet Jaxer's *father* stunned her into stupefied silence. She only looked down at herself when she heard Deacon's low growl.

She narrowed her eyes at Jaxer. "You really want to piss me off? Right now?"

He grinned. "It's a perfectly appropriate look for the court."

"It's see-through," she said. The diaphanous blue gown hung in paper thin wisps of material, wrapping snuggly around her body, and only a few well-placed patches of tiny, glittery gemstones preventing the room from seeing all the bits she normally kept covered in public. "Are there *flowers* in my hair?"

"You look stunning," Jaxer said.

Deacon growled again and she felt him take a step forward. "Don't." She raised her hand, without looking away from Jaxer. "We don't have time. Jaxer, change this look now, or you are on your own trying to safe Faery while everyone and their pixie tries to kill you."

"Fine. But this would have been more impressive." He flicked his fingers at her.

The rolled her eyes at the dismissive gesture before looking down to see what he'd done. She was still wearing a dress, but at least it wasn't see through anymore. It was made of thicker, glittering material, this time in a flowing pink color that changed to pale blues when she moved. She wasn't much of a pink person, but it wasn't a bad color. The biggest problem was the skirt—it fitted snug to her legs, all the way to her ankles.

"I will fall over if I try to walk in this," she said. Although it was glamour and she technically knew she was still just wearing her jeans and t-shirt, Jaxer was so good that she *felt* like she was wearing this outfit. She took a step forward and nearly tripped as the material contracted around the lower half of her legs.

"Nope," she said. "Not going to work. I can't wander around Faery walking in tiny baby steps."

"You're being very picky about all this," Jaxer said.

"Stop putting me into inappropriate clothing then," she said.

"This is appropriate to the court."

"But not appropriate to a bodyguard. Which is what I'm going to be doing while I'm there. Guarding your body."

"Ah, I knew you cared."

"Jaxer," Deacon growled in warning.

Jaxer ignored him. "How about something like this?" he said and wiggled his fingers at her.

"You don't need to do the hand gestures, do you?" she asked, before risking another look down.

"No." He grinned. "But it's fun."

"This isn't supposed to be fun. We're in a hurry." She took in this outfit. "Finally!"

He'd put her into a pair of tight-fitting leggings and a thigh-length tunic that was belted around her waist with a thick gold cord. The leggings were a dark blue. The tunic still a glittery, diaphanous material—but not see-through!—and the entire thing felt flexible and easy to move in. The thigh-high boots were even flats instead of high heels she wouldn't be able to run in. She didn't run much, but if she had to, running in heels was a great way to get a twisted ankle. She'd done that more than enough over the years.

"Thank you," she said. Then frowned. "There are still flowers in my hair, though, aren't there?"

He shrugged. "They look pretty."

She sighed. "Okay, now Deacon."

Deacon had swung the cloak on already, pinning it into place with the brooch at his left shoulder.

She raised her brows. "Wow. That looks good on you. Even with the jeans and t-shirt." She titled her head to one side. "It actually looks like it belongs on you. That's weird."

"Probably some magic in the material," he said with a shrug. To Jaxer, he said, "If you put me into a see-through dress, at least make sure the color suits my skin tone."

She laughed. Jaxer snorted, but from the flat line of his mouth, Deacon had obviously robbed him of the joke he was about to play.

Jaxer flicked his hands in a dismissive gesture at Deacon, not really looking at him. Cary turned to see the results, half-wondering if Jaxer would put Deacon into a see-through outfit anyway. She had to blink a few times to absorb what Jaxer had actually done.

"Wow," she murmured again.

Deacon was dressed like a warrior from ancient times. Thick brown pants tucked into mid-calf boots topped with fur. His tunic was a deep shade of red, embroidered with gold thread and blue and green jewels. A thick gold and jewel encrusted belt circled his waist, low on his hips, with a short sword hooked into a scabbard on his left side. His hair, normally cut loose but short hung longer now, to just above his shoulders and the black waves made her fingers ache for an excuse to touch him. Rather than flowers, Jaxer had placed a small diadem on his head, gold and also jewel encrusted, which came down low on his brow. The small, golden crown brought out the gold color in his eyes, reflecting the inner light.

The only thing that remained the same was the simple purple cloak and the silver brooch.

"You look like you just stepped out of a novel about ancient Irish gods," she said. "And I mean that in a good way. Well done, Jaxer."

She glanced back in time to see him roll his eyes. But then he frowned and nodded at Deacon. She looked back. Nothing had changed.

"What?" she asked.

"His cloak isn't changing," Jaxer said. "I'm trying to adjust it to match the rest of the look—more gold and embellishments. It's not working."

Everyone looked at the Nags who'd been silently watching the show.

"There is enough magic in the garment already," Wisat said.

Liruk said, "It will make a bigger impression on the English—"

"And Irish," Wisat added.

"Courts," Liruk continued, "just as it is."

Jaxer frowned a little but shrugged and flicked his hands at Deacon again without looking at him. Cary feared the worst but when she studied Deacon, the only change was an extra sword on his right hip.

"Shame those are glamour and not real," she commented. "Although, would you even know how to use a sword?"

"Not as well as my grandma," Deacon said. "But I could mostly keep someone from cutting my head off."

"Well that's good," she said, her mouth flattening.

"He can use the swords if he needs to," Jaxer said. "My glamour has weight to it."

"Meaning?" Cary asked.

"You see and feel it all, right? You feel like you're wearing the clothes you see, not the clothes you actually have on."

"Yeah."

"So does everyone else. Except brownies, of course."

"Or course," she said.

Jaxer once again ignored her aside. "The rest of Faery will see this outer look, assume it's all real, and that gives it a reality. Which means he can use the swords if he has to because anyone seeing them will assume they're real and that gives them a kind of solidity."

"Your magic is scary," she said.

He grinned in reply.

She glanced back at Deacon. "You ready?"

He shrugged. "We'll see when we enter Faery."

"That's not helping." To Jaxer, she said, "We'd better go now. How do we get there?"

With the Nags standing over them, she felt the ticking clock in the back of her mind. She wasn't even entirely sure what it was ticking down *to*, but whatever it was could end the world, and it was her job— unofficially in this case—to stop that.

Even if she didn't have the first clue how. But Protectors kept all hell from breaking loose, and this was one of those moments. Again.

axer took them into Cary's backyard to open the portal into Faery. The dogs followed, so Cary took a moment to give each a head scratch and some hugs and kisses. "I'll be back before you know it," she told them. "Be good for Angie."

Pickles woofed, which Cary took to mean they would. Buck bumped his big head against her thigh, which she took to mean have a save journey. And Fred hopped in a circle, jumped at her, and bounced off her leg, which she took to mean, yay, does this involve food?

The Nags remained as Jaxer opened a door-shaped gap in reality. Beyond the opening, Cary couldn't really see anything except a grayish swirl of fog. Bright colored lights danced in the fog, eerily magnetic, making her want to move closer and see what those lights were. And suddenly, she understood how humans got tricked into entering Faery.

She took a deep breath and unconsciously touched the little good luck charm on the necklace she seemed to wear all the time now—the charm was a little gold-plated Fatima Hand, worn with the fingers pointing up for good luck, given to her as a gift from a girl she'd saved earlier in the year. Jasmine had gotten the necklace from her aunt's shop and assured Cary it was inexpensive so Cary wouldn't feel the need to return it. Angie had touched the necklace and told Cary there was actually a little magic in it, just a touch of good wishes with real magic behind the sentiment. Both Angie and Cary had spent a bit of time with Jasmine and her family over the last months, for meals, and both of them had gone to Jasmine's big fourteenth birthday party. After some careful study, Angie realized Jasmine had just a touch of innate magic. Her aunt had the same spark. It wasn't a lot. But it was enough to bless charms and pass around the kind of good luck infused in Cary's charm.

Without a lot of conscious thought, Cary kept putting the necklace on every day. Mostly because, in her life, she could use all the *good* luck she could get.

Jaxer paused in front of the doorway into Faery and turned to face her and Deacon. "This first part of the journey is going to be the hardest. I'm not in danger here."

He paused to let the information sink in but he didn't have to. Cary had already worked that out when the colored lights started luring her forward.

"My Protector magic isn't flowing yet," she said, to assure him she understood. "Angie said she closed her eyes and that helped. Should I do that? And Deacon? Should Deacon close his eyes?" She frowned. "How the hell will you lead two of us with our eyes closed through Faery? I'm picturing a lot of falls and banged knees."

Jaxer's mouth lifted on one side. "Fortunately, I only need you to close your eyes. Deacon's magic brooch should keep him from succumbing to the madness." He glanced at the Nags and raised his brows. "Right?"

Liruk nodded. "That was the point, Mentor."

"He should be able to travel without the magic taking hold of his mind," Wisat said, in a decidedly more consoling tone.

Jaxer shrugged. "Your choice," he said to Deacon. "Since I can't cover the brooch and cloak with glamour, I'm inclined to think they're telling us the truth."

Deacon almost smiled, the edges of his mouth lifting. For just a split second, Cary saw Deacon and Jaxer as they likely were before the whole mate thing had come up. Friends about to step into danger together and sharing an understanding of what was to come.

"Shame, though," Jaxer said.

Or maybe she was just being overly romantic.

"How am I supposed to move through Faery, then?" she said. "And when will we be in a place where your life is in danger?"

"Why can't Cary protect me in Faery?" Deacon said. "Shouldn't her magic work to keep me safe?"

They all looked at the Nags again.

"Will the fact that he's already protected by the brooch mean my magic won't work?" she asked them. Frankly, that had never come up before. When someone needed protecting—whether they could normally protect themselves or not—her magic worked. But because Deacon was already technically safe with the brooch on, Faery posed him less harm.

Still, the place was full of dangers even without the magic tugging at his brain and animal half. He'd need protection from all those other things. Right?

Liruk and Wisat exchanged another look. "Faery is different, Protector," Liruk said.

"And no Protector has entered Faery before," Wisat said.

Cary sighed. "You don't have any idea."

Well, they'd warned her before this that there was no telling how her powers would work. She faced the doorway with its gray fog and swirling colors. She put Deacon behind her and moved toward the lights, toward the magic, watching for the pull and tug, the lure she'd sensed right after Jaxer opened the door.

The lights were still captivating, still interesting and hard to stop watching. But she could look away. She stopped on the threshold, Jaxer next to her, Deacon behind her, and stared into the realm beyond for a long moment.

"Well?" Jaxer finally said. "Do I carry you with your eyes closed or can you walk?"

"I'll do the carrying if that's necessary?" Deacon growled.

Cary ignored them. She reached out to touch the fog, smacking

Jaxer's hand away when he swiftly tried to stop her. "Stop that," she said when he tried to pull her back again. "I'm testing this."

"How do you feel?" Deacon asked.

"How do you feel?" she asked back, not turning to look at him, but keeping a hand on his arm as she leaned closer to the doorway.

"I'm worried about you," he said.

"No lure into the world?" she asked. "Not feeling compelled to follow all the swirling lights?"

"What lights?" he asked.

That startled her enough that she faced him. Putting her back to Faery was probably a bad idea, but Deacon's comment required eye contact. "What do you see when you look through that doorway?" she asked.

He shrugged. "Some hills and trees. Lots of open space, deep grass, and blue sky."

"No gray fog and dancing iridescent lights?"

He shook his head. "Is that what you're seeing?"

"And the lights were calling me into the fog earlier. Tempting me to follow them."

"Are they now?" He took hold of her shoulders, as if to keep her from the lights he couldn't see.

"Nope," she said. "Not in that compulsive way they were earlier. I still sense the lure but it doesn't feel necessary that I follow. I'm leery and aware of the danger. There was a moment, right after the doorway opened, when I wasn't."

"That's good? You're channeling the Protector magic?" Questions. Not statements.

"Depends on what it means that you see something different." She raised her brows at Jaxer. "Which one of us is Faery messing with right now?"

"Both of you," Jaxer said. "It's what Faery does to non-Fae. But the fact that you're not feeling compelled and overwhelmed is a good sign. And the fact that Deacon hasn't shifted to charge out into the wild is another good sign."

"Wow. The place could do that to him even before he's stepped inside?" Her heartbeat thumped a little faster as adrenaline pumped through her blood.

"That's his temptation," Jaxer said. "At least, it's the temptation for his leopard."

"Why is my temptation gray fog and dancing lights?" she said with a frown. "Why not… I don't know. A pizza restaurant. Or a winery?"

"A coffee shop even," Deacon said.

She nodded and pointed to Deacon while looking at Jaxer. "Or that. I haven't had nearly enough coffee yet today. That would have been very tempting. The smells alone might have pulled me through without a thought."

Jaxer's brow creased, just the barest hint of a frown. "I don't know," he said after a moment. "You're right. Pizza or coffee would have been more tempting." He glanced between the doorway and Cary. "Maybe the magic just doesn't know what to do about you, so it defaulted to a more general lure?"

"Is that…good or bad?" She blinked. "Or just a guess?"

"A guess. A complete guess," Jaxer said. "I haven't a clue. Faery magic tempts people in, lures them with something they love deep down. Do you love dancing lights and mystery deep down?"

She snorted. "Not that I've noticed."

"You do keep jumping into the middle of trouble all the time," Deacon said.

She waved that away. "That's just my job."

"A job you got after jumping into the middle of trouble," Jaxer reminded her.

"The demon. Should *not*. Have kicked. The puppy," she said. How many times did she have to explain that to people? "Also, I was tricked into this job, and we both know it."

"I know no such thing," Jaxer said.

"It is past time to go," Liruk put in, her tone sharp. "You will miss the window of time and chance to fix this if you don't go now."

"Hey," Cary snapped, "I'm off the clock here. You don't get to tell me what to do. I'm walking into Faery, and I don't know if I'm coming out. Forgive me if I have some questions."

But in truth, that clock in the back of her mind was ticking louder with each passing moment. Liruk was right. She was stalling. Maybe not consciously, but she was hunting up excuses because she was scared. Really scared. The kind of scared that had her stomach tight and her heartbeat pumping and her mouth dry and the bad kind of adrenaline surging through her system.

She looked into the doorway. Gray fog and dancing lights still swirled on twisting eddies. Despite admitting out loud to her real temptations. No pizza restaurants had appeared. No cozy tables with bottomless pots of coffee on top of them. No donut shops or ice cream vendors. None of the things—all food related she noticed—that might really tempt Cary to wander into danger unaware.

Either Faery knew something about her that she didn't. Or Faery couldn't understand her at all.

Straightening her shoulders, and hoping with all her might that the second thing was true, she stepped toward the doorway. Deacon held her hand and stayed behind her, letting her protect him from the magic so she would be safe against it too.

Boy, she hoped this worked.

"Jaxer," she said as he moved up next to her.

"Yes?"

"If I go crazy in Faery, I just want you to know…"

"Yes?"

"I'm going to blame you."

She stepped into the swirling fog.

11

The fog cleared slowly, fading away the farther she moved forward. Lights still danced, teasing at the periphery of her vision, and voices whispered just beyond her ability to hear them clearly, urging her to strain to catch their meaning. She leaned forward once, listening hard. Then straightened and shook off the compulsion. She didn't need to know what the dancing lights and whispering voices were saying. In fact, she was pretty sure she didn't want to know.

Deacon held tight to her hand, staying behind her. He leaned in. "How are you doing?"

"So far, so good." She made a face. "I think. Do I still seem like myself?"

"You haven't started chasing lights yet, so I'm going to say yes."

She snorted.

"Definitely yes," he said.

That was a relief. "How are you doing?"

"Fine. The sun is warm. The scents of the forest are strong. And my leopard is resting contentedly without any need to go racing off into the jungle."

"So the brooch is working. That's good."

"And your magic must be working as well, keeping me safe despite the brooch."

"Yeah. Yeah?" She wasn't sure. Maybe Faery was just fucking with her.

Jaxer appeared out of the fading fog and gestured. "This way. We'll have to make a few transitions in and out of your realm to reach the English court."

"You couldn't have mentioned that earlier?" Stepping into that doorway once had taken a lot of her courage, and now he expected her to do it again? And again?

"It'll be easier from now on," he said, his tone gentle. "You'll know what you're stepping into."

"I still don't have the faintest clue what I've stepped into," she snapped as she followed him in a direction she assumed was forward.

She glanced back but could no longer see the doorway or her backyard. She was well and truly inside Faery now with no way out until Jaxer opened another door. Panic trickled through her bloodstream. She punched it down and focused on keeping Deacon safe. That helped them both and she knew how to deal with that.

Though the fog had faded, her surroundings were still baffling.

Like a smudged painting, started by an impressionist and then just smeared and twisted, the surroundings refused to take solid shape or become much of anything. There were the suggestions of maybe hills, sometimes trees, though not the lush verdant jungles of Deacon's view. Some vaguely brown and green colors that might have been shaped as lines before being melted like old crayons. A few brightly colored smudges and some illuminated spots, like lights or suns or maybe even stars. The ground under her seemed to lose shape and solidity if she looked at it, too. If she didn't, it felt as solid as a dirt path through the woods—some give, a little rough, but solid nonetheless. When she looked, though, things seemed to roll and buck and move. A little like being in an earthquake. The colors were gray, brown, white and a little yellow but all swirled together. And any sense of substance went out the window. Without warning, she was walking on clouds, on water, on air.

She stumbled more than once, her body trying to find some stability even as it sensed itself falling into the swirl of colors and air her mind saw. Deacon held her hand tightly, catching her around the waist once or twice to keep her up.

"Don't look down," Jaxer said over his shoulder. "How's your mind doing?"

"Depends on what you consider sane," she said. "This place is bonkers."

"Sounds sane to me," Jaxer said, facing forward again. "Faery is bonkers."

"I'm still just walking through a jungle," Deacon said.

"Any compulsion to run after a darting prey animal?" Jaxer asked.

"No. Not even seeing any, but not interested in hunting either."

"Cary, any interest in wandering off and exploring all the weirdness?" Jaxer asked her, keeping his gaze forward.

"Not even a little bit. I can't get out of here fast enough."

"Good. Faery magic is a lure not a repulsion. At least that's the way it's supposed to work on humans. Your Protector magic must be working."

"Maybe," she muttered as something darted in front of her face and then dashed away, so fast even the sense of color was lost on her. She shook her head. "Are there other things here checking us out?" she asked.

"Some. Mostly they're staying away. Why?"

"Something just buzzed me," she said under her breath. She did have a sense of being watched but there wasn't a sense of threat in it—which surprised the ever-loving hell out of her. This whole place felt like a threat to her.

And maybe that was the point. "You suppose Faery is trying to freak me out on purpose?" she asked. "Because I'm a Protector and I'm not supposed to be here? Rather than lure and seduce, the place really wants to eject me as quickly as possible?"

Jaxer didn't answer for a long while. "Anything is possible here. But we're still within the North American sector—not where the Nags reside and reign, but still a less hostile part of Faery. If the magic is working to scare you off, then it isn't just the Fae themselves who object to Protectors. It's the very realm, down to its essence."

"That doesn't sound…good," she said.

"Maybe it's just you," Deacon said in a reasonable tone of voice.

"Gee, thanks."

He chuckled and the sound actually settled her nerves, which were jumping around so much she felt like her skin was going to burst.

"I didn't mean that to offend," Deacon said. "I mean, because you can absorb magic. Maybe it's not so much the Protector part of you but the more innate part of you that's causing Faery to fear you."

The very suggestion that an *entire realm* of wild magic and creatures of myth might be afraid of *her* was so laughable, so absurd, she forgot for all of two minutes to be worried.

"That's beyond ridiculous," she said. She might even have laughed if she'd had the concentration for it. She was too busy trying to stay upright and not look at her feet to really laugh. But inside, she was laughing at the idea. Hard.

Jaxer didn't comment, one way or the other. And it was his silence that finally stopped her amusement.

"Wait," she said. "You're not taking that idea seriously, are you Jaxer?"

"We're almost to the place where we step out of Faery for a minute," he said, ignoring her question.

She frowned at his back, opened her mouth to say more, and found herself stumbling from the weird swirling world of Faery into a bright hot afternoon, surrounding by grass and trees and…skyscrapers poking over the tops of the trees.

"Hey, are we in Central Park?" She turned in a circle. Sure enough, she spotted tall buildings rising above the trees in the other direction as well.

She came to New York to visit her sister when she could, but she'd only managed a handful of visits since becoming a Protector—which had started only a few months before her sister married right out of college and moved here permanently. So Cary wasn't an expert on the place. She wasn't certain exactly where they were inside the park, but there was no mistaking this was Central Park. She was pretty sure one of those tall buildings was the famous Dakoda building. Maybe? She'd have to check with Valerie.

They'd apparently stepped out of Faery and into a huge expanse of open grass lawn, some low hills and a few scattered trees around the edges. The smell of heat and grass permeated everything. The area was filled with people, gathered on blankets or just resting in the grass, kids running around playing, groups talking and laughing, some joggers passing on a nearby paved path. No one was looking in their direction.

"Why didn't any of these people notice we just appeared out of nowhere?" she asked.

"They see what I want them to see," Jaxer said, grinning at her. "Glamour remember."

She glanced down at her outfit, feeling like she'd stepped out of Renaissance Faire compared to all the other people surrounding them in their summer dresses, shorts and t-shirts, yoga pants and tank tops. Well, there was that one guy in his business suit, but even that was very very New York.

Actually, as she thought about it, New Yorkers probably wouldn't notice her and Deacon's distinctly Ren Faire clothes. They'd probably just think they were actors or…interesting fellow New Yorkers.

The humidity hit her in the next moment, the afternoon heat heavy with the oppressive weight of damp air. "Wow, and I thought we were having some hot days," she muttered. "When do we go back into the madhouse?"

Jaxer snorted at that. "Be sure to tell Tatianna that's what you call Faery when you meet her, will you? I'd love to see her expression."

"We're in enough trouble here as it is," she said. "I'm not going to aggravate the queen of the English court." The thought of meeting *the* Tatianna was too overwhelming to think about so she decided not to. She had other worries to keep her well occupied just then.

"Are you settle enough to go back in?" Jaxer said.

"We're not taking this detour for my sake, are we? I'd rather just get where we're going and be done with it."

"Not the type to break up travel with a few choice layovers?" he asked.

"No."

"Fair enough. We are not taking the detours for your sake, though. We have to do this to get where we're going."

She narrowed her eyes at him, but he seemed sincere. Which for Jaxer could just as well be an act. Or magic. She didn't argue, though. She didn't want to waste time.

"I'm ready when you are," she said, waving a hand for him to get on with things.

"Okay, here we go."

He opened another portal into Faery and gestured her and Deacon inside. She took hold of Deacon's hand and stepped through with Jaxer at her side, Deacon at her back.

And almost fell on her face in the sudden darkness. "Shit," she muttered, squeezing Deacon's hand. "You still there?"

"Here," Deacon grunted. "Can't see. But here."

"Can't see anything either."

No pinpoints of starlight, no faint glow, no nothing. She blinked a few times and the pervasive black was there with her eyes opened or closed. She cursed again under her breath and without thinking reached to her side where Jaxer had been. She connected with his arm, the smooth texture of his silk shirt settling her. The arm felt like Jaxer and knowing she was in contact with both her companions helped stave off some of the primal panic at sudden blindness.

She pulled in a deep breath, let it out slowly, calming her pulse. She could manage this. It was probably worse for Deacon, a shifter with excellent night vision who wasn't used to being without his sense of sight even at night.

Although, his sense of smell was even better. "You scenting anything?" she asked him, squeezing his hand so he'd know she was talking to him.

"Faintly—roses and ice. It's a strange combination."

"Sorry for the blackness," Jaxer said, not sounding sorry. "Should have warned you. This passage moves us into a new section of Faery. We're almost to our exit."

"Wait," Cary said. "How? We're not moving?"

"The passage is," Jaxer said.

"Whoa." Her stomach rolled. Could you get motion sickness if you weren't moving but just aware that something around you was?

A bit of light broke into the solid wall of black, making her wince. Amazing how fast she'd gotten used to not being able to see. The growing point of illumination suddenly felt too bright. She squinted as it got closer, brighter, and then it broke over her like a wave.

The scent of salt, ice, and a sharp bite of something metallic hit her first. The air was cool and crisp, a lovely relief after the New York humidity. Eventually, the brightness faded enough that she could see again. She narrowed her eyes and stare for a long moment before she could adjust to *what* she was seeing. Icy covered gray mountains, a flat pool of water with steam rising over its surface, a blue and cloudless sky overhead.

"Uhm?"

"Iceland," Jaxer said.

"I've never been here before." An asinine, and obvious, statement, but it was all she could think to say. Iceland. Wow.

"Wait till you hear this," Jaxer said.

He stood very close and she realized she hadn't let go of his arm yet. She was still clutching Deacon's hand as well. She eased her grip on both men, but kept her hand entwined with Deacon's. Jaxer didn't step away, but he turned to gesture at the sky.

"It's about an hour earlier than it was when we left your house," he said.

"Huh?" She looked up. "But... Huh?"

"Couldn't be a time zone thing," Deacon muttered. He was also studying their surroundings, but he looked a lot less shell shocked than Cary felt.

"Time works weirdly in Faery," Jaxer said. "We exited here before we entered in your backyard. Nothing to do with time zones. If this was just an effect of time zone changes, it'd be later here. Though not dark this time of year."

Cary shook her head. "How can you tell?"

"I'm old and experienced," Jaxer said, giving her a little bow. "I know my way around time paradoxes."

She pressed her lips together in a tight line. She was not amused. "Can we just move on?"

"You don't want to take a dip?" He gestured to the hot pool. "The water is lovely here."

"No. Thank you."

He grinned. "Fine. Here we go."

Another portal cut into reality. She pulled in a deep breath and held tight to Deacon's hand again. He moved close enough that she could feel his heat along her back.

Jaxer hesitated outside the portal, not stepping through for a long moment. Cary wasn't going to walk in there without him so she waited, watching as he stared into the realm beyond. She looked to see what he was seeing. But there was nothing there—literally nothing. She couldn't see blackness or gray fog or anything at the moment. She was *aware* of the hole in reality, and she couldn't see beyond it, but she couldn't see into the portal either. That was as disorienting as the blackness. Maybe more. She'd been able to *understand* blackness.

She turned away so Faery couldn't mess with her mind any more than it already had and watched Jaxer watching the space beyond the portal.

"You sure you want to do this?" she asked quietly after another few moments.

For all everyone had been concerned with getting her and Deacon through Faery without them going crazy, it was Jaxer taking the real risk at the end of this journey. He wasn't welcome where they were going. Cary still didn't know what kind of greeting he was expecting. But the fact that he'd wanted her along to protect him made her certain it wouldn't be good.

"Even the Nags think I have to go," Jaxer said, his voice oddly emotionless. "I haven't been through this part of Faery in centuries."

He shrugged. "I don't notice time very often. I'm feeling the years just now."

With his free hand, Deacon clapped Jaxer on the shoulder. "We've got your back. But if you don't want to go, we won't."

Jaxer turned slowly to look at Deacon, frowning slightly. "Thanks," he said.

Another of those brief moments, where Cary could just see their former friendship. Damn but she wished they could go back to that. Just as she wished she and Jaxer could go back to their emotionally uncomplicated friendship.

Both men turned away from the moment without further comment and Jaxer squared his shoulders.

"Okay," he said, almost to himself. "Okay."

He grabbed Cary's hand, a gesture that startled her, squeezing tight. Then they all moved into the portal.

12

There was a long, disorienting moment of nothingness, as if her senses weren't working at all. No sight, sound, light or dark. It wasn't the sensory deprivation of the portal between New York and Iceland. It wasn't the thick fog or swirling lights on the way to New York. She couldn't even feel Deacon or Jaxer's hands in hers, though she was still aware on some level that they had to be there. She tried flexing her hands, tightening her grip, but she couldn't even feel that.

Was this what it was like to die? This loss of all sensation?

She knew her heartbeat was pounding hard, and breathing was difficult because of the adrenaline rush and fear, yet even that felt… dulled and distant. Something happening to someone else.

Maybe more like an out of body experience? But then, didn't you *see* yourself and the rest of the world during those? She'd have to look it up when she got home.

If she got home.

Finally, a faint sensation clawed through the emptiness and woke her nerve endings. She sensed the tight tight grip of someone holding her right hand—Deacon. Then someone holding her left—Jaxer. She made a conscious effort to pull in a breath, and felt her lungs fill and her chest expand.

And then everything burst into life around her. So suddenly, so completely, she gasped and almost lost her hold on her companions.

"Holy hell," she muttered.

"Yeah," Deacon said, taking a step closer to her.

"I warned you," Jaxer said.

Cary nodded. He had tried to warn them. But she doubted anything he'd have said could have prepared her for the world around them. The immense, golden, iridescent glory surrounding them defied description anyway.

There were things that looked like trees, but with glowing rainbow trunks and golden leaves. At least some of them. Others were more solidly colored in reds and browns and greens, but the trunks were green and red while the leaves were brown. And still others that looked like trees in her realm, brown trunks, green leaves, although the shapes of the leaves were strange and specific. Was that a leaf shaped like a dog?

From some of the trees, vines like ropes of sparkling Christmas lights hung to the ground. In other places, the trees towered so high, Cary couldn't see the tops. The grass underfoot was green and blue and scattered with pinpoint flowers in a myriad of pastel colors atop golden stems. And what looked like fireflies or starlight danced in between the grass blades.

The temperate air itself seemed to sparkle with a kind of iridescence, shimmering in the diffused sunlight—sunlight that seemed to come from everywhere at once instead of from a single source, like a sun. There were no shadows anywhere, not even under the trees. It weirdly reminded her of a child's drawing. All sparkle and imagination, but no contrasts between shadow and light, no actual depth in the use of bright and dark.

To add to the weirdly child-like impression, the place smelled like...

"Is that cotton candy?" she asked, sniffing. "And maybe chocolate chip cookies? Or is that just Faery fucking with me?" If it was, Faery had finally gotten something right.

"No," Jaxer said. "Those are smells Oberon likes, so those are the smells that fill Faery. When I left, the place smelled primarily like curry spices and cheeseburgers."

"That's…an interesting combination," Cary said.

"Tell me about it." Jaxer snorted.

She noticed he sounded a little more American than usual, his accent bending toward the Pacific Northwest and away from its usual vaguely Irish or sometimes English. Jaxer had chosen neither for this visit. And she couldn't help but wonder if he was claiming neutrality with the American bluntness.

She also wondered if that would work.

From the corners of her eyes, she spotted dancing, flitting, moving beings, but she couldn't catch a good look at them to see what kind of Fae were checking them out. They could have just been birds or bats for all she could see. Whenever she turned, the little things flitted out of sight.

"Should we have been expecting a welcome party?" Cary asked, finally releasing her tight grip on both men to turn in a full circle.

Certain parts of the garden seemed to dance away from her gaze so she couldn't focus on them. She'd spot something that might have been a living thing, turn to look at it, and it would be gone. Whatever *it* was. Sometimes the its were large enough to worry her. Sometimes they were human-sized. Sometimes so small, she felt more like she was trying to catch sight of a bug. But none of the moving things stayed still long enough to give her a good look.

"We're being watched and monitored and studied," Jaxer said. "But they won't approach or engage unless ordered to. Apparently, the queen and king want to see me."

"How can you tell?" Cary spun fast trying to catch sight of something big just to the left. Nope. Missed it. Damn.

"We're not being swarmed," Deacon said.

Jaxer nodded.

"Is that one of the possibilities?" Shit. That didn't sound pleasant.

She sure hoped her Protector abilities were working here. Speaking of which. "Are my Protector abilities working here?"

"Have you gone screaming crazy yet?" Jaxer asked.

"Not that I can tell, but given what I'm glimpsing from the corner of my eyes, who knows."

"Faery's presenting itself to you as it is," Jaxer said. "No illusions. Well, none that aren't normal. This is just what the English court looks like. So either you're channeling your Protector magic, or the place wants you to see it this way."

"I'm not sure that second option is good for us," she muttered.

"Probably not. But then again, nothing here is going to be good for us."

"Gee, you're just a bundle of reassurances today," she said and flashed him a scowl.

He grinned in return. Which was actually pretty reassuring.

"How you doing?" she asked Deacon.

He shrugged. "I'm seeing what you're seeing so I suppose that's good. The smells are pretty intense and sweet. A lot of sugar and vanilla in the air. It's making my nose itch. And my leopard is on full alert. But I feel in control of myself and my animal half, so I'm assuming that's…good?"

They both looked at Jaxer. He lifted his shoulder. "I assume so, too. At least for the moment."

"So, when do we know if I'm functioning as a Protector here?" Cary asked, still trying to catch sight of the beings watching them. She had a feeling this had become a game, at least for them, because she very faintly heard the sounds of laughter like bells dancing on a breeze. Though there weren't any breezes. The pleasant temperature permeated the garden, but the air itself didn't move. No currents or eddies. An odd bit of stillness that also made her think of a child's creation—a playworld missing some of the basics of nature.

It also made her realize there weren't many other sounds outside of the laughter and hers and Jaxer's and Deacon's voices. A very very faint sense of sound like a bell came and went, but otherwise, there was no bird song, leaves rustling, water falling sounds. Even her own footsteps as she turned seemed muted.

"We'll know when someone tries to seduce Deacon or kill me," Jaxer said blandly in answer to her question. "We should present ourselves to the queen and king. They're waiting." He lowered his voice. "Tatianna doesn't wait well even though she has eternity."

"Unless the conspirators succeed," Cary muttered.

That earned her raised brows from Jaxer. "This way."

Deacon took her hand again as they moved through the weird landscape and she couldn't bring herself to argue with the contact. They'd probably both be better off with their hands free if things went wrong. But she needed the comfort of touching him.

Though she didn't know where they were going, she still took the lead, keeping just ahead of Jaxer and Deacon so she could protect them from any threats. Jaxer murmured directions, ensuring they got to where they were going, but he remained carefully just behind her.

They stepped onto a stone path—stone that was a light gray color, which was an oddly normal thing in the otherwise topsy-turvy landscape—that twisted through the trees and felt like it was taking them deeper into Faery. Cary got the impression that was relative. The entrance they'd walked through to get here was just one of many. Distance and time and space were probably pretty flexible concepts here.

As if to prove this point, they seemed to be walking for a very long time along the stone path. It moved from being rough and cobbled, to a smooth, thin road of blocks. Yet still they walked. And all along their route, things hovered just out of sight. Watching them. The hairs on the back of her neck spent so much time at attention in her awareness of the danger, she wasn't sure they'd ever settle. She wasn't sure her nerves would ever settle again.

She really hoped they didn't have to stay here too long. Faery, or at the very least, this part of Faery was giving her the creeps.

That sensation did not diminish when she finally stepped from the trees into a huge, open area, paved in smooth marble and surrounded by white columns. Overhead, the sky remained blue and cloudless.

Trees just outside the columns bent a little inward, providing an edge of cover. But mostly the huge space was open and filled with light. So much sparkling golden light, she couldn't see to the opposite side.

And here, finally, were beings that didn't rush away from her direct gaze. Dozens of tall, willowy beings, with faintly human features and shapes, but there was no way anyone would confuse these creatures for humans. They were beautiful, ethereal in their strangeness, stunning and seductive. Pale skin to dark as ebony, hair ranging in length and color from none at all to an iridescent purple Cary kind of envied. Their clothing was elaborate and grand, but impossible to affix into a single style. Some wore flowing, gauzy material. Some heavy leather and chainmail—couldn't be iron-based metal, though, so she wondered what it was. Still others rich velvets and silk. And was that person wearing a human-like business suit? She blinked a few times at that. The contrast with everything else was so stark and odd, her brain balked. Especially because something about the man in the business suit seemed…familiar. Weird.

The silence in the clearing was oppressive. Even the faintly almost impossible to hear sound of bells had stilled. Cary's ears rang with the silence. No one moved. Nothing fluttered. There was still no air movement or breeze. Gold and silver and precious jewels winked in the diffuse light, but that was the only sense of life among the myriad collected there.

"Okay," she murmured. "Now what?"

Jaxer lifted a hand and gestured to the far side of the clearing. "We present ourselves to the queen and king," he said.

Cary blinked and the light that had been blocking her view of the far side of the clearing finally dropped. She gasped. She couldn't help it.

"Cary Redmond," Jaxer said, "may I present Queen Tatianna and King Oberon of Faery."

Cary swallowed hard. She hadn't moved. But they were suddenly standing in front of the two leaders of this court. And she felt rooted to the spot, unable to think or speak or process any of what she was seeing. Her poor little brain wanted to pack things in and go on vacation. Somewhere nice. Maybe Hawaii.

Deacon's hand tightened in hers. She squeezed back.

Holy hell.

What had they gotten themselves into?

Describing Tatiana and Oberon felt a little beyond her powers of language and imagination, but her brain still tried to settle on some solid way to think of them. Eventually, she got around to glowing gorgeousness.

Tatiana gave the impression of pale and dark beauty combined—mostly a lot of pale, though Cary was hard pressed to say which parts were pale. Her mind really couldn't quite wrap her brain around the queen. And she'd thought meeting Deacon's mom had been intimidating!

She blinked a few times and Tatiana settled into a vaguely human-shaped entity with pale skin and hair and darker clothing made up of shadows and silk, possibly in blues, greens, and browns, but the colors melded and shifted into something she couldn't name. There was a halo of light around the queen's body that made the edges of her blurry. And she seemed to be holding a scepter, but the stick of gold and flashing color came in and out of Cary's focus so she couldn't be sure.

Oberon took less time to settle into something Cary could vaguely imagine. He was darker overall, dark hair and skin, paler clothing but still in darker jewel shades than whatever it was that covered Tatiana. He gave the impression of being stunningly handsome, but it was more an impression, a feeling, than any feature or actual look she could see with her eyes.

In fact, a lot of her sense of the queen and king emerged as more of a feeling than through a visual impact. Her eyes kept trying to make sense of them but had to rely on this *sense* of what they were rather than being able to *see* them.

The experience was all together the most disorienting experience Cary had ever had. And that included channeling a baby god's powers on accident.

Jaxer bowed low in greeting. Cary didn't trust her limbs and coordination to bow quite that deeply, and she didn't have the first clue how to curtsey properly, so when Jaxer introduced her in a formal tone, she dipped her head and lowered her eyes, leaning forward as far as she could without feeling like she might fall over.

His introduction of Deacon was significantly more elaborate than the simple, "Cary Redmond" she'd gotten.

"Deacon Jones, son of Maria Jones, queen of the Pacific Northwest leopard shifters, son of Evan Jones, consort to the leopard queen."

From the corner of her eyes, Cary saw Deacon bow. He executed the same deep, graceful, formal gesture that Jaxer had. Bastards with their innate grace. She probably looked like a gangly teenager next to them. Ah well. Too late to be anything but what she was.

A long moment of silence followed. It was hard to tell if the queen and king had even heard the introductions.

With her nerves stretched too taunt and her awareness of the danger Faery posed to them all, she broke the silence. "We've come to save Faery."

If she couldn't be graceful and she couldn't even wrap her mind around the vision of the queen and king, at the very least, she could keep the conversation moving in the right direction.

Her pronouncement broke the silence, all right. Which, she supposed, was sort of the point.

A wave of noise traveled through the court from just behind her all the way to the back of the clearing, picking up sound and intensity as it went. There weren't as many laughs as she would have expected. She'd just claimed that a human, a shifter, and an exiled faery were going to stop the destruction Faery—that Faery could even be destroyed—and she'd thought for sure that would earn them, at the very least, a few guffaws.

But apparently, the court took the statement seriously. The sounds of worry and anger spread fast. She couldn't tell if the sharp, angry-sounding twittering was actual anger. She couldn't understand the words being spoken. She assumed because this was the *English* court, that most of the Fae here spoke a version of English that she'd be able to understand, but again, this was Faery so who knew. By the time the sounds got loud enough for her to hear individual words, there was too much noise to make out what anyone was saying anyway.

The cacophony carried on long enough that Cary wanted to fidget. The queen and king hadn't so much as moved, not during the introductions and not following Cary's pronouncement and not in response to the rising anxiety filling the court. They remained like statues in the same positions they'd been in from the start.

Where they even alive? There as a lot of light around them, and glow and sparkle and magic and awesomeness in the literal sense of that word, but without movement, they might as well have been magically encircled marble or spotlighted statues in a museum.

After what felt like an excruciatingly long wait, something finally changed. She couldn't see it at first in the queen and king, but the court began to quiet. Silence descended once again, slowly but completely.

With the silence came another change. Like the sun dipping just behind the horizon, the impossibility of looking directly at the queen and king seemed to ease away. She could sort of see them now, her impression of them coming into sharper focus. They were still hard to look at, hard to discern clearly, but her visual sense of them came together better.

"You are a Protector," Tatiana said.

Cary startled at the sound of her voice. It was higher than she'd expected, softer, and a lot more gentle. She'd been imaging something deep and reverberating. Instead, Tatiana sounded faint, as if she were smaller and less substantial than the trees around them.

The disconnect between what Cary had expected and what immerged from the queen took her a moment to process and so she was slow to answer. Finally, she said, "Yes. I am. And I realize I'm not supposed to be here. The Nags…my bosses send their apologies. But this was important."

A sharp, and quickly cut off, laugh seemed to come from the direction of the queen and king, but Cary couldn't tell if one of them had made the noise or if it had come from someone else. She couldn't see beyond them. There could be a whole other part of the court back there.

That was a creepy and scary realization.

"The Nags is a good name for that particular group of Fae," a deeper and more booming voice said.

Oberon's voice. And *his* voice was exactly what Cary had been expecting to come from him. All power and depth and weight. That at least was something she could settle with.

"I suppose most people consider their bosses nags at some point in time," Cary said by way of trying to hold on to some diplomacy. She didn't want to throw her bosses under the bus, but calling them the Nags was habit, and if it amused Oberon, that was probably good for her. At least they weren't sending her packing—or breaking her mind—just yet.

"Why do you think Faery is in danger?" Oberon asked.

"Ah, well, that is something of a story." She looked at Jaxer. "You want to explain." She subtly nodded behind them. "Or shall I?"

"Will we get privacy if we ask for it?" Jaxer addressed the queen with his question.

"Done."

Cary glanced over her shoulder. The clearing was empty. Whether the court had fled or Tatiana had magically moved them, Cary couldn't say. But there were no longer any other beings in the wide open, column circled space. And it had only taken a blink for the place to clear out.

That was impressive.

"Explain now, Jaxer," the queen said in her soft, high voice. "Why have you finally returned to us?"

That didn't sound like a threat.

"And why," Oberon added in his deep voice, "shall we not kill you where you stand?"

Ah. There was the threat.

Well, at least that gave Cary a reason to be here.

"A brownie named Borir traveled to the human realm to find me," Jaxer said. "With a story that forced me to break my exile. I would have stayed away if I didn't believe this was serious."

The glow around Tatiana dimmed at that. Interesting. But since Cary could barely look at the queen, attempting to read her moods and reactions from her glow was probably a stretch. Maybe she just moved between darker and lighter phases, like a moon?

"Serious enough to bring a forbidden Protector into our midst," Oberon said.

Jaxer bowed his head slightly. "So serious that I wanted to survive our initial reunion long enough to explain."

Oberon grunted a noise that Cary couldn't begin to interpret. Amusement? Annoyance? Something caught in his throat?

"I know Borir," Tatiana said. "Why you? Why did our dear subject not come directly to me?"

"Ah. Now, there's the tale," Jaxer said.

His accent had changed again, lilting ever so slightly toward the Irish. She wanted to frown at him but was too terrified she'd give something away she wasn't supposed to. She might not be able to read Tatiana and Oberon's reactions, but she had no illusions that hers were all that mysterious to them.

"Do tell," Tatiana said, as she leaned ever so slightly forward.

Cary felt a very distinct nudge, a physical push at her shields—which she now knew for sure were up. Since she rarely felt her shield, or anything coming into contact with it, the fact that she'd felt the nudge was disconcerting, her sharp inhale in reaction was hard to hide. She narrowed her eyes at the queen, then the king. But of course, she couldn't read their expressions. Trying to just make sense of them was more than enough for her poor brain.

She waited for another nudge, another push, and when it didn't happen, and Jaxer began his story without anything weird happening, she decided to let it go. The Potector shield was working, or at the very least *there*, so she and her companions had some level of defense. As she couldn't be sure how Tatiana and Oberon would take the news of members of their court conspiring to destroy Faery, having any protection at all felt like a very good thing.

"Your highnesses," Jaxer said formally, with his Irish accent now on full display, "my story begins with a little light treason."

14

"It all began with a walk in the garden," Jaxer continued. "And talk of an ancient curse."

In a lilting, richly cadenced rhythm, Jaxer related the story of Borir, minding his own business, tending the trees, overhearing the highborns discussing their plot. As Jaxer told it, Cary could practically see the events happening, almost feel them, live them along with our terrified brownie hero. She found herself hanging on Jaxer's every word, breathless in anticipation, anxious over what would happen to poor Borir, even though she knew. She'd been the one to save him! None of that seemed to matter. Jaxer spun the story into a kind of magic all its own. And she was captivated.

Especially when he got to the part she didn't know yet.

"The Lachlinain is not something just any faery could access," Oberon said as Jaxer's recitation hit a natural break. "Not even a highborn."

"Ah, but we both know there's a reason for them to think otherwise," Jaxer said. "Me da was charged for crimes against the court when he had me and refused to kill his beloved wife as a way to earn the court's forgiveness."

Cary tried not to gasp out loud, she really did, but she must have

94

made some noise because Tatiana's attention shifted, very obviously, to Cary. The queen didn't speak. But she stared at Cary while Jaxer continued.

"And unlike my mother, who was stripped of her immortality, my da was forced to continue with his. So that he would watch his wife die. But from a distance. For he was charged to guard the ancient curse. He was burdened with the stewardship of the Lachlinain."

Cary's eyes widened with each statement. Holy hell! His father was the *guardian* of the very thing that could end Faery. That was…big. Especially since it was pretty obvious Jaxer's father would have a grudge against Faery. Particularly the Irish and English courts for what they'd done to him and his wife.

She wanted to ask questions so bad she could barely hold them back. Only the feel of Tatiana's gaze on her, the weight of the ancient queen's stare, kept Cary quiet.

"He cannot shirk this duty," Jaxer continued. "The geas placed upon him prevents it. Physically, he must protect the Lachlinain from all who might wish to release it. Ah, but even that might not have been enough for a man who'd had the love of his life, his family, all stripped away from him. Would it? So the court tightened their hold, and ensured he was bound irrevocably to this duty."

How? *How*? Cary was bursting with her need to ask. She pressed her lips together, willing the words to stay inside. She didn't dare interrupt now.

"You were saved," Oberon said. "Thanks to this court's choices."

"Saved, eh?" Jaxer's tone held more bitterness than he'd allowed out so far. But he quickly buried the emotion under his storyteller's cadence. "Yes, the young prince of two worlds was the key. The key to all. Control him, and Faery is balanced. Like the Irish court, the English court wanted me. Needed me. Everything depended on it. But both had a claim and neither could force the issue. That was the rub. Being of two worlds, being of both and neither court, I was free to choose my allegiance."

And yet both courts had given him fair reason to hate them and not choose either. They'd essentially killed his mother and cursed his father into a life Cary was pretty sure sucked based on the ominous tone Jaxer had used to describe it. It was all she could do not to reach back and take his hand, to give comfort somehow, pointless though it would be at this stage.

"My da knew you wouldn't kill me. Or strip me of my immortality to punish him. You couldn't. You needed me. Needed the new blood, the new magic. Without it, this world stagnates and fades away into shadows and smoke. A place as insubstantial as mist on the moors. But the court gave him a promise, one that, even could he break the geas to guard the Lachlinain, would make him choose to continue his duty. You promised him that I would be protected. Not an outcast you happened to need but didn't want. I would be welcomed to the court with full honors. And be protected from all enemies."

He paused. The weight of the pause filled the clearing. Cary could barely breathe as she waited.

"And so it came to pass that this halfbreed son of two feuding courts was able to claim a high place in the English honor roll. As well as the Irish. I was given free rein, so to speak, of two different courts, with no burden of exile or abuse hanging over me. My father accepted his geas willingly, so that his son would be blessed. And so it was and has been. For centuries."

Tatiana, her gaze still on Cary, said, "Ulieran will guard the Lachlinain until the end of time. You see, our wayward heart's son, no one will get through him to release destruction upon our realm. Because to do so would destroy the only thing left Ulieran loves." She turned her gaze, then, to stare at Jaxer. "You."

The twisted, manipulative, terrible truth hung between the queen and Jaxer in a silence so deep Cary felt it in her bones.

But...

She let the story's details mix and mingle in her brain. Didn't this mean Jaxer was as safe here in the English court as he'd be at home? They couldn't kill him, despite Oberon's threat, no matter what he did, or his father would be released from his obligation to guard the Lachlinain. Or at least would no longer have the psychological reason to stick to it. The physical compulsion of a geas might be harder to overcome.

Cary knew geas weren't things to be taken lightly. You couldn't just *not* do them. That was the point. The person under a geas was forced to carry out their quest.

It occurred to her suddenly that a geas was an Irish thing, not an English thing, and she was about to ask questions, only to realize she'd be derailing her own attempt to logic through the situation. So she got back to sorting through what she had just learned.

Without the assurance of Jaxer's life, Ulieran would have a very good reason to look for loopholes and ways out of his burden. Ways to get around his own punishment. There were always loopholes in these kinds of things. And with eternity to consider his options, and nothing to lose by trying it, he would likely eventually free himself of his geas.

Or bring down Faery in the effort.

The rub indeed, she thought. Holy hell.

"So," Cary said into the silence, facing Jaxer to confirm all this out loud. "If they can't kill you because it's your life that keeps your father from trying to get out of his curse, and he's the one protecting the Lachlinain from getting out and destroying this realm, why did you need to come here? I can see why Borir might come for you, if he was worried. If he knew all of these details. But wouldn't staying away, remaining safely alive in a part of Faery these courts can't access, be all the guarantee needed to ensure the Lachlinain isn't released? Isn't being here among enemies, where someone might try to kill you…isn't this the very thing that could unleash the curse by freeing your father of his burden?"

"Ah, but there's more, love," Jaxer said. "The years between that decision and now have not seen the situation unchanged." He looked at Oberon. "Have they?"

More? This already twisty tale got twistier? Where the hell did it end? No wonder Jaxer had always deferred telling her about his past with "it's complicated" and leaving it at that. The damned mess *was* complicated.

And, of course, Jaxer being Jaxer, he would not have let all the damage done to his family stand without doing *something* in retribution. Just to make things worse and more complicated.

She didn't even try to hide her exasperation and accusation when she said, "Jaxer, what the hell did you do?"

A sudden, harsh, startling sound burst through the clearing, sending the few birds who'd been hiding silently in the trees scattering into the sky with shrieks of fear. The sound pierced Cary with a similar shard of fear.

The sound of Tatiana, queen of the English court of Faery…

Laughing.

15

ary turned to face the queen, wide-eyed and stunned. Tatiana's laughter was horrible. Not the melodiousness of her high, light voice, but a harsh, rusty, grating noise full of things that didn't sound particularly like amusement. Cary wanted to cover her ears, but figured that might be offensive. And she was pretty sure they were in enough trouble as it was. What with Tatiana laughing that terrible laugh and all.

She did wince, though, and found her hand back in Deacon's. Oh. Was the sound hurting his sensitive ears? Probably. He squeezed tight, and she took a step in front of him. But Protector powers probably wouldn't work against the laugh. It wasn't a threat. Just…a very unpleasant sound.

Tatiana slowly stopped laughing. "You know your mentor well, child," she said, her voice again that lovely, sweet sound. "And that amuses me. Because so few do."

"Thanks?" she said and asked at the same time. Was it good or bad that she'd amused a faery queen? She assumed bad because, well, Faery.

"He broke with both courts," Oberon said. "It is all you need know.

Once that was done, returning meant death. No matter the promises made to his father."

"Not quite," Tatiana said. "The break only solidified your desire to kill him, my love. It didn't ensure his execution."

Jaxer gave his queen a slight bow. Oberon growled.

There was more to all this than just Jaxer having broken with the courts. Cary would bet a month's salary on it.

But as the silence descended, she realized no one was going to explain. She'd have to grill Jaxer about it later.

In the meantime, she said, "So… Given what Borir overheard, I think we can all agree that, for the moment anyway, killing Jaxer would be a bad idea. Right?" She stared hard at Oberon. There was no discernible reaction from either king or queen to her comment. Which wasn't reassuring. "And I think we should probably meet with Ulieran to make sure he hasn't changed his mind about ignoring geas loopholes."

This was met by more silence.

Cary sighed. Really, did she have to do everything? Her job here was supposed to be stand around and make sure Jaxer wasn't killed. But she didn't have an eternity to wait on things getting done. Faery wasn't the kind of place a human should hang out in for very long. And Deacon didn't need to be here for an extended period of time either. Which meant they had to make sure this Lachlinain wasn't going to get out.

And yeah, yeah, if she were honest, she'd admit she was kind of anxious to meet Jaxer's father. His *father*! The baby stories alone would be worth the risk.

The silence stretched her nerves, but she held her tongue and stared —as best she could—at the royal couple, trying not to fidget. She wasn't always the most patient of people and she hated waiting. She wanted to nudge Jaxer, urge him to push the matter so she didn't have to. She glanced at him from the corner of her eye.

He wasn't giving away much. His expression was neutral, and like the queen and king, he didn't move. There was a focus in his gaze, as if he were hearing something she didn't, and he was listening carefully. If she hadn't known better, she'd think he and the royal couple were carrying on a silent conversation that she and Deacon couldn't overhear.

And if the faeries could do that, and Jaxer hadn't seen fit to warn her, she was going to give him an earful.

She squeezed Deacon's hand, glancing back at him with raised brows. She was itching to ask if he could smell or sense anything with his super shifter abilities, but she didn't want to be the one to break the silence. He shook his head, almost as if he understood what she was wordlessly asking—if he did, that was both sweet how well he knew her and maybe a little disturbing; he seemed to be able to read her thoughts through her scent more often than she liked—and didn't have any answers for her.

Suddenly and without warning, bird song started up in the clearing. Descending like a booming crash into the middle of all that ringing silence. She jumped with the first noise, so unexpectedly normal in a forest. First a single little twitter, then a few chitterings, a barking-like honk, and finally a hoot. An owl? Was that odd since they were night birds? Did they even have nighttime here? Given they had bright daylight with no shadows or visible sun, what would night look like?

With the bird song, the tension in the clearing relaxed, and from the corner of her eyes, she saw Jaxer finally move.

She was about to open her mouth and ask a question when, as suddenly as the normalcy had flowed into the clearing, the surroundings suddenly went dark. Pitch dark. A blackness without light. She gasped, and clenched Deacon's hand. Panic made her heart pound painfully hard in her chest.

And then…light.

They were no longer in the clearing.

Cary blinked and turned in a circle. They were in a stone structure of some kind, the floor made of large, flat rectangles of gray stone, the walls gray stone bricks. There were no windows to give a clue what was outside the structure, but the air was fresh and clean like a breeze did flow through the place. She couldn't feel any air currents, but then she hadn't since getting to this part of Faery. She took a deep breath, trying to settle her racing pulse, and smelled a faint wood-burning scent but no longer got the cotton candy and chocolate chip cookies that had been permeating the air up to now.

There were torches lining the walls, flickering their orange light around the single room, bright enough to give light while still leaving the high ceilings in darkness. At least, she thought there was a ceiling overhead. She couldn't see anything that looked like sky. She had a sense of night, but probably only because it was dark inside the structure.

It was cooler here, almost chilly. A noticeable change from the more comfortable warmth of the clearing. Goosebumps raised on her arms and she was grateful for the longer sleeves of the outfit Jaxer had created for her. While she knew she was still just wearing a t-shirt, and the long sleeves were an illusion, Jaxer's illusions were solid things and she felt like she was wearing clothing more appropriate for this colder air.

She frowned a little, glanced down, and realized she had a cloak on now, too. Not something she'd been wearing before. It was pinned at her throat with a brooch similar to, but significantly simpler than, Deacon's. Hers was just a simple silver with some beautiful knot-work but no jewels or adornments.

She raised her eyebrows at Jaxer. He grinned and winked.

"Thanks," she mouthed. No one had spoken aloud since they'd blinked and appeared in a new place and it felt weird to break that silence. To Deacon, she mouthed, "Okay?"

He nodded, but his gaze kept roving their surroundings. And there was a faint yellow glow in his eyes. That was worrying. That only happened when his leopard was near the surface.

She put a hand to his chest, making him meet her gaze. She nodded at his eyes and frowned.

He cupped her cheek, running a finger over her jaw line. With his free hand, he touched his own brooch and mouthed, "I'm fine."

She let out a long breath, not completely reassured. But he wasn't shifting so this would have to do.

She turned another circle, taking in their surroundings. The room was a long, tall, open rectangle. There didn't seem to be any doors, there was no furniture, no wall hangings or rugs. No signs of anything that might be comforting or make the place more comfortable. Nowhere to hide. Just a big, open, stone room.

And, she realized, no Tatiana or Oberon either.

Shit. That couldn't be good. Could it?

She looked at their surroundings with new eyes. Was this a prison of some kind? Where they stuck here?

And if so, how the hell had the queen and king magicked them here if Cary's powers were still working?

Where her powers even working?

"How?" she finally said aloud, though very quietly. Still her voice sounded shockingly loud after all that silence. "Where?"

"Wait for it," Jaxer murmured. He'd turned to face one side of the stone structure, staring hard into the shadows near the top of the building.

Cary faced the same direction and placed herself in front of Jaxer. Deacon came up behind her, close enough she could feel his heat but not touching her. A sound like wings flapping, claws scrambling against stone…

A huge creature dropped from the shadows, only a few feet in front of them.

Cary gasped, despite herself, despite knowing something had been up there. She cursed her surprise and stepped forward again once she realized she'd stepped back. That was damned irritating. She glared at the giant being as it pulled up to its full height in the torchlight and gave her a clear view.

Well over seven feet tall, maybe eight, the creature had a man's face, torso, and arms. The skin on his human parts was dark brown and thickly muscled, covered with short, crisp black hair. His eyes were black and wide, his features sharp and long. His shoulder-length hair was dark dark brown, with two streaks of pure white stretching from his temples. He was handsome, but in a harsh and unforgiving way, the predatory look in his black eyes too deadly to ignore.

His legs were shaped like a giant eagle's, covered in brown and white feathers, wickedly sharp talons for his feet. The claws topping his talons tapped on the stone floor as the creature stepped closer. Behind his back stretched two huge black and brown wings, the feathers smooth and glossy. His wingspan was easily twenty feet or more, the tips stretching almost the full width of the stone room. At each wing tip, two sharp claws poked out of the feathers. And Cary finally noticed his human hands were also tipped with long, sharp claws instead of regular fingernails.

The creature held his wings wide for a moment longer, before flapping them once gently, and folding them against his back. The movement created a soft breeze, brushing her with a faint, musky, avian smell which was both pleasant and earthy. In their resting position, the folds of his wings rose above his head, giving him a sort of black feather halo. With wings back, the creature took another two steps toward them, then stopped. And stared with his black, pupilless eyes.

Chills rose on Cary's arms under her long sleeves and the new cloak Jaxer had glamoured up for her. She ignored the warning shiver. She was afraid any movement might set off the predator in this being and send him into attack mode.

"You seek the guardian of the Lachlinain," the creature said, his voice echoing in the tall room, deep but with a faint piercing note near the end when he said the name of the curse. "Why have you come?"

"Mostly," Jaxer said quietly, "to make sure you were okay."

The creature turned his gaze to Jaxer.

Jaxer stepped closer to Cary so that she could just see him from the corner of her eyes. His lips were lifted in a very slight smile.

"Hi, Da," he said.

1 6

*A*h, Cary thought.

And also, Oh boy.

She wasn't sure whether to be relieved that they were talking to Jaxer's father, or whether she should be terrified because he wasn't at all what she'd been expecting, and it was hard to tell looking into his eyes if he even recognized Jaxer. Which would be heartbreaking if he didn't. After all he'd done, taking on this guardian position to ensure his son was safe, and then not even know him? That would be the ultimate punishment.

Her fears were banished a moment later when the guardian's expression softened and he opened his arms wide. "Got a hug for your old man?" he asked.

Cary thought she might cry. Jaxer gave his father a real hug, not that male, back-patting thing, and suddenly she was all sentiment and emotion. So sweet!

She sniffled and leaned back into Deacon. He didn't comment, but he did wrap a comforting arm around her waist.

When the reunited father and son pulled back, Jaxer stared up at his father for a long moment. "You look good, Da."

"You're surprised?" His father chuckled. The sound was a deep, rumbling thing of beauty.

Jaxer shrugged. "Hard to know what to expect after all this time."

"How're the Americas treating you?"

"Better than Europe did."

His father's expression darkened. "You shouldn't have returned. Why didn't Oberon try to kill you?"

"I came back for a reason. Nothing flippant. And…" He turned and motioned to Cary and Deacon. "I brought friends to have my back."

Cary grinned at the fact that Jaxer called them both friends. She waved a little at his father. "Hi."

"Da, this is Cary Redmond, Protector of Portland, and her mate, Deacon Jones, heir apparent to the Pacific Northwest leopard clan."

Cary almost choked on Jaxer introducing Deacon as her mate. He hadn't been very good at admitting that out loud before now.

"Cary and Deacon, my father, Ulieran of the English court, Guardian of the Lachlinain."

"It's a pleasure to meet you," Deacon said.

"Pleasure," she muttered.

"It's my honor to meet you both," Ulieran said, with a slight dip of his head. "Jaxer's friends." He raised his brows at his son. "You brought a Protector into Faery? And you survived? I'm impressed."

Jaxer shrugged. "She's a good Protector. One of the best I've trained."

"Her skills work here?" Ulieran stared at Cary now, assessing her as if she were something under a magnifying glass.

That was a little rude.

"As far as we can tell, they do. But no one seems to be attacking us. Just yet."

"Well, there was that one thing Tatiana tried," Cary said.

Jaxer's gaze turned sharp. "What?"

"You know, when she leaned forward. I don't know what she did, but whatever it was it bounced hard against my shields."

"Wait. Tatiana threw magic at you?"

"Yeah." She looked between Jaxer and Deacon. "You guys didn't notice?"

"Hard enough you *felt* it?" Jaxer asked.

"Yeah. That part was weird, I suppose." She glanced past Jaxer to his father. "I don't often feel anything against the shield. I just stand there and nothing gets through."

Ulieran raised his brows again.

"Tatiana," Jaxer said slowly, "the most powerful wielder of magic in the English court. Threw magic. At you. And you *felt* it. Through the shield." He paused. "How's your skin?"

She shrugged. "Tingling a little I guess, but... Oh." Her eyes widened. "Oh, shit."

"Yeah," Jaxer said.

Deacon's hand tightened on her waist. "Damn," he murmured.

"I'm missing something," Ulieran said.

"But the shield was working," Cary said. "So not much would have gotten through. And I can apparently hold on to a little for a long time without any risk. And I'm sure it was too little for her to notice. I shield from magic all the time without trouble. It's fine. I'll be fine. Everything will be fine."

Did she sound as frantic as she felt? She'd known coming into Faery that this was a risk. The entire place was magic. But her shields had been up and working almost from the start because of the danger to Deacon and then to Jaxer once they got here. She was certain of it. Her skin hadn't started really tingling until after Tatiana's attack. Right? She frowned. She couldn't actually remember. The process of moving through different parts of Faery had been so overwhelming. And then landing into the English realm and all its weirdness... She'd been pretty distracted.

Still, she would have noticed her skin tingling like mad. She always noticed when she finished a job and her skin got that weird sensation that they knew now meant she'd absorbed some magic. It made sense she hadn't felt or noticed it before now. It was reassuring actually. Right? It meant her shields *had* been up this whole time. And they were only relaxed now because Ulieran wasn't a threat. And that's why she could feel the tingling.

Right?

"Wait," she said. "If we're not in danger anymore, and my shields are down, does that mean I'm absorbing ambient magic now? What-ever Tatiana threw at us, that got mostly blocked. But now…" She made a face.

Jaxer frowned.

Deacon cursed under her breath.

"I'm still missing something," Ulieran said. He looked from his son, to Cary, to Deacon and back to Jaxer. "Perhaps we should settle in to some more comfortable surroundings for this discussion." He waved a hand, his sharp claws leaving sparks in the air.

Cary blinked and the dark stone room was gone, replaced by a smaller, informal living room with a large stone fireplace to one side of the room and a set of overstuffed couches and chairs cluttering up the center. Thick woven rugs covered the wooden floor. A sideboard oppo-site the fireplace held what looked like a pot of tea and some cups. The fire crackling in the grate smelled like peat instead of wood and it cast the only light, giving the space a warm, flickering coziness.

But like the stone room, there weren't any windows or doors that Cary could see.

Ulieran gestured to the couches. "Have a seat. Would you like some tea?"

Somewhere in the back of her mind, Cary remembered a warning about not eating and drinking in Faery. She couldn't place it exactly. And she might be getting the warning mixed up with the story of Persephone going into the underworld. Without access to the internet to check, she couldn't be sure. But just in case, she said, "No, thank you. I'm fine."

Jaxer lifted his chin in a slight nod that his father didn't see, a gesture Cary took to mean she'd done the right thing not accepting a drink.

Once they were settled and Ulieran had a cup of tea steaming between his claw-tipped fingers, the questions started.

Ulieran's first was to ask why Jaxer had risked coming back. Jaxer explained everything in a much more straightforward and blunt way than he had to Tatiana and Oberon. No rhythmic storyteller's cadence, no dramatic pauses and rich language. Just a simple recitation of the facts: Borir had run to the human realm to find him after overhearing conspirators plotting to unleash the Lachlinain and destroy Faery, and even Jaxer's bosses thought he should come to the English court to ensure disaster didn't happen.

"A fair enough explanation for why you're here," Ulieran said, turning his tea cup in his hands without sipping. "Could have been a trap."

"Which was why I brought Cary," Jaxer said.

"Ah yes. The Protector." He flicked a narrowed look at Cary before returning his gaze to his son. "And that neatly brings me to my next question. Would anyone care to explain the earlier exchange? The fear that Tatiana had thrown magic at the Protector. I should think that the Protector's ability to block Tatiana's spell, whatever it was, would be a relief."

Jaxer sighed. "It's complicated. With Cary."

"She's human, yes? She smells human."

That comment might have been more disturbing if Cary hadn't been spending so much time with shifters lately. What bugged her more was the way they were talking about her like she wasn't in the room.

"I'm human," she said, not hiding her annoyance. "And a pretty ordinary one at that." She shrugged. "Except for the one little thing."

"What 'little' thing?" Ulieran turned his attention on her.

The intensity in his stare made her gut tighten. It didn't feel quite like a threat, but he wanted this answer, wanted this bit of information more than just to satisfy curiosity.

She glanced at Jaxer. "Do I admit it out loud here? Is that safe?" She realized she'd already mentioned absorbing magic, but she kind of hoped Ulieran had missed that.

"I think he'll need to know," Jaxer said.

"Yeah, well I needed to know your father was cursed to guard the

Lachlinain before we got here, and yet I still didn't know that until the court."

Jaxer rolled his eyes. "We didn't have time."

"We seemed to have had plenty of time." She gestured at their surroundings. "Since we're sitting here with the guardian and no one is trying to release the Lachlinain at the moment."

"No one could release it," Ulieran said. "Whatever the little brownie overheard, I have not been successfully recruited into a conspiracy, and so it was idle talk."

"Idle enough that they sent hobgoblins to kill Borir?" Cary asked him. "All the way into my realm?"

"They may not realize their talk is idle. They may assume I'll be recruitable, given… But I'm not. So there is no danger."

She wanted to ask about the "given" part he hadn't finished, but first she needed to know, "Could they kill you?" Speaking bluntly now because anything else seemed a waste of time.

"No," he said just as bluntly. "Oberon and Tatiana can't even kill me."

"Why not?"

"It's part of the geas. I'm indestructible."

"Ha. I've been that too. It doesn't last."

He raised his brows high, leaning farther back in his chair as he studied her. And she realized his wings were draped in such a way that they circled around the narrow-backed chair, giving him a place to lean without his wings getting in the way. That was clever.

"How were you indestructible?" he asked. "A human?"

She waved a hand. "Had to do with a baby god. Long story. And off topic. How does the geas make you indestructible?"

"I have to be able to keep the Lachlinain contained. Anything less than my indestructibility would make it vulnerable."

"Doesn't that make you a threat to the court? If even the queen and king can't kill you, couldn't you take over, using the Lachlinain as leverage or a threat or something?"

"That would also violate the geas. I physically can't violate its compulsions."

"That's only mostly true, or we wouldn't be here," Cary said. "There are always loopholes. After all these years, someone thinks they've found one. Or you've found one and haven't admitted it out loud."

"You've neatly turned the conversation away from my original question," he said. "Well done."

"Thank you. Have you found a loophole in your curse?"

"I have. I wouldn't use it."

"Why not?"

"My son is alive and well."

She smiled at that, just a little. Their whole family situation was tragic but the obvious love was sweet. "So was this just a trap to get him here? To kill him? Or have Oberon kill him?" She glanced at Jaxer. "I'm still waiting for an explanation on that, by the way."

Jaxer sighed. "I might have disguised myself as the king and... played a little mischief with the court. For a few years."

"Years?"

"Give or take a century."

"Jaxer. What *exactly* did you do?"

"Nothing worse than I did in the Irish court."

She closed her eyes. "None of what you tell me is going to be good, is it?"

"It was fun at the time."

"Right." She opened her eyes. "So... Oberon wants to kill you. And someone important in the Irish court wants to kill you, too?" She glanced at him and he shrugged, confirming her suspicion. "Which is why you've avoided coming back for several centuries."

"Also, I supported the Nags when they began creating the Protectors," Jaxer said. "That didn't go over well either."

"Apparently. And so Borir looking for you and bringing you back here puts your life in danger, and your life is the only thing that keeps your father from using the loophole in his geas and unleashing the Lachlinain, but the Nags thought we needed to come here to prevent the destruction of Faery. And... I'm still not seeing why we didn't just avoid the place."

"I'm not either," Jaxer admitted. "I thought it would be more obvious before now. And it isn't. Which is why I think there's more to the story than you're admitting. My bosses are good at premonitions. They urged us to hurry here." He held his father's gaze. "What were you about to do?"

Ulieran's gaze flickered and he blinked very slowly before lifting his mug to his lips. The silence stretched out.

Along with Cary's nerves. The whole thing didn't make sense. The more she learned, the less sense all this made.

Why the hell had Borir been allowed to overhear the conspirators? Why had he been allowed to get all the way to Portland to find Jaxer? The route wasn't straight, as she'd experienced getting here. The hobgoblins trying to kill him could have reached him at any point. In a location where Cary wouldn't have been conveniently on hand to keep them from killing Borir. If it really was all just a trap to get Jaxer here, if Borir had been used as a dupe, why on earth would the Nags have encouraged—even helped!—her to come here with Jaxer?

None of this made logical sense. And while she knew better than to try to assign human logic to faery motivations and activities, the illogic of their current situation couldn't just be waved off as "faeries don't make any sense to humans."

"You still haven't explained Ms. Redmond's 'little' uniqueness yet," Ulieran finally said.

"And we're not going to until you explain what you almost did," Cary said. "We rushed here to stop the destruction of Faery. Trap or not, there was a countdown ticking, an urgency for us to get here. And yet…now that we're here, there doesn't seem to be any frantic rush anymore. You claim the Lachlinain is safe. It wasn't, though, was it. Up until we stepped into the English court, that curse was about to unleash. How? Why?"

"How?" Ulieran's shrug was casual and urban. His wings shifted with the movement where they rested around the back of his chair. "As I said, I found a loophole in the geas. It was inevitable with so many centuries to think about it in detail."

"I figured as much. You can break your geas at any time, then. What happens if you do? Are you still indestructible? Can you use the Lachlinain, or does breaking the geas just leave it vulnerable?" She paused. "Sometime soon I'd like to know exactly *what* the Lachlinain is, by the way. But I can wait on that until we sort through the rest of this. What I'd like to know now is the 'why?' Why were you going to break your geas now?"

He glanced at his son, holding his gaze for a long time. "The why… Now, that's a story."

Cary groaned. Not more stories. Couldn't anyone just cut to the chase here?

Ulieran's lips twitched. Not quite a smile but there were hints of amusement in the gesture, as if he'd understood her annoyed groan. "Not a long story," he assured. "Well, technically, it is, but I'll give you the short version. Some parties in the court have come to me with stories of Jaxer being killed, assassinated at the king's orders." He shrugged. "I didn't believe. Many have attempted that ploy over the years. I would know if my son was dead."

He paused long enough Cary worried that was all he'd tell them. Then he let out a long breath.

"This time, though," Ulieran said quietly, "this time the conspirators showed me something that made me more willing to listen to their argument."

"Which was?" Jaxer asked. "Clearly not me dead." He gestured at himself, as he was very much still alive.

"This was a…note. A message left in a bespelled box." He met Jaxer's gaze. "From your mother."

Jaxer sat a little straighter in his seat.

"It was apparently delivered here after her death by one of the Fae who came to me, Eriana, one of the few your mother would have trusted to bring the message into Faery. Eriana presented the box to the queen, asking that it be given to me." Ulieran glanced at Cary and said, "Most Fae, even highborn, can't come to me without the aid of the queen. Some are able to manage it. But very few. And the ones who've come to me before this were not Fae my Grenelle would have associated with, nonetheless trusted with her last message to me."

Jaxer cleared his throat. "What did it say?"

"Eriana assumed the queen had given me the box," Ulieran said quietly, "centuries ago. But Tatiana withheld the missive. I thought, for all these years, Grenelle had died alone without…" He swallowed visibly. "Without having anything more to say to me." He looked at Jaxer. "Even when you returned to Faery, you brought no message from her. I assumed…"

"She hadn't sent one," Jaxer finished. "She didn't through me. I don't know why." He sighed and looked away from his father. "Or maybe I do. I was very angry at the time, watching her age, watching her die like a human when she was so much more."

Cary wanted to take offense at that, but bit her tongue. Probably a bad time to get pissy about a little species insult.

"She should have had as long as any faery, but they stripped her of that. They cursed you. And they left me…"

"They left you," Ulieran said, "so that our realm would remain stable. She didn't leave you."

"She died. That feels like she's left, Da."

"Her note said…" He paused another long moment. "Her note said she'd been content with her life. She praised you and the man you'd grown into. She had missed me and wanted me to know."

"She never bonded with anyone else. She remained loyal to you."

Ulieran smiled. "She admitted as much. She sent drawings of herself, self portraits over the years as she aged, and there was amusement in her words as she described the changes time brings when one grows old."

"I never saw her resent the aging," Jaxer said. "Or having had her powers stripped."

"But you did?"

Jaxer nodded.

"She said as much. That your resentments ran deep and that she hadn't been able to help you release them, even though she tried."

Jaxer didn't meet his father's gaze.

"There were personal things. Words between lovers. I won't share those. But she ended with a warning. And it's that warning which had me considering what I might do to break the geas."

"Which was?" Cary asked before she could stop herself. She was caught up in the story, leaning forward in her seat as she listened.

Ulieran kept his gaze on Jaxer. "She'd had a premonition of disaster."

Cary looked at Jaxer. "Your mother had premonitions? Like the Nags? Even after her faery powers were stripped."

"Even after," Jaxer said. "Her visions weren't quite the same as the Nags. They were erratic and she never sought them. She certainly couldn't call them on demand the way the Nags can. But she had a few during her last seventy-five years." He met his father's gaze. "She didn't tell me about this one."

"You died in this one," Ulieran said. "She couldn't bring herself to tell you, or warn you, for fear your efforts to avoid the fate she saw would send you careening into it." To Cary, Ulieran said, "That's the way of it with death visions. The paradox. That knowing how you will die might drive you to do the very things that eventually lead to that death even though your efforts were all in an attempt to avoid your fate. If you'd never known or seen the death vision, you might have avoided doing the things that make the vision come to pass."

Cary wrinkled her nose. She hated paradoxes. They made her head hurt. "I've heard that one before," she said. "It doesn't seem to come up with the Nags and their premonitions, though. They send me to help and I do."

"But perhaps that's only because of *what* they tell you," Ulieran said. "Do you have any idea what they *don't* tell you?"

No, she thought. No, she didn't. But did she even want to know?

Given the paradox they were discussing, she was leaning toward happily embracing her ignorance. At least where a death vision was concerned.

Ulieran turned back to Jaxer. "She detailed the vision for me in the note. Some of it is hard to countenance, things she didn't know how to make sense of. Fiery demons from other realms. Vampires and magic and mechanical things made of iron and steel unlike anything she would have known about hundreds of years ago."

"Have you been able to keep up with technological advancement in the human realm from here?" Cary asked.

"I have," he said. "It doesn't violate my geas to open a viewing portal. I've watched your world change."

"Why?" Jaxer asked.

"It was where you chose to live. Where some of my happiest years were spent. I have a soft spot for the human realm."

A brief silence descended before Ulieran continued. "There was more to the vision. But two elements gave me pause. They involved her vision of the destruction of Faery coinciding with these mechanical marvels she couldn't understand."

"You think that's now," Cary said. "At least in this era."

He nodded. "And she described our son being in the middle of the conflict, a lynch pin of sorts, but more... More that he was the key to the tipping point. Things would go one way or the other based on his decisions."

"Well that sucks," Jaxer said.

Ulieran lifted his mouth in a faint smile. "Yes, she thought so too. She didn't want you to have the responsibility of that future. Any more than she wanted the death she'd seen for you to come to pass."

"I'm not particularly keen on either of those things myself," Jaxer said. "Did she describe *how* Faery was destroyed?"

"The Lachlinain," Ulieran said simply.

"And did she mention how you came into all this?" Cary asked. "Since you're the guardian of the curse and all."

"She said I didn't appear in the vision. She's not sure what that meant."

"But you worry it means you're dead by the time I have to make whatever decisions I have to make," Jaxer said.

"Or she was simply too caught up in worry for her son to see the full scope of the vision," Ulieran said. "She couldn't control this particular skill, couldn't direct it when it happened. She had blind spots that affected her focus. Often things were missed."

"But she would have been looking out for you in the vision. If only to see how you managed over the centuries."

Ulieran shrugged. "Perhaps I do die before all this comes to pass."

"You're taking the end of your life very casually," Jaxer said, his voice thick and deep.

"My son, among the humans, it's the way of it. Children outlive their parents. It's natural. The parents hope for it because they want their children to live long lives. Grenelle and I wanted that for you, too."

"It's not natural to faeries, though," Jaxer said, a touch of anger in his tone now, "and you'd do well to stop talking about your death."

Ulieran narrowed his eyes. "Realize that that may well be the very decision you have to make, son. The reason Grenelle couldn't see that part of her vision. It may come down to my life, or the continued existence of Faery. But if Faery is destroyed, the human realm will follow. My life is nothing to that."

"It's not nothing," Jaxer said. "Don't say that ever again."

The silence that followed had Cary wanting to fidget but afraid to move.

When the tension grew too much for her to bear, she finally spoke. "You said two elements in her vision gave you pause. If Jaxer's decisions determining the fate of Faery was one, what's the other?"

Ulieran continued to stare at his son, who was pointedly *not* looking at him, as he answered. "She saw more signs that would portend when the time of destruction was upon us. A harmless brownie in danger. A shifter of royal blood with golden eyes. A human who sucks up all the magic in the world."

He finally turned his gaze on her and Deacon. "One of you is a shifter of royal blood, who also happens to have golden eyes. The other... You said there was a little thing that made you not quite normal for a human. Have I guessed correctly, Ms. Redmond? Are you the woman who can suck up all the magic in the world?"

18

Cary felt a little lightheaded for reasons she couldn't entirely explain. Maybe the fact that Jaxer's mother had known what Cary would be centuries before Cary was born? Or maybe it was just the fact that Ulieran had been suspicious about her this whole time.

Or maybe it was that she was smack in the middle of a vision about the destruction of a realm made of magic…and she absorbed magic.

Oh boy.

"We've only just figured out I can do that, absorb magic," Cary murmured. "I mean, we figured it out a few months ago, but considering it's been with me my whole life, that's a long time to go without knowing." She pulled in a deep breath. "And I have no idea how it works or how to disperse the magic once I absorb it."

"How are you still alive?" Ulieran asked.

She met his gaze. "I became a Protector. The shields, the power I channel, are designed to block everything, including magic. Nothing is supposed to get through those. That's the point."

"But Cary sometimes gets hurt," Jaxer said quietly. "She shouldn't get hurt while she's protecting someone."

"That's how we finally figured it out. Sort of." She sighed. "Okay, to be honest, the wizard who is trying to kill me actually had to tell us.

But then we worked out the details. Or at least, what we can work out. There's not a lot of information about my…uniqueness."

"Most people like you die early," Ulieran said.

"So I've been told." She blinked. "But…wait, you know about humans who can absorb magic? Have you met any? Do you know… how all this works?"

"I'm afraid not. Tatiana might. Though I'd hesitate to ask her. She might not take it well that you're in her realm. Being a Protector is already several strikes against you."

"I noticed."

"I have encountered the phenomenon once over my long life, but only the once. And he died shortly after coming into contact with magic."

"What happened?" Cary rubbed her arms, not sure if the tingles were magic absorption or fear.

"He attempted to step into Faery. All that magic… I don't know exactly what happened. Just that the reaction was deadly. And not something I'll ever forget."

"I don't want to know any more, do I?"

"Probably not."

She looked at Jaxer. "Is that happening to me right now? Maybe I should get out of Faery for a bit since I'm not protecting anyone right now."

"You're still protecting Deacon, remember," Jaxer said quietly. "Just like during our journey here."

"Yeah, but my skin is tingling now."

"Worse than normal?"

"No. Just the usual. But it hasn't gone away yet."

"We need to get her out of here," Deacon said. He was staring at Ulieran. "There's more to this story."

Ulieran nodded. "A lot more, I'm afraid. I fear Grenelle's vision is coming to pass. In ways the conspirators whose plot brought you here didn't anticipate. And since my son's life hangs in the balance, I have a vested interest in seeing things play out quite differently. But we'll need Ms. Redmond alive, if we've any hope."

"Me? Why me? What don't I know?"

Ulieran smiled kindly, she suspected, to offset his next words.

"Quite a lot," he said. "But don't take offense. There's a lot I don't know either."

"Two things," Cary said, "before we find a way out of here. First, what were you about to do before we arrived? Second, what *is* the Lachlinain? Exactly."

Ulieran glanced at Jaxer. "Before you arrived… After reading your mother's message, her warnings and the details of what was to come…" He let out a long breath. "I was considering releasing the Lachlinain myself and destroying Faery."

"Da!" Jaxer practically came out of his seat. "What the hell for?"

"To protect you from having to make the decisions you will have to make. I hoped by undermining Grenelle's vision, you would survive and be safe. Faery is old. Growing weak and decrepit. That decay will infect many realms. It is, perhaps, better to remove the gangrenous limb now and save the whole."

"Destroying Faery will likely destroy those other realms. Including the one I live in," Jaxer said. "That's why we're here. And it would destroy you."

Ulieran wings seeming to sag under a great weight. "I worry much less about me than I do you. But you're here. Alive and well. And determined to stop this thing. Any chance of preempting Grenelle's vision have been taken from my hands, and probably for the best. I fear this is what Eriana and the others were attempting from the start."

"Meaning?" Cary asked.

"They arranged for the brownie to overhear their threats and run to Jaxer. To get Jaxer here so that the predictions could come to pass. If I didn't release the curse myself after reading Grenelle's message, they needed you all here to make the destruction inevitable."

"Wait, how could they even know about me and Deacon?"

"You think the queen hasn't kept tabs on her wayward love? You think she hasn't followed everything Jaxer has done and everyone he's associated with since he left? No. She tracks us all. And if she knows a thing, there are others who will learn it too. Her guards. Those close to her in the court."

"So," Cary said, "this was a trap to get us here. Though, maybe not for the reasons we thought."

"Just so. A plan with many chances to fail. But that's why there have been several contingencies and alternatives put in place along the way. No matter what happened, there are those who want to see our realm dead for good, and they are using all methods at their disposal to see it done. And so we must find a way to stop them."

"You'll help us?" Jaxer asked.

"I will always help you, my son. As much as I am able."

"That means not releasing the Lachlinain," Jaxer said.

"I won't attempt to now."

"Good," Cary said. "Now, what does the Lachlinain do, exactly? That might help us work things out."

Ulieran met and held her gaze for a long time. The blackness in his eyes widened and the intensity grew, and suddenly Cary saw the predator again. Not the loving father, but the guardian who kept this curse at bay. She wanted to drop her gaze and fidget and maybe run away, but she held still and waited. Running away from predators was a great way to ensure they attacked.

"Perhaps it would be better if you saw," Ulieran said finally.

"No," Jaxer said, standing now. "It's too dangerous for them both."

"Perhaps. But they need to understand." Ulieran ran his claws across the air in front of him and the cozy sitting room vanished, leaving them all standing in the middle of the huge stone room again.

Cary blinked and narrowed her eyes. "Glamour or something else?" she asked.

"A little of both," Ulieran answered.

Which wasn't really an answer. She didn't stop glaring.

"Come. You and the Lachlinain should meet."

"Me?" Cary took a step away from him. "Why me?"

Ulieran's black eyes pierced her, keeping her frozen like a rabbit in an eagle's sights. "Because you share a common trait. It also eats magic."

Well, that didn't sound good.

He turned and headed toward one side of the long room. Cary hesitated to follow.

"You don't have to," Deacon whispered against her ear. "This isn't your fight, even if Jaxer's mother saw us here."

Jaxer leaned closer and said, "You don't need to do this," echoing Deacon. "My father isn't telling us everything. I'm not convinced of his explanation for why he almost released the Lachlinain but then didn't after we arrived."

Cary turned to him. "You're not? You don't…" She lowered her voice. "You don't trust him?"

"It's not that. I think he's hiding something and probably thinks he's doing it for our own good—my own good. I think he was being honest when he said his intentions had to do with protecting me. I just don't think he told us the whole story."

Great. As if the story wasn't complicated enough. Now she had to worry about all the stuff not said. She was starting to hate Faery.

"I'm not sure if I'm still in Protector mode," Cary said. "Will this Lachlinain be dangerous for you or for Deacon? That might help."

Jaxer looked in the direction his father had gone, disappearing into the shadows at the far end of the long room. He nodded. "Oh yeah. It's dangerous to all of us."

"Okay. Okay, then. I can do this." She blinked and looked at Jaxer again. "Do you think your mother was serious about the 'all the magic in the world' part of how she described me?" Cary really really didn't want to absorb all the magical power in the world. It sounded painful. And also probably deadly. And none of that sounded good.

"Probably an exaggeration," Jaxer said.

He didn't sound nearly as reassuring as she'd have liked. She pulled in a deep breath and straightened her shoulders. "Let's get this over with. I'd like to step out of Faery for a bit. I'm getting a bad feeling about being here."

Deacon took hold of her hand and squeezed as they started forward. He remained just a little behind her, but through his touch, she could feel his tension humming through his muscles. He was poised to pounce, coiled and ready to leap. Given what was happening, that was both comforting and terrifying. She held his hand tighter to ensure he didn't jump away from her.

As they moved deeper into what had looked like shadows, Cary realized her ability to see a few yards in front of her didn't change. She glanced back and the shadows had deepened behind them so that she could no longer see the spot in the room where they'd been standing. It reminded her of walking in fog. Her circle of visibility remained the same distance but the fog kept that visibility limited to a small area. Even the sound was muted inside their circle of faint illumination. The only difference between the shadows and a thick fog was that the shadows were so dark she couldn't even see hints of what lay beyond.

She looked more closely at her surroundings, the parts she could see, and realized nothing had really changed. The parts of the room she could see looked exactly like the area where she'd been a few minutes earlier. She was certain they were moving forward, but the illusion made it seem as if they weren't actually making any progress, like moving the wrong way on an escalator. Walking but not getting anywhere.

She opened her mouth to ask if they were, in fact, moving at all, when Ulieran appeared out of the shadows before them. His wings were slightly spread, giving him a large black halo around his body that brought out the predatory glint in his dark eyes. She tried not to gasp or step back, but the instinct to move away from the threat he posed was strong. Normally, she was good at getting between bad guys and good guys and basically ignoring the threat the bad guys posed because she knew they couldn't get through her shields. But nothing in Faery felt guaranteed and she didn't entirely trust her shields here. Her more basic survival instincts—instincts she wasn't entirely sure she'd had before this moment—kicked back strong against walking toward the giant bird of prey that was Jaxer's father.

"This way," he said, his deep voice a soothing contrast to the scariness of his direct gaze.

Geez, why was she suddenly so afraid of him? She'd just been teary-eyed over his sweet reunion with Jaxer. And now she couldn't seem to stop seeing him as someone just waiting to swoop down and rip her apart with his very sharp claws. Was she really afraid of him or was something else affecting her? Was this instinct? Or was some aspect of the magic here getting into her head?

Was something here trying to prevent her from seeing the Lachlinain?

Damn it, she really hated Faery.

1 9

ary braced herself against the fear pumping in her blood. Deacon could smell it, she was sure. Hell, Ulieran probably smelled her fear. And that wasn't good because Deacon's instincts might push him to attack the threat to her, and Ulieran's instincts would prompt him to fight back. That would keep them in Faery longer while she had to break up the fight. Her skin was crawling now from being here too long. She needed to calm down, see the stupid curse that could destroy Faery, and then get out of here to regroup before anything bad happened.

At least anything worse than what already seemed to be happening.

"We almost there?" she asked. She frowned at the slight squeak in her voice. Gee, that sounded brave and confident. She rolled her eyes at herself and tried again. "How much farther do we have to go? This room of yours doesn't seem to…end."

"It's as large as it needs to be," Ulieran confirmed.

His still sounded as reasonable and as safe as he had while they were sitting in the imaginary living room around the fire having a chat. The comfortable calm of his voice wasn't doing much to dispel her sudden worry, though.

"But we're almost where we need to be," Ulieran continued. "Just this way."

"Da?" The single word held a great many unspoken questions.

Ulieran met his son's gaze. "You'll all be fine. It's contained."

He turned back into the shadows but stayed close enough for her to see now, staying just at the edge of where the shadows swallowed up the light from the torches on the walls.

After another few yards, he stopped again, and Cary almost groaned. If this was another pause before reaching their destination, she was going to start sounding like a kid, asking "are we there yet?" over and over again.

He faced Cary. "Brace yourself, Ms. Redmond. I'm not sure what you'll see. The Lachlinain isn't like anything you would have encountered before. It will appear to you in a way your mind can fathom, but it still might not make much sense."

"So, basically like everything else in Faery? Got it."

Ulieran grinned suddenly. The expression did wonderful things for his face, bringing out his sharp handsomeness and diminishing some of her growing fear at the predator she kept seeing in his eyes. Some, but not all.

To Jaxer, Ulieran said, "I see why you like her."

He didn't wait for Jaxer to respond before facing the shadows again, swiping a clawed hand through the air, and parting the blackness like a curtain to reveal a glowing room beyond.

Cary's heart pounded so hard, she had trouble breathing. Fear and panic had her rooted to the spot for a long moment, unable to move forward.

She literally couldn't seem to move forward.

It took her several moments and a couple of deep breaths to realize it wasn't her panic that had her stuck.

"Why can't I move?" she murmured. She pushed a leg forward, through sheer will, but it was like moving through thick, sludgy mud. The very air seeming to push her backward.

"You okay?" Deacon asked.

He stepped up beside her, and she noticed he wasn't having any trouble.

"You're not feeling stuck and having trouble moving forward?" Cary asked. "Because I'm having a hell of a time here."

Deacon's eyes narrowed. "Jaxer? What's wrong? What's happening to her?"

"Da?" Jaxer asked, clearly as confused as the rest of them. He moved to stand in front of her and to the left, watching as she tried to force herself through the dense air. He didn't seem bothered either, moving around as if he was just walking through ordinary air and not a quickly solidifying gelatin.

"What the hell?" Cary pushed herself forward another step, leaning into the resistance.

"Can you move backward?" Deacon asked.

She brought the foot she'd just forced forward back again.

And she ended up flying backward a few feet, landing hard on her ass.

She blinked in surprise. Whoa.

"Cary!" Deacon was beside her before she finished her blink. "Are you hurt? What happened?" He glared at Jaxer and Ulieran. "What the hell is happening?"

"Interesting," Ulieran said under his breath. "Are you hurt, Ms. Redmond?"

"Nothing that won't heal," she grumbled as Deacon helped her back to her feet. She rubbed her ass. "Ouch," she said. "I'm still waiting for an explanation." To Deacon, "You didn't feel anything? No resistance or anything?"

"Nothing." He held her shoulders, looking her over. "Anything but your lovely ass bruised."

She grinned at the compliment because she hadn't been expecting it. "No. I'm fine. Really. Just startled."

"What did that feel like?" Ulieran asked. His black eyes were narrowed to slits as he looked between her and the glowing hole in reality.

She tried to lean one direction, then another, to see through that rip, but all she saw was a bright blue light that prevented her from seeing beyond. She blinked a few times. "It was like trying to walk through mud," she said. "But the minute I relaxed my efforts to move forward, by taking a step away, it was like something snapped...or no, wait. It was more like...I'm not sure how to explain it exactly. Recoil? That's not quite right either."

She moved toward the glowing opening again, stopping when she reached a point where moving forward got difficult. "Right here. This is where it starts." She forced her leg forward. This time she felt a slight vibration in the resistance. She leaned into it again.

"You know what it reminds me of," she said, almost to herself. "Bringing two magnets together with the same charges pointed at each other. Positive to positive. And you can force them only so close before they bounce backward or swing to the side. Repelling each other." She looked up at Deacon. "Did you do that in school? Play with magnets to see how they moved?"

"Not that I remember," he said. "We may have. It's been a while, though."

"You feel repelled by the Lachlinain?" Ulieran asked. He sounded interested, not worried.

Cary nodded as she concentrated on taking another step toward the glow. "Yeah, the magnet comparison is a good one." The vibration of forcing herself close to the glow moved through her bones now, and she could feel the point approaching when she wouldn't be able to move forward anymore. "What does this mean?"

"I'm not entirely sure," Ulieran said. "It's never happened before. But then, the Lachlinain has never encountered someone who absorbs magic before."

"Great," she muttered, forcing herself one more step closer.

"Perhaps your nature repels it, just like your example of the same charged ends of a magnet," Ulieran said.

"So... I can't get close enough to see it?" She looked at Deacon. "Can you? Can you step through that glow and tell me what you see?"

"You want him to do that without you in front of him protecting him?" Jaxer asked, frowning at the glow.

"Have you seen it?" she asked Jaxer. "What do you see?"

"It doesn't matter what Jaxer sees, or what your mate would see, Ms. Redmond," Ulieran said. "Their experiences would always be very different from yours, even if you could get closer."

"So I can't actually get near the thing, whatever it is, because… I repel it." That wasn't very flattering.

The guardian shrugged.

"Well, hell." She stopped trying to force herself toward the glow, but she was still leaning forward into the resistance. She glanced at Ulieran. "Is this anything to do with the Protector magic I'm channeling? Could it be that rather than the magic absorbing thing?"

He looked thoughtful. "I've never had a Protector here either. It could be that magic that's causing the resistance. Perhaps the danger beyond is so extreme, your Protector nature is preventing you from going forward."

"But it's not stopping Deacon or Jaxer," she said. "If I'm protecting anyone from the curse, thus triggering my magic, it would be them. And I'd be able to easily get between them and the danger. That doesn't seem to be what's happening."

"Then you've answered your own question," Ulieran said. "This reaction is most likely nothing to do with the Protector magic."

She waved at the glow. "If we're not going in, I guess you can close that now."

"Brace yourself," he said again.

Cary leaned against Deacon, letting his sturdy strength take her weight as Ulieran swiped his claw across the glow, sealing the rip in space like closing a zipper. When the light cut off, plunging them back into a flickering darkness, all the resistance Cary had been pushing against collapsed. She stumbled, grateful she'd been leaning into Deacon already or she would have dropped onto her ass again. He held her close, keeping her upright as she found her footing.

"Well that was weird," she said.

"We need to get you and Deacon out of Faery for a bit," Jaxer said. He faced his father. "Will you send us back?"

"Of course." He paused. "It's good to see you again. I'm glad you're well."

"Shame it's the end of the world," Jaxer said, his smile forced.

"Heed your mother's warnings." Ulieran settled his hands on Jaxer's shoulders. The guardian was so tall, Jaxer looked like a kid in comparison. "Your decisions will have an impact on all that happens now. I would have preferred you not have this responsibility. But it's too late for me to change the course we're on. I received Grenelle's message, and her warning, too late."

Cary wonder if maybe that had been on purpose. Tatiana had kept the message all this time, refusing to pass it on to Ulieran. Maybe she'd done it for a reason. Had Ulieran known this fate was coming years ago, would he have done something to release the Lachlinain sooner?

A question no one could answer now.

Jaxer and his father hugged again, then Jaxer stepped back to join her and Deacon. "I'll see you soon, Da," he said, lifting a hand in farewell.

Ulieran didn't answer as he flicked his fingers in the air, and the stone room vanished from view, leaving her, Deacon, and Jaxer once against standing in the now empty clearing where they'd meet the queen and king.

2 0

They emerged from Faery onto a grassy lawn in the middle of Hyde Park. Jaxer had to tell her it was Hyde Park because she'd never been to London. As far as Cary was concerned, they could have been anywhere in the world. But the large park in the heart of London made sense.

"Not back to Iceland, huh?" she said.

"I needed a cup a tea," Jaxer said with a shrug.

Taking in a deep breath, she spun in a circle, letting the reality of her own realm settle her humming nerves. She was tingling all over, like she'd come into close proximity with lightning. The sensation wasn't unpleasant, it didn't hurt, but it wasn't comfortable either.

Glancing down, she smiled. "Ah, I kind of liked the Ren Faire clothes." But her jeans and t-shirt and hiking boots were a much better fit for the middle of the day in the center of London. Wait… She blinked at the bright sunlight. "Middle of the day? How long were we in Faery?"

"A couple of days in this realm have passed while we were there," Jaxer said as Cary pulled her cellphone out of her back pocket to check.

Fortunately, these were Marianne-made jeans and the pockets were magic. She could keep her phone, wallet, and keys in the pockets without causing weird bulges and without worrying about them falling out when she was jumping in between good guys and bad guys. She hadn't even had to worry about breaking her phone when the Lachlinain bounced her on her ass.

Pockets were great. Magic pockets were the best.

As she waited for her cell to turn on because somewhere along the way it had shut itself off—probably safer in Faery anyway—she glanced at Deacon. He was back to ordinary street clothes as well, but he was still wearing the cape and brooch. She nodded at them. "I think it's safe for you to take those off now."

He shrugged and deftly removed the brooch, swung the cape off, and rolled the whole thing into a bundle. "It's comfortable. I forgot I was wearing it."

"Seemed to work," Jaxer said. "No sudden appearances of your leopard."

"It was a close thing when that Faery curse tossed her on her ass," Deacon said, a faint growl in his voice.

She patted his arm as her cellphone dinged on. "I was fine. My ass is well-padded."

"And I like it just the way it is, without bruises," he said.

His eyes darkened as he looked at her, his gaze dropping to her butt, and she felt her pulse jump in reaction. She had to force her gaze away from him so they didn't embarrass themselves in the middle of the park. Well, she'd be embarrassed to start making out with her boyfriend in public. Deacon probably wouldn't care.

She risked a glance at Jaxer. He was staring off into the distance, at a group of people sitting on a hill picnicking, and the kids playing in a small playground just beyond the grassy area. He was pointedly *not* looking at her and Deacon.

Glancing down at her phone, she realized she had a whole bunch of texts waiting for her. And three voicemails. The voicemail was from her mother. Probably wanting to know where she was and to nag her about getting married, so she ignored those for the moment and opened up the texts. She'd give her mom a call when they had a quiet moment.

One of the texts was from Marianne saying she was having fun in New York but was looking forward to coming home next month. That was such a relief, Cary felt her shoulders sag. She'd support Marianne if she moved. They all would. But she would really miss having her friend around all the time.

Two texts were from Lucy, one checking in since Cary had missed her training session, and a second saying she'd talked to Angie so call her when she got back.

The last three were from Angie, asking her to call as soon as her phone worked.

Cary frowned. "Angie wants me to call her. She sent three messages about it. I hope it's not the dogs." Her cellphone had an international plan with good rates on long distance calls—which she never used but had thought would be a good idea at the time—so she dialed through, biting the bullet on the expense.

Angie answered her own cell on the second ring. "Is your mind still intact?" she asked.

"Hello to you, too. What's wrong? Why three messages to call you?"

"Intact then," Angie said. "Your mother's been calling you for days, and I was afraid she was going to come down here and move in until you got back. Since I had no idea when you'd be back, I've been stalling."

"What did you tell her?" Cary glanced at Deacon and he raised his brows. She shrugged. He could hear the conversation perfectly well—privacy was difficult around a shifter with super shifter hearing.

"That you and Deacon had gone on a little summer holiday to the beach and the cell service probably wasn't good. She believes the excuse, but she's annoyed you didn't tell her yourself."

Cary closed her eyes and let her breath out slowly. "Didn't realize I'd be gone long enough for my mother to notice." To be fair, she did usually at least message her mom when she traveled, but she traveled so rarely, because of work, she hadn't thought about it this time. "Sorry she's been pestering you."

"No, that's not a probably. The problem is your sister is pregnant again and your mother is officially more worried than thrilled, although she tried to hide that at first."

"Don't tell me, you got the entire story?"

"On the third call." Angie sighed. People talked to Angie and told her things, even when they weren't her clients. People tended to trust her with their private lives, which always amazed her.

"Sorry about that." Cary knew why her mom was worried. This was Valerie's fourth baby in less than six years. As far as Cary knew, Valerie had a good marriage. Her husband made a good living, so they could support the kids. But still, Valerie having so many kids in such a short period of time seemed…well, worrying. She'd claimed to be done with kids after her last one. "I'll call her back as soon as I can."

"How are things going with you?"

"Oh fine. Only got knocked on my ass once. Absorbing Faery magic doesn't seemed to have caused me any damage. And the hit I took from Tatiana happened while I was in full Protector mode, so I only felt it a little."

"Where are you now?"

The fact that Angie took all that in stride proved just how well she knew Cary and understood Cary's life. This was why Cary loved her friends. "London. Hyde Park according to Jaxer. I needed a break from Faery. Jaxer needed a cup of tea."

"And Deacon?"

"He needed me to not get knocked on my ass anymore."

Deacon nodded emphatically in agreement.

"Hi Deacon," Angie said without bothering to raise her voice.

"Hi Angie," he said back, his lips quirking in a slight smile.

"He says Hi," Cary told her. "Thanks for the heads up on my mom's calls and the news about my sister. How are the dogs?"

"Perfect. Currently napping after a romp in the backyard."

"Give them hugs and kisses for me. Thanks again."

"No problem. Don't forget to call your mother."

"Right. Thanks."

She disconnected and considered the three voicemails from her mother. This was going to be a long conversation. And even after her mother stopped fretting over Valerie, she'd start asking Cary why they hadn't met Deacon yet. That had become a regular part of their conversations lately, since Cary had officially told her parents that Deacon existed. Cary didn't have a good answer. Especially since she'd met Deacon's family already. She'd just been stalling.

"How long can we stay out of Faery before we have to go back and stop the end of the world?" she asked Jaxer.

"We have an hour or so."

A little girl ran up to him, her gap-tooth grin wide. "Hey, are you an elf, sir? Like them ones in the movies mummy likes?"

Jaxer smiled and shook his head.

"You look like one," she said, her gaze narrowing as she looked at him from the side of her eye. Her blond hair was tied back in a messy ponytail peppered with grass, a small dirt smudge streaked her cheek, and her leggings and t-shirt had a few grass stains. She put her hands on her hips as she looked Jaxer over. "You are one of them elves. I'm sure of it."

"Not an elf," Jaxer said, but he edged away from the little girl.

Kids saw through his glamour. Like brownies, it was almost impossible to fool human kids into believing the façade. They saw right down to the real being beneath.

So Jaxer avoided kids like the plague.

Cary moved forward just enough to put herself between the little girl and Jaxer. "I think your mom is waving to you," she said, and nodded back toward the group of picnickers.

"Hey, you're American. Do you have a huge car?"

"Not... No." Cary blinked at the girl.

"Shavon," her mom called, getting up to hurry over.

"Better go," Shavon said with a cheeky grin. "Nice to meet a real elf," she said to Jaxer, and skipped back to her mother.

Cary didn't hear the conversation, but from the look on Shavon's mom's face, she was getting a warning about talking to strangers.

"You okay?" she asked Jaxer.

He scowled. "I am not an elf."

"I know, I know. Let's go get that cup of tea. We have some things to discuss." Her stomach growled. "And food. I need food."

THEY FOUND A COFFEE SHOP THAT SERVED FOOD A FEW BLOCKS outside the park. Cary spent a lot of time gaping at her surroundings, since this was her first trip to London, and she almost got hit by a double-decker bus because she looked the wrong way before crossing the street. Both Jaxer and Deacon's scowls ensured she paid more attention after that.

The tea was fantastic. The scones delicious. The cheese, onion, and chutney sandwich a little weird and soggy. But since she was starving, she ate everything put in front of her.

"So now what?" she said once her stomach stopped yelling at her for not feeding it for three days even though it had technically only been a few hours. "Your father isn't going to unleash the Lachlinain anymore. Not on purpose anyway. What happens now?"

"We find the faeries who were trying to manipulate him into breaking his geas and turn them over to Tatiana," Jaxer said.

"Easy as that?" Cary asked. "This all seemed a lot more dire when we first went into Faery."

"It was dire. And may well still be. The conspirators are still on the loose, and my father is keeping something from us. I'm not sure what, but something to do with my mother's vision."

"The brownie was a set up," Deacon said. "They arranged that because it fit your mother's vision."

"Poor Borir," Cary said to no one in particular.

"And they could have known about you," Jaxer said to Deacon, "because Tatiana keeps tabs on me." He pursed his lips as he looked at Cary. "The thing is, no one would know about Cary. I mean, they'd know she was the last Protector I've trained, but they wouldn't know she'd be the one to fit the vision. They couldn't have known the 'human who can absorb all the world's magic' would be among my traveling companions, even if they'd assumed I'd enlist Cary to come with me."

She scowled. "I can't absorb all the magic in the world," she mumbled around a mouth full of currant scone. "That would definitely kill me." She swallowed. "I think."

"Likely," Jaxer agreed.

"You think the wizard had anything to do with this?" she asked. "Or Sheldon? He was back at the Bookstore, did I mention that?"

"Renee told me," Jaxer said. "But I don't know how either the wizard or Sheldon would get in touch with anyone from the English court. My people don't venture into the new world very often." He snorted. "Not the ones welcome at court anyway. Only exiles like me spend a lot of time in the human world. And none of them seem to be part of this mess."

"That probably leaves out the vampires telling on me too, huh?"

"Faeries and vampires don't get along, even if they do meet," Jaxer said. "Faeries taste too good."

She laughed, suddenly enough to startle the quiet older couple sitting nearby. She winced and apologized before returning to her tea and the subject at hand. "So, maybe the conspirators didn't know about me and figured that part of the vision could be ignored?"

"Possible," Jaxer said, frowning. "My father didn't know about you, but he suspected."

"Was telling him a mistake?" Deacon asked.

"He would have figured it out," Jaxer said. "Especially when Cary couldn't get near the Lachlinain."

"We could have written that off as the Protector magic," Cary pointed out. "He can't know how it works in detail, right?"

Jaxer stared at the table. "I'm not sure what he knows and doesn't. It's been a long time and he's been confined in that place, mostly alone, for so many years…"

"He seemed genuinely happy and relieved to see you," Cary said quietly.

Jaxer nodded but continued to stare at the table, his gaze distant.

"You don't trust your father?" Cary asked, but she didn't have to. It was in Jaxer's tone.

"I want to," he admitted. "But I don't. Not after what he's been through in the last few centuries." He lowered his voice. "Even before I left for the Americas, we rarely saw each other. Tatiana didn't allow it. He's been cut off from most of his people, his world, confined with a curse that could end everything. Knowing the love of his life, the person he was willing to sacrifice everything for, was dying, or dead. I can't imagine what that did to him." He met Cary's gaze. "And that's the problem. I don't know what his punishment has done to him, to his logic and the way he thinks. I don't know what reading my mother's letter, after all this time, has done to him." He shook his head. "I still love my father. But I can't afford to trust him. Not with all of Faery at stake."

"Tatiana and Oberon obviously don't trust him, or they wouldn't require a geas…" She paused, remembering her earlier question. "Wait, I've been meaning to ask, isn't a geas an Irish thing?"

"And Scottish," Jaxer said. "And Tatiana is capable of invoking one. But yes, they are mostly an Irish thing." His mouth quirked into a quick grin. "I'm not the only thing that ties the two courts together."

She snorted, glad to see he still had some humor in all this. She couldn't imagine what he was going through. Having to re-experience his mother's loss, to know he couldn't trust his father now even though he wanted to… Her parents might sometimes be a pain in her ass, but she trusted them explicitly. There was no question on that. The only reason they didn't know about her real job was to keep them safe, not because she didn't think they'd keep her secret.

Thinking about her parents reminded her, though, that she still had to call her mother.

"Do you have a plan to find the conspirators?" she asked Jaxer.

"If Tatiana will allow me to visit with my father again, I'll ask him directly. Eriana is at least one, since she brought my mother's message to him. If I can't see him again, I'll go to her and try to get the information from her. Because nothing has happened yet, their punishment won't be that severe." He rolled his eyes. "Conspiracies against the throne are so common in the court, if the queen and king punished every conspirator in the worst way possible, there wouldn't be any courtiers left. I think Tatiana goes easy on them on purpose."

"Why on earth would she do that?"

"It amuses her," Jaxer said. "And gives her something to do. Eternity is a long time if you don't have something to keep you occupied. And since she doesn't leave Faery, she needs to find her amusements there."

Cary narrowed her eyes. "Are we going to get to the end of this and discover it was just some big game Tatiana was playing to entertain herself?"

"That's entirely possible," Jaxer said.

"I might have to hate that woman."

"Join the club."

She snorted. "So our plan is go back to Faery, try to talk to your father, and then go talk to this Eriana person. Right. In that case, I need to call my mom before we go back."

"How are you doing?" Jaxer asked, narrowing his eyes. "Tingling skin? Need to unleash all that pent up magic?"

"I never get that last one until I unleash stuff," Cary said, "and even then I have no idea how it happens." Still. Which was a problem. "I don't suppose anyone in Faery can tell me how to deal with releasing the magic in a way that doesn't kill me or the people around me?" So far, she'd only killed bad guys. But she couldn't count on that always being the case. It would be nice to know how to get rid of everything she absorbed on purpose instead of on accident.

"Not sure anyone who could help you would," Jaxer said.

"And probably better not to ask," Deacon said. "The less the court knows about you, the better."

"Like the vampires," Jaxer said. "It's better if they think you have control over that skill."

"Oh well. Worth a shot." She sighed. "Anyway, to answer your question, I'm feeling just fine. My skin stopped tingling while we were still in the park." She pressed her hands against the table and levered herself up. "I'd better go call my mother, now. After which I'll probably be glad to run away to Faery again." She loved her mother, but there were moments... "You two keep yourselves occupied. I'll be back in a few minutes."

2 1

"**W**hat aren't you telling her?" Deacon said once Cary had stepped outside the little coffee shop. He kept one eye on her where she stood just outside the large front windows, London pedestrian traffic flowing past her, but his main focus was on the faery across from him.

A former friend. A romantic rival. And in that moment, a liar.

Except Deacon wasn't sure what he was lying about.

"I don't know what you're talking about," Jaxer said. He met Deacon's gaze, and the look was steady.

Deacon wasn't buying it. He tapped his nose. "Super shifter smelling, remember?"

Jaxer cursed and glanced out the window at Cary. Then back to Deacon. "It's personal. Nothing to do with this situation."

"It's to do with that Fae, Eriana. The one we need to talk to. Your scent changes every time her name comes up. It has since the meeting with your father."

"As I said, it's personal. It won't come into this."

"Bullshit. Spill or I tell Cary and let her beat it out of you. I'd enjoy watching that, so don't tempt me."

Jaxer's gaze flicked to the windows again. "She can't actually beat on me, you know."

"She's been practicing with Lucy a lot. And Lucy could kick your ass, even with the handicap of being a mundane human."

Jaxer smiled a little. "I'm glad Cary's been going to her more. She spent years avoiding Lucy's training."

"You're changing the subject."

"You started it by bringing up Lucy."

"Jaxer…" Deacon let his leopard out, just a little, the growl in his voice a warning. His mate was in danger here. A lot of danger. He had no intention of letting her go back into Faery if Jaxer continued keeping secrets this way.

Jaxer shrugged, as if none of this was all that important. Deacon flared his nostrils. Jaxer might be trying to look unconcerned on the outside, but his scent told a different story.

With an eye roll, Jaxer finally said, "Fine. There's history between Eriana and me. And it's not good. She won't be happy to see me, and I'd rather not see her either. But I'll do what has to be done."

Jaxer's scent told a story of anger, hate, and even more complicated emotions. Complicated enough to make Deacon raise his brow. "You going to be able to turn her over to Tatiana?"

"If she's trying to end Faery and the human world in its wake, yes. Yes, I will be able to."

"Why would she want to?"

"That's the million dollar question, isn't it? I haven't a clue." Quieter, he murmured, "A lot must have changed in the last couple of centuries, though, for her to want that."

"She was your mother's friend?"

Jaxer glanced up from where he was picking at a tiny divot in the wooden table. "A…protégé more like. She was originally one of the Tuatha de Dana, the Irish court, like my mother."

"How did she end up in the English court?"

"Long story. But she took to it like she'd grown up in it." He looked back down at the table. "Even with the change of loyalties, my mother trusted her, all the way to the end of her life. But that was a long long time ago."

"Will Eriana talk to us? Given your past with her." Whatever the hell it was.

"She will. She wanted me to come, or she wouldn't have arranged for my father to see my mother's message after all these years. She's part of whatever is going on. We have to talk to her."

But Jaxer smelled a lot less certain than he was trying to sound. There were a lot of tricks Jaxer could pull using glamour, including fooling Deacon's sense of smell if he really wanted to. Either Jaxer didn't want to, or he was too upset to remember he could.

Neither possibility boded well for their next journey into Faery.

BY THE TIME CARY HUNG UP WITH HER MOM, SHE HAD A WHOLE NEW set of worries to nag at her. Ones that, really, had to take a backseat to saving the world. For now at least. But once that was done, if the world hadn't ended, Cary needed to talk to her sister about this new pregnancy and why their mother thought Valerie's marriage was failing.

She studied the people pushing past her on the narrow sidewalk, the noise of traffic buzzing by on the narrow, one way street. She could almost forget they were driving on the wrong side of the road when there weren't cars going in the opposite direction. The warm afternoon had all of London turned out in short sleeves and summer dresses and shorts. Or maybe they were just the tourists. Cary couldn't really tell. Most of the people who passed had distinct English accents, but there were enough other languages and accents going by as well to keep her guessing.

Shame her first visit to London had to be so brief. And was over-shadowed by the fate of the world hanging in the balance.

She started to turn back into the coffee shop when a familiar tingling started down her spine, that sense that someone nearby needed her particular skill set. She frowned, turning in a slow circle, until her instincts urged her to the end of the block, where an even narrower road made a kind of alley between the buildings. The sidewalk was only about a foot wide here, and a lot quieter than the walkway outside the coffee shop. But it was broad daylight. And there were still a lot of people passing on the street behind her.

Which made the mugger holding a knife on the woman a few yards away either incredibly stupid, or dangerously desperate.

Cary jogged forward as the man hissed, "Give it over, cunt. Now, if you don't want me to slice you through."

"Well," Cary said, as she forced her way between the man and the trembling woman, "that's pretty rude. Although, according to a friend of mine, the English and Irish don't have the same connotations for the word 'cunt' as we Americans do. But that didn't sound like a friendly use of the word, so I'm going to stick with my original assessment that it was rude."

Her little speech had the usual result of throwing the bad guy way off his game. He glowered at her, his knife lowering a few inches.

"At any rate," Cary went on, "holding knives on people is also pretty rude, and I'm not going to let you hurt the poor woman." She glanced over her shoulder.

The "poor woman" was several inches taller than Cary, her dark hair pulled back into a messy ponytail, her pale skin red from either a sunburn or anxiety, and her light brown eyes narrowed as she stared mutinously at the man. Despite still obviously shaking, she started yelling at him in a language Cary thought might be German.

"Yeah, she doesn't sound like she's going to 'hand over' anything," Cary said turning back to the mugger. He was a skinny, wiry little man. His tan pants, used-to-be-yellow t-shirt, and the knit cap covering his head had all seen better, cleaner days. And his stench wasn't to be ignored. Cary tried not to breathe too deeply. "Seems like a good time to be on your way," she said.

"Stay out of this, Yank. Or I'll cut you, too."

"Sure sure." Cary sighed and waited for him to try.

He lunged at her, knife high, bounced off her shield hard, and ended up sprawled on his ass in the street.

"What the bloody hell...?" He glared up at her.

"I've been training," Cary said vaguely, which only made the man's scowl deepen. She shrugged. "Going now?"

"Stupid fucking cunt…"

Cary shook her head. "So rude. Go away or I'll call the cops. I'm sure they don't look kindly on tourist muggings. Bad for business I'd imagined."

"It's fucking London," the man hissed. But when he scrambled to his feet, he ended up on the tiny sidewalk opposite instead of charging them again.

So, not as dumb as he looked.

He pointed his knife at her, his eyes narrowed, and wiped his free hand across his face, smearing dirt and snot across his pale cheek. Gross.

"Watch yer back, bitch," he snarled. "I finds you in the dark and yer dead."

"If you find me in the dark, it means the world hasn't ended because I stopped it. You should be more grateful."

"Here. Yer crazy." He spit in their general direction and hurried off, tucking his knife out of sight into his pants' pocket.

Cary sighed again. He was just going to hunt up another victim. And there wasn't a lot she could do about it. That was the part of her job that sucked.

She turned to face the German tourist and got pulled into a hard, fast hug. Cary chuckled. This part of her job wasn't the worst. The woman shook her hand hard, nearly pulling Cary off her feet, and talked at her in rapid-fire German. Cary caught the word "Danke", so she assumed the woman was thanking her.

"No problem," Cary said.

"How did you stop him?" the woman asked, in accented but perfect English.

Cary blinked, adjusting to the language change. "Ah, oh, I just… As I said, I've been training pretty hard lately. Martial arts."

"You were brilliant," the woman said. "I didn't even see you move. I have to join my party, now. Thank you again. Danke."

The woman shook her hand once more, hard enough to knock Cary off balance again, before hurrying toward the busier sidewalk. Cary rubbed her shoulder as she watched the woman disappear. Then she returned to the coffee shop, thinking London could probably use its own Protector. Or two.

Shame the rest of Faery didn't have the same desire to help humans as her bosses did.

2 2

She'd barely made it back to the table before Jaxer said, "What kept you?"

"I was talking to my mom," she said at the same time Deacon said, "She was talking to her mother." She grinned at Deacon.

Jaxer rolled his eyes. "You walked off from in front of the window."

"Oh, I just had to go rescue a tourist from a mugger. No biggie. So when are we going back to Faery?"

"Any problems?" Deacon asked.

"Nope." She shrugged. "Just a guy with a knife and a German with a hell of a solid handshake. I'm pretty sure if I spoke German, I'd have learned some new curse words today, too."

"Any tingles?" Jaxer asked.

"That sounds more like innuendo than it should," she said, pretending to scowl at him. He didn't take the bait and smile back. She huffed out a disappointed sigh. "They were both mundane. There was no magic thrown. I'm fine. What the hell is going on? You both look way too serious. Okay, well, I mean, yes, we have a pretty serious situation facing us. But we also have a plan—which is better than I normally have at this stage—and we're all of us still alive. That's a

148

good thing." She narrowed her eyes. "Have you two been fighting while I was gone? I can't take you anywhere."

Deacon squeezed her arm. "Nothing to worry about." He met Jaxer's gaze. "Right?"

"Nothing," Jaxer said. "Let's get back to the park so we can talk to Eriana."

"I don't suppose she can come out of Faery to talk?" Cary asked as they stood.

Deacon picked up the bundle of his cloak and brooch from the table, which reminded her…

"Wait, who paid?" she asked.

"I did," Deacon said. "Credit card," he said when she raised her brows.

"Thanks."

"You're welcome."

Jaxer let out an obnoxious sigh. "If you two are done making moon eyes at each other—"

"I told you once before, we do not make moon eyes," Cary said.

They headed back out onto the street. "We have things to do," Jaxer finished, ignoring her interruption. "And no, I doubt Eriana will leave Faery. She used to enjoy the human world, but as far as I know, that ended a long time ago."

"As far as you know? She was a friend of your mother's, right?"

Cary automatically tried to take the lead on the narrow sidewalks, because that's where the Protector had to be to do any protecting, only to realize she didn't have the first clue how to get back to Hyde Park. The twists and turns of the streets, the tall buildings that were all new to her, and the fact that traffic was going the wrong way down the various narrow roads, disoriented her. She'd been too busy gawking on their way to the coffee shop to make note of their direction.

She rolled her eyes at herself. "Uhm, anyone else know where we're going?"

Jaxer took the lead without a word.

"So, friend of your mother's?" Cary nudged him in the back. "Do you know Eriana well?"

"Not anymore," he said. And didn't say anything else.

"Jaxer…"

"Later." He threw the single word over his shoulder, his tone sharp.

She frowned at his back, then frowned at Deacon, her brows raised in question. Deacon gave a slight head shake that could have meant anything, but she took the hint. This was a conversation that had to wait.

Was this what the two men had been discussing while she was dealing with the crisis of her sister's potentially failing marriage—or at least, her mother's worry about her sister's potentially failing marriage —and was this why they were both so serious?

Since talking on the noisy, crowded street, wasn't on option, she bided her time. Pedestrian traffic lightened somewhat as the sidewalk alongside the park widened. They ducked through a wide gate, taking a path that lead between a cool statue and fountain garden and an open, grassy hill dotted with a few shade trees. The sun was moving west, into late afternoon, casting longer shadows across the paved walking path. It was warmer than it had been when they'd first arrived, but a pleasant breeze kept things comfortable.

The park was filled with people still. Clustered on the grassy hill, strolling down the path, wandering the statue garden snapping pictures on their phones. While there was room to walk, there wasn't room to open a portal into Faery without being seen.

"Uh," she said, trotting to walk next to Jaxer. "How far are we going and how are we going to go into Faery with all these people around? More glamour?"

He'd managed it before, getting through the transfers to this part of the world as well as taking them out of Faery in the middle of the park. But still, all these people everywhere… It was hard not to feel hemmed in.

"We'll use that copse of trees for cover," Jaxer said, nodding to a clump of oaks.

The copse didn't look thick enough to provide much cover ordinarily, but given Jaxer particular skill set, she supposed the spot would do.

As they stepped into the middle of the small patch of trees, Cary glanced around. No one was looking at them. Yet. But then they hadn't glamoured up their Faery clothes yet either.

Deacon swung his cloak over his shoulders and affixed the brooch up near his left shoulder again, then they both looked at Jaxer expectantly. Jaxer, on the other hand, was staring at a point behind Cary's back. Almost as soon as she noticed his stare, a prickle of awareness crawled over her shoulders. She spun to face whatever it was, moving forward to get between a possible threat and her companions.

The ordinary looking woman standing twenty feet away did not look like a threat.

Which either made her a really scary person, or she was just some random park goer who'd stumbled into their patch of trees.

Cary didn't move from her position in front of the men.

A beat, maybe two, of silence filled the copse, a silence so loud it covered the other noises from the park, blanketing them in eerie quiet. Then the sounds from around them rolled in again.

And Jaxer said, "Hello, Eriana. Long time no see."

The woman smirked and settled her hands on her hips. "Not long enough."

Well. Guess there was some history there Cary didn't know about. She raised her brows at Deacon in question. He gave a little head shake. Cary glared. This is what they'd been talking about while she'd been out saving tourists and dealing with family crises. She knew it. And she was going to ring the story out of the both of them just as soon as they had some quiet time to talk.

For the moment, she turned back to the woman who was a highborn Fae and former friend of Jaxer's mother to study her. In her human guise, she was really quite average looking. Longish, straight brown hair framed a pale face and hazel brown eyes. No ethereal paleness like Tatiana, no dark shining beauty like Oberon. Just…ordinary pale with a little splotchy pink around her cheeks and chin. Her hair didn't glow in luxurious waves, no shampoo model luster, just brown hair. Even her eyes were ordinary enough despite the brown having that touch of green-gold in it. Her lashes were dark and long but nothing outrageous and obvious. Her mouth had that pretty heart shape to it that probably made wearing lipstick fun. Except she wasn't wearing any makeup at all. She was dressed in tan walking shorts and a white t-shirt, her figure average—not too thin, not too curvy. She was even an unremarkable height, just a few inches shorter than Cary.

There wasn't anything about her that said she was other than an ordinary human woman, out for a walk in the park on a sunny afternoon. Not a hint in any part of her outer appearance that she was one of the legendary Fae.

The disguise was so complete, either Eriana was a pretty ordinary looking faery, or she was as good—if not better—at glamour as Jaxer.

Cary glanced back at her former mentor. He hadn't moved. And he hadn't taken his eyes off the newcomer.

After another few beats of silence, Cary finally broke. "Hi," she said, giving Eriana a little wave. "I'm Cary. This is Deacon. We're friends of Jaxer's. Well, sort of. They used to be friends." She pointed at both men with her thumbs. "And Jaxer was my mentor. But okay, that's probably more information than you need right now. Funny you should show up. We were on our way back into Faery to talk to you."

She closed her mouth before admitting she hadn't been looking forward to another trip through the scary magical wonderland.

Her rambling broke the staring contest between Jaxer and Eriana, lightening the growing tension a little. Eriana tilted her head to study Cary. "I'm not sure if I'm pleased to meet you or not," she said. "But you're right. We do have to talk."

"Here?" Cary asked. "Or somewhere more comfortable?"

"This is comfortable for me. In your world." She wrinkled her nose. "The place stinks. I'd rather not leave the park."

"Fair enough." She glanced between Jaxer and Eriana. "Who wants to start?"

"We don't have much time," Eriana said, "so I'll be blunt."

"A first for a faery," Cary said with an approving nod. This earned her a glare from Eriana which she supposed she deserved. "Why don't we have much time?"

"They'll find me soon." Eriana turned her attention to Jaxer. "The situation isn't what you think."

"It never is," he said.

"Who's 'they'?" Cary asked.

Eriana ignored her. "I ensured Borir overheard that conversation. I urged him to find you and bring you back."

"We suspected as much." Jaxer's voice was surprisingly calm and neutral.

He must be pissed. Cary studied the two Fae. There was more between them than just Jaxer's mother. Feelings they were both trying to hide, but the anger was palpable from both sides.

"I didn't like doing it," Eriana said, sounding defensive.

"I wouldn't think you'd want me here. Out with what you're hiding."

"I'm not trying to end Faery. I'm trying to protect it."

"By urging my father to loose the Lachlinain?" Jaxer didn't try to hide the bitterness and anger in that statement.

"For your father to be free of his geas, Faery has to be destroyed."

"Which kills him as well as everyone else. Which likely destroys the human realm as well. As my father loves this realm, he's not likely to destroy it just to kill himself. There are easier ways to die."

"Not for the Curse Guardian," Eriana said.

Wait, were they saying Ulieran was suicidal? Cary opened her mouth to ask, then snapped it shut, afraid to interrupt and slow down the conversation.

"I discovered Tatiana had kept your mother's message from your father only a short time ago. After I'd already begun to worry about him. I found the box and brought it to him myself, with some help. I thought it would stop him from considering the worst, thought..." She lifted her hands in a shrug. "Thought it would motivate him to continue guarding the Lachlinain and not give in to despair."

"By letting him read about my mother's vision of the end of Faery?" Jaxer said, an actual growl in his voice now.

Wow, he was pissed. Cary wasn't sure she'd ever seen him this angry.

"By letting him see you would be in danger if he continued on the way he was going," Eriana snapped.

"What way was he going? What were you worried he'd do? And why now?"

Eriana looked off into the trees. Beyond their sparse protection, people strolled past as the sun drew closer to the horizon. A cool breeze made it almost chilly in the shade. Cary started to envy Deacon his cloak.

"He…" Eriana started, then sighed. "He's been growing increasingly convinced you were dead. He could see you, follow you, but he…he couldn't believe his own eyes." She met Jaxer's gaze. "I knew you wouldn't, couldn't come back without a life or death reason."

"Since coming back tempted a death sentence," Jaxer said.

"And whose fault was that," Eriana snarled. "Trouble of your own making."

"I had help in creating that trouble."

"Enough. I don't have time to argue with you."

"Why?"

"Yeah," Cary finally stepped into the conversation. "You said 'they'd' find you soon. Who are they? And why shouldn't they find you."

"It's a long story," Eriana said, her gaze remaining firmly on Jaxer.

"*We* have time," Cary said. "Who are 'they'?"

"They are the enemy." She flicked a glance at Cary before settling her full attention on Jaxer again. "Not me."

"We could argue that point," he said quietly. "But for different reasons. Answer Cary's question."

Her eyes narrowed, and for the first time Cary saw something more than ordinary in them, a spark of emotion that lit up the hazel depths and gave power to that gaze. Scary power.

"Your pet Protector," Eriana sneered. "Do you always do what she tells you to do?"

Jaxer didn't answer. Cary wasn't sure if that was a good tactic or not and wanted to open her mouth to defend her mentor. Only Deacon's soft touch on the back of her hand stopped her.

Cary really didn't like this woman very much.

After the silence stretched, Eriana let out a frustrated huff, and glanced away. "They are the ones trying to destroy Faery. They took your mother's vision seriously and want to end everything."

"How did they learn of my mother's vision, when you claim Tatiana has kept the message hidden away all this time? That you only discovered this fact recently."

Yeah, Cary thought, mentally fist bumping Jaxer.

"One of them, one of the conspirators, he sometimes took me to your father, when I went to see him."

"Did you visit him frequently?" Jaxer's tone softened.

"When the queen would allow it. How else to you think I knew he was in trouble?" Eriana's tone didn't soften.

"Who?" Jaxer said after a moment. "Who can reach him when you can't?"

"Me," a deep voice said from behind them.

Damn it. Cary spun and put herself between the newcomer and the rest of the group. She was now protecting Eriana as well, instead of protecting against Eriana. Unless, of course Eriana was still a threat. Cary had no idea what to make of the faery yet. But at the moment, she had bigger things to worry about.

Much bigger.

23

For about thirty seconds, the man in front of Cary looked like an ordinary human man in a business suit. She frowned a little, remembering the Fae in Tatiana's court who'd been dressed in a human business suit and how he'd looked so out of place. Was this the same man? The same Fae?

But before she could study him, the man smiled, showing a lot of teeth that didn't typically belong in a human mouth. And then he changed.

Growing taller and wider until the business suit shredded.

In place of the unassuming business man stood someone as tall as Deacon, as wide as a grizzly bear, and sporting leather armor studded with plates of silver and gold, twisted and braided in ways that made the metal sparkle like jewelry in the dying sunlight. He was the biggest, thickest, meanest looking highborn faery Cary had ever seen.

He was flanked by three equally large and mean looking Fae. And two of the hobgoblin who'd chased Borir into her realm.

They were all wearing the same thick leather armor, covered in silver and gold links. Silver and gold weren't strong enough to serve as much protection, but Cary had a feeling there was magic in that chain-mail that belied the soft metals used to make it.

"Nice transformation trick," she said, nodding at the former businessman. "Must have practiced a long time to get that down so well." She waved at the two hobgoblins. "Hey."

The former businessman-turned giant faery wasn't holding any weapons. But the faeries and hobgoblins flanking him were all armed with long swords, the blades glimmering with a bright purple light, glowing from within. The hilts were wrapped in leather, a thin wire of gold twisting over the top, and the guards were made of the same glowing metal as the blade.

Because of the Fae's allergy to iron, Cary was certain those swords weren't made of steel. But that magic glow proved whatever the hell they were made of, it probably wasn't weak.

"Well, this is fun," Cary murmured. "And you would be?"

The man flicked a glance at Cary, then summarily dismissed her and focused his full attention on Jaxer and Eriana.

Rude.

"Eriana," the man said, "by order of Queen Tatiana, you are being placed under arrest for conspiracy to overthrow the crown."

"Grim, you bastard," she hissed. "You think you can have me charged with your crimes? The queen will hear the truth!"

"Not if you've been killed resisting our efforts to bring you in."

"Yeah, I'm not sure which of you is the bad guy here," Cary said. "Although, I'm thinking the guy named 'Grim'—Grim? Really?—is likely not in the good guy category. But at any rate, I'm not letting anyone kill anyone just yet."

Grim ignored her. "Take her," he ordered his soldiers.

The hair on Cary's neck tingled, but she didn't glance behind her to see what the others were doing. She faced down the very large soldiers charging toward her, waiting patiently. When they slammed against her shield and were tossed backward onto their collective butts, she nodded.

"Okay, then," she said, "at least we know for sure you're not the good guys."

Protector magic was really good at picking out the bad guys. Cary wished she could take some credit for that, but she just channeled the stuff. In this case, that was for the best. She still wasn't sure Eriana was a "good guy," but this confirmed the group after her were definitely not friends.

"Cease this magic, witch." Grim finally turned his attention to Cary, along with the full weight of his dark green-eyed glare.

"No." She grinned.

His heavy brows lowered in a scowl that could have scared a corpse. "You have no place in this. You will not interfere with the execution of my official duty."

"Since your official duty seems to be to have Eriana charged with crimes you're looking to commit..." She glanced back at Eriana for confirmation. The faery hesitated a moment, as if she wasn't sure what Cary wanted, then nodded and glared at Grim. Cary faced him again. "Yeah, since you're trying to falsely accuse and/or kill Eriana, I'm going to say your duty isn't actually official—at least not handed down from Tatiana; I hope—and is in fact a bad thing. I stop bad things from happening. So I'm not lowering my shield. You're just going to have to deal with that."

She grinned again when Grim's scowl worked its way into confusion. She had that effect on people. And faeries apparently. Dark spots of red formed on his high cheekbones, turning his dark brown skin ruddy. The heat of anger made his green eyes spark. Grim did not like being confused.

But bad guy confusion tended to work in her favor. "Shall we exchange names?" she asked, glancing around as Grim's soldiers clambered to their feet. "Or would that be too friendly?"

One Fae charged her again, his eyes flaring a strange bright green-blue, and light like sparkling glitter surrounded him. He smashed against her shield like a bug, his nose smooshed flat, and slid back to the ground. Cary pressed her lips together so she wouldn't laugh. This wasn't a laughing situation. It was, in fact, a sort of scary one since she didn't trust Eriana and all these faeries had a lot of magic to throw around. But that bug-smash-against-her-shields thing was always funny looking.

"I said I wasn't lowering the shield," she told the man on the ground as he shook his head. "Did you think just charging it again would somehow change my mind?"

"He thought he'd broken it," Eriana said.

"He did?" Cary glanced back at her.

"He hit it with a spell that apparently didn't work." Eriana glanced at Cary now, her eyes narrowed. She didn't say any more, which was good. Wouldn't want to give the enemy too much information.

"Ah," Cary said and faced the soldiers again. "That was the green-blue flare in your eyes and the glitter around you, was it? Casting out some magic. Cool. But yeah, that was never going to work." She looked at the others. "Better not to try. You'll just get hurt."

And Cary would probably absorb at least some of that magic. Since she was already worried about the amount she might be taking in just by going into Faery, she really didn't want to risk taking in a lot more.

"Tatiana's will cannot be denied," Grim said.

"Except you've made it clear this isn't her will," Cary said. "She wants Eriana brought before her, not killed. And you'd like to kill Eriana. And I'm really confused about what's happening here, so I don't want anyone who might explain it all to end up dead. Which means you can't kill her. I won't allow it."

"*You* won't allow it?" Grim's cheeks turned red again and his brows lowered dangerously.

Wow, he was good at that scowling thing. No wonder his name was Grim. Did he get the name first and perfect the look to go with it? Or was it the other way around? She opened her mouth to ask, but didn't get it out before Grim pulled a sword out of thin air and aimed it at her, like a very large, accusing finger. Where the hell had the sword come from?

Blue-white light shot out of the tip of the sword, slamming against her shield and lighting up the darkening clearing. The hit was so strong, she had to brace to keep from being pushed backward. She spread her feet farther apart and leaned into the pressure, squinting her eyes against the glare. Damn, that was going to draw attention. The last thing she needed were innocent bystanders wandering into the situation and being used as bargaining chips.

"You hiding this from the locals?" she asked Jaxer. The glare intensified and she raised her arm to cover her eyes.

"I am," he said. "But we need to take this fight out of this realm. There are kids here. They'll see through my glamour."

"Shit. How exactly do we do that without putting Eriana into the hands of the bad guys?" She glanced back at the faery in question. "And by the way, I'm still not sure you're in the good guy category. I do, however, need answers from you."

Eriana lifted her lip in a dismissive sneer.

"Nice," Cary said. "When I'm saving your life. Guess we won't be friends." Which, since she might still be a bad guy, made sense.

"How're you doing?" Deacon asked. He was standing right at her shoulder, not touching her but ready to help if needed.

"Fine, fine," she said. "Pretty bright in here. But otherwise, I've got this."

"Lot of magic."

"Noticed." She grunted when the light flared brighter and turned from blue-white to solid white. "But already doing my thing. It'll be fine."

Given they had an audience, she stuck to being vague. Still, she'd never worried about magic attacks before. They were just one of the many things her powers blocked, and she'd been blocking magic for years without any issues. Now that they knew she absorbed some of it though, she got edgier around these jobs. Which kind of sucked. She'd preferred her ignorance. In her case, ignorance had ensured she didn't balk when doing her job. Balking could get people killed.

The light finally died down. Cary blinked in the darkness that followed. Spots swam in front of her vision, making pretty designs and swirling colors. Several moments passed before she blinked away the spots and could see Grim again. He was scowling, of course, and looking at his sword. He even shook it a little, like it was broken and shaking it would fix it.

She did chuckle then. She just couldn't help it. "Your weapon isn't broken," she said. "I've just got super shields. Like a superhero. Only without the cool superhero costume." Which she probably wouldn't wear anyway because she didn't like the way her thighs looked in skin-tight leggings. Maybe something like Batman, where it was all thick, movable body armor. She could make that work. So long as there were pockets in it.

She was wondering if that was something Marianne could make when Grim interrupted her train of thought.

"This will not stand," he snarled. "Eriana the traitor must appear before the court. The queen will not be denied."

"I'm not denying the queen." Technically. "I'm denying you a chance to kill Eriana. That's two different things. Now, head on back to the queen and tell her you couldn't bring Eriana to her because you threatened to kill her. I'm sure Tatiana will be very interested in that fact."

Instead of listening to reason, all of the soldiers charged again, various colors flaring out from their swords. She winced as they tried to hack away at her shields. The reverberation along their arms must hurt.

"Can we just stop now?" she asked, but they were all making too much noise to hear her. She shook her head. "Got any ideas?" she asked Jaxer. "Given the limits of your glamour, and the people still walking past?"

Although, as she looked around, she realized it had gotten dark while they were waiting out Grim's determined attack. There weren't many people walking by anymore thankfully. The park was clearing out for the night, and that meant most of the kids were probably gone, which meant Jaxer's glamour would hide this confrontation longer.

"There's still a few kids," he said. "Teenagers in the distance."

"Damn it." Teenagers were the worst. Young enough to spot something wrong with Jaxer and his magic, but close enough to being adults, they couldn't see through it fully. Combine that with their curiosity, and they could walk right into the middle of danger without any self-preservation awareness at all.

"We need to get out of this realm," Jaxer said.

"Somewhere that doesn't endanger Eriana further? Where?"

Jaxer sighed. Long enough, and with enough emotion, Cary heard it clearly over the noise of the attacking soldiers.

"We need to take refuge in the Irish court," he said. "I have to face Danu."

Cary's eyes widened.

Oh boy.

2 4

The lights and noise of the attack stopped suddenly. Cary blinked, glanced up, and realized Grim had stepped as close to her as her shield would allow.

"You've interfered where you should not have, human," he growled, his voice low.

"I beg to differ," she said. "Saving lives and stopping the end of the world is exactly where I should be interfering."

"You don't even understand what you're meddling in."

"Well, that's true," she muttered.

Grim glowered at her. He was epically good at glowering. "For your arrogance, you will suffer," he said.

"I've heard that one before, you know. Bad guys tend to say the same things over and over again. It's like you guys have a book or something. Do you have a book? Do they hand that out when you decide to do something nefarious? 'Here, you'll need these clichéd lines to spout when someone's gotten in your way.' Is that what happens?"

His glower shifted into confusion again. She loved doing that to bad guys. And since it was one of the few offensive things she could do, she did tend to wield her confusion skills as often as possible.

Grim took the confusion poorly. He lifted his sword and swung it around, aiming at her neck.

Eriana gasped. Deacon made a noise Cary couldn't decipher.

The sword hit her shield about a foot from her neck and rebounded hard, sending it flying from Grim's grip. She met his gaze and tried to put on an innocent expression.

It didn't work.

He cursed her and reached for her throat with his bare hands. When that didn't work, he motioned for the others to charge her again.

So stubborn.

"We'd better leave," Cary said to Jaxer. "They're not giving up and going away like smart bad guys. Can we get to the Irish court from here? Or do we have to venture into English Faeryland first?"

"This way," Jaxer said.

She glanced back, and did a double take. "Oh. Wow. That was fast."

A doorway had appeared cut into one of the trees. A narrow passage, but it had a real wooden door and knob and everything. That was different. Jaxer held the door open and gestured Eriana inside.

She paused at the threshold. "I'm not welcome with the Tuatha anymore," she said, staring into the tree doorway.

The edges of the opening glowed green, but the interior was dark and from her angle, Cary couldn't see inside. She wondered what Eriana was seeing.

"Neither am I," Jaxer said, "but it's this or face Tatiana before we're ready." He gestured to Cary and Deacon. "Let's go."

Cary backed toward the doorway, keeping Deacon and the other's behind her as she faced the Fae soldiers.

"Stop them!" Grim shouted.

The group redoubled its efforts to break through her shields, launching at her at speeds that blurred their large shapes. One jumped high and dropped down onto her head—stopping several feet in the air above her before being tossed away. Four of them, including Grim, tried to circle around her, attempting to attack from behind the tree as the fifth charged her directly while the one who'd tried to jump on her head got back to his feet.

Cary shook her head. "You can't just come in from behind and get at us," she grunted. What good would shields be if you could just circle around and come in from behind? Really.

She watched the attacker in front of her bounce off the shield and hit the ground hard. The Fae's head came up and she shot a bolt of something white and sparkling from her palm. It flared against Cary's shield, dissipating in a wide circle of glitter and color. That might have been pretty if Cary wasn't certain it would have killed her.

"Cary, move it," Jaxer called.

She glanced back just as Deacon stepped through the doorway, Jaxer hovering at the threshold, waiting for her. She trotted to him, keeping the attackers in her peripheral vision. They edged closer, swords drawn, moving more slowly as her shields contracted and they could reach ground they hadn't been able to get to before. Grim raised his sword and aimed it high, firing up into the tree over their heads.

Cary squealed and instinctively ducked when a huge branch loudly cracked off of the tree and dropped toward her. It stopped a foot overhead, the leaves rustling and falling in a semi-circle that showed one edge of her shield.

"This isn't over," Grim said. He snatched one end of the huge tree branches and, one handed, swung it at her. It shattered against her shield, sending splinters and sharp spikes of wood flying around the copse.

Whoa. Grim was strong.

"You're still reading from the bad guy dialogue book," she said, covering her anxiety with bravado.

Jaxer stepped inside the doorway, holding the door for her as she followed him. She faced the soldiers until the wooden door closed shut. The last thing she saw was all six of them rushing the tree.

She waited, watching the closed door.

"They can't open it," Jaxer said. "They're Tatiana's guard. They aren't allowed in Danu's realm."

Cary nodded, though she continued to stare at the door a few minutes longer, just to be sure. When she was certain no bad guys would attempt a sneak attack, she turned to face the others.

Oh. Wow.

Her mouth actually dropped open.

Unlike the English realm, which had been all glitter and sparkle and strange swirling colors, the Irish segment of Faery was the lushest, greenest forest Cary had ever seen. Green leaves and vines and moss covered oaks, maple, and heather trees. Thickets of blackberry brambles and patches of stinging nettles beneath the trees. The soil was a rich deep brown, almost black. The air was crisp and damp. And here and there, circles of mushrooms grew against felled trees or up against a mossy trunk base. Everything smelled of the woods, rich and loamy.

A slight movement from the corner of her eye made Cary spin. A startled deer raised his head, his antlers large and symmetrical above a stocky body covered in white fur. He was a magnificent animal, all power and grace as he stared. He snorted at them before turning and trotting deeper into the woods. For reasons Cary couldn't fathom, she took a step toward the animal, as if to follow him.

Jaxer grabbed her arm. "Don't. That's…a trick."

"Huh?" She faced him, blinking a few times.

"The stag. You follow and you'll be running until you waste away to a husk."

"Oh. Ew. Yeah, I'd rather not do that." She shook her head. "Does that mean I'm not protecting anyone right now? Am I soaking up Irish Fae magic?"

"Probably," Jaxer said with a sigh. He looked at Deacon.

Cary followed his gaze. Her eyes widened. Deacon's brooch was glowing softly in the muted green light under the trees. His purple cloak had also taken on a richer texture, though it was still unadorned. And Deacon himself looked…different. Taller and broader, if that was possible. His tanned skin glowed and the gold in his eyes brightened.

"Are you okay?" she asked him.

He frowned at her. "Why?"

"Is your leopard under control? Not feeling any need to shift and go for a run? Follow that stag into the trees? Any of that?"

"Not more than I did in the English court."

She glanced at Jaxer. "What's happening?"

"I don't know," he said. "Unless…"

"What?" she and Deacon asked at the same time.

"Your father is Welsh," Jaxer said. "And your grandmother's Scottish."

"What does that have to do with the land of the Tuatha?" Deacon asked.

"Nothing directly. But… There are arrangements."

"Huh?" Cary asked.

Jaxer shook his head. "It could be nothing. Maybe it's the brooch."

"What are you two talking about?" Deacon asked.

"You look like a king," Cary said bluntly. "Not just your usual large and gorgeous self. You're literally exuding a visible aura of power right now. Kind of sparkly and golden. Almost like…like you belong here."

"A trick of the realm," Jaxer said, but he didn't sound as confident as he had with the stag. "We'd better get moving. Danu isn't any more patient than Tatiana."

"Oh boy," Cary sighed. She narrowed her eyes at Eriana.

The faery hadn't moved or commented since the door had closed. She stood in the middle of the forest, staring straight ahead, her back straight, her head high. But she no longer looked perfectly ordinary either. Her brown hair now hung all the way to the middle of her thighs and would have overwhelmed any hair model with envy. Glorious didn't begin to describe the length and weight and luster. Her hazel eyes were now much more pronounced and electric against skin that was several shades darker than she'd had in her human guise, and glowed with a richness that made it seem like she was lit from within.

Her features had changed a little too, moving her away from ordinary and average to so stunning she was hard for Cary to look at. The changes were subtle, though, nothing Cary could put her finger on directly. But now, Eriana *looked* like a highborn faery who belonged in the court of Tatiana and Oberon.

Except, Cary remembered, she was originally one of the people of Danu, which meant…

She was home.

Cary glanced down at herself, to see if she'd achieved any cool changes. But, nope. Just herself. In her ordinary clothes even. Jaxer hadn't bothered to glamour her up a cool Ren Faire costume.

She pulled her ponytail around to look at her hair. Still ordinary blond-brown. And if those split ends were to be believed, in need of a haircut. Given that everyone around her looked like royalty now, she felt markedly underdressed.

She gestured to herself. "Do I need something a little more formal to meet your goddess?" Danu was considered more than a queen to her people. She was their goddess and she was worshipped as such. Revered and feared as much as Tatiana, but for different reasons.

Jaxer blinked and shook his head. "Sorry. I forgot." He glanced away as if he'd forgotten again the instant he'd spoken.

Cary scowled, but when she glanced down at herself again, she realized he'd given her a new look—he just hadn't bothered with the dramatic hand gestures this time. Her lovely green tunic and brown trousers weren't exactly the elegant gown Eriana gave herself with a sweep of her hand, but they suited Cary better. She even got her own cloak—a modest blue—and another pretty silver brooch with Celtic knots swirling the surface. No swords or weapons, but that was probably for the best since she didn't know how to use a sword if she wasn't protecting someone. Her magic would give her the skills if she absolutely needed them. But without that boost, she was about as good at wielding a sword as she was at doing her own plumbing—which was to say she was not good at all. Although, technically, that flooding hadn't been her fault.

"This'll do," she said of her new outfight. She still felt pretty ordinary compared to Deacon and Eriana, but at least she blended in better with her surroundings now.

Jaxer didn't comment. He was staring into the woods, his brows lowered, his frown the only thing that marred his complexion. Like Eriana, he seemed to have grown more gloriously gorgeous in this realm. His blond hair lay thickly down his back, much longer than he normally kept it, and several braids hung down around his face. His blue-green eyes were luminous and otherworldly in a way he usually disguised. He'd changed his clothing again, too. This time to a style similar to Deacon's but his red tunic was accented with silver designs, and he didn't have any armor or obvious weapons like the sword that hung at Deacon's hip. He hadn't bothered with a cloak or outer covering. But he was now wearing a large flat silver torc around his neck and silver bracers on his forearms, all intricately pattered with Celtic knots and swirls.

When no one moved immediately, even though Jaxer had said Danu was impatient, Cary spun in a slow circle. Their surroundings hadn't changed. Except the door in the tree had vanished. Without it, there was no obvious way back to the human realm. That momentary realization got her pulse pounding. She tried to ignore the punch of fear, but it beat in her bloodstream, a steady reminder that she was human in a world that wasn't typically kind to human visitors.

At least here there was bird song, and air movement, and the sunlight overhead felt real. There were shadows under the trees, sun dappling the dark soil, and the way everything had a faint halo of light surrounding it could almost be ignored.

"Aren't we…going?" Cary said. "Isn't Danu waiting? Shouldn't we move?"

"We don't have to," Eriana said.

The first thing she'd said since they entered Faery. Cary blinked. Her voice had deepened and was so melodious it brought unexpected tears to Cary's eyes. Just her voice. For no reason at all.

That did not calm Cary's heartbeat.

"She's approaching," Jaxer said quietly.

Cary let out a breath—at least Jaxer sounded the same—and placed herself in front of the others, between them and the direction Eriana and Jaxer were staring. It was habit, getting between people she wanted to keep safe and the unknown. She hadn't stopped to consider until after she'd moved that maybe no one else was in danger, and she'd just put herself in peril.

The underbrush in front of them rustled as something substantial moved through it, approaching them slowly but with an inevitability to it that started Cary's pulse hammering again.

Too late to move now.

25

low mist rose from the damp, dark ground in front of them. And from the depths of the trees, a glowing white deer appeared.

Unlike the stag, this doe was ethereal and didn't look even a little like an ordinary animal. She was huge, the size of a red deer, maybe larger, and her white fur was flawlessly pristine. Green eyes that should have looked wrong on a deer held a great deal more intelligence than an average deer would have displayed. On top of her head, the doe wore a crown of gold and precious gems entwined together in intricate Celtic knots. The gold threads were thin and delicate, making the entire piece look like it might fall apart at any moment. But the piece didn't move on the does head at all, even when the animal dipped her head in what could only be interpreted as a regal greeting.

Cary looked over her shoulder to see both Eriana and Jaxer had dropped to one knee, their heads down, gazes focused on the ground. She gave Deacon a panicked look. Should they kneel? He shook his head slightly, not taking his gaze off the doe. It occurred to Cary that he was a predator in his other form. And deer were natural prey animals. And Deacon's eyes were starting to glow. Which always meant his leopard was near the surface. He stared at the doe intently, his shoulders back, not even ducking his head in greeting.

Suddenly, Cary was a lot more worried about Deacon than she was about the formalities of greeting a goddess. "Deacon?" she asked quietly. "You…okay?"

He nodded again, not taking his gaze from the doe.

"Sure?"

Another brief nod.

This couldn't be good.

But if he was in danger, if this was Faery getting to him, wouldn't that trigger Cary's powers and stop whatever was happening? Shouldn't she be protecting him from Fae magic right now?

She faced the doe again. If anything, the animal had grown larger, and the glowing halo encircling her had intensified.

A voice like quiet thunder filtered through the air, coming from the direction of the doe, though the animal didn't move her mouth. "You have returned to me, my wayward son. And you bring back my daughter. Why have you come?"

Jaxer didn't lift his head when he said, "I returned for sanctuary."

"From the other half of you. From the ones who stole my beloved Eriana."

From the corner of her eye, Cary saw Eriana visibly wince. There must be one hell of a story behind that.

"It's complicated, revered Danu," Jaxer said.

And Cary noted his accent was much more Irish now. No longer the bland American he'd used in the English court. That, all by itself, was a fascinating reveal.

"Will you grant us sanctuary?" he asked the goddess.

"Will I have a story in return?"

"You will."

"Then you have it. Tell me the tale."

All without raising his head or rising from his knees, Jaxer told the entire story of events that had brought them here. He spoke again in that lyrical, sing-songy rhythm of a true storyteller, and once again, Cary found herself captivated. Turning a bit so she could see him better, eager for the exciting conclusion to the tale—which of course she wasn't going to get because they had no idea how all this ended.

Even with the retelling, she still didn't have a clue what was going on. The fact that Eriana seemed to have been working with traitors to the English court, but then maybe she was working against them, the fact that Ulieran was hiding something from them and his sanity seemed to be in question, the mystery behind what the English queen and king did and didn't know, how all of this worked together with Grenelle's vision, why Cary and Deacon were even in the vision, and how all of this would end depending on Jaxer's choices… None of it made a lot of sense to Cary. The unknowns far outweighed the knowns and, like Faery itself, the possibilities played with her mind.

When Jaxer got to the part about Cary and the Lachlinain repelling each other, the doe raised her head from intense attention on Jaxer to stare with her bright green eyes at Cary. Cary swallowed hard. Was it good or bad that she was a natural repellant to the curse? She couldn't begin to read the doe's expression, or interpret what she might be thinking. Though even if Danu had presented herself in a more human form, Cary doubted she'd be able to read the goddess's thoughts. Still, the stare was intimidating and Cary wanted to fidget so badly she had to dig her nails into her palms just to keep still.

The doe turned her attention to Deacon as well, and the green light in her eyes flared brighter. Cary glanced back at Deacon. His eyes were glowing entirely yellow now, his leopard right at the surface, ready to break free. Cary bit back a curse. She took a step to the right and back, putting herself more directly between him and Danu. Although, she wasn't entirely sure which one of them she was protecting from which in that moment, she did know getting between them seemed like a very good idea.

Danu blinked and looked back at Cary. Jaxer had paused in his retelling, and the silence in the forest was heavy. Everyone seemed frozen in place, waiting.

And then, though Cary couldn't say why, she swore the deer smiled. It was impossible. The animal's mouth didn't really move, maybe a little quirk near the back, close to her cheeks. But nothing that blatantly said *smile*. Still, Cary couldn't shake the sense that Danu was smiling.

At her.

She glanced back at Deacon. The yellow in his eyes had faded back to his normal golden shade. Not even a hint of that dangerous glow anymore. He blinked and shook his head slightly, then pulled in a deep breath.

What the hell had just happened?

"You need a threat, Protector," Danu said, her voice a quite roll of distant thunder in the silent clearing. "And I am that threat."

Uhm. Had Danu just purposefully created a situation that would allow Cary's powers to work? That was…

Nice?

Cary swallowed hard and kept her attention on the goddess. "You okay?" she asked Deacon again.

This time, in a voice gravely and harsh, he said, "Better now. What happened?"

"How long have you been on the edge of losing control?"

"Not long." He paused. "I think."

Oh boy. "Everything's fine now." She hoped. "But I think maybe I'll just stay right here."

Danu tilted her head to one side as she studied Cary. The golden diadem stayed in place as if it was a part of the animal's head and not a separate piece of jewelry. Cary noticed, as she studied the goddess in return, that the deer's hooves were also gold. Sparkling, matching her diadem gold. And the aura surrounding the animal seemed to have brightened in the last several minutes. Or maybe Cary's eyes were just getting tired staring at an actual goddess.

"Why do you smell of the gods, little one?" Danu said, her intensely green gaze on Cary. "You are not one."

Cary almost snorted at that. A more obvious statement had never been uttered.

"Yet, there is a very faint trace." Danu stepped forward a few more paces.

Cary's heartbeat thundered but she held her place. It took a great deal of willpower not to drop to her knees and bow her head, though. When you talked to a goddess, it felt weird to *not* bow. Holding Danu's green gaze wasn't particularly comfortable either. But because she'd gone to all the trouble of creating a threat that would allow Cary's powers to work, Cary didn't want to ruin all that good work by abandoning her position protecting Deacon.

The doe raised her nose and sniffed gently at the air. "Yes. Very faint."

"There was an incident with a baby god a few months back," Cary said. "Well, technically, she wasn't a baby yet since she hadn't been born. Although, she has since. Her surrogate family is doing well, according to their last email. Apparently, the baby goddess is adorable and has learned to coo at their dog."

Danu's huge green eyes blinked once. Cary realized she hadn't been blinking regularly.

"It was months ago, but maybe that's what you're smelling?" Cary finished lamely. Confusing and baffling this particular entity seemed less like a strategy and more like a relapse of her awkward teen years. Like she didn't know how to behave so she ended up acting like an idiot.

"Tatiana tested you," Danu said after a long beat.

And Cary was grateful for the change in subject. "I don't know if you'd call it a test or an attack. But yes, she threw something at me. Or tried to." She shrugged.

"Had she wanted to destroy you, you would likely not be here."

Cary sighed. "Yeah, I got the feeling she pulled her punch."

"You are rare," Danu said, taking another step toward her. "I can see the power flowing into you, through you. And some of it doesn't flow out as it should. The reason you can deflect the Lachlinain."

"Uhm." She didn't know what else to say to that. She glanced at Jaxer, but he was still kneeling with his head bowed. No help there.

"Some of that power is of Faery. Not my domain. The domain of other gods."

"And I understand you didn't approve of their use of that power to help humans. But I have to admit, I'm grateful for it."

"You would be dead without it."

"Well, that too."

"You retain more magic than you release," Danu said.

She'd ignored Cary's statement about being against the creation of Protectors. Maybe she didn't feel she needed to comment on the obvious.

Danu studied her quietly for another moment before saying, "You have not learned how to release what you absorb."

Well. So much for keeping secrets. Why had Jaxer even had to bother telling Danu their story? Obviously, the goddess could just sniff the air and figure everything out without having to be told.

Cary pressed her lips together and rolled her eyes. "It's a work in progress," she said.

"I can teach you," Danu said.

Cary's head snapped up. "You can?"

"For a price."

Her shoulders sagged. There was always a catch. "No, thank you. I'll work it out."

How, she wasn't sure. Even the Nags didn't know how to help her. Angie had been trying, but she'd been working on intuition and a comfort with magic, not with any actual facts. And so far, Cary had failed miserably at even sensing the magic building in her body. Outside of the tingles she got in the wake of protecting against a magical attack, she generally felt normal. It was hard to grab hold of and release something you couldn't sense or feel.

"You fear the price?" Danu asked.

"I know a catch when I hear one. And deals with faeries never go well for the non-faery." She resisted glancing at Jaxer, but it took a great deal of willpower.

"There is a price for everything, little one," Danu said. "That is *life* for mortals. Choices, and tradeoffs, and prices to pay for each."

"Sure. I'm just choosing not to accept this price."

"You fear what you will owe me?"

"Damn right I do."

"Wise for so young a being."

Cary did snort at that. "I'm not sure I'd call it wise. More like punch drunk. But I do eventually learn my lessons."

"You selected a good protégé with this one, my son," Danu said to Jaxer without looking away from Cary.

"She's an excellent Protector, Revered One," Jaxer said. He didn't lift his head.

"Good. She will need to be in the times ahead." Danu raised her head, towering over their group, seeming to grow larger and more radiant by the second. "You will have sanctuary here. But you can't stay for long. There are things to do. And you, my children both have enemies here. You will do well to leave before they learn of your presence."

It was on the tip of Cary's tongue to ask why Danu didn't just forbid these enemies from attacking Jaxer and Eriana, but she kept her mouth shut. She didn't want to draw the goddess's focus again if she could help it.

The goddess had other ideas. "Come to me when you're ready to pay the price for knowledge, little one," she said to Cary. "I will help you."

"Thank you for the offer," Cary said. She had no intention of taking Danu up on it, but it never hurt to be polite.

"My cherished son," Danu said, turning back to Jaxer.

Cary glanced at him, still slightly behind her so she could protect him if he needed it. He'd bowed his head even lower as the goddess turned her attention on him.

"You have a choice to make," she said. "You must heed your mother's visions, and her warnings." Danu paused. "And you must return to your father. Soon. He grows weary in his task. His resentment has not abated since your mother died."

Jaxer nodded. "I know."

"Neither has yours," Danu added.

Jaxer bowed even deeper. "I miss her."

"She would not be pleased with your reaction to her death."

Cary opened her mouth to defend Jaxer. But Danu continued before she could.

"She would be proud of what you have done since leaving us."

Jaxer's head snapped up. Obviously, he hadn't been expecting that either. "You don't approve of Protectors," he said.

"No. I do not. I don't know that the humans are worth our time. They destroy their realm. They do not manage their people or their lands. They war."

"We war," Jaxer pointed out.

Cary kind of liked the noun being used as a verb in this case. It seemed to fit. But she wasn't sure pointing out that the Fae also went to war would go over well with Danu. Again she was wrong.

"We do. And that is our problem. We still fight and scramble for influence and territory. From the beginning, the Tuatha have fought. And then we retreated here. And yet still we do not settle. Our people grow restless. A time of conflict approaches. Your father is a tool in that conflict."

"What?" Jaxer asked.

"Wait, what?" Cary said at the same time. "You mean, here? In the Irish realm? How?"

"The Lachlinain affects us all," Danu said. "All of Faery."

"Yes, but…"

"It is not just machinations in Tatiana's court that have gotten us here. And once unleashed, there is nothing that can stop the Lachlinain from destroying us all."

"I still don't know why anyone would unleash it if that's the case," Cary said. Why anyone had created it in the first place was another question. Or had it even been created? It was a curse. Someone probably made it. Right? So many questions rivaled to get out she ended up asking none of them.

Fortunately, Danu heard them anyway. "Our realm grows tired and old. Rotting. We all feel it."

"The reason both you and the English court needed Jaxer," Cary said quietly. "To help balance magics?"

Danu dipped her head in affirmation. "Young are still not being born. Not among the more powerful beings. The realm grows stale. The magic will end. Our time will end. One day. And there are those who feel we should take back the human realm and make it ours again."

"It was never ours," Jaxer said. "We shared it with humans always. Always we had a separate place to exist. Here."

Danu said, "Always is only a blink when an eternity of slowly rotting faces you. Some would see us change everything." She paused, lifting her head as if scenting the air. "And some would be right." She lowered her head again, focusing on Jaxer. "You still have anger toward us. But your choice to support and train human Protectors, that requires this realm. Magic from Faery. Did you know it's one of the things keeping us alive?"

"What?" Cary and Jaxer asked at the same time. Again.

Cary was so stunned, she actually took a step closer to the goddess, only stopping when Deacon grabbed her arm to hold her back.

"Magic flows into and out of this realm from our North American brethren. It is a breath of freshness. But too many fear and hate humans. They will not abide that choice. They would prefer to take. Not share."

Bastards, Cary thought but she kept that to herself.

Why she bothered, she wasn't sure since Danu seemed to read the reaction without needing to hear the word. "They are not friends of your people," Danu said, sounding almost amused.

"If Faery is destroyed, won't that destroy my realm?" Cary asked. "That's what I've been led to believe. What good is that to the Fae? To destroy both places?"

Danu's deer tail twitched. It was the only movement in the goddess's otherwise still body. "The magic here will be destroyed with the release of the Lachlinain. But only for those remaining here. Only for this realm. Your realm will shiver, but it will not break. Not if enough Fae escape to it."

"Wait, you're saying they're going to invade my world and then… burn the boats so no one can get back? Then what? Destroy all the natives with disease?"

Humans had done that to themselves already, during several invasions and colonization periods. None of that had been good. And Fae doing the same thing to humans wouldn't end any better. Her realm might survive the destruction of Faery only to become uninhabitable for humans.

"Fae and humans have lived side by side before," Danu pointed out. "Always." She glanced at Jaxer. "It is an option. To abandon a dying realm for one full of life. To take over and lead where your people have lost their way."

"We've always been a disaster," Cary said, scowling. "But it's our world to be a disaster in. Sharing is one thing. Invasion another."

"The Protectors couldn't stop it," Danu said. "Your source of power…their source of power would be destroyed with Faery."

Cary actually gasped aloud. She hadn't considered that.

"You, though," Danu said quietly—if the ground-shaking rumble of thunder that was her voice could be considered quiet. "You would still…protect. You would steal and use what they do not want to share."

"Yes, the magic. But that would kill me. So I couldn't keep protecting anyone."

"Maybe. Unless you learn to use and release the magic you take."

That offer again. A tempting one she didn't dare take. "I think I'll go with keeping Faery from being destroyed."

"That you cannot stop. It is already being destroyed. It destroys itself. Slowly, but inevitably. It's the nature of things. To break down. To rot." She nodded at a downed tree nearby, covered with moss, the bark soft and weak. A patch of mushrooms grew in the side of the fallen tree like little steps. "Rotting to feed the whole," Danu murmured. And she met Jaxer's gaze. "Rotting to feed the whole."

"What can we lose and still save the whole?" he asked, picking up on her comment.

"War will destroy some. The fallen will feed the ground. Blood will renew the realm."

"You're saying," Cary said slowly, "that the only way to save Faery is war? War within Faery? War with the humans?"

Danu blinked again, and her eyes went from bright green to white, as white as the rest of her fur. "War will destroy. War will heal. War is inevitable. But when is not." She blinked again. "And how is not."

"Huh?" Cary asked.

The doe raised her head, scented the air, and blinked, her eyes going green again. "Sanctuary is granted," she said again. "But the time draws near for your choice, my beloved son. You understand now? Faery is dying. And only blood will fix it. Only death."

"I don't understand," Cary said, her voice squeaking. This conversation had only confused the situation more. Except for one point. Both Faery and her realm were still in danger.

Danu didn't acknowledge Cary's comment. She dipped her head again, in a regal nod—which was impressive from a deer—and turned casually to disappear back into the woods, fading into the mists.

No further comment. Nothing. Just…casually walked away after telling them death and blood were their only choices.

Well, that sucked.

2 6

"What the hell?" Cary said aloud, scowling at the spot where Danu had disappeared. She turned to Jaxer. "Did any of that make sense to you or clarify anything? Because I'm still pretty baffled. Are the Fae going to invade my realm and destroy Faery so they can't come back? Is that really what she was telling us? Because that's not good if that's what she's saying. Really really not good. Plus, I thought destroying Faery would destroy my realm. That's what everyone else has been telling me. So how do they get around that?"

Jaxer stood, finally, and looked at Eriana. Cary and Deacon turned toward her too. She was still kneeling, but she was staring up at the sky. And a tear dripped down her magnificently smooth cheek.

"Eriana?" Jaxer asked, his voice quiet.

"I'd forgotten," she said. "What it's like to be in her presence. I betrayed her. Yet she allowed me sanctuary." More tears flowed.

There didn't seem much any of them could say to that. Deacon came up behind Cary and wrapped his arms around her. Everyone remained silent for a long moment as Eriana cried. They had things to discuss. Plans to make. They had to get back to Ulieran and ensure he didn't release the Lachlinain after all. And Cary really wanted to stop the Fae from invading her realm because that just seemed like a terrible terrible possibility. The Fae had escaped to Faery and limited their ties with the human realm millennia ago because the two species couldn't live together without fighting. Humans had iron, a powerful weapon against the Fae. But the Fae had magic which the average human couldn't even fathom. Another war, now when humans had things like nuclear weapons... That really would destroy her world.

She blinked. Maybe that's what everyone had meant when saying the destruction of Faery would mean the destruction of her realm. The Fae and humans had lived side by side in different realms for a long time. Pushing them back together in one, with no option of the Fae being able to return to a separate realm, would start a conflict with no good outcome. Not for anyone.

Oh, she really had to stop that.

At last, Eriana rubbed the tears from her cheeks and rose. She faced them. "Thank you for your patience. Coming back was...surprising."

"We can't stay long," Jaxer said. "I have people here who want to kill me, too."

"What that hell did you do with yourself here, Jaxer?" Cary asked.

He grinned at her. "Caused a lot of trouble. I was good at it."

She snorted. She believed that.

"Some of that trouble was unnecessary," Eriana said.

A chill entered her voice, making Cary raise her brows. One day soon, she'd love to hear the story between Eriana and Jaxer. She had a feeling it was a juicy one.

"Oh, it was necessary," Jaxer said, his tone also taking on a haughty bite. "And I proved my point, didn't I?"

"Kids," Cary interrupted, "while I'd *love* to hear this, we need to stop the invasion of my realm and the destruction of Faery first, please. Then you two can argue and spit at each other all you want. And I'll watch, with popcorn, because that sounds like a fun way to celebrate the world not ending."

Jaxer made a face at her. She grinned at him. It was nice to give him some of his own sometimes. She rarely got the chance.

"We can't go directly to my father without help," Jaxer said, getting the conversation back on track.

"And we can't go to Tatiana," Eriana said. "Or Grim."

Cary sighed. Since Tatiana's guards had come for Eriana, and Cary had gotten in the way of their murderous plans, yeah, that route to Ulieran was off limits now. "Who else can get us to him?" she asked. "You went without Tatiana's permission to bring him his wife's message. Who took you then? Grim?"

Eriana held Jaxer's gaze when she said, "Oberon."

Jaxer, to Cary's amazement, growled. A serious, eyes narrowed, deep from the throat growl.

Wow.

A very tense silence followed while Jaxer and Eriana glared at each other. Cary raised her brows at Deacon. Deacon gave a brief head shake. Cary moved out of Deacon's arms and shifted her weight to balls of her feet, in case she had to get between the two snarling faeries.

While this was a really interesting soap opera to watch, and her curiosity was killing her, they really did have to get moving. Cary's nerves were tingling again. And she couldn't tell if she was absorbing ambient Faery magic, or she was just sensing the approach of danger, because this was Faery and everything here was bizarre and strange.

The mist that had come with Danu was thickening around them, rising higher, casting the trees into a ghostly dimness and muting the sunlight. What had been a light dappled forest a few moments ago was cooling into a quiet, eerie landscape of wavering shadows in diffuse light.

"Uh," she said, looking into the trees. "I think we need to take this argument somewhere else." Her pulse started to pound, though she couldn't pinpoint the reason for it. Her every sense lit up with a need to run. And run fast. She motioned Jaxer and Eriana closer. "Get behind me. Something's coming."

Jaxer moved without question. To Cary's surprise, Eriana did too—she'd expected an argument from Eriana.

Silence descended as they all moved back to back, studying the woods, waiting tensely. Almost without thinking, Cary stretched her arms out and back, holding Deacon on one side and Jaxer on the other, willing them all to stay close and within her ability to protect them.

Rustling in the trees, beneath the cover of fog was her only warning before a rush of…something charged from the woods. Slamming against her shields and baying in anger.

She blinked a few times before she could make sense of what had attacked. They were sort of wolves, but larger than real wolves, and not entirely shaped like a wolf. And they weren't werewolves—at least not the kind Cary had dealt with in her realm. Even the werewolves who hadn't mastered their shifts never ended up in forms like the pack snarling at them. These creatures were like composite animals made up of wolves, hyenas, and a hint of scorpion thrown in just to really complicate matters.

"She loosed the Othries on us," Eriana hissed from behind Cary. "What the hell did you do to her?" This last Cary was pretty sure was directed at Jaxer, but she was too busy staring in horror at the animals circling them.

They were gray, covered in sharp, stringy hair, their long ears tufted at the pointed tips, their open snouts revealed wickedly sharp teeth. Their eyes were red and too large for their faces. Their shoulders were hunched and huge compared to their hips, and their legs were too long in proportion to their bodies. They had long tails, but instead of fur, the tales were covered in scales and tipped with a sharp pointed claw that dripped something Cary was suspiciously afraid was poison.

So, yeah, nothing to worry about there.

One of the beasts stalked up to her, rising on its back legs in a way that didn't look like it should have been physically possible for the animal, and stuck its snout as close to Cary's face as it could get. It snarled, bearing his teeth, saliva tripping from his black lips. Cary tried not to breathe too deeply. She'd thought vampires had bad breath. They had nothing on these things.

"Uhm," she said, leaning away from the beast snarling at her. "What are Othries?"

"Deadly is what they are," Eriana said.

"Okay, well, that's pretty obvious. Who controls them?"

"I do," a new voice from the woods said. A woman as tall as Deacon but thinner than Angie, so thin it actually looked painful, stepped from the thick fog. "And no magic can stop them. They will get through and rip you to shreds, and I will laugh."

"Well, hello to you too," Cary muttered.

She'd had bad guys say some pretty rotten stuff to her over the years, but that had to rank up there with the most blunt. She kind of liked it. No point in beating around the bush when they were surrounded by snarling, poison dripping beasts with really really sharp teeth. And bad breath.

She leaned to one side so she could see around the still standing and snarling Othrie in her face and get a better look at the woman.

Some would call the woman willowy, but only if willows were really sick and might be dying. The thinness was almost hard to look at. Like she was made of sticks instead of bones and muscle. Her hair was stringy and gray like the creatures she commanded and hung around her like a veil. Her eyes were red and very large in her face. Her features were angular and pointed, her cheeks hollow, her huge eyes sunken. Her skin was as pale as any vampires but with a gray cast. Her legs and arms, even her fingers, looked disproportionately long compared to her short torso. She wore tattered trousers and tunic the color of the fog—which had continued to thicken until the area was dark as twilight.

With growing horror, Cary realized the being in front of her was…

A wraith.

A real, honest to god, wraith.

The things that haunted nightmares and portended death and called eerily from the darkness. Hearing or seeing a wraith was a sign of impending doom.

Wraiths were just a step away from being ghosts.

Cary was terrified of ghosts.

She fisted her hands to hide the sudden tremor that moved through her entire body. A litany of panicked curses rolled through her mind. Shit shit shit shit shit shit shit shit…

As far as she knew, ghosts couldn't get through her shield, but she'd tried to avoid dealing with them since becoming a Protector so wasn't entirely sure. She'd encounter them only a very few times over the years. And they hadn't gotten through her shields then. But she'd never been sure if that was her powers or not.

If anything could get through her shields, though, it would be a ghost. Mostly because that was just Cary's luck. A Fae wraith wasn't technically a ghost. It wasn't the spirit of someone who'd died. It was a being that heralded death, could curse someone with illness and death, and walked with Death like a friend. And it was close enough to a ghost to send Cary's heartbeat into overdrive, her breathing so erratic she was a little afraid she'd pass out.

"I've got you," Deacon said quietly, wrapping an arm around her waist. He was still technically behind her and within her protection, but his arm kept her from dropping to her knees.

For which she was extremely grateful.

"I smell your fear, humon," the wraith said. Her voice was a whispered hiss on the fog. The way she pronounced human made the hairs on Cary's arms stand up for no good reason. "I am the bringer of death."

"Jaxer," Cary said, clearing her throat so she could talk around the panic while keeping her gaze on the wraith. "I'm going to kill you for getting me into this mess. With a wraith. A fucking wraith!"

Jaxer's hand wrapped around hers, a support on her other side. "You're fine. She can't get at you. She's a threat to me, and you can keep me safe."

Cary nodded, working to slow her breathing. "Right. Good. Good. Then I'll kill you."

"Fair enough," he said, not even sounding amused.

The snarling beast in Cary's face dropped to the ground, giving her an even better view of the wraith as she approached. She moved like a marionette with her strings cut, awkwardly loose limbed, like bits might fall off at any moment. The horror of watching her approach made Cary see spots. She'd faced many things in her six and a half years as a Protector, including demon gods and ghouls and a really ticked off wizard out to kill her. But this was, by far and away, her worst nightmare come to life. The panic holding her in place was a living thing that crawled through her system like the poison dripping from the Othries' tails.

The closer the wraith got, the more the panic consumed Cary. She could *smell* her own fear, pumping from her in a stink of sweat and musk to rival the Othries's breath. Some terrified part of her screamed at her to run. The wraith reached toward her with a long-fingered hand, fingers tipped with ragged, dirt incrusted gray nails. Whispering, words Cary couldn't quite hear, but a whispering, hissing through her mind. The terror pumped adrenaline into her blood.

Run!

But running would be the worst thing—she wouldn't be protecting anyone at that stage, which would leave her vulnerable. And if she ran, she wouldn't be the only one to die. Deacon, Jaxer, even Eriana… All their deaths on her conscious because she failed and fled.

Well, on her conscious for the few minutes she had before she died herself.

Cary feared that failure almost as much as she feared ghosts. Maybe more. Because despite the adrenaline-fueled panic, the terror-driven need to escape, she didn't move. She couldn't. She was frozen in place. A deer in the headlights.

Which, as it turned out, was a really useful instinct for a Protector.

She stood her ground, despite her terror, and the wraith came up solidly against her shield. Pushing at it, trying to force her hand through, all she did was contort her fingers and break her already ragged nails.

Cary tried not to look at the wraith's hand too closely. Meeting her red eyes was hard, but not as hard as watching her nails crack and shatter.

"What are you?" the wraith said, her voice sliding out like an echo.

"About to crap my pants in fear," Cary said. "But also not moving. You can't get through me." Thank every magical hair on the Nags' heads! "Jaxer is mine and I will keep him safe. No one dies here today."

The beasts started howling, the noise so loud, Cary winced and barely resisted covering her ears. The wraith sent up an ear-piercing screech, joining her Othries in a chorus that sent a chill straight into Cary's soul. She glared over her shoulder at Jaxer. If not for the noise, she would have asked what the hell he'd done to this being. And *why*?

The noise dropped and the wind picked up, tearing around them in a frenzy of stinging dirt and broken branches, leaves and sharp bramble thorns. Cary squinted against the fury. None of it got through to her, none of it actually touched any of them. But between her ringing ears and her rushing pulse, that didn't matter. The sound of the chaos was enough to set her teeth on edge. Like listening to a storm rattle the windows—pretty sure you're safe inside, but still worried the windows will shatter at any moment and let the whole thing in.

The torrent of wind was joined by rain, then lightning, and the shocking clap of thunder. Inside the noise of the storm another howl rose, a keening, soul-crushing scream. The sound wasn't coming from the wraith. But the wraith smiled at Cary, her gray teeth ragged against black gums.

"The banshee," Eriana shouted over the noise. "Jaxer, what have you done?"

"Nothing to the banshee," he shouted back.

Cary couldn't speak. A banshee was screaming at them. That... wasn't good.

"My sister only calls when someone will die," the wraith said. "There is no escape. You are doomed."

"I've heard that before," Cary said, her voice choked. "In fact, I hear it all the time. I'm always doomed. I'm always a dead woman. Someone is always going to exact their revenge. And yet I just keep going. Maybe, just maybe, all of you bad guys could just stop!"

She shouted the last word loud enough to rival the banshee's scream, screaming herself into the chaos. The word was filled with her terror and her panic and all the build up of emotion overwhelming her.

Her skin felt like it was going to burst from the pressure. Her blood seemed to bubble through her veins, pulsing faster and faster. The weight of everything bore down on her. Too much. She had to break free. She had to make it all stop so she could catch her breath. She let all of that need, that overwhelm, that pressure out. In that single, loud, long shout.

And to her absolute amazement, everything around them stopped.

Just…stopped.

The tossed dirt and leaves and branches froze in mid-air. The banshee's scream cut off abruptly. The wind dropped like a stone. The lightning and thunder ceased. The beasts stopped howling. The mist stopped spinning around their feet. And the wraith froze in mid-laugh. Literally, she looked like a movie paused at the moment she was about to cackle. The beasts also looked frozen in mid-motion, some of them in awkward enough positions, Cary was certain they weren't holding them on purpose.

"Uhm," Cary said.

"Huh," Jaxer said.

"What just happened?" Eriana whispered.

"You okay?" Deacon asked Cary, leaning in close to her, his arm still wrapped tightly around her waist, holding her upright.

She blinked at the scene. "I honestly don't know."

"How does your skin feel?" Jaxer asked.

"Huh? Oh. Uhm. Better actually. The tingles had turned into fire ants crawling on me, stinging me, and the pressure and fear of…" She swallowed and gestured at the wraith. "I, uh…" She blinked a few times. "Did I do this? Cause, this isn't the kind of thing Protector magic does."

"But Faery magic can," Jaxer said.

"Huh?" she said again.

Her brain was having trouble working. Her body wasn't exactly cooperating either. She tried to take her own weight and found she couldn't stand upright on her own. If Deacon hadn't been holding her, she would have dropped hard to the ground. Her eyes grew heavy and a need to sleep overwhelmed her.

"Uh oh," she said. "I'm getting really tired, really fast here."

"Don't pass out yet," Jaxer said. "I need to get you somewhere safe first."

"I'm not sure I'm going to have a lot of say in this." She listed sideways and Deacon lifted her off her feet, cradling her against his chest. "Good thing you're strong," she murmured, her head drooping against his shoulder. She couldn't open her eyes anymore.

"Cary? Cary?"

Was that Jaxer or Deacon? Both? Whoever it was they sounded worried.

She'd have to deal with that when she woke up.

"This way," Jaxer said, opening the darkened cottage's front door. "There's no park ranger using this one at the moment. We should have some privacy."

Deacon carried Cary inside, ducking under the low doorframe. The cottage was so small there wasn't much to it. A single main sitting area with a couch facing a stone fireplace to the left, a small open kitchen to the right, a couple of doors near the rear of the house, and a single, unmade bed at the back of the room tucked into a little nook. The ceiling was low, but he could still stand at his full height. The wooden floor was worn but clean. The place smelled faintly of dust, peat, and human sweat, but all faded. No one had used the cottage in weeks, maybe several months.

There was still a pile of peat bricks and a few fire starter sticks next to the fireplace. "Get a fire going," he told Jaxer. The air was damp and chilly, though not cold. At least, not to him. Cary might feel differently if she were conscious.

He swallowed his worry and carried her to the bed, settling her as comfortably as he could, then removing the purple cloak still wrapped around his shoulders and laying it across her. He tucked the brooch into his jeans pocket before he knelt beside the bed. Brushing her hair from her cheek, he studied her.

Her skin was pale, but the color had started to return to her cheeks. Her breathing was slow and steady. And, to his relief, strong. Her heartbeat was steady as well. She was just knocked out cold. He set his forehead against hers for a moment, pulling in her scent, trying to settle his racing pulse. When both his human and his animal half were convinced his mate was fine, he left her to join the others in front of the fire.

"Well," Jaxer said, his gaze on the dancing flames. "That was a thing."

The scent of burning peat reminded Deacon of his grandmother's house in Scotland, a comfort he needed at the moment. "She absorbed too much magic, didn't she?" he asked quietly.

"What happened?" Eriana said. She stared at Jaxer, her jaw tight.

"Cary has been absorbing magic since she went into Faery," Jaxer said, not turning to look at anyone. "We thought she could get away with it while she was protecting us, Deacon..." He snorted. "Me. Because her Protector shields keep her from pulling in too much."

"But there were periods of time where she was inside Faery when none of us were in danger," Deacon said.

"I don't understand." Eriana faced him now.

Deacon waved away her question. He didn't know this Fae and he certainly didn't trust her. He wasn't going to go into more detail about how Cary's magic worked. It left her vulnerable if too many knew how to get around the Protector magic.

Jaxer apparently felt the same way, because he avoided mention of Cary's shields and instead said, "She absorbs magic. Faery is magic. The attack was filled with magic. Tatiana tested her with magic... She's been taking in more than a human body should be able to tolerate."

"And she had to release it or die," Deacon said, very quietly to keep from bellowing out his rage. That his mate had been so close to the breaking point was intolerable. He could barely keep his temper in check, and only did so because he didn't want to wake Cary until she'd had more time to rest.

Jaxer finally looked away from the fire to glance at him, his eyes narrowed and leery. "You still in control?" he asked.

"Mostly," Deacon said. "It's not the residual effects of Faery doing this to me, though, if that's what you're worried about."

"Your eyes are glowing."

"My leopard is very very angry right now."

"She'll be okay."

"I know. Which is why I'm still sitting here."

"And technically, the release of magic was good."

"Unless it knocks her out for days. Then we have to face the potential end of Faery and a Fae invasion without our best shield."

While he didn't always like it, and her job gave him literal nightmares—nightmares he'd kept from her because he didn't want to burden her with them—she was a superb Protector. She was probably the bravest person he knew. She'd held off things he'd thought for sure they wouldn't survive. And he didn't think they'd do nearly as well holding off a Fae invasion without her. In fact, he was certain that without her, they'd fail. He hated it, because he didn't want his mate, the woman he loved fiercely, in danger. But they couldn't fight this fight without her. Even without the predictions in Grenelle's vision, Deacon felt that truth in his soul. Every instinct he had, even his overly protective and stubborn leopard knew, they needed Cary.

And it was his job to keep her safe, so she could save the world.

His mother would approve.

"I can help ease her out of her healing sleep," Eriana said, her voice quiet.

"Without it hurting her?" Deacon asked.

"It won't hurt her." She didn't look at Deacon as she said, "I've a few healing skills I can bring to the task." Quieter, she said, "I've been keeping Ulieran sane for centuries. I can manage one human."

Jaxer's head snapped up. "What?"

The faery's shoulders seemed to hunch further in on themselves and she didn't turn toward either of them. "He's not been the same since word of Grenelle's death reached him. You know that."

"You've been healing his mind?" Jaxer asked.

Deacon couldn't read the emotion in his words, Jaxer had kept his tone too neutral for that, but his scent was full of emotion. Pain, anger, regret, grief. Rage and guilt. Gratitude and horror. All of it a miasma of textures and tones. Deacon didn't have the human words to explain what he smelled and how his body interpreted it. But the musky punch, the heat of burning ozone, and the sweet undertone of rotting detritus seemed close to describing the complex mixture of Jaxer's scent, the even more complex mix of his emotions.

"We hoped…" Eriana lifted her chin but still wouldn't meet Jaxer's gaze. "Oberon and I decided it would be best for all if Ulieran were sane enough to continue his duty."

"He could have lifted the curse," Jaxer said. "He could have convinced Tatiana to release my father."

Eriana didn't say anything to that, only pressed her lips together.

Her scent was another complex journey for Deacon's senses. But he didn't know her well enough to read the meaning underlying some of her emotions. There was, like Jaxer, a lot there, though. One thing did keep jumping out from the complexity, though. From both of them.

Jealousy. Hurt.

Love?

If that's what he was picking up, it was a bitter sort of love, one they seemed to feel reluctantly and resented. Or maybe he was misinterpreting whatever that chemical signal was, because the way they dealt with each other did not speak to softer emotions.

And Jaxer's feelings for Cary hadn't abated as far as Deacon could tell. Which was one more complication they didn't need at this moment.

"If it won't hurt Cary," he said, to bring the conversation back to the present, and his injured mate, "we should heal her. We'll need her to stop the invasion."

"And to hold back the Lachlinain if Ulieran decides to release it," Eriana said.

"I think you and my father both have kept things from me," Jaxer said. "You need to tell me everything. Now."

"After Cary," Deacon said. "No point in repeating all this. She'll need to know for what's ahead."

Jaxer glared at Deacon, but only a moment before his shoulders relaxed and he nodded. "Thank you," he said.

Deacon frowned. "For what?"

"For keeping me grounded," Jaxer said ruefully. "For…being here."

Deacon nodded, understanding. They'd been friends once. They weren't now. And Deacon had come on this journey for his mate. Still. He wouldn't abandon Jaxer to all this. He had his back. That was, at least, some kind of progress toward a peace between them.

"Heal her," Deacon said. "Gently or I won't be able to keep my leopard from objecting." He let Eriana see how close his animal side was to the surface, holding her gaze before she quickly looked away. "Then we'll talk."

And make a plan to save two worlds.

2 8

---

*C*ary groaned and rolled to her side. She could definitely sleep for another few hours. Or days. Mmm…days. That sounded good. Right.

Why the hell was she awake again?

Wait…

She sat up suddenly, everything that had happened rushing back. Deacon's arms came around her, pulling her against his solid, sturdy chest.

"I've got you. You're okay. How do you feel?"

"Groggy." She took stock of her senses, her body, looking for telltale aches and pains. No more tingling skin, she realized. "Otherwise fine."

She blinked in the flickering light. She was sitting on a cot in the middle of a small, but cozy room. Eriana stood nearby, staring at the ground. Jaxer sat on the floor near the head of the bed. Deacon sat beside her on the mattress. There was no banshee screech or wraith wail filling the air. Just the crackling of a wonderful smelling fire in a stone fireplace in an otherwise very quiet room.

"What happened and where the hell are we?" she asked, leaning into Deacon.

197

"Dublin," he said. "Phoenix Park. An unused park ranger's cottage. We're safe."

She heard the unspoken "for now" at the end of that sentence. "Who's going to explain?"

Jaxer did. "You released a lot of magic, stopped the banshee and wraith in their tracks, and we got you out of Faery before you could absorb any more." He didn't move from his spot on the floor. "Danu's sanctuary extends to the human realm here in Ireland, so we're safe enough from Tatiana's guards for the moment."

And there was the spoken "for now."

Cary let out a breath through pursed lips. It lifted the tendrils of hair on her forehead that had escaped her ponytail. She swiped a hand across her head in an attempt to smooth her hair back a little. She probably looked the worse for wear, and in front of Eriana that was annoying. Especially since Eriana hadn't gone back to her very ordinary human guise and was still sporting her frighteningly beautiful faery exquisiteness. Jaxer seemed to have settled at even-more-extraordinarily-stunning-than-usual too. Closer to his real appearance, she thought. And was grateful he toned it down most of the time. He was hard to look at this way.

So instead, she focused on Deacon. Who was just as stunning, but she was a lot more comfortable basking in his gorgeousness. "Why am I awake? Shouldn't I still be unconscious?"

"Eriana healed you. As much as she could. You'll probably still be a little wobbly for a few hours. A little food will help."

Her stomach growled, with its usual perfect timing, which made Deacon smile. She made a face. "Do we have any food?"

"There's some tea and a tin of biscuits in the cupboard," Deacon said as he rose. "Cookies," he corrected. "The tin is sealed so they should still be okay. We'll have to leave the park and head into the city for food once the sun comes up."

"Cool." Cookies and tea would have to do until then. If she didn't feel like she'd been recently run over by a truck, she'd be looking forward to seeing Dublin. "Shame I keep seeing all these cool cities for such a short period of time in such rotten circumstances," she said, mostly to herself.

"We can come back on an actual vacation if you want," Deacon said from the small, open kitchen at one side of the cottage.

Although, the single countertop, three cabinets, mini-fridge, and really nice wood-burning stove didn't seem to qualify as a real kitchen, she supposed it fit the space. The electric kettle worked at least, and in the firelight, everything seemed cozy and clean. She gave a passing thought to the park ranger who would eventually call this place home before returning to Deacon's comment.

"I'd love a vacation here. If I can get out of work." She sighed ruefully. For at least another five months, that wasn't an option. The farthest the Nags had allowed her during her Seventh Year trial was Eugene, and they'd argued with her over that.

"Next year, then," Deacon said, his back to her as he dropped tea bags into four mugs.

There was a tone in his voice that worried her a little. But she didn't feel comfortable bringing it up in front of Jaxer and especially Eriana, so she turned the conversation back to their current predicament.

"We're safe in Dublin long enough for Deacon and I to eat and for me to recover," she said, "but then we need to get to Ulieran. And the only way to do that is to ask Oberon. Do I remember that right?"

Jaxer frowned but nodded. He did not look at Eriana.

"And according to Danu," Cary continued, "we're going to have push back from the Fae who want to destroy Faery and take over the human world?"

Another nod.

"Do we know who all these Fae are?" Cary looked at Eriana when she asked.

"I know a few of the conspirators," she said. "But the conspiracy is larger than that. I've never known all of them."

"Is Tatiana involved directly or indirectly?"

Eriana gasped. "Of course the queen isn't involved."

"Her guards came after you. She's as aware of the rot in her world as Danu is. How did you discover she hadn't handed over Grenelle's message to Ulieran? Are you sure you haven't been manipulated into setting all this into motion?"

Eriana looked at her, blinked twice, then looked away frowning. "But…"

"But Oberon has been helping you," Jaxer said. "And you have never believed he would lie to you."

"He didn't," she snapped, glaring at him for a moment before looking away. "You did."

"To prove a point."

"By violating my trust?"

"By proving you couldn't be trusted," Jaxer hissed.

She snarled at him again, slicing the air with a dismissive hand as she returned to the fire.

"Okay," Cary said into the tense silence that followed. "There's a lot going on between you two and maybe that needs to be settled before we finish this. Out loud so I know what the hell I'm getting into when we go back to Faery. Eriana, how did you betray Danu and end up in the English court? What's the problem with Oberon? And what the hell is going on with Ulieran? The truth, Eriana, not some half-baked-I-can't-tell-you-buts. I'm getting really tired of being confused. And given that we have to stop an invasion and a war, and there's four of us against who knows how many Fae, and I have no idea if the queen and king of the English court are for or against this invasion yet, I need answers and the truth."

"Our issue has nothing to do with this," Jaxer said.

"I beg to differ," Cary said. "You two snarling at each other and Oberon somewhere in the mix is gonna be a thing very soon. Especially since we have to go to him to get to Ulieran. Spill. Or I'm going back to Portland and letting you try to hold back a Fae hoard on your own. I miss my dogs."

And she was grumpy from…well not understanding any damned thing going on. Her body was still sore from whatever she'd done to stop the wraith, she was still shaken from facing the closest thing to a ghost you could get without actually facing a ghost, the banshee's cry still haunted her because she was worried it meant someone close to her would die soon, and she was hungry. Really really hungry. If someone didn't clear up at least some of her confusion soon, she was going to scream.

Deacon brought her a steaming mug and sat down next to her on the small bed, resting a circular tin of shortbread cookies on the mattress between them. She gobbled three cookies down before sipping her unsweetened tea. The cookies were glorious, and the tea quenched her thirst even though she normally hated unsweetened tea. Who knew? Her muscles started to relax, but she didn't let up on glaring at Jaxer and Eriana. Waiting them out as she gobbled another two cookies. They were small. And she was hungry.

Deacon had left Eriana and Jaxer's tea on the small countertop. Jaxer rose to get his, hesitated over the second mug, then brought it to Eriana. She took it with a reluctant nod of thanks.

So, they could be polite to each other if required. At least there was that. But still the silence stretched.

Cary woofed down two more cookies before she started to get annoyed again. "No one is talking. I am waiting. And we can't go anywhere until the sun comes up." She looked at Deacon. "What the hell time is it anyway? And day? What day is it?"

"It's three thirty in the morning. The sun will be coming up in another hour or so, but nothing will be open in the city until at least six thirty. It's Friday, at least, so some places will open for breakfast."

Friday. The hour or so they'd been in Faery talking with Danu and facing the wraith had taken another day and a half in the human world. Missing out on all that time didn't sit well with Cary. Some primitive part of her brain balked at losing so much time. She reached into her jeans pocket to pull out her cellphone and realized it was still charged. It must be doing time hops in Faery too, because her battery did not last a week under normal circumstances.

"I need to call Angie," she said. "What time is it in Portland?"

"Around seven thirty Thursday night," Deacon said.

"She'll be up." Cary glared at Eriana and Jaxer. "You have a two-minute reprieve. Then I want the story. All of it."

29

Cary made her call to Angie quick. Angie was fine. The dogs were fine. Everyone missed her. The Nags hadn't shown up to ask where she was. And her mother had stopped calling the house looking for her. So Portland, at least, was managing without her. For the moment. She promised Angie a full explanation of her current adventure after she got home, then hung up feeling just a little homesick.

She looked up from her phone to face the rest of their little band again. Flickering firelight cast a warm glow on everyone. Which only highlighted the ethereal beauty of the two Fae.

She snarfed down the cookie Deacon handed her and nodded at Jaxer. "Okay, your reprieve is up. Spill. Everything you haven't told me." She glared at Eriana. "You too. In fact, you start. Since you seem to be key to Ulieran's part in all this."

Eriana lifted her top lip in a snarl that, unfortunately, did nothing to detract from her gorgeousness. That really wasn't fair.

"I have been *helping*," she snapped at Cary. "This entire time, *I* have been trying to avert disaster. I went to the English court *for* Grenelle. My mentor asked a great favor of me and I went." She pressed her lips together and faced the fire, cradling her mug without drinking the tea.

"My mother asked you to switch courts?" Jaxer said. "You never told me."

"There's a lot I never told you," she murmured.

"Yes," he said, his voice dull. "That I'm aware of."

"No arguing yet, kids," Cary said. "Finish the story first."

"When Grenelle knew her life was nearing its end, she asked me to go to the English court and beg permission to see Ulieran. The message I was to deliver was only one part of my purpose there. As I was angry with Danu for what she'd done to Grenelle, and angry at the Irish court for pushing Danu to destroy Grenelle, I was happy to abandon them. I…made my feelings known when I left."

"That's why you feel like you betrayed Danu?" Cary asked.

"I chose her rival over her. Even though what Tatiana had done to Ulieran was…worse than what Danu had done to Grenelle. At the time, I didn't consider it so because Ulieran was still alive and would remain alive." She shook her head and set her mug aside. "I ingratiated myself into the English court so that I could have permission to see Ulieran regularly. Oberon talked Tatiana into allowing the visits." She glared at Jaxer. "He's always been my ally in court."

Jaxer looked away, not commenting.

"Why did Grenelle send you to watch out for Ulieran?" Cary asked. "Just because she trusted you? Why not charge Jaxer with the task since Ulieran is his father?"

"I wasn't allowed to see my father very often," Jaxer said. "I did apply for the privilege, but was denied more often than allowed. Mostly as punishment for the… Well, I wasn't exactly a predictable member of the court."

Eriana snorted at that. "If Tatiana weren't so charmed by your story-telling ability, she would have cast you out centuries ago. Everyone loved you, despite your mischief. And that was half the problem."

Well. That was an interesting reveal. "You managed to both charm and piss off the queen?" Cary said. "That sounds just like you."

He snorted, a reluctant chuckle, and shrugged. "What can I say?"

"Having nothing to say was never the issue," Eriana said dryly.

"Finish your part, then we'll get to Jaxer," Cary said.

"I'm a healer," Eriana said. "Grenelle helped train me. She knew I could help her husband. And that my skill would be welcome in the English court. She was right. They didn't have a healer of their own anymore. The last... He walked into the human world and disappeared."

"That's the equivalent of a Fae committing suicide," Jaxer murmured. "It's easier to find ways to die here than it is in our own realm. Especially if you bring value to your court. No one will want to kill you."

Cary raised her brows. "Is that why you originally left Faery behind for the human world?" That idea had never occurred to her. Jaxer didn't seem like the suicide type. But...given what she was learning about his history, she was no longer sure she understood him as well as she'd thought.

"No," he said. "I left to piss everyone in Faery off."

"Ah. Well, that does sound more like something you'd do."

His mouth quirked in a little smile. "I wanted to help humans and went to the North American Fae when I heard they were going to make Protectors, despite the objections of the rest of Faery. I specifically went to America to become a part of their efforts."

"With the side benefit of it pissing everyone else off, of course," Cary said.

"Of course. That was the icing on the cake as they say."

Cary chuckled, then chomped up another cookie. She'd lost count of how many she'd eaten, but the tin wasn't as full as it had been a few minutes ago.

"Okay, let me just make sure I've got the story in the right order," Cary said. "Grenelle is dying. Ulieran is cursed to guard the Lachlinain. Grenelle sends her healer protégée to the English court to keep an eye on her husband, who she knows is likely suffering under his curse."

"And who will suffer further when he feels his love die," Eriana said. "That's what worried her most. That once she passed, Ulieran would lose his hold on his sanity." She dropped her gaze to the wooden floor. "She was right about that. His grasp on sanity has been…tenuous at best since her passing. Only knowing Jaxer was still alive and causing chaos kept Ulieran from giving in to his demons. And many of his enemies, or those wishing to cause mischief, knew Jaxer was his…" She paused and narrowed her eyes. "Achille's heal? Is that the saying?"

Jaxer nodded, but didn't comment.

"Yes, Jaxer was always Ulieran's soft spot," Eriana continued. "I helped him hold on to his mind as best I could. Healing where I could. But…the mind is more difficult than the body to heal. And there was only so much I could do. Only so much Tatiana allowed me to do. He was made guardian as a punishment, and she wanted him to suffer under his curse."

Cary watched Jaxer as Eriana told this part of the story. He hunched a little further around his mug, his expression closing off so that Cary could no longer read his emotions.

"You didn't know a lot of this?" she asked him.

"That he was having difficulty holding on to his sanity? I was aware it was a possibility. I didn't realize how dire the situation was, because he hid his desperation from me. And I had no idea Eriana visited often and kept him sane. No one saw fit to tell me."

His last sentence was spat with a venom Cary had rarely heard from her mentor.

"Okay," she said. "So Eriana has been keeping Uleran sane, or helping anyway. But you didn't know Tatiana had hidden Grenelle's last message from him until recently? How did you miss that?"

"Oberon was with us almost every time I had a session with Ulerian," Eriana said. "And when it wasn't Oberon, Grim took me. Ulieran and I weren't free to talk about Grenelle in front of them, and so we didn't. Only recently was I given more than a few moments alone with him, when Oberon had to leave me with him for a longer period of time than usual. Ulerian was…in a very bad place and the healing took much longer than usual. Everyone was worried about him—punishment is one thing; actually loosing the Lachlinain another—so I was given privacy to work on healing more of his pain. And that's when we discovered he'd never received Grenelle's last message. The anger was, ironically, good for him. It gave him a reason to continue and not give in to the despair."

"Until he read Grenelle's note," Cary guessed. "And found out about Jaxer's part in her prediction of the end times."

Eriana nodded. "I wasn't privy to what was in the message. I didn't know about her vision for our demise. She didn't share her worries with me. I only knew the message had been her last words for her husband and son and that it was a crime Ulieran had been denied that message so long. I... I had to defy the queen to get him the message. And I had to deliver it without Oberon knowing. Which is how I ended up in the middle of the conspirators unwittingly."

"Meaning?" Cary asked carefully.

"Grim—he's one of the leaders of the conspiracy. He can travel to Ulieran without Tatiana sending him. He's been... He's been whispering to Ulieran. Feeding his mind with fears. I didn't know that when I went to him. I didn't know he was working to convince Ulieran to unleash the Lachlinain. I had thought him extremely loyal to Tatiana. And I didn't realize Grenelle's note would push Ulieran closer to the choice to destroy Faery. I thought it would bring him peace." She finally looked up and met Jaxer's gaze. "I was *trying* to help. To honor your mother's last request of me. I have always been on her side and your fathers."

"But not mine," Jaxer said.

"Yours as well. Until you broke that trust."

He looked away this time, not meeting her gaze. And Eriana turned back to the fire.

Cary so wanted to dig into that, but they needed to focus on the problem at hand. "So Tatiana's guards have been conspiring to end Faery and invade the human world? All of them or just some?"

"Just a few," Eriana said. "Enough though. And they have allies among the high Fae."

"Are the queen and king on board with this plan or have they been deceived as well?" Cary doubted there was anything that went on in the court that Tatiana wasn't aware of. But maybe she was wrong about that.

"Tatiana cannot be involved," Eriana said emphatically. "Destroying Faery will destroy her and Oberon. They can't escape into the human world and survive. Neither can Danu. They're all too tied to their realms and the magic there. Some of their people could make the transition but others would perish."

"Did Ulieran…" Cary looked at Jaxer a long moment before finishing her question. "Did Ulieran delay his plan in order to see Jaxer one last time? Will he still release the Lachlinain to save Jaxer from making whatever decision it is he has to make?"

Eriana's gaze flickered to Jaxer, too. "That's what I fear. I went to Ulieran, with Oberon, after Jaxer's visit. Before I came to find you in London. He is more at peace than I have ever seen him. He seems…happy."

Cary sat up straighter on the cot. "Oh shit."

30

"He's going to do it," Deacon said, echoing Cary's fears.

With people intent on suicide, there tended to be that moment, right before they went through with it but after they'd made the decision, where they felt peaceful and at ease. The last moments of life filled with acceptance that it would all be over soon.

Eriana nodded.

Desperation and adrenaline surged into Cary's blood. She started to stand. "We need to get back now. We can't wait."

Eriana raised a quieting hand. "We have a little time. I promised him that Jaxer would return. That Jaxer wanted to come back and see him again and that he needed to hold on for that visit." She winced when she glanced at Jaxer this time. "I'm afraid I used his feelings for you to stall. But I knew you'd come."

"You were right," Jaxer said. "You did the right thing."

Cary settled back onto the bed, but her body still vibrated with renewed worries. "He'll wait as long as it will take?" she asked. Because getting there around Tatiana's guards, even getting to Oberon to ask for passage, that was going to take some doing.

"He will." She pressed her lips together before saying, "He knows we'll need Oberon to bring us there, and he knows the…complications between the three of us."

Cary narrowed her eyes as she ate another shortbread cookie. "I think maybe we need to understand this complication better now, too. And not just because my curiosity is killing me."

Jaxer gave her a look she chose to ignore. She raised her brows at both he and Eriana, waiting.

They both looked away, equally mutinous expressions on their faces. It might have been comical if the situation weren't so dire.

"Look," she said into the silence, "I get there's something more personal going on here and I wouldn't normally pry… Well, okay, I *would*, but I'd also understand if you didn't want to talk about it. But this thing between you two and Oberon, it's the thing that could get Jaxer killed in Faery, and the thing that complicates us getting Oberon's help. And we need Oberon's help if we're going to stop Ulieran from destroy Faery while the Fae invade my realm. I'm very very motivated to stop Faery from invading my realm. Which means I need to know why Oberon wants to kill Jaxer and why he's a sensitive topic between you two. Silence will not save the world here. And I mean to save the world."

Again.

Jaxer stared at her for a long moment, emotions moving through his expression she couldn't read. Finally, he smiled. A soft, approving smile. Cary frowned. And his smile turned into a grin.

"I'm proud of you," he said. "You are, by far, one of the very best Protector's I've ever trained. And if anyone can save the world, it will be you."

"Ah, Jaxer. That's really sweet. It's not going to distract me. But it's really nice of you to say."

His chuckle was resigned. His smile fell away as he said, "This story…none of us come out of it looking good, and that's why neither of us wants to go into it. It's done, over a long time ago."

"But the pain lingers," Eriana said.

"The pain lingers," Jaxer agreed.

"That doesn't satisfy my curiosity even a little bit. Spill. Before I finish this tin of cookies—" She glanced down. Only three left. Oops. She'd eaten a lot. "Before I finish what little food is in this place and start getting hungry again. I'll be a lot less patient the hungrier I get."

Jaxer sighed, but he didn't look at Eriana when he said, "I was jealous. For good reason. And did something I shouldn't have. But it proved my point, and confirmed my fears."

"It was a betrayal," Eriana said, her tone icy.

"Maybe. But only to prove I was being betrayed."

"This isn't clarifying things, kids," Cary said.

Her condescension drew a scowl from Eriana. Jaxer ignored it.

"He came to me in the guise of Oberon," Eriana said. "He pretended to be the king, his glamour so thorough, I had no idea he wasn't Oberon."

"And you went into his arms like you belonged there," Jaxer said.

Ah! Cary finally caught on. "You two were…involved, but Jaxer thought you were cheating on him with Oberon and to prove it he used his glamour to trick you."

Wow. No wonder they were both pissed. And angry and hurt and bitter. Jaxer was right. None of them came out of that looking good. It was on the tip of her tongue to ask Jaxer how he could be such an ass, violating Eriana's trust that way. But then, Eriana had obviously been cheating on him with the king. So…

Yeah, neither of them looked good. Both betrayed.

"I assume Oberon wasn't pleased," Deacon said.

Jaxer snorted. "Impersonating the king is frowned upon."

An understatement, Cary was sure. "Another reason why you had to abandon the English court?" she asked. "Not just to come to American because it suited you. You *had* to leave."

"I could have taken refuge in the Irish court," he said.

"Except you'd pissed off at least one wraith intent on killing you there," Cary pointed out. She shivered at the memory of the wraith, and Deacon wrapped an arm around her shoulders. She moved the cookie tin so she could lean into him. She didn't care if the gesture made her look weak. She hated ghosts. She was still buzzing with the fear of having faced an actual wraith.

Jaxer shrugged. "I'd burned a few bridges," he admitted.

"So you ran away," Eriana said. "You didn't stay to deal with the situation."

"That you'd betrayed me with Oberon? That situation?" He snarled the last word. "What was there to say? The damage was done. To both of us."

Eriana pressed her lips together and looked at the fire.

Okay. So. She'd gotten her answers and they were doozies. And this wasn't a hurt that was going to heal overnight. Especially since it had apparently been festering for the better part of two centuries. But they did have to deal with Oberon and that meant having to set all this trauma and heartbreak aside for a short time.

"Is there anyone besides Oberon we can go to?" she asked, just to be sure. The idea of putting that triad together didn't thrill her. She had her hands full already with the whole end of the world and Fae invasion thing.

"Tatiana," Jaxer said, his voice dull, "whom we can't trust. Oberon, whom we can't trust but who might still help us for Eriana's sake. The guards who are working to destroy Faery." He paused. Then shook his head. "There are, maybe two more Fae—both courtiers—capable of going directly to Ulieran without aid, but neither are trustworthy enough to take us."

"One, Fomen, is part of the conspiracy," Eriana said. "So he wouldn't be much help."

"Fomen is trying to bring down the court?" Jaxer sounded surprised. "Of the two, I would have assumed it was Bethanir."

"She's too vain," Eriana said. "Attached to the glitter of Faery. She'd never sacrifice all that magic just to conquer a few humans she considers beneath her anyway."

"Still. Fomen. I wouldn't have expected it."

"Grim has promised him he'll rule. He's stupid enough to believe that lie."

"Will this Bethanir take us to Ulieran?" Cary asked. "If she thinks it'll save Faery?"

"She won't deign to help you," Eriana said. "She won't even

acknowledge you. She is the highest of the highborn Fae. A child of Tatiana and Oberon's child."

Ah. Cary was kind of impressed by that pedigree, but she didn't want to admit it out loud. "So, you're both sure we're stuck with Oberon? No other options you can think of? There has to be others or ferreting out the conspirators wouldn't have been difficult."

"There are lower Fae allowed there," Eriana said. "To clean and bring food and tend the gardens around the cursed hall."

Cary assumed the "cursed hall" was where Ulieran lived and the Lachlinain resided. It was the first time anyone had given that strange place a name.

"Any of the lower Fae that could sneak us in?" she asked.

"They don't have the power to," Eriana said without hesitance.

Cary sighed. "We're going to have to go to Oberon, aren't we?" she asked, not really expecting anyone to say otherwise.

No one did.

Through the windows, the rising sun had started to lighten the surroundings, casting a pale pink-orange glow on the inside of the small house. She looked at her cellphone. Still too early for anything to be open. And, to her supreme sadness, all the cookies were gone.

"Okay, so I need to eat and sleep a little more—so long as you're sure we've got time before Ulieran does anything irreversible?" She waited for Eriana to look at her, to meet her eyes when she confirmed they had time. "Good. Then I'm going to sleep another couple of hours because channeling as much magic as I did is exhausting. Then we're going to eat. *Then* we'll go back to the English court and save the world. Deal?"

Jaxer quirked his mouth in a semblance of a smile and nodded.

"Do you need sleep?" she asked him. "You look tired, too." When he winced, she apologized. "I know it tweaks your vanity. But you do. You should sleep." She looked at Deacon. "You too. We have time. And this little bed is big enough to hold us both if we sleep sideways." To Jaxer. "You're gonna have to take the couch or a chair. I'm too tired to be noble and give anyone else the bed."

His smile grew. "I'll be fine."

She set aside her tea mug—she'd actually finished the whole thing, even without sugar in it; that was a testament to her thirst—and the now empty cookie tin and stretched out on the bed, letting Deacon spoon up behind her, his back to the wall. He wrapped her in his arms, the position surprisingly cozy and secure despite the narrow mattress, and she let herself relax into his heat. Her eyes were heavy and she was desperate for a little more rest. Even the worry couldn't keep her awake.

But it did follow her as she drifted off, nagging at the edges of her dreamless sleep.

31

When Cary woke, the cabin was well lit by sunlight, the fire in the grate had died, and Deacon's arms were still securely around her. That was nice. She'd have loved to have stayed just like that for another few hours.

But hunger and duty called.

She rolled onto her back so she could see Deacon. His eyes were open. "Did you sleep at all?"

"I did. I woke when you did."

She narrowed her eyes, studying him. It'd be just like him to stay up keeping guard, but she didn't see any exhaustion dragging at him, so she had to assume he'd at least rested. She glanced at the others. Jaxer had stretched out in a chair in front of the now cold fireplace. Eriana was curled up on the couch. Neither had moved at the sound of voices.

"I need to eat soon," she murmured to Deacon. "Cookies and tea don't seem to be enough. Mores the pity."

He smiled. "It's after nine in the morning. Something will be open now."

"Oh good. Do they have scones here? I love scones."

"Yes, but not the kind you're used to. Smaller and not as sweet. But still really good."

"Have you been to Dublin before?"

"Once when I was younger. I was visiting my father's family in Wales and Scotland, and we came over to Ireland for a visit. As I remember, they have some excellent coffee here."

Her eyebrows shot up. "Coffee..." She nearly moaned. She really needed some coffee.

He patted her hip. "Up we go. The bathroom is that door on the left." He nodded to one of the few doors off the main room. "I'll wake our estranged lovers and we'll get going."

"Their story was really sad," she whispered, glancing back at the two sleeping faeries.

"Not all romances end well," Deacon said, his voice even lower than hers.

She wondered what romances he was thinking of. He'd had an ex-girlfriend to rival the worst of the worst in exes. But he hadn't been in love with Sasha, which was, as it turned out, the heart of the problem. She couldn't help but wonder if he was thinking of that, and how Sasha had tried to kill her, or if he was just thinking about Jaxer's piss poor history with Eriana.

She'd have to ask him later, when they had more privacy. And time.

If the world wasn't in the middle of a Fae war of course.

After morning ablutions and Cary finger combed her hair into some semblance of order—no one else seemed to need to do anything to still look well groomed, which pissed her off—they made their way into the center of Dublin, by foot until they reached the Luas, then the light rail to City Center, and on to a large café restaurant in the heart of town. The two-story building, in all its rich woods and brass accents delighted Cary as much as the spread of food.

"Scones!" With jam and butter. And coffee that was like drinking heaven.

She didn't bother to speak much until she'd worked her way through two cups of coffee, two scones, and a plate of eggs and Irish rashers, which was just bacon but thicker and not smoked. And also yummy. Deacon had an Irish breakfast and a large glass of milk. Cary tried not to gag at the fried tomato and blood sausages on his plate. Turned out the "black and white pudding"—blood sausage and sausage without the blood added—were pretty good. She wouldn't eat a whole plate of them, but they tasted nice with her eggs. She wasn't crazy about the baked beans, though.

Jaxer picked at an Irish breakfast, mostly just pretending to eat as far as Cary could tell. Eriana didn't even pretend. She drank a pot of tea and didn't bother with food.

Well, they could face the impending end of the world on empty stomachs if they wanted, but if she was going to risk death, she intended to do it on a full stomach.

She contemplated the French press holding the last of the coffee, figuring no one else was drinking it and it would be a crime to waste it. Besides, she was low on sleep. And three cups were her normal morning amount. And really, she needed more coffee.

She was mid-pour when a well-dressed, four-foot-tall man walked up to their table and tipped an invisible hat at them. "Well, and good morning to you, strangers. Long time no see."

"Tom!" Cary greeted with enthusiasm.

The leprechaun was an old associate of Jaxer's. She couldn't call them friends, because they hated each other. But they had worked together in the past. And Cary adored Tom and the way he got under Jaxer's skin.

Except the last time she'd seen him…

"Hey, you were working for the bad guy last October," she said, narrowing her eyes at him. "What side are you on this time?"

"The side that would hate to see yer world invaded while Faery was destroyed," he said easily. "Will I have a seat so we can talk?"

"Hmm." She glanced at Jaxer, who was glaring at the leprechaun, before gesturing for Tom to join them.

Tom grinned crookedly, snatched a seat from another table, and settled himself at theirs, helping himself to a cup of tea from the pot on the table. Where he'd gotten the cup from, Cary hadn't seen. Sneaky leprechaun.

"How do you know what's happening?" she asked Tom without preamble.

The tables around them were crowded with summer tourists and crammed close enough together she was going to bump someone when she pushed back from the table to leave. That didn't give them a lot of privacy for talking, but the din of background noise from all those chatting tourists also seemed to make eavesdropping even on the table right at her back difficult. She figured if they spoke quietly enough, they wouldn't have to worry about the mundane humans surrounding them overhearing anything.

"Didn't Danu herself send me," Tom said. "She wanted you to have backup. As you might guess, she'd not be pleased with the destruction of Faery, despite its troubles. And she knew getting back to see Ulieran without the aid of Tatiana or Oberon would be complicated."

Cary snorted at the understatement. "We were going to go to Oberon." She tried not to flick a glance at Jaxer or Eriana, because she didn't know how much Tom knew about them or their past.

Apparently more than Cary had, though, because he did look at the two faeries and said, "Oberon, huh? You sure that's a bright idea?"

"No," Cary said with feeling. "But he seems to be our only option."

"Well, now, and don't I have a brilliant solution for you then."

"Am I going to like this solution or hate it?" Cary asked.

Tom barked out a laugh. "You'll adore it, love. Me and the lads are going to get you in. Infiltrate the lair of the enemy so to speak."

"Huh?"

His grin widened. "We leprechauns have a way of getting into places, don't you know? Even places we're technically not allowed to go." He waggled his eyebrows at her and sipped at his tea.

"You can sneak into the…" She groped for the word Eriana had used to describe the place. "The cursed hall. In the English realm. Without drawing Tatiana's wrath?"

"Or even her notice," he said. "One of the benefits of being beneath the notice of the English court is yer *beneath* the notice of the English court."

"Okay. I think. But this sounds like a better plan than Oberon." She looked at Jaxer. "Right?"

"Last time he showed up, he was working for a demon," Jaxer said, still glaring. "I wouldn't trust him to clean the toilets in this place."

"Well, and you shouldn't at that. Not the toilets anyway. I'd dodge out of that duty and fast. Too many tourists in here."

Jaxer lifted his lip in a snarl.

"But you can trust me to get you in to your father," Tom said, his expression suddenly serious. "I give ye my word, Jaxer. I'll get you there safely."

Jaxer's glare fell away at that. He sat a little straighter in his chair. "Danu really sent you, then?"

"Sure I wouldn't tempt fate going to the cursed hall without a nudge from my goddess." He sounded wry enough, Cary believed he was being completely honest.

Jaxer must have believed his sincerity, too. "Fair enough. If you can get us in, I'll take the help. I'd prefer the Irish contingent in this anyway."

That brought back Tom's grin. "And why wouldn't you." He set aside his tea cup. "Now. I'll meet you all back at the park. We have some preparations to make. Don't be too long with paying the bill. We have a realm to save."

He tipped his invisible cap at them and headed away, straightening his suit jacket sleeves as he walked toward the restaurant's curved stair case, and smoothing his long hair back in its low tail, an unnecessary gesture as he didn't have a hair out of place. He attracted the admiring glance of more than one woman as he went.

One little girl tugged at her mother's sleeve and said much too loudly in a very American accent, "Mommy, that's a leprechaun!" Her mom tried to hush her, obviously embarrassed. Tom turned at the top of the stairs and winked at the little girl, a twinkle in his green eyes. This started the little girl giggling into her hand.

Cary shook her head. He was too charming for this realm. But she was glad she could put him back into the good guy category. At least this time. She'd hated seeing him working for the bad guys. Even if Jaxer had relished it.

She glanced back at Jaxer. Given that Tom seemed to know what had happened between him and Eriana and Oberon, it was no wonder he didn't like the leprechaun much. Tom, being Tom, likely threw that disaster back in Jaxer's face whenever the opportunity arose.

"You going to be okay working with Tom?" she asked him.

"He's still not my favorite person and I still don't trust him," Jaxer said. "We'll have to watch our backs."

She shrugged. Leprechauns were notoriously sneaky. She'd intended to watch her back around them anyway.

"But I believe Danu sent him. And he'll get us to my father. After that... Well, just remember he'd do anything for gold, so don't drop your guard."

"Okay." She glanced at Deacon. "You ready?"

"As I'll ever be."

"Then let's head back into Faery."

She tried not to shudder as she finished her coffee. Even that deliciousness wasn't enough to settle her now jumping nerves. Fear crept through her blood, making her recent meal turn a little. The ever-present worry that she'd fail and someone would die churned in her gut.

She'd failed once and someone had died—when she'd been facing the very demon Tom had been working for the last time she'd seen him.

Was that a bad omen?

Boy, she really really hoped this didn't turn out to be the time she failed completely.

And everyone died.

A group of five leprechauns were waiting for them in the large woods beside the U.S. Ambassador's residence in the middle of the park. Cary and the others skirted a patch of stinging nettles and joined the small group in the middle of a clearing. The dark soil was damp from a rain Cary didn't remember, but the oaks weren't drip on them, and the woods smelled loamy and rich. If not for the occasional glimpse of a large white mansion through the trees, Cary could easily forget they were smack in the middle of a huge metropolitan city.

Tom greeted them with a head nod. "One of the lads is scouting out the gaff," he said. "Should be back soon. Then we'll head out."

Cary blinked a few times at him. It was the first she'd ever seen him in anything but a swanky, well-tailored suit. He wore a pair of green canvas trousers, a thick flannel shirt, and rubber boots that covered his calves. Even his long hair was tucked up under a knitted cap. This was not the charming, wealthy rogue image he usually presented.

She shook her head, trying to make her current impression mesh with the Tom she was used to. "Why are you dressed like a farmer?" she asked.

He grinned, and the other four leprechauns chortled.

"Ai, the English Fae assume we all look this way," one of the others said.

"And we likes to play into their prejudices, like," another said.

"So, not the Kerry green top hat and buckled shoes of the American image, then?" she asked.

That earned another laugh. "If we were infiltrating the American realm, we just might have to pull out our top hats and green suits," Tom said. "But for today, it's the farmer's lofty apparel."

"Well, you still look good," Cary said.

Tom winked and set a finger to his brow. "Right you are, so."

She grinned. Even his accent was more pronounced. More country, Jaxer would say.

One of the leprechauns, the only woman in the bunch, stepped up to Jaxer and took his hand in hers. She was dressed exactly the same as the other men in the group but her long brown hair was plaited in two thick braids that hung across each shoulder. Her age was as impossible to guess as Tom's—because they were immortal and so didn't age— but she gave the appearance of older rather than younger.

"I never got a chance to tell you, love," she said, patting Jaxer's hand, "how much we missed yer old mum. She was a fine, fine woman. One of the best of the People. And I miss her every day."

"Thanks for that, Grainne," Jaxer said, his voice very quiet. "She always had nothing but the best to say about you, too." He smiled a little. "It's why she used your name when we were pretending to be humans while I grew up. You were her favorite."

The leprechaun, Grainne, sniffled and patted his hand harder. "Fine woman," she repeated. And then released Jaxer to rejoin the others.

Cary watched Jaxer carefully. He'd taken the conversation better than she would have expected, given all the things he'd had to deal with on this visit. But then again, maybe he was just covering up his reaction with glamour and good acting skills. He wouldn't want to show Tom anything less.

She didn't have much time to ponder the exchange, though, as a stairway leading down into the earth opened up next to Tom and another leprechaun poked his head out of the hole.

"All's ready to go, lads," he said.

"Any of the guards about?" Tom asked. "Especially herself's personal guards? Danu warned to steer clear of them."

"Some of them are involved in trying to unleash the Lachlinain," Jaxer said. "There won't be any help there."

"Good for us, then, that they all seem to be about other business," the leprechaun standing on the stairs said. "There's a kerfuffle of some kind going on down the court. Lots of comings and goings and muttering about disasters. Couldn't pick up the full story, but I'd say our time to stop whatever we're going to stop is running out. Sounds like a battle is brewing."

"Right then," Tom said. "We'd better get moving."

"You're sure you trust them," Eriana said to Jaxer, her gaze on Tom. She didn't exactly look hostile, but her expression wasn't warm and open either.

"No," Jaxer said. "I don't trust them even a little bit."

"Smart man, that," one of the leprechauns said to Tom, giving him a chuff on the shoulder.

"But the sneaky bastards can get us to my father and that's where we need to be."

"Ah, yer old mum would be proud," Grainne said with a fond look for Jaxer.

Cary pressed her lips together so she wouldn't grin. This wasn't really a grinning moment. But still.

Deacon unfurled his cloak, sweeping it around his shoulders and pinning the brooch back into place. His eyes were their normal golden color, but there were creases at the edges, and a few extra lines bracketing his mouth as he held his jaw tight. He looked as worried as she'd ever seen him. And given what they'd been through over the last eight months, she'd seen him pretty worried a few times.

She took his hand, for comfort as well as to give comfort. As she stared at the stairs leading down into Faery, she kept remembering the sound of the banshee screaming, and how the wraith said she'd had nothing to do with encouraging the banshee. Someone in their small party was destined to die. She tried to shake off the superstition. She wasn't Irish. She didn't have to believe in the banshee scream. But...

Fear had her heart pumping as she watched Jaxer follow the leprechauns down the staircase, letting Tom and the others take the lead. She should have gone first, probably, to act as protection and so her powers would work. But she didn't know where they were going. And frankly, she was scared. Scared to return to Faery. And scared of facing the Lachlinain again.

Scared she wouldn't be able to stop the looming disaster.

Deacon squeezed her hand. "You'll be protecting me from the effects of Faery," he said under his breath, near her ear. "You'll be okay even before we get to the cursed hall."

"You've got your cloak and brooch to do that," she muttered but she appreciated the thought. Her nerves and fears must be pumping out a lot of pheromonal signals to his super shifter senses. Or maybe he just knew her well after all these months.

Eriana followed Jaxer down. Leaving Cary and Deacon for last. She took a step toward the stairs, but Deacon stopped her.

He removed the cloak and wrapped it around her. "I'll keep the brooch because I don't want to lose control and be useless to you. But the cloak also seems to have some magic to it that's been keeping me in control. Protections from Fae magic. It'll help you."

He adjusted the cloak on her shoulders and flipped a heavy section of it over one shoulder so it would stay in place. The material smelled like him and was warm from his body. It felt like being enveloped in a big, yummy Deacon hug. She drew in a deep breath and then stretched up to kiss him, hard.

When she drew away, she cupped his jaw in her hands and held his gaze for a long moment. "So you know, and not because I think we might die, although that's a possibility, but... So you know. I love you."

"About time you said that," he murmured with a slight smile. "I love you, too."

"Thank you for your patience." She straightened her shoulders, the weight of the large cloak a comfort. "Okay, let's go save the world."

"Again," he said, and let her lead the way down the stairs.

3 3

he trip through Faery took longer than Cary had been expecting. Up to now, they'd been hopping in and out of areas without a lot of walking required, so she'd sort of assumed they'd just step through some hole and end up where they needed to go.

Instead, they trekked through the same woods—or at least they looked the same—as the place where they'd met Danu and the wraith. Cary tried to ignore the echo of the banshee scream in her head, but that memory dogged her as they went farther and farther into the woods.

"Got to reach the right doorway," Tom said. He'd fallen back to her side to update her, letting Grainne and the leprechaun who'd been scouting the way take the lead.

"How much longer?" she asked.

"Not long now," Tom assured. "Nearly there."

She could feel her skin tingling, but so far it didn't seem to be overwhelming her. Still, she wasn't having to protect anyone yet—apparently Faery had given up on trying to seduce Deacon's leopard out—which left her vulnerable. And it looked like she might just be more of a sponge for magic than she'd thought. She'd come into Faery working under the impression that she had to have magic tossed at her in order to actually absorb it. After all, she'd gone for twenty-six years without issue before that demon kicked puppy Buck and she'd become a Protector. Only then did she start absorbing any magic, and then only when it was thrown at her, and that was mostly offset by her Protector shields.

But Faery had disabused her of the idea that magic had to be thrown at her. She could feel the magic here soaking into her skin, her cells. More now even because she'd released some of what had been building up when she'd faced the wraith. She was aware of the process in a way she hadn't been before, aware that with every step she took, more magic seeped into her body. When surrounded by enough, it seemed, she could just pull it out of the ambient air.

Good to know. Bad to have happening at the moment. But if she survived, it was good to know a little more how all this worked.

It crossed her mind to wonder if she could purposefully pull in magic, but since she still didn't know how to release it on purpose, trying that seemed a little stupid.

"Is the cloak helping?" Deacon asked. He was a step behind her and to her right, a steady presence that reminded her she wasn't alone in this.

"A little, I think." Though, it was hard to tell because she didn't have a lot to compare what she was feeling to. "Still, it'll be good to get there," she said. "Have the shields up and all that."

She was purposefully vague because Tom didn't know she was a Protector. Or at least, he hadn't before this particular trip. She realized a little late that Danu might have told him what she was, and why they needed to reach Ulieran. Up to this adventure, Tom had thought she was a slightly inept but powerful sorceress whom Jaxer had taken under his wing to train.

But...

Some of the Fae here knew why Jaxer had gone to the Americas, that he'd gone to help the Nags create Protectors. So maybe Tom had known all along?

Well. That would be a surprise and not a pleasant one either.

She gave Tom a look from the corner of her eyes. His expression gave nothing away. He was too busy scanning their surroundings and didn't seem to be paying much attention to the exchange between her and Deacon. She didn't buy that for a moment. But she didn't dare broach the subject just yet. They had enough to worry about.

"Stay lively, lads," he called to the other leprechauns. "We're making the transition." This to Cary.

"Huh?" she said. And a moment later, her question was answered when the woods around them bled away into something entirely different.

Here, the trees were weirdly colored and glittering again. The bird song and breeze had stopped. The light from the sparkling vines was muted against the pervasive sunlight that didn't cast shadows. When Cary looked behind her, all she saw was more of the strange forest, no hint of the verdant green stretch of woods they'd just been walking through.

A winged creature flittered past and Cary realized it had a human shaped body under the overlarge butterfly wings. The creature ignored them as it bounced here and there in the still air. The strong scent of chocolate chip cookies and cotton candy surrounded her again, making everything smell both delicious and a little too sweet. The kind of sweet that gave her a headache after too long.

A rumbling in the distance drew her attention, but she couldn't see what was causing the sound through the pink and purple tree trunks.

"Welcome back to the English realm," Tom said, his voice quiet.

"What's that sound?" Cary asked, also speaking quietly.

"Must be whatever kerfuffle Sean warned us about," Tom said.

Cary assumed Sean had been the scout. "Should we check it out first?" she asked.

"We're here to sneak into the cursed hall and stop the release of the Lachlinain. We'd best stick with that and leave the rest of the English to their own business."

Cary hesitated. Her instincts were always to run in and make sure none of the good guys got hurt. But she was here to specifically stop the end of Faery so her own world didn't get invaded. Tom was right. The Fae would have to take care of themselves.

"This way," Sean said, directing them away from the distant rumbling and into a section of the strange forest that grew stranger as they went.

The vines tangled. The light turned a more orange, muddy shade. The sparkles on the trees started to look like eyes winking at them, watching them. The bright, luminous leaf colors shifted to something darker, their shapes morphing into sharper edges, and thorns and spikes appearing along the trunks. Thorn covered roots started popping up, wrapping around the trees and crowding the narrow dirt path they followed.

"Careful of them thorns," Grainne called over her shoulder. "Nasty bit of work those things."

"Poisonous," Jaxer murmured. He walked a few paces ahead of her, his gaze tracking their surroundings. "Watch out for anything that looks like an insect too. They won't be nice little butterflies."

"Sharp teeth," Tom said with a knowing nod.

Eriana, walking steps in front of Jaxer, said, "Even the bark and leaves here are dangerous. Touch nothing."

Cary's knee-jerk reaction was to look at the soil and question whether it was safe, but she bit her tongue and kept the comment to herself. Since she and Deacon couldn't fly—and she didn't think the leprechauns could either—she didn't really want to know if the ground itself might be poisoning them.

Things moved at the edge of her vision, glimpses of color or just the flitter of motion. She resisted trying to spot the things this time around. Pointless. And after the warning about teeth, she wasn't sure she wanted to see what was watching them.

She kept a wary eye on the ground and thorn covered vines, though, carefully stepping around and over the vines when they crept across the path. Patches of moss covering the base of the trees pulsed as they moved past. And here and there, Cary spotted what seemed to be black tulips opening and closing in a strange rhythmic pattern. The sucking, slurping sound coming from the black tulips made Cary's stomach roll.

She shivered and looked away.

They'd slowed their progress significantly since entering this section of the woods, and with each careful step, Cary grew antsier. That ticking clock counting down to disaster had grown louder in her head since they'd re-entered Faery. Louder and louder with each slow inch forward they took. Every instinct in her screamed to run toward the cursed hall, run as fast as she could. Ulieran wouldn't wait long. They had to reach him before he unleashed the curse.

They had to get there.

Get there. Now. Before it all ended. Before she was too late.

Run.

Run!

She was up on her toes, the urge to run overwhelming, when she noticed a vine along the ground edging closer to her, its thorns vibrating. The sight stopped her cold. Maybe her need to hurry came from the surroundings, not the approaching confrontation.

Ah. That wasn't good.

"You feeling the need to rush?" she asked Deacon.

"Like if we don't move quicker, we won't make it in time?" Deacon said. "Yeah. But…" He nodded toward the side of the path.

A vine with what looked like eyes dotting its length was stretching toward them at an unnatural angle, and a blood red flower that appeared to have teeth opened about midway up the vine as they neared.

"Yeah," Cary said. "Slow seems a more survivable idea."

"Don't look into them eyes either," Tom said. "They'll mess with ye."

"I'm already being messed with," Cary muttered, letting out a slow breath. What she wouldn't give to have her Protector shields working right now.

Which made her wonder… "Do you suppose my shields are working now since the surroundings are a threat?" she asked Deacon.

She couldn't feel them, but then she couldn't usually anyway. And she was being fucked with by the weird forest, but maybe that wasn't something her Protector magic could stop? Normally it would, though. She frowned. This was exactly the kind of situation in which it seemed like Protector magic should work. At least, she'd have thought so given how dangerous all these plants were. But if her magic was working, it wasn't working in the ways she'd have expected.

That did not bode well for the upcoming confrontation.

"Maybe," Deacon said, answering her question. "But I'd rather not take chances on maybes." He edged closer to her to avoid a vine that seemed to swing toward him in the nonexistent breeze. "Are you still…?" He motioned to her skin.

"Yeah. Unfortunately." Her nerves still popped, the tingles not painful, but not comfortable either. The sensation of soaking up magic remained. "Though it's not getting worse or stronger. I'm hoping that's a good sign." It *could* mean her Protector shields were up and blocking some of that magic absorption. Right?

Deacon grunted a noncommittal sound.

Tom glanced at her, his eyes narrowed. She ignored the look. Even if he figured out what she really was—or had known all along—they didn't have time for her to explain.

She glanced at a vine with those winking eye-like nubs and suppressed a shudder. She didn't want to say anything aloud right now anyway.

"Much farther to go?" she asked Tom, keeping her voice a mere whisper.

"Not much," he said. "But the path is narrowing. This isn't a way most can come. Or care to risk."

"Yeah, starting to see why."

"Sorry to say, it's going to get worse," he murmured.

She looked ahead to where he nodded. A wall of interwoven vines filled the path in front of them. Thorns the size of small swords covered the vines, lacing together to form what seemed to be an impenetrable barrier. And all over the vines, in between the sword-sized thorns, those black sucking tulips slurped at the air.

Cary groaned. "Well shit."

34

"I think I hate Faery," Cary muttered as she stared at the black tulips and giant thorns. "I mean, I don't want it to be destroyed. But this is not ever going to be my first choice of vacation destinations."

"Agree," Deacon said dryly.

"Is it just me, or are others having flashbacks to Sleeping Beauty?" she asked, studying the wall of death ahead of them.

"I am not playing the Prince Charming roll in this," Deacon said. "Jaxer can do it."

She snorted. "You kiss some random princess, and I'm going to kick your ass."

"You're my only princess. And I would happily fight a dragon for you."

"Fortunately for us both, I'm not on the other side of this disaster." She paused, wincing slightly when she said, "You don't suppose there *is* a dragon in there?"

"I really hope not."

"Me too," she said, with feeling. "I don't have a sword. And dragon fire is hot." She'd had to hold off dragon shifter flames a couple of times before. That had been interesting. A real, non-shifter dragon wasn't something she aspired to meet on a narrow path surrounded by deadly plant matter.

"Are you two finished?" Eriana snapped.

Cary turned to look at her, eyebrows raised. "You in a hurry to get into the middle of all that?" she asked.

"We have to get to Ulieran, so yes, yes I am."

"After you, then," Cary said, scowling at the healer. Geez, she was snappy.

Eriana just grumbled under her breath, but, Cary noticed, she didn't move toward the wall of thorny death.

Cary glanced back at it, and tried not to whimper. "Jaxer, you ever try coming this way to see your father?" Knowing there was a back door, deadly as it appeared, she'd be surprised if he hadn't tried to get through at those times when Tatiana denied him visits with his father.

"I didn't know it was here," he said, sounding irritated. "I probably would have tried if I'd known. How in the name of Danu did you know about this?" he asked Tom.

"Sure, don't we know all the back ways into everywhere," Tom said as if that was obvious.

"There's a path," Sean said. "Follow the red roses. Takes you right to the cursed hall."

"Really? Red roses?" Cary tried not to groan as the fairytale references stacked up.

"So you've gotten through this?" Deacon asked.

"No! Sure, why the feck would I want to go in there?" Sean said.

"No gold in the cursed hall," Tom said. He and Sean nodded as if this explained everything.

Cary pulled in a deep breath and straightened her shoulders. "I suppose I should take the lead." One of the thorn swords moved a little. She sighed. This was going to be fun.

"Deacon, you should shift," Jaxer said. "It'll be easier to slide through."

He nodded. "You?"

"Don't tell me you can shrink down to some diminutive size with wings and flitter through this," Cary said.

Jaxer shrugged.

She narrowed her eyes at him.

His grin flashed briefly. "No," he finally said. "But if I could, I would."

"Take this," Deacon said. He handed Cary the brooch he'd pinned to his shirt. "Every added layer of protection helps."

"You need it," she protested, pushing his hand back.

"Won't do me any good in a minute. I can't pin it through my fur."

"Don't destroy your clothes," she said, pretending she wasn't worried about…everything as she took the brooch from him. It was warm in her palm. From his body heat or its own magic, she wasn't sure. She cupped the large circle tight in her fist rather than pinning it through the cloak she was wearing—she didn't know how anyway.

Deacon's chuckle sounded forced, like he was trying to pretend he wasn't worried either. "Just this once."

Unlike most leopard shifters, Deacon's pedigree meant he had actual magic at his disposal. Most shifter species didn't. Their ability to change forms was biology, not technical magic. But Deacon was the first born of two first born parents who were also the first borns of first born parents for seven generations back on his mother's side. His mother had a degree of magic as well. But Deacon's was something even stronger because of being the seventh first born of first borns. Birth order mattered in leopard shifters. And Deacon's was truly rare.

Which meant there were things he could do that most shifters couldn't. She didn't even know most of what he could do. She wasn't sure he did either because he'd refused to use that magic most of his life. So normally, when he changed forms, he did so like an ordinary leopard shifter. If he was dressed and didn't take the time to strip, he shredded his clothes. When he shifted back to human, he was naked.

Except he didn't need to shred his clothes, and he could magic up clothes on his body when he returned to human form if he wanted to. He hadn't bothered to reveal that fact to her until *after* she'd seen his mother do it.

She held his gaze a moment, blinked, and then she had to look down to see him. In his leopard form, he was a magnificent cat. Black, glossy fur, eyes so gold-yellow they glowed, body muscled and deadly strong. He was large for a leopard but still smaller and sleeker in this form than his human form. Looking at him like this, she was glad Jaxer had recommended it. Slipping between sword-sized thorns would definitely be easier.

He bumped his big head against her thigh, then waited for her to take the lead.

She turned back to Tom and the other leprechauns. "Thanks for your help getting here. We really appreciate it. I can't ask you to come the rest of the way." To Sean she said, "Just follow the red roses, right?"

"We'll go all the way," Tom said before Sean could answer. "We've brought you this far. Who knows, you might still need our particular skill sets." He winked at her.

"I appreciate it, Tom, really I do. But I can't ask it of you." She glanced back at the vines of thorns and sucking tulips. "Not through all this."

"If Faery's destroyed, we'll be out a home and have to see friends die," Tom said, sounding as serious as she'd ever heard him. "I love yer realm, Cary, but this is our place. And I'll defend it as surely as I'd defend me gold."

What could she say? He was right. "Okay. But please let me protect you through this…" She gestured to the wall of thorny vines.

She tried not to show any of her doubt. Protecting is what she did, what she'd been doing for years now. She'd trusted her shields to work in some of the most dangerous situations she'd been in and they'd never failed her.

But with all the interference of Faery magic, the way her body was soaking up the magic, she doubted her shields for the first time since becoming a Protector. It was not a pleasant feeling.

"I've seen your shields work," Tom said. "We'll let you take the lead. But we've got yer back."

She faced the black wall of death and spotted the single red rose that marked the start of their path. Had that been there a moment ago?

Shit.

She shook off her fear, or at least tried to, wrapped the cloak tighter around her so it wouldn't snag on any of the thorns, and started forward, stepping into the darkness of the choking vines just at the red rose.

A path did open up in front of her, narrow but manageable if she ducked and moved slowly. She stopped a few feet in, startled when one of the sucking black tulips dropped down in front of her and spit something at her. She blinked at the tiny spike hovering in the air a foot from her face. After a terrifying moment when the spike seemed to push closer, it turned directions and flew into the vines.

Cary let out a breath.

She took one more step forward, and the tulips released a barrage of little spikes, from all directions, raining down on them like a tiny, malevolent storm.

Cary half closed her eyes, half watched the shower of pointy death as it flowed over and away from them. She'd always been grateful for her shield, but she thought that moment might rank up there with one of her strongest moments of gratitude.

The spikes rolled over the invisible barrier and back into the vines like actual water, moving fast into a flood-like flow. She felt like she was standing inside a glass bubble, watching the hurricane, hoping the glass didn't break.

Behind her, someone gasped. Someone else cursed. Actually, a few very colorful curses hissed out. Some she was going to have to remember. They were both evocative and perfectly suited to their current predicament.

Over her shoulder, to Jaxer, she said, "Well, the shield works. That's good."

"Yes. And I'm glad I didn't try this in my misspent youth."

She snorted. Turning a little to look at their scout, Sean, she said, "You didn't mention poisoned darts. A warning might have been nice."

"Didn't know about the bloody things, missus," he said, staring up with wide green eyes at the sharp rain of spikes overhead. "Didn't dare come into this tangle before, like. Fecking hell but they're vicious little bastards. Whenaya think they'll stop?"

"Got me." To Jaxer, "Should I just move forward? I mean, we don't technically have to just stand here and wait them out, right?"

Jaxer gestured forward. "After you."

"Ha!" She glanced down at Deacon, who was staying just behind her, but close enough she could touch if she needed to. "You okay?"

A quiet hissing growl was her only answer. It was enough.

She moved forward, slowly, giving her shields time to readjust position and meet the attack without any of it getting through. They'd moved as a group another few yards into the viney tangle before the tulips stopped firing darts at them. Cary spotted another red rose at a split in the narrow path. The rose hung on a vine in front of the path that got darker and thicker with threatening sword-thorns. The other path moved into a greener, lighter area of the tangle. In the lighter direction, the path was wider and more welcoming. The tulips no longer made their horrendous sucking sound. The giant thorns angled away from the path.

Cary didn't have to know fairytales to understand why that was a trick.

"Trying a bit hard, isn't it?" she said as she started down the dark and more forbidding path. "I mean, they could have been a *little* more subtle when constructing the wrong trail."

"You're sure it is a wrong path?" Eriana asked.

"If you're not, I wonder you've survived Tatiana's court this long," Cary said.

"I knew it was," Eriana said, with a little snort. "I'm just surprised you did."

"Yeah, I'm smarter than I look," Cary muttered, easing forward so her shields could push aside the thorns trying to angle across their path. "Anyone have a guess what might have happened if we'd gone down the pretty path?"

She winced when a few of the thorns scrapped together, sounding like actual metal on metal even though they looked like they were just plants.

"Death and despair," Grainne said quietly. "Death and despair, love."

"Yeah, kind of figured." Given that the "safe" path was still trying to kill them, she was probably better off not knowing what would have been waiting on the wrong path.

"Likely you'd have just been lost in the tangle forever," Jaxer said quietly. "No way out until you starved. Faery likes to trap and kill slowly."

"That's gross," she said matter-of-factly. "No wonder the real fairy-tales were always so bloody and violent."

"We're a bloody violent sort, we are," Tom said.

Another red rose appeared a few feet ahead. There was no obvious alternate way to go. But the reassurance that they were still on the right path was nice.

A fine mist rose from the ground as they moved past the rose, eerily reminding Cary of the mist that proceeded the appearance of the wraith. She moved a little closer to Deacon, staying in front of him, but letting her hand brush the top of his head.

This mist didn't thicken into an impenetrable barrier of fog, though. It just remained a swirl at their feet, covering the ground like a translucent blanket.

For some reason, her heartbeat kicked up, pumping a new wash of adrenaline through her blood. A warning shiver traveled down her spine. But she couldn't see a source for her newfound hit of terror. Just the swirling mist at their feet.

They passed another two roses, and with each one her heart hammered harder and the fear crawling into her bloodstream increased.

What the hell?

"You feeling this?" she asked Jaxer. "You?" she said down to Deacon.

Deacon's response was a predictable grunt since he couldn't actually speak in his leopard form.

Jaxer said, "If you mean am I getting more terrified as the moments pass? Then yes. I'm feeling that."

"Fecking hell," Sean muttered.

"Keep yer eyes sharp, lads," Tom said, his voice low. "Something's coming."

If it was a ghost, Cary was going to scream. She didn't care that her shield was working and would stop it. She was still going to scream. A lot.

The sound was clogging her throat, clawing at her lips, trying to get out even without a visible sign of the source of her terror.

The mist at their feet swirled in little eddies. Cary realized with a start it was warm. In fact, the air all around them was getting warmer, danker. The path ahead opened up, the vines separating to make a clearing, though they still stretched overhead in an arc that blocked out any view of the sky.

And the dark shadows had turned a strange and forbidding shade of…red.

That couldn't be good.

She knew they didn't have demons in Faery. Faery had its own monsters. Monsters that came in all different shapes, and sizes, and abilities.

But when she finally got a look at the monster that moved out of the tangle of thorns into the clearing, her first response was…

"You have got to be fucking kidding me. A dragon? It just had to be a dragon."

3 5

The creature was large, but not quite as large as Cary would
have expected. Which wasn't in any way, shape, or form a
relief. It was still the size of a small house and could swallow her in a
single gulp.

It was a dark reddish-purple color, the scales along its back and
sides shimmering with faint iridescence. A thick body, with a long
neck, and stocky legs ending in claw-tipped, four-toed feet. From the
angle, and with the thick vines blocking some of her view, Cary
couldn't see its tail, or if it even had one, but it had wings folded along
its sides. And there were spikes along its spine, though they were flattened against its back at the moment.

Its eyes were huge, and black, with a glow of purple at the center
that reminded her of a camera lens for some reason. Its snout was long
and narrow with raised nostrils from which a slow stream of smoke
emerged. And when it opened its mouth to make a hissing sort of
growl at them, it revealed teeth as long, and sharp, and pointed as the
sword-sized thorns covering the vines.

So. Many. Teeth.

"This is one of those moments," she said, mostly to herself, "when
being a teleporting superhero would be really useful."

"Or at least having a very strong sword," Deacon said.

He'd shifted back to his human form in that fast-as-a-blink way he was capable of. With clothes, she noted from the corner of her eyes. She didn't want to take her attention from the big, giant threat standing a few yards away to make sure.

"I can't use a sword," she said. "Despite Lucy's best efforts."

"I haven't used one in about twenty years," he said. "So not sure that helps."

"You can at least manage one without cutting your foot off, though."

The dragon shifted its weight and Cary swore she felt the ground tremble.

"Grandma was big on us learning the basics," Deacon said.

"Never considered learning to sword fight a 'basic' before this moment."

The dragon took one step closer to them and then crouched, putting its huge head on their level. Its mouth pointed directly at their group. A source of heat Cary couldn't spot—but could guess at—sent the surrounding temperature spiking. Sweat beaded on her brow and dripped down her back under her shirt. The cloak Deacon had given her suddenly felt very heavy and much too warm.

She gestured with her arms to make sure everyone was behind her. A few curses and one quite colorful prayer to Danu assured her everyone was standing back.

"Her name is Maloria," Eriana said, her voice very quiet. "She's Oberon's."

"And she doesn't like Eriana very much," Jaxer said.

"There's a story there," Cary commented.

Her heartbeat pounded so hard in her chest she was worried about passing out. She'd faced demon gods and dragon shifters, armies of supernatural bad guys, and a supremely dangerous ex-girlfriend of Deacons. But somehow, a real, honest-to-god, fairytale dragon with black eyes and a name seemed so very much worse.

Not as bad as the wraith had been. But a pretty close second.

"Not one we have time for," Jaxer said. His voice was quiet and low as well.

No one seemed to want to speak above a murmured. She wasn't sure why. It wasn't like the dragon hadn't already noticed them.

A few small little bursts of fire puffed out of Maloria's mouth. Nothing like a stream. More like warm ups for the big show.

Cary settled her stance, keeping her legs braced and her body ready to take the fiery hit. She'd withstood dragon shifter fire before. She could do this.

"Don't suppose you could glamour us up a solution?" Cary murmured as one of the warm up fire balls emerged from Maloria's half-open snout. A bigger burst than the last.

"Dragons see through glamour," Jaxer said. "Same as brownies."

"Well. That's useful."

"You don't run away," a voice as deep and terrifying as an ocean trench emerged from the dragon's mouth.

Oh good. She talked. "Yeah. About that," Cary said, trying not to be her usual, irritating-to-the-bad-guys self. For some reason, she just assumed a dragon deserved more respect. Maybe it was the potential fire stream. "See. You're a lot bigger than us. And you have wings. I'm not sure where we'd run away to."

"Everyone runsss," Maloria said, a sibilant hiss in her ground-shakingly deep voice. "When faced with a dragon."

"I imagine they do," Cary said. "To be honest, if I weren't so terrified right now, I might run away. But my legs aren't working so..." She shrugged. "I guess I'll just stand here."

"You are a Protector," Maloria said.

Cary's stomach bottomed out. The dragon knew what she was? That couldn't be good. Cary's mind curled up into a little ball in the corner of her skull and whimpered. A dragon, after a wraith and a banshee, was just one step too far for her. She only barely recognized the fact that Tom and the other leprechauns would know for sure what she was now. She couldn't worry about that, though, because she was too busy panicking over the fact that a dragon knew. Which meant the dragon knew exactly how to kill her and holy shit a dragon—*a dragon!*—knew how to kill her.

"For what it's worth," Cary said, hoping to stall the inevitable. "We're here to stop the end of Faery."

"Yessss," Maloria hissed. "The end timesss dawn." Another burst of flames puffed from her mouth. "Sssuch a weak and sssilly crew to stand here now. Claiming to be heroesss. Claiming to be worthy."

"Oh no," Cary said. "You misunderstand. Not claiming anything of the sort. Not worthy. Not heroes. Just..." She sighed and shrugged. "Just in the wrong place at the right time with a useful skill."

"Ussseful," Maloria said. "Yessss."

Cary winced as another fire ball burst from the dragon's mouth.

"Food is ussseful," Maloria said.

Cary tried not to shiver, but she failed miserably. She really really didn't want to be a dragon hors d'oeuvre. The torture of waiting for the flames to burst over her was almost as bad as the heat. Anticipating being fried seemed like it might be as bad as being fried, although she didn't particularly want to find out. She was sure the delay was on purpose, though. A little dragon game.

"Hisss faery toy would be tasty," Marloria said. "Very tasssty. Tatiana would be pleased if I ate the healer."

Cary let out a slow breath. Obviously having an affair with Oberon wasn't good for anyone involved. Except maybe Oberon. Since he wasn't here anticipating being eaten by his own pet.

"They play gamesss with lives," Maloria said. "Moving piecesss and destroying like godsss."

"Yeah, I remember something about that from my reading," Cary said. This felt like a non sequitur but since it didn't involve being digested, she'd take it.

"Your livesss," Maloria said, and took one step closer.

Cary braced for the attack. Boy, she hoped this wasn't the time her Protector shields failed. With Eriana in definite danger of being eaten, it should mean that even if Maloria knew how to get around Cary's magic, she wouldn't be able to. At least, that was how it had always worked before. How her magic was supposed to work.

But since this was Faery and nothing had gone exactly as usual here—well, except for all the fairytale clichés they'd had to face in the last hour—Cary worried.

Maloria opened her mouth, lowered her head, and Cary had to work hard not to close her eyes against watching her own death approach.

The fire emerged in a wash of immensely hot blue flames…that Maloria swept sideways and up, covering the surrounding vines in heat so intense it melted them instantaneously.

Cary blinked a few times when she realized none of that searing heat was actually being directed at them.

All around the clearing, vines melted and dropped, turning to ash when they met the mist still covering the ground. Cary looked up, expecting to see the flaming debris dropping onto them. But it wasn't. More ash like gray snow fell from above, building up in a layer on top of her shield. It was like being inside a snow globe, but the snow was outside the glass.

By the time the dragon's stream of blue fire stopped, the vines around them had been destroyed utterly. Leaving plainly visible an inclined path up to what looked like an honest-to-god gray stone castle with turrets and parapets and even a strange black and purple flag fluttering from the point of a single tower.

"Uhm," Cary said because that was basically all her brain was capable of at that moment.

"I will eat the dead when the fighting isss done," Maloria said. "Will you be among the corpses, Protector?"

Before Cary could answer—and really it was going to take her at least another hour or more before her ability to speak rationally returned anyway—the dragon spread her wings. The span was huge and impressive, and for a moment, all Cary could see. Giant wings. Tipped with spikes along the trailing edge.

With a single down beat, the dragon launched into the sky, pumping those magnificent wings in a few strong strokes, before gliding away on an invisible updraft.

"Uhm," Cary said again, staring at the purple dot of the now-distant dragon as it disappeared into the sky. A sky that was no longer bright blue but gray and dim and tinged with red.

Deacon leaned close to her. "Did the dragon just help us?"

"I think that depends on your definition of help," Cary murmured, remembering Maloria's comment about eating the dead.

"The cursed hall," Tom said.

His comment pulled her gaze back from the sky. There was an awe in his tone Cary had always assumed he used only when faced with significant stacks of gold. To be fair, the castle was a pretty impressive sight. And if there was a moat of lava around its base, she was going to start laughing. Hysterical laughter. Brought on by a broken brain.

"Now what?" Sean said, his voice a little higher and squeakier than it had been a few moments ago.

"I guess we'd better go in," Cary said. She glanced back at the leprechauns. Every one of them had gathered together in a tight clump, including Tom. Even the two with darker brown skin were pale as parchment now, and their eyes were all huge as they stared up at the castle.

Tom caught her gaze and whistled softly.

"You don't have to go," she said. "You've done more than enough to fulfill your promise to Danu. You got us here and showed us the way in. You don't have to do anymore." She glanced at the group huddled around him. "You can leave."

Tom straightened his shoulders. "Sure, Cary, where are we going to go now?" He nodded over his shoulder. "That noise in the distance? The battle is underway."

She turned her attention to the steady booming noise she'd heard after they'd arrived in the English realm, a sound she'd stopped hearing in all the terror of spike-spitting flowers and actual fairytale dragons. Now, she realized it had gotten louder, and was more obviously fighting. If she listened carefully, she could hear shouts and the sound of clashing swords.

"Who?" she wondered aloud.

"Danu's warning against herself's guards?" Tom said. "It's them and their allies that's started it all. Them against the members of the court that don't want to die with Faery. It's the ones who want to invade your realm, who'll be able to live there, battling the ones who can't leave. The final fight before Ulieran releases the Lachlinain."

He exchanged a look with Grainne. She was holding Sean's hands in hers, patting him absently as if to calm him, but Cary had a feeling the gesture was as much to self-sooth as to give comfort.

Tom met her gaze again. "It's an old tale here, I'm afraid. Who gets a say in what happens next. The weaker Fae are subject to the stronger, and everyone fights for a better place. We've all a part to play in this outcome. Like the old fairytales. The real ones. The ones with blood and carnage."

"Lovely," Cary said.

"If Tatiana's guard and their ilk succeed, Faery ends and yer world will be wrecked. We can't do much in the battle itself. And we've nowhere to hide from it."

"It's why Danu sent us," Grainne said. "Why we agreed to come."

"Besides," Sean said, finally looking away from the castle, "I'll not have the English court—" he spit on the ground, "—determine me fate or the fate of me lands. We're with you, Cary. To the bitter end."

"And beyond that," Tom said, some of his usual charm flowing back into his grin, "I figure the safest place in all of Faery right now is at your back. Given yer one of those Protectors and all."

Cary sighed and rolled her eyes. "Have you known all along?"

"No. No, your secret was safe from me. Danu had to tell me." He shrugged. "Can't say as I believed her either. But I should've known."

"I'm not sure if that's a compliment or insult so I'm going to assume a compliment and we'll move on."

Tom grinned, neither confirming nor denying her assessment.

"We do need to hurry now," Eriana said, her tone urgent and not snappy as it had been earlier. "Ulieran… He knows the battle is underway. And that we're near. He's waiting on us."

"How can you tell?" Cary asked, frowning at the faery. Was she glowing? That didn't seem right.

"The healing linked us," she murmured. "This close, I can feel his emotions." She shivered.

Cary sympathized with that shiver. She wouldn't have wanted to feel Ulieran's emotions, not that directly. Especially not right now.

She looked up at the castle, staring at the dark gray stone, the sounds of a distant battle echoing in her ears.

And with that echo, her memory dredged up the sounds of the banshee again. Her imagination added that scream to the sounds of battle, and the vision of a dragon gobbling up the dead.

Boy she really hated Faery.

3 6

ortunately for Cary's sanity, there was no mote of lava circling the castle. Probably, after the vines and dragon, someone must have thought a mote of lava was an unnecessary expense. There was, however, a drawbridge they had to cross, but the little trickle of water in the rocky, barren streambed beneath hardly qualified as a barrier.

The area around the castle was equally as barren, a waste of scrubby black brush and rocks. None of the lush green of the Irish court, or even the colorfully weird English court. No plants. No trees. No scent of cotton candy and cookie dough or even the deep loamy scent of the earth. No birds or pretty winged insects flitting about. She did spot a few winking red spots that might have been eyes hiding in the castle walls, but she never got a good enough lock at the things to be sure.

And really, she didn't want to know.

The air was heavy and still. If she focused on her sense of smell, she picked up a faint hint of something that reminded her of melting metal. The scent coated her tongue, too much like the taste of blood. She glanced at Deacon. His nostrils flared. His eyes glowed yellow. He held his human form. But his animal was close to the surface.

Without a word, she handed him back the brooch. He silently pinned it back into his shirt, not putting up even a token protest.

No one spoke.

At the end of the drawbridge, a giant wooden gate had been raised so that only the bottom spikes were visible. The spikes slotted into divots in the stone walkway, which, when the gate was lowered, would have given it a great deal of strength and stability. Beyond the raised gate was a dark tunnel through the thick outer castle wall. She peaked inside the darkness, hoping to spot any scary attacks or booby traps ahead of time, but all she saw was thick stone bricks arching overhead and the dim light from the courtyard beyond.

Ready to jump at the least movement, she was almost disappointed that nothing leapt out at them as they passed through the short tunnel and emerged into a small, dark courtyard.

There was nothing in the courtyard either. No plants or decorative statuary or fountains. Just stone cobbles on the ground, the surrounding stone walls, and across from the tunnel, a large, arched wooden door. The door was studded with metal bolts and held together by strips of thick dark metal. The hinges and spiral door pulls were also metal. Metal that Cary was pretty sure was iron.

Which surprised her given the Fae allergy.

Although, maybe that was the point.

When none of her companions reached for the door pull—and in fact Eriana and the leprechauns hung well back from the door—she figured she'd been right about the iron. Jaxer stayed close behind her and to her left, but he didn't reach for the handle either.

Because she needed to stay in the lead anyway to keep everyone safe, she took hold of the door handle in one hand and pulled. She'd expected resistance. Some difficulty. Rusty hinges. Maybe even a lock she'd have to break. But to her surprise, the large door swung open easily. Even the heavy weight of all that wood didn't make opening it much effort.

The door swung outward almost of its own accord.

Like they'd been expected.

Well that couldn't be good.

She dragged in a deep breath and straightened her shoulders, afraid if she hesitated too long, she'd balk and not go in. Her every movie-trained instinct was screaming at her to run away. Fast. Because whatever was through that door was going to be scary, deadly, and might even want to eat them.

Sometimes being a Protector meant facing your fears.

Sometimes it just felt like being the dumbass heroine in a slasher film, walking into danger in high heels and with no weapons, instead of running away like a smart person.

She forced down her more intelligent "run away" impulses and stepped through the door. It was pitch dark inside, too dark to see until everyone had moved past the door. Once it swung shut, however, a dim glow from surrounding wall sconces rose in flickering firelight, casting a faint orange light across the stones.

Verifying that the inside of the castle was another Faery mind-fuck.

The flickering torch light revealed the castle interior to be that single windowless corridor stretching out in front and behind them. The corridor where she, Deacon, and Jaxer had first met Ulieran.

She turned in a slow circle, her gut clenching. Yup. No sign of the door they'd just walked through. Nothing but the long corridor and the deep shadows of the high ceiling. Shadows she couldn't see into.

No visible signs of a way out.

She wanted to close her eyes. She wanted to scream. She did neither as she faced forward again and waited for Ulieran.

But it wasn't Ulieran who stepped out of the shadows.

A huge, leather armor clad Fae stalked out to stand in front of them. He had a glowing purple sword drawn.

"You can't stop the inevitable," Grim said, his deep voice echoing in the endless corridor.

"Oh good. You." She sighed. And *of course* the guy named Grim was here right now. If the fairytale references didn't stop stacking up, she really was going to go laughing into hysteria.

"You will not stop the war, witch," he said. "You cannot stop the Lachlinain. The end of Faery is inevitable. The human realm will be ours. And your people will bow before us as gods."

"Well, that's not happening on my watch," she said. "But let me ask you something."

Grim blinked. His green eyes bright in the dim, flickering torchlight. The purple glow dancing on his sword cast a strange illumination on his heavy-lidded scowl.

She ignored the scowl. "Is Tatiana in on all this or not? I mean, she dies if Faery dies, right? I can't believe she wants her realm destroyed. She can't live in the human realm. So…you've basically committed treason, right? Or have I been misinformed? And if this is real treason, is Tatiana out there fighting against your crowd now, or… What?"

Grim's scowl continued to deepen, until his face looked like he was going to explode with anger. "You. Never. Stop. Talking."

"Asking questions helps me learn," she said primly. "If you don't want to answer, fine. No need to be rude."

"You die now, witch."

"You tried that already," she reminded him. "Remember? Magic lights, glowing sword attacks. Doesn't work."

"It will work here where the rules of both realms do not apply."

"Actually, no. It won't. But go ahead and try, waste time."

She waited for him to charge in, head lowered and sword high. Or maybe throw some magic at her in an attempt to break her shield even though he had to know that wouldn't work. She would have preferred answers to her questions, but she supposed they had to go through the motions.

But Grim didn't charge in and attack. His eyes narrowed. And he smiled. The smile revealed a lot of teeth. Sharp, pointed teeth.

That couldn't be good.

Behind him, dropping from the shadows, Ulieran appeared. He straightened to his full height and folded his wings behind him, towering over Grim.

Cary looked at the two Fae. Ulieran wasn't attacking Grim. He was standing *with* him.

"Da?" Jaxer asked, stepping forward. He remained behind Cary, but only just barely.

"Faery must die," Ulieran said quietly, smiling softly at his son. "If

I am to join your mother. I want to join her now. It's time. And you'll be safe in the human realm. You've done well there. This is for the best."

"Sending half of Faery in to invade the human realm is for the best?" Jaxer snapped. "After all the human world gave us? The safety. The good life we had? You'd take part in assuring its destruction?"

"It's time for me to die, son," Ulieran said. "Faery has rotted. It can't be saved. Even your blessed birth couldn't stop the decay. The human world will be better for this too. Everyone wins."

"No. Da, no. That's not how this will work." Jaxer made a move to step in front of Cary to get to his father.

She grabbed his arm and pulled him back, ensuring he remained behind her. To Ulieran, she said, "I understand you want to be with your wife. I do. I know you miss her terribly. But this isn't the way. My realm won't be better in the wake of an invasion. It just won't. And so many will die if you do this. So many innocent Fae. Please reconsider, Ulieran. Grenelle wouldn't want you to do this."

"Her vision…" Ulieran's gaze turned inward. He blinked his black eyes as he stared at something none of them could see. "She knew Faery would rot. There was no way to stop that."

"There is, though," Cary said urgently. "There has to be. There is another way."

Ulieran looked at Jaxer. "That choice you have to make? My son, now is the time. Will you help me? Will you kill me?"

Jaxer gasped. His eyes widened. "No," he whispered. "No. You can't mean…"

"I tried to do it myself," Ulieran said sadly. "I didn't want you to have to make this choice. But…I cannot die. Not while I'm the curse guardian. And I will always be the curse guardian. But you can kill me. You can. You can choose to release me. I'm sorry. I'm truly sorry to ask this of you. But it must be done."

Jaxer shook his head. "No. No."

"Don't worry," Ulieran said softly, his tone kind and loving. "You're strong. You'll be fine."

"That's not what I'm…" Jaxer took a deep breath. "No, Da. No."

"It'll be fine," Ulieran said. "Your mother saw it."

Grim, where he stood in front of Ulieran, smiled at Cary again. Showing off his pointed teeth. "You see, witch. You can't stop this. It's been fated. Your realm will be mine. And you will die."

Ulieran straightened, letting his wings spread behind Grim. Cary braced herself for the attack. She'd stop this. Somehow, she'd stop this.

Ulieran reached forward.

And tore Grim's head off without a word.

Blood sprayed across the cobbled floor, green blood that looked shockingly black in the flickering torchlight. Grim's body remained standing for several, horrifying, silent moments before it dropped to one side, landing with a heavy thud that made Cary want to gag.

Ah.

His flaming purple sword clattered to the stones, a foot in front of his body, continuing to glow though its owner was just a husk.

Ulieran tossed Grim's head aside as if discarding an old apple core, not paying attention to where it landed. He didn't even glance at Grim's body. He held Jaxer's gaze the entire time. And his expression was gentle. Loving even. As green-black blood dripped off his talons and over his chest.

Cary was so shocked, so utterly stunned, she couldn't even blink for long moments. The whole thing had happened so fast her brain couldn't catch up.

When words did emerge, they came from Eriana first. And she sounded...matter-of-fact and calm.

"Why?" she asked.

"Grim wasn't a good leader," he said. "He was too selfish. There are others who will do better."

Eriana nodded, as if she understood.

Cary didn't understand. "I don't understand," she said, some of her shock abating enough she could form the words.

If she didn't look at Grim's headless body, ignored the lump in the shadows that was his head, and kept her focus up—on Ulieran—she could almost think. Though there was still a part of her mind that was rocking and jabbering nonsensically in a corner of her brain.

"What don't you understand, Protector?" Ulieran asked, kindly.

The kindness, the patient tone of voice against the swift and sudden violence he'd just committed, was downright disconcerting. "What you're doing, Ulieran," she said, giving in to her own confusion. "Why go along with a battle over Faery and then kill the leader of that upris- ing? Why decide to destroy Faery and yet kill the person who'd helped you get to this point?"

"He had nothing to do with me and my decision," Ulieran said, then shrugged. "Well, he did provide a diversion. Tatiana and Oberon have been too preoccupied with his treason to focus on me. And his efforts signaled that the time was right. I suppose he was useful in that." He spread his hands wide. "But this was always coming. My love saw it. She saw that we would be together again. But Faery, as it is, would end."

Cary didn't miss the "as it is" part of that sentence, but she didn't want to draw too much attention to it yet. In case Ulieran had just misspoken. But if the "as it is" came directly from Grenelle, there was still a chance for this to end without invasion and destruction.

Visions always had loopholes.

"You told us Grenelle didn't see you in her vision," Cary said instead.

Ulieran spread his hands. "A small omission. Jaxer wasn't ready to hear yet. It is time now, though." He gave Jaxer a look so full of love it actually hurt Cary's heart to see. "I will miss you, my son. You and Grenelle were the best things to ever happen to me in my long long life. And I love you."

"Please don't do this," Jaxer said. "Don't. We can find another way to break your curse, to release you from this…"

Ulieran closed his eyes. His wings, still spread to their full span, trembled faintly.

Jaxer lunged toward him again, but Cary held him back. And when his struggling grew difficult for her to control, Deacon grabbed him.

"Let me go, damn it." He cursed and swung back at Deacon.

Both men were supernaturally strong, and Jaxer was desperate. His swing connected with Deacon's jaw, rocking his head backward.

"Jaxer," Cary snapped. "Stop that."

"We can't let him—" He spun to face her, snarling. But he stopped his tirade abruptly and his eyes widened.

Cary was almost afraid to look. She turned back to face Ulieran slowly, even as she felt a strange push against her Protector shields, strong enough she was forced back a step before she could stop herself.

That by itself should have warned her. And yet, she was still shocked, stunned.

Once again brought to silence in awed horror.

Behind Ulieran a dark shadow loomed large, growing and twisting like a living thing. Inside the darkness, she swore she saw flashes of purple light, sparking and then being subsumed by the shadows. There was something thick about the blackness. Solid. A presence. And Cary found she had to squint against light that wasn't there even to look at the stygian cloud. It wasn't glowing. It wasn't bright. And yet she had to narrow her eyes as if against a glare.

The shadow grew taller, and spread wider behind Ulieran until it blocked out all of the corridor behind him.

Another push against her shields forced her back two steps. She braced against the shove. Deacon released his hold on Jaxer to steady her. She started to protest, afraid Jaxer would try to dodge around her now and go to his father. But he didn't move. He stood in the same shocked stupor that had overwhelmed her.

Tom's voice whispered through the hall, bouncing off the blackness in a strangely muted echo.

"The Lachlinain."

3 8

The shadow spun and twisted faster, its movements speeding Cary's pulse. She stared at the curse that would destroy Faery, the curse that had thrown her on her ass the last time she'd gotten close to it. She hadn't seen it that time. She wasn't sure what she'd expected to see when she finally—if she finally—got a look at it.

But it looked exactly like a Faery-destroying curse should look. Like a black hole, sucking in all light and matter around it. Except this wasn't just devouring the light.

Cary could actually feel the magic ebbing past her, toward the shadow, a stream of power flowing in a low stream toward the waterfall of darkness. The curse *feeding* on the magic. And as it fed, the shadow grew, the movement of its twisting darkness sped, tightened into tendrils of black.

Those tendrils began to wrap around Ulieran.

"No," she murmured and took a step toward him.

She wasn't sure what she was thinking, what drove her to move toward the guardian—maybe to protect him from the shadow winding around him. She wasn't really even thinking. The move to get to him, to help, to save was all instinctive, and she couldn't have credited any conscious thought to the action.

Because if she'd been *thinking*, she would have remembered that getting too close to the Lachlinain—in her case—was a very bad idea.

The backlash slammed against her and she flew backward, careening into Deacon and the leprechauns, all of them crashing against the hard floor in a heap.

"Fecking hell," Sean muttered. "What the feck was that?"

Cary scrambled to her feet, ignoring the pain in her hip to put herself between Jaxer and Eriana and the danger again. They were the only ones still standing and she'd left them vulnerable when she'd been tossed on her ass.

Stupid mistake.

"You okay?" Deacon asked.

He was at her back so fast she startled—though why, she wasn't sure. He moved at shifter speeds. Of course, he joined her again that fast.

"Fine. Feeling stupid for jumping forward is all." She glanced back at the leprechauns. "Everyone okay?"

"Grand," Tom said. He scowled at Ulieran and the Lachlinain. "We're all banjaxed. But otherwise, we're fecking grand."

The tendrils were wrapping tighter around Ulieran, poking into him now, arrowing through his body as well as around it. He dropped his head back on his shoulders, mouth open, and the shadows dove inside.

"No!" Jaxer yelled. "Da, stop!"

Eriana grabbed Jaxer this time, holding him back as he tried to lunge toward his father again. There were tears streaming down her cheeks, but her expression was impassive, almost emotionless.

Ulieran showed no signs of having heard Jaxer. His arms and wings were spread out to the side, his legs braced, as he absorbed the shadow, the darkness winding around and through him, consuming him.

Helplessness swamped Cary. What did she do now? What could she do? She couldn't reach Ulieran to stop what was happening. She couldn't get near enough to protect him, even from himself. She wasn't even sure she could have protected him since he was doing this willingly. And that was probably the worst feeling of all

"What do we do?" she asked aloud, panic embarrassingly obvious in her voice. "How do we stop this?"

Her heart pounded with adrenaline, fear coursing through her. She couldn't think. She needed to think, damn it. What could they do? How did they stop the Lachlinain from eating all the magic?

The shadows absorbed fully into Ulieran, and he convulsed, his wings sweeping close around him. His upper body tossed to one side, then the other, while his feet stayed firmly planted, as if he couldn't move them. For the first time, Ulieran made a sound. He screamed. The deep, loud echo of his pain pierced Cary's skull. She slapped her hands over her ears, and still the sound bit into her, burying deep with the horror of what she was watching.

A purple glow flared briefly around Ulieran, lighting him up like the sword Grim had carried. He dropped his head, opened his eyes, and looked at Jaxer.

For one brief moment, the man who was her mentor's father looked back at them.

Then the blackness sucked all the light back in, swamping the man, consuming him completely.

Leaving behind a huge, black shape with wings and the vague outline of Ulieran. But nothing of the man remained. Even his head was faceless, not so much as a glow where eyes or a mouth should be. A solid blackness against the dark corridor behind him.

She could only see him because of the way other light bent around him. If there'd been no torchlight in the hall, she wasn't sure she'd have been able to spot the new monster at all. It really was like looking at a black hole, except this one repelled her.

What it did soak in, however, was the magic surrounding them. The flow Cary had felt earlier was intensifying. As the stream grew, the power rushing faster toward the black hole of the curse, she started to see it. Wisps of magic, a sparkling white light, running in rivulets toward the Lachlinain. Streams that were growing into rivers.

The leprechauns gasped. Sean cursed roundly. Jaxer dropped to his knees. Eriana murmured a prayer to Danu.

"He's doing it," Tom said. "He's taking in all the magic. He's going to destroy the place."

Cary watched the magic whipping past her legs. A torrent now, a current buffeting against her, threatening to push her over.

Some of that rushing power hit her legs and instead of washing past, soaked into her. Not much. Only a little. But she felt the tingles along her nerves as she took in little sips of the rushing whitewater river of power. It didn't hurt. It wasn't overwhelming her. Yet. Her Protector shield held most of the magic at bay.

She looked up suddenly, staring into the darkness that had been Ulieran.

"It also eats magic," she murmured.

The being's wings flittered.

"I can stop it if…" She swallowed. "I can starve it." She met Deacon's gaze. "If I take the magic in first. I can starve it."

"What? No."

Jaxer leapt to his feet. "That will kill you. And still destroy Faery."

"I don't intend to keep what I pull in," she said. "I'll release it back once the curse is starved."

"This will not work," Jaxer said.

"Not while my Protector shields are still up," she said.

He held her gaze and shook his head. "No. No. You can't. Cary. There's too much magic."

"You will die long before you can starve that," Eriana said. "Your human body will not be able to take in enough. Faery is too big."

Damn it. "Is there a way to isolate the cursed hall from the rest of Faery. Even temporarily? Keep the magic here cut off from everything else. I don't need long. Just long enough to starve the curse. If there's only so much magic for either of us to absorb, I can do this."

"Can that be done?" Deacon asked.

Jaxer and Eriana exchanged a look. "Tatiana and Oberon could do it," Eriana said.

"So long as Tatiana wants to save Faery and hasn't been part of the conspiracy to end it," Jaxer said.

"If she has been," Eriana said, "then we're all dead anyway."

"Worth a shot," Cary said. She motioned Tom closer. "I need you all to get to Tatiana. I'm sorry I'm sending you into a battle. Try not to get killed. I need you to tell her to cut this place off, the magic off, from the rest of the realm. Isolate us here as long as possible. A bubble with no magic in or out."

Tom looked at the growing blackness. The being's outlined shape had nearly doubled in size now. "Not much time," he muttered. "Not much chance of this working."

"No," Cary said. "But it's a chance. And if it doesn't work, you and the others need to be somewhere you can get out. Get into the human realm before this one dies."

Tom met her gaze. "This is pure madness. You know that right?"

She nodded. "Yeah. I'm open to other suggestions."

He snorted. "I've got nothing for ye but to offer a flagon of whiskey and toast to the end of the world."

"Let's try my way first." She shrugged. "If we're not dead at the end of this, one way or another, then we can do your thing. I'll probably need the whiskey at that stage anyway."

Tom's charming grin ticked up the corners of his mouth, despite the fear darkening his green eyes. "I've always liked you, Cary. Even when we were on opposite sides of a line."

"I feel the same, Tom. Look after yourself. Try not to get killed."

"Same," he said bluntly. "Come on lads," he said to the other leprechauns. "We've got to reach that bleeding English queen and talk some sense into her."

Grainne rushed forward and gave Cary a quick, surprisingly strong hug. "Look after yerself, love." Then she hurried off after Tom, not looking back.

Tom tipped an invisible hat to Cary, flashing a quick, fleeting smile. And then the leprechauns disappeared through a crack in the air that Cary couldn't see. Sneaky bastards.

She pressed a hand to her stomach, hoping they'd be okay. She looked back at the black hole of the Ulieran-shaped Lachlinain.

No matter how this ended.

3 9

She watched the monster grow as the slow, creeping dread of what she needed to do swamped her.

"It goes against everything in me to not protest this," Deacon said, his gaze also on the monster.

"I know. But I need to. And I need your help."

He faced her. "If you don't do this, everything ends and dies."

She nodded. "It might still. This might not work."

He took her face in his hands and kissed her, hard. "I love you. If we die here, we die together. Trying to save the world."

"Worse ways to go."

He snorted. "I'd have preferred in our old age, after spending a day watching our grandkids play."

She sighed and held his wrists. "Me too."

Later, she was sure she'd be surprised by the feeling of nostalgia that overwhelmed her then, that sense of possibilities lost. She'd be even more surprised at how much the thought of kids and grandkids appealed to her, so long as she had that family with Deacon. If they survived, she'd have some things to think about.

The echo of the banshee's cry sounded loud in her mind.

She straightened away from Deacon. "How will we know if the

leprechauns have convinced Tatiana to cut us off from the rest of the realm?" she asked Jaxer, still staring up at Deacon.

"I'll feel it," he said, his voice quiet. "But it won't matter. Cary, this can't work. Look at him."

She turned to see that the shape that had been Ulieran had grown even larger.

"It's too much. Even if Tatiana stops the flow now. There's too much here. It's too late. We're all dead."

"What kind of mentor are you?" she snapped. "You want to save your father? Get your head out of your ass and help me."

His head jerked back as if she'd physically slapped him. He scowled at her. "What makes you think he can be saved now?"

"If I starve the curse, it'll die. He'll no longer be the curse guardian. He can be free."

"To kill himself," Jaxer snarled. "If the death of the curse doesn't take him with it."

"Eriana's a healer. She can save him. We just have to get the fucking curse out of him." She leaned forward, putting her face in Jaxer's. "I can do that. I can starve the fucker out."

Jaxer met her gaze. "Not while you're protecting us. Not while your Protector shields are up."

She straightened. "Exactly."

She glanced back at the growing curse. The sparkles of white magic were rushing past in huge swaths now, so fast Cary could feel the heat of it building. The glow brightened the hall, making the light-less black that had been Ulieran even more stark in comparison.

Letting them out of her protection went against her instincts as much as letting her risk death went against Deacon's. She knew what she had to do, but taking those steps back, leaving the others vulnerably…

She let out a long breath. "Can you all keep it occupied? Distracted? It's going to fight back. I'll need time."

"You focus," Deacon said. "We'll handle Ulieran."

She cupped his cheek. "I love you."

He kissed her palm, then unpinned the brooch the Nags had given him and let it fall to the stone floor. He spun to face the curse as his leopard.

Cary took four steps back from the others. Because she could feel so much magic, she actually felt her shields abruptly end. And the power of Faery rushing past slammed into her like a stone wall. She dropped to her hands and knees, head bowed as the magic overwhelmed her.

"It's done," Eriana shouted. "Tatiana has cut us off from the rest of Faery."

Cary couldn't tell the difference. The flood of magic swamped her, leaving her awash in a hurricane. At first, the power beat on her, pummeling her nerves, her bones and body. The tingling along her skin thick and pervasive, a single block of pain. Then the magic started to soak into her skin.

She closed her eyes, forcing herself to focus, to see herself pulling in the power. Not just passively absorbing it, but sucking it up, eating it, swallowing it, taking it all in. She jerked her head back as that magic filled her, building and growing.

Room. She needed more room for it. More spaces for it to fill.

She forced herself up onto her knees. Magic rushed into her, harder and faster. She grunted and got one foot under her, slowly pushing up, standing through sheer will. She spread her arms wide and braced as she opened more, took it in. Took it all in.

Distantly she heard fighting, the hiss and roar of Deacon's leopard. A sound like a sword clashing against a sword. She blinked her eyes open.

Jaxer held Grim's dropped sword, and he was wielding it like he knew what he was doing, against a sword of blackness held by the Lachlinain. The monster swung his huge weapon in long, sweeping arcs that Jaxer deflected and countered. The size difference would have been comical if it weren't so terrifying.

On the other side of the curse monster, Deacon leapt at the darkness, knocking the huge being to one side long enough for Jaxer to slash across its chest. The monster swung toward Deacon. But Deacon was already several yards away, crouched low and ready to leap again.

Eriana stood to one side of the room, twisting her hands in a pattern that reminded Cary vaguely of something Angie would do. A ball of purple light formed in the center of her hand and she tossed it on the ground at the monster's feet.

Cary wanted to shout out, to tell her to stop feeding the beast with more magic. But then she saw what Eriana's spell had conjured. A multitude of Jaxers, all holding flaming swords. It was glamour, still magic, but the illusion distracted and confused the creature. It spun in a circle, swinging its sword at all the different enemies who didn't really exist. The illusion gave the real Jaxer an opening and he lunged in, sword raised, running the being through the chest.

The monster roared. Cary realized it was the first sounds she'd heard from the thing.

And then power slammed into her again, hard. Rushing from the curse beast now, taking up residence in a less besieged body—hers.

She screamed and braced against the torrent. Pulling it in, willing herself not to resist, not to fight or release the magic. Soak it up. Take it all.

She heard her name shouted over the noise in her head. She couldn't open her eyes anymore though, to see who was calling to her. She was a sponge, bloating and filling. She had to take it all. Every last drop.

Another sound, like a scream and a roar rolled into one.

Just barely, she heard someone shout, "It's working!"

Her body felt like it would break apart, but she kept taking in more. More. More. All of it.

Every. Last. Drop. Hers.

She knew her mouth was open, a part of her aware she was still screaming, but she couldn't hear her own voice, couldn't hear anything anymore over the rush of power, the storm of magic. Her cells bubbled with it. Her skin grew tight. Her skull ached. She couldn't breathe but that no longer seemed relevant.

More.

All of it.

She kept taking it in, kept pulling at the magic, willing it into her, willing her body to contain it.

The flood of power slowed, and still she focused on sucking up the last of it. None could be left behind. None could be ignored. She would have it all. There would be nothing left.

Then she felt it, around the fullness, the tightness about to burst apart, she felt the echo of denial, the roar of resistance, the last, ringing shout of refusal to die. She didn't know who made that noise—her or the Lachlinain. But the feel of it choked her.

She held everything for one last second, one last moment. The magic broke parts of her, popping inside her like so much carbonation. She still held on.

One. Final. Second.

Before she let it all go, the release so fast, she split apart, split open. She screamed again, the sound lost in all the noise of magic and power.

Yet still, over all of it, she heard the banshee's shriek.

4 0

---

eacon stared up at the curse beast, his pulse pounding hard through his veins. He was acutely aware of his mate's vulnerability. That awareness only sharpened as he watched the dark shadow being hold out its hand and a long shadow blade grow from its palm. Despite the weapon's ephemeral appearance, Deacon had a feeling it would cut as quickly as steel.

Jaxer, standing beside him, swept up Grim's dropped sword. He didn't say a word as they stared at the being that had been his father. He held the sword in a solid one-handed grip, steady and low and waiting. Deacon had seen Jaxer with sword in hand before, a long time ago. He knew the faery could use the weapon.

The question was, would he use it against the beast?

"Aim for his heart," Eriana murmured. "It will be the area where the Fae and the Shadow are most vulnerable to injury."

She carefully didn't call the creature by Ulieran's name. The knowledge still hung in the air between them all. Even when the creature swung the sword over its massive head and swept the blade down in an arc designed to cut all three of them in half.

Jumping aside easily, Deacon repositioned himself to one side of the beast while Jaxer moved to the other, dividing the creature's attention. Eriana, weaponless as she was, moved farther back. She glanced between Cary and the creature, frowning fiercely, her lips pursed. Deacon couldn't be certain what she was thinking, but given her only weapon at that moment was magic, and there were two people in the room who soaked up magic, he imagined that complicated anything the healer wanted to do in this fight.

He couldn't concern himself with that, though. His full focus had to be on keeping the curse beast distracted. From the corner of his eyes, if he didn't look at it directly, the white hot lines of power were visible to him, and he could see them flowing into the beast, but also away from it, toward Cary.

He didn't dare look at her. Not now. Not in this form. Not when she was in danger. But even knowing she was doing something so dangerous nearly drove him mad.

He took out that fear and anger on the curse beast, charging in, swiping at its legs, testing its speed and skill. The creature was fast. Not as fast as he was, but fast enough to be troublesome.

Despite the look of shadows, its body was solid enough. He got a good hit across the beast's calf, leaving a gash behind. But to his frustration, the wound sealed immediately, the darkness closing over it so thoroughly there wasn't even time for it to bleed.

Not that Deacon had even scented blood.

Eriana had said to aim for the heart. He wasn't going to take the monster down by belting its legs. The move did throw the creature off center as it swung around to slice at him. He leapt out of range, using his speed to keep the monster distracted as Jaxer drove in with the sword, also taking a swipe at the creature's leg. Grim's glowing purple sword plunged into the shadows, and emerged covered in green blood. But the wound once against closed instantly.

The creature spun to face Jaxer. Deacon lunged at it, coming in low, pulling its attention. The beast swung its shadow sword, the blade whispering over the top of Deacon's head as he crouched, then he jumped beyond the beast's reach.

Jaxer dove forward, plunging his sword into the beast's leg again. It turned, its sword whistling toward Jaxer's chest. The faery dropped low and rolled away, coming to his feet again with a battle grace he rarely showed.

Using his speed, Deacon feinted and dove, swiped and jumped, trying to keep the creature occupied while Jaxer continued to take hits at the beast's legs and arms. But still, they were fighting a being that had been his father. And Jaxer was pulling his punches.

Deacon couldn't blame the faery. But he wanted to curse at him to stop taking it easy on the beast. Fortunately for both of them, Deacon couldn't speak in this form.

Eriana, on the other hand, had no such limitations. "You're too restrained, Jaxer. The heart, damn it. Aim for the heart."

The beast's sword changed direction mid-swing to swipe at the healer. She grunted and dove away, more awkwardly than Deacon would have expected given she was Fae. The sword missed her by inches. She twirled back up to her feet easily enough, dusting off her tunic and curses in a Fae language Deacon hadn't heard in decades. When the beast took a step toward the healer, Jaxer lunged in again, pulling his sword across the beast's lower back.

The move brought the beast's attention back to him, and the shadow sword clipped over Jaxer's hurried crouch, barely missing him.

Deacon jumped forward again, landing high on the beast's shoulders, between its wings and clamping his powerful jaws onto the creature's neck. The monster tasted like nothing he'd encountered before. Darkness, and revenge, and so much magic. But not flesh and blood. Not even the stranger blood and flesh of a Fae.

While Deacon didn't make a habit of biting the Fae, it had come up before, and this was not what they tasted like. This was…beyond his experience, and he didn't have words to describe it. But the texture of the Lachlinain coated his tongue and mouth, making him gag.

He bit down harder, fighting his need to let go. The creature reached for him with its free hand. He resisted the pull at his nap, the scrambling fingers, thick as his legs, for as long as he could, keeping the beast off balance.

Jaxer lunged forward again, this time driving his sword into the creature's hip. The beast didn't make any sound, didn't appear to notice the wound. In fact, it had remained eerily silent throughout the fight.

Its fingers finally found purchase in Deacon's fur and jerked hard, tossing him aside like an irritating fly.

Deacon spun in the air and hit the ground on his feet, crouched low. The area he'd bitten, where he could swear he'd removed a chunk of whatever made up the being, was whole and undamaged by the time he'd landed.

Damn it. They weren't doing anything but irritating this thing.

From the corner of his eyes, he could see more magic flowing away from the beast now, toward Cary. The creature was still huge, but not as large as moments ago. This was working. They just had to keep it occupied, give Cary the time she needed.

He pulled in a deep breath, then leapt at the thing's head again, high and straight over the top, swiping at the side of its face in passing. Another distraction so Jaxer could stab it again.

As his paws hit stone, he heard Cary scream. He was rushing toward her before his brain caught up with his instincts. Everything in him wanted to go to her, to help, to save, to protect. But that would distract her. And his job was to keep the beast distracted. That was how he helped her.

When she screamed again, he roared in denial.

He channeled his need to help her into his attacked on the monster. A frenzy of rushing, claws and teeth slashing at whatever bit of it he could reach. The creature's sword caught him once, slicing a line along his side that hurt like hell. The wound slowed him for a few seconds, and he felt something dangerously like poison seeping into his body through the opening. Some of the shadow creeping in.

To heal the wound and stop the poison, he shifted back to his human form, using his internal magic to change instantly. The shift healed his wound. He could still feel the taint in his blood, but when he shifted again, his body took care of that.

Poison could kill an average shifter. And Deacon had a feeling this particular poison worked fast given the speed it had seeped into his blood. But he was no average shifter. He didn't use the innate magic often. He hadn't worked with it or trained in its use. He refused to, much to his mother's frustration. But that magic was a part of him whether he liked it or not. It sped up his shifts.

And it healed his body more rapidly than the creature's poison could work.

Still, it was a danger they hadn't anticipated. He shifted to human once again, long enough to call, "Don't let that sword cut you. It puts some of the curse into your blood."

He was the leopard again before Jaxer could grunt his response.

He jumped high over the monster's head, taking another shot at the back of its skull. The creature backhanded him, sending him slamming hard against the stone wall, knocking the air from his lungs. He sucked in a breath, giving his body a split second to heal from the bone-breaking hit, before jumping back into the attack.

The creature swung its massive sword at Jaxer again. Eriana called out a warning. The faery dove aside, but the shadow blade cut close to his head. Deacon roared, Eriana screamed.

The creature turned its attention to the healer and reached for her.

"Eriana!" Jaxer swung to his feet and slashed his sword across the creature's arm, neatly severing its forearm. Still the monster didn't make a sound.

It swung its own sword once over its head and swept it across the space Jaxer had been standing. Fortunately, the faery moved almost as fast as a shifter.

Deacon took advantage of the opening and plunged in again. Even with only a single arm, the beast batted at them easily. But the loss of the limb distracted it. Threw it off balance.

And the magic continued to flow away from it in faster and faster waves.

Cary screamed again.

The sound pierced Deacon's skull. He turned toward his mate. She was braced against her own battle, surrounded by a light so bright he could barely see through it. Her head was back, her eyes closed, her arms flung out to the side.

In his head, he shouted her name. Aloud, he roared.

The light barreled into her, a storm of magic that tasted of sparks and heat, a bitter tint like rot just at the edges. And all of that poison poured into her. She seemed to glow from the inside, the incandescence filling her.

Because he couldn't help her, couldn't risk going to her, he spun and attacked the monster again. This time, he managed to knock the creature backward a few steps. It was smaller now. He was certain of it. The knowledge gave him a vicious sort of satisfaction and he ramped up his attack, taking the frenzy of his panic and fear out on the creature. He dove in, all claws and teeth and anger, tearing and biting. Leaving wounds now. Leaving holes.

He managed to knock the beast to the side, and this time, Jaxer went for the chest, slashing a deep wound. The creature didn't bleed, but the wound didn't seal shut this time.

From the corner of his eye, Deacon saw Eriana doing something with her hands and a moment later, a multitude of Jaxers circled the monster, an army of identical faeries with flaming purple swords. The monster spun, swinging at the new enemies circling him.

Jaxer leapt forward, stabbing his sword through the creature's chest.

Finally hitting it in the heart.

For the first time in the entire battle, the beast roared. The noise pierced Deacon's sensitive ears, but it was a sound he savored, snarling his satisfaction. He attacked again, ripping at the beast's wings, slashing through the delicately thin stretch of shadow beneath the line that would have been bone on Ulieran.

Cary screamed again. A sound so devastating, Deacon was brought to his knees, choking on loss.

"Cary!" Jaxer called out to her.

"Don't stop," Eriana called. "It's working! Look."

Deacon dragged his gaze from his mate. The creature was shrinking, the shadows hardening. The power rushed out of it, faster and faster, the white lights swarming from the beast toward Cary in a torrent of magic.

Deacon's vision went hazy, then, and blood lust swamped him. His enemy was wounded and he was ready to kill. He charged in, dimly aware of Jaxer at his side. As the faery continued to hack away at the beast, Deacon tore and ripped at every part of the shadow he could reach, snapping at that flesh that wasn't flesh, tearing it away.

The more they battered at it, the smaller the creature shrank. Until Deacon tasted blood. Not the strange taste of the creature, but actual blood.

Fae blood.

Jaxer swung the sword around in a wide arc and plunged it through the being's throat.

Blood sprayed across the floor behind the beast, the green blood of a highborn faery. The shadows tightened into tendrils of smoke, coalescing and shrinking. A sound like denial ripped through the hall, though it didn't come from a physical body anymore. Beneath the thrash of the blackness, Deacon could see flesh again, the dark skin of Ulieran showing through the twisting shadows.

Jaxer pulled his sword free and stabbed again, right through Ulieran's heart.

The sound of denial and resistance echoed so loud, Deacon had to crouch and cover his ears. He watched the remains of the shadow rise high over them, spinning fast, spitting out light, and shrinking down to a pinpoint. That point of darkness hovered in the air for what felt an eternity, refusing to fade, refusing to give in.

And then in a blinding flash, the darkness exploded outward.

Deacon closed his eyes against the glare, but still his vision danced with spots when he opened his eyes again.

He rose and spun, hunting the shadows. None of the darkness remained.

Then a sound broke through his body, ripped out his heart... His mate.

Her scream a devastation that tore his world apart.

41

Deacon swung toward Cary just as she released the magic she'd been gathering and the storm of that release flattened him. The power flew out from her, ripping through the hall, filling it with light, stealing the oxygen as it went. It flung Jaxer against the stones, the sword flying free from his grip. It tossed Eriana against the corridor wall, pinned against the corner where the wall met the floor.

Pressure like an ocean pressed Deacon into the stone floor, so much weight, he thought it might crush him. He couldn't breathe, couldn't move, as the magic battered him.

And then, as suddenly as it had barreled over him, the pressure lifted. Oxygen rushed back in. Everything opened up in one blinding wash. He could swear he felt Faery itself take a great, big, gulping breath.

The release was like a wash of warm, sweetly scented, fresh air blowing through the hall.

In its wake, everything fell silent and still.

Deacon blinked and looked around, realizing he was seeing the world through his human eyes. He glanced down at his hands where they pressed against the stone. The backlash of magic had forced the shift. Something that had never happened before.

But he didn't have time to question it. He rushed to his mate, dropping beside her fallen body.

She wasn't breathing. He pressed his fingers to her throat. No pulse.

"Jaxer! She's not breathing. Cary's not breathing." He turned toward the faery.

Jaxer was crouched over his father, cradling his father's head in his lap. The curse guardian was bleeding from so many wounds, he was soaked in his own blood. His wings were in tatters, his face ashen, his green eyes closed. The wounds in his neck and chest weren't healing.

"Eriana," Jaxer called. "You have to heal him. You have to save him."

Despite his wounds, Ulieran tried to shake his head.

"I can only save one," Eriana said. She stood between him and Jaxer, her gaze darting between them. "I can't save them both. I won't have time." She turned toward Jaxer, then back toward Deacon. She looked panicked in her inability to pick a patient.

Deacon pressed his mouth over Cary's trying to breathe life back into her. He started chest compressions, desperate to get his mate's heart pumping again. Damn them all. Fuck them all.

"Cary," he said. "Cary, don't leave me. Please. Don't leave me." He held her nose and breathed into her mouth again. Then went back to compressions.

"Jaxer," Eriana said. "This is your choice. This is the choice your mother saw."

"No," he shouted. "No."

Deacon breathed for Cary again. Then went back to chest compressions. In his head, he cursed and roared and denied. But he didn't say any of that out loud. He could no more demand Jaxer pick Cary over his own father, than Jaxer could demand Deacon pick Ulieran over Cary. Instead of arguing, Deacon focused on Cary, on restarting her heart. On breathing for her.

He willed life into her, willed her to stay with him. With each breath, he poured himself into her, with each measured pump of his hands on her chest, he demanded she live.

He blinked when a shadow fell over him. Eriana crouched next to Cary and motioned him away.

"Give me room," she snapped. "We've not much time."

She bent over Cary, her head bowed, her hands hovering over Cary's chest. A faint blue glow circled the faery's hands. She closed her eyes and set her hands against Cary's chest and forehead. The glow encompassed Cary's entire body.

Deacon sat back on his haunches to watch, his nerves stretched to breaking. He could barely breath for himself, but he willed air in and out of his lungs in an attempt to start his mate's breathing again, still trying to force life into her body by sheer willpower alone.

Inside, his leopard was raging in denial, and a slow, creeping sense of doom swamped him. He refused to see it, to acknowledge it. She would live. She had to live.

Jaxer stumbled onto his knees beside Deacon. Tears streaked the faery's cheeks, streaming down his face unnoticed as he watched Eriana work on Cary.

Silently, and without looking back to Ulieran's body, Deacon gripped Jaxer's hand. Holding tight. They didn't lock at each other. No words were spoken.

In the silence, Deacon's every sense was focused on his mate. He couldn't hear her heartbeat, her breathing, and the longer he was denied those sounds, the closer he moved toward madness. The closer he moved toward despair.

He couldn't judge time, but the moments ticked by. Too many moments. Too much time.

She was dead.

Gone.

The knowledge hit him like a battering ram. And he shattered inside, broke apart. Denial still raged through him, but the devastation of it left only bleak emptiness in its place.

His mate was gone.

Jaxer's grip tightened on his, though he was only vaguely aware of the gesture. His senses were shutting down, his own body consumed with grief so choking, so overwhelming, he curled forward into it and shut his eyes.

He wouldn't survive the loss. Couldn't survive it.

He'd follow her.

He had nowhere else to go.

And then, a sound like bells and glory and heaven itself echoed in the quiet hall. A single, gasping intake of breath.

Deacon snapped his eyes open. The sound of her heart beating. The second, deep indrawn breath. He scrambled forward, grabbing at her hand.

"Cary? Love. Talk to me." He brushed hair from her face, cupping her cheek in one hand. "Love. Can you speak?"

She blinked her eyes open and looked up at him. And Deacon had never seen anything more glorious in his life.

"Ouch," she murmured, her voice harsh and rough.

Then her eyes fluttered shut and she passed out.

4 2

ary kept her eyes closed for a long moment as awareness rose. She could feel a mattress under her, soft and familiar. She smelled Deacon. And her dogs. And something green and floral. Faint light glowed against her eye lids. Her body ached, just *ached* every-where. But it was the dull ache of stiff muscles. Bearable. Not too bad.

Not as bad as…

She snapped her eyes open.

"What the hell happened?" she said. Her voice croaked out and she had to swallow to wet her dry throat.

A straw against her lips startled her.

"Drink," Deacon said, sitting on the bed beside her.

She sipped at the gloriously cold water, sighing. Then she smiled up at him. "Hey. We're alive."

He made a face as he set the water bottle aside, and grunted some-thing that wasn't words but conveyed a great deal of feeling.

"Aren't we?" she asked, glancing around.

They did seem to be in her bedroom. The curtains were closed but the light level indicated it was the middle of the day. Deacon felt alive, warm and strong, his wonderfully masculine scent wrapping around her like a big hug. He had circles under his eyes, and a furrow between his brows that seemed deeper than usual. There was a paleness to his tan skin, and a few creases around his mouth from the tightness of his jaw.

If they were dead, would he look so exhausted?

Buck and Pickles were sitting on either side of her bedroom door—their guard positions. Fred was curled up at the foot of her bed. He crawled forward when she noticed him and snuggled against her side, laying his head on her stomach to stare up at her with his big brown eyes. He wasn't technically allowed on the bed, but she couldn't bring herself to shoo him off. Instead, she hugged him closer, burying her fingers in his fur.

He felt alive. She felt alive. Surprisingly.

When Deacon leaned over and pressed a kiss into her temple, his heat seeping into her, along with his wonderful smell. She pulled in a deep breath, letting his solid presence settle nerves that felt achy and tired.

"We're alive," he said, his voice very deep. "But you weren't for a few minutes, and I haven't recovered from that yet."

"What happened?" she asked again, quietly.

"You starved the Lachlinain," he said.

"It's…gone?"

"According to Tatiana, yes."

"Ulieran?"

Deacon pulled in a deep breath, his mouth tightening. He shook his head.

She felt a tear leak over her cheek. "How's Jaxer doing?"

"Better now that you're awake," her mentor said from the doorway.

She smiled at him, though she could still feel the tears dripping across her temple. "I'm so glad you survived."

"You scared more years off my immortal life than any other protégée I've ever had, Cary," he said.

She snorted. "I seem to be good at that." With Deacon's help, she sat up against her hard wood headboard. Deacon propped some pillows behind her and she leaned into them gratefully.

"How do you feel?" Jaxer asked, coming to sit on the bed, opposite Deacon.

Her dogs didn't object, which was interesting. And Fred scooted to a position midway between her and Jaxer so they could both pet him. The fact that Jaxer did run his fingers through the dog's fur without thought was…new.

She also noticed Deacon didn't growl at Jaxer. Or object to him sitting on her bed. Deacon didn't even scowl.

Wow. They must have really been scared.

"I feel pretty achy," she answered Jaxer, "but not so bad, all things considered. How did Faery fare?" She tried to make the question light and smile at her own alliteration, but she didn't have it in her after hearing about Ulieran. She wanted to hug Jaxer, offer condolences, but none of that felt enough. Or quit right for the moment. He was holding his distance, not leaning in for a kiss or even touching her. She couldn't read him at that moment, either. Couldn't tell if he'd want her sympathies.

After all, her plan had killed his father.

"It's still standing," Jaxer said. "And if you're up to some visitors, there are…people here who'd like to see you."

"First, how long have I been out?"

"About ten days," Deacon said. "And we were in Faery for about a month."

"Geezuz. My mom and dad?"

"Angie kept them distracted for the time we were in Faery. They're in New York right now, with your sister. When your mom called, I told her you got sick after our 'vacation' and couldn't talk. She wasn't very happy with that excuse. But once I promised her I'd fly you to New York as soon as possible, she got very chatty and happy."

"You talked to my mom?" They hadn't met yet. Cary had been avoiding it. And since her parents lived a three-hour drive away on the coast, it wasn't as hard as it might sound. They knew Deacon existed, but none of her family had met him yet.

Looked like that was all about to change.

"You told her you'd fly me to New York?"

"I promised her," Deacon said, with feeling. "As soon as the Nags approve, and you're recovered, we're going. I'm not going to break my first promise to your mother no matter what happens."

She leaned in to kiss him. "Where is Angie?"

"Angie, Marianne, and Lucy will be here soon," Jaxer said. "I let them know you'd woken up before coming in. They've been worried, and have been here off and on when they could manage it around their work."

"Marianne is back in town?"

"Has been for a few weeks," Deacon said. "Remember, we were gone for a while. And you've been unconscious for a week and a half."

She groaned. "I hate Faery."

"You might want to keep that quiet over the next few minutes," Jaxer said, though he chuckled.

She closed her eyes and let out a breath. "Who's waiting?"

"You ready for them?"

"Almost." She looked at Jaxer. "First, how are Tom and the other leprechauns? Did any of them...?" She couldn't finish the sentence, just in case.

"They're all back home in Ireland. I imagine they've been drunk on whiskey since returning."

Relief made her shoulders sag. "I owe Tom a few drinks. Wonder if I should wait for him to sober up first?"

Jaxer smiled, but the expression looked forced. "The songs will be better if you jump in while they're still drunk." He made a face. "Don't ask them about the dragon, though."

"What happened with the dragon?" She sat up a little straighter.

"Nothing to them directly. Apparently, she was full by the time they got there."

"Ew."

Jaxer gave her an I-told-you-not-to-ask look.

She stared at her closet, trying not to think about what the dragon had filled up on.

The closet door was open and clothes spilling out onto the floor. She glanced around her room. Random stuff was piled on her dresser haphazardly. The side table next to her bed had the water bottle, a few empty mugs, and a crumb-covered plate stacked on it. The chair in the corner held her leather jacket, the cloak the Nags had given Deacon, her jeans, and a dog toy. There were shoes kicked into another corner. A dog bone in the middle of the floor between her bed and the door. And dog hair on her blankets.

Visitors about to descend on her, and her bedroom was a mess. Lovely.

"Okay. I'm done stalling. Bring them in." She gave mental permission for her visitors to find her house. Whoever *they* were.

But she could guess.

When the newcomers materialized in her room, she sighed. She'd guessed right.

Tatiana materialized at the foot of her bed, looking regal, but decidedly more solid and *viewable* than she had when Cary first saw her. She was as stunningly gorgeous as Cary remembered, only Cary could actually make out why now. Long long pale hair, straight as a veil down her back and plated with colorful, jewel-colored flowers. A halo of flowers covered her head too, though the flowers were in colors not normally found in nature. Her pale skin blended in with her hair, but she had slightly darker eyebrows and her eyes were an electric green which kept her from looking like a ghost.

Cary suppressed a shiver.

Tatiana was still dressed in a gauzy, shadowy dress of swirling dark colors. But the golden scepter she held was now a solid, glittering thing that didn't fade in and out of existence. She still glowed, a faintly purple light circling her, but the glow didn't blind.

Danu, looking much earthier than Tatiana, materialized by the window. She appeared as a human woman this time, complete with curly red hair hanging down her back, pale freckled skin, and a dark green velvet dress that hugged a lovely, curvy figure. If not for the golden diadem buried in the red curls and the white glowing aura that surrounded her, she'd have looked like a pretty ordinary human woman.

A lot more ordinary-human in appearance than Tatiana had bothered with.

Somewhat to Cary's surprise, Eriana tapped at her bedroom door moments after the queens had appeared.

"May I join you?" She waited just outside the doorway, as if uncertain of her welcome.

Cary frowned a little. She hadn't given Eriana permission to find her home. To Jaxer, she mouthed, "How?" And nodded to the healer.

"The Nags," he murmured back, thankfully understanding her question.

Ah. Well, if her bosses wanted someone to find her place, she supposed they could arrange that since they had arranged the glamour to begin with. Later, she'd ask them why.

For now, Cary waved Eriana into the room. The dogs didn't even glance at her. Pickle's full attention was on Tatiana. Buck's attention was on both queens. Fred was asleep.

"What are you doing here?" Cary asked Eriana. She glanced between the healer and Jaxer, her eyes narrowed.

"She's been helping you heal," Jaxer said.

And that answered the question of why the Nags would let Eriana find Cary's house.

"You would have required a lot longer healing sleep if she hadn't helped," Jaxer continued. "You did some serious damage to yourself with that stunt you pulled."

"Hey." She sat up a little straighter. "I saved Faery with that little stunt." She looked to the two queens, suddenly a little uncertain. "I did *save* Faery, didn't I? I mean, I didn't die for nothing, right?"

Danu's smile was gentle and kind. And maybe even a little mischievous as she flicked at glance at Tatiana. "You not only saved Faery, Protector," she said, meeting Cary's gaze. "You renewed it."

Cary pursed her lips. She blinked a few times. Glanced between the two queens. Frowned. "Yeah, that's going to require a lot more explaining."

"The magic you pulled in and released?" Jaxer said.

"I remember it." She scowled at him. Those last moments were etched in her memory. Especially the pain part. She'd have preferred that memory not be quite so clear.

"Filtering it through you—and the Lachlinain—and then releasing it out into the greater realm… It was like opening a window and trading out stale air for clean," Jaxer said. He glanced at the queens.

Tatiana, though she didn't smile, said, "It worked better than even having new magic brought in by the birth of a new Fae. And the effects have spread throughout the realms."

"All areas of Faery felt the renewal," Danu said. "The rot creeping through our worlds has been…pushed back."

"But not fixed completely," Cary said. Danu's phrasing was too careful.

"No," she agreed, her gaze again moving to Tatiana.

Tatiana didn't so much wince as flicker, like her solidity wavered. "It has helped our realm. Even if you didn't intend it. But it isn't a permanent answer. We can't ask you to attempt it every few years."

"No," Cary and Deacon said at the exact same time.

"No, you can't," Cary said firmly. "Mostly because dying sucks and I don't want to do that again, thank you very much." She raised a hand when Danu opened her mouth. "At least not until I'm an old old lady." If she managed to make it that long. Which, given her job, was certainly not looking good.

As if thinking of her job called them, her bosses materialized into the room, appearing near the dogs. To Cary's utter amazement. Pickles and Buck both shifted positions just slightly so that they were sitting in front of the Nags. Guarding them. Fred looked up. Barked once in greeting. Then laid his head back down and closed his eyes.

"She has done what was needed of her," Liruk said. "But she is not here to rescue the realm. She should not even be asked."

Cary narrowed her eyes at all of the Fae. "Is that what this is? You're hear to ask me to…what, die on a regular basis to renew Faery? Yeah, no, that's not happening."

"No, it is not," Deacon agreed, a growl in his voice.

"Not die," Danu said. "Such sacrifice would not be necessary every time."

"No," Cary said, pointing at both queens. "I'm not doing that again."

"You destroyed the Lachlinain," Tatiana said. "That should not have been possible."

"Cary does impossible things all the time," Jaxer said, sounding annoyed.

She glared at him. He glared back. That made her grin. He rolled his eyes.

"Our Protector is not required to do more for Faery," Wisat said.

"And we will not ask it of her," Liruk said. "No one will."

Liruk sounded firm. And fierce.

The tone made Cary do a double take at her. Liruk gave her one of the kindest and most approving looks she'd ever given Cary.

Well, that couldn't be good.

Damn, her dying must have really upset her bosses if Liruk was coming to her defense. The cynical part of her wondered if they'd been upset because they cared, or because it meant they'd lost a Protector and would have to start over with someone new.

Because she was still tired and achy, she chose to believe they cared.

"We all know Faery cannot continue on as it has been," Danu said. "The rot isn't gone. Just pushed backed. More is required, or we will simply find ourselves here again in another century or two."

"Well, I'll be well and truly dead at that stage, so I don't care what you people do," Cary said.

"But your children will be alive," Tatiana pointed out. "Your grand-children."

Since Cary still had some thinking to do on that topic, and since no one was even sure if she and Deacon would be able to conceive, she chose not to rise to that bait. "I'm sure you all are smart enough to think of a solution that doesn't involve me dying regularly sometime in the next two centuries. Plenty of time to mull over an answer."

Danu and Tatiana exchanged a look.

Cary knew for certain she wasn't going to like what they said next.

Except this time, she was wrong.

"We may have already come to a solution," Tatiana said.

"Though others in the realms will not approve," Danu said, sounding indifferent to that fact.

"What?" Cary said, eyes narrowed.

"We will make Protectors," Danu said.

"What?" Cary said again.

"We will expand the work that the Fae here have been doing," Tatiana said. "At least into our realms." She faced the Nags. "You are prepared to help us?"

The question might have almost been an order, but Tatiana changed her tone at the last moment.

Liruk still narrowed her eyes at the queen. "It will require some discussions," she said.

"And a council meeting," Wisat added.

"But…" Liruk and Wisat exchanged a look before Liruk finished. "But if the council approves, it could be arranged."

"The movement of magic through Protectors has been helping Faery for two centuries now," Danu said. "More of that movement can only be good for all the realms. Expanding into Ireland. And England. It will be something."

"And you all would have Protectors then?" Cary considered that. She nodded. "I approve." She made a face. "Not that my opinion matters on this. But I figure more Protectors in my world is better than fewer."

"Indeed," Danu said.

"Is that why you all came to visit?" Cary asked, glancing around the room. "Just to tell me you had things to discuss amongst yourselves?"

Wisat smiled. "We came to ensure you were feeling better," he said.

"And ensure they—" Liruk flicked a glance at the queens, "—didn't get the wrong idea about your participation in Faery business."

That was sweet of them. And really unexpected. "Thanks, guys."

"Are you feeling better, Protector?" Wisat asked.

"Just a little sore. Considering what happened, I'll call that much better." She glanced at Eriana. "I didn't do any permanent damage, did I?"

"Nothing that couldn't be healed, no," Eriana said. She was quiet, her demeanor subdued. But she smiled at Cary when she answered.

Cary took a closer look at the healer. She'd returned to her more human look, though now her hair was cut really really short, in that adorable pixie look that only women with the right bone structure seemed able to make look both cute and sexy all at once. Apparently, Eriana had the right bone structure. Or she'd glamoured herself up the right bone structure.

Jaxer, too, was back to his usual look. Gorgeous, maybe a little too gorgeous, but not that overwhelming Fae beauty both he and Eriana had sported in Danu's realm and beyond.

Cary decided she liked these looks on the two faeries a lot better. Easier to take, really.

"Thank you for helping me heal," she said to Eriana. "I appreciate that."

Eriana waved her thanks away without commenting. Her gaze kept flicking to the queens and then jumping away. Occasionally, she glanced at the Nags, and there her gaze rested longer.

Cary's curiosity peaked, but she needed one more question answered first. "Is Borir back in Faery, or is he still at the Bookstore?"

"Borir has been returned to his home and his duties," Tatiana said. "And he has been commended for his bravery in seeking Jaxer out."

Cary raised her brows at that. She still wasn't sure which side of all this Tatiana had been on. But it seemed the queen was going to take the winning side now that the uprising was put down. Since Tatiana had done what needed to be done to cut the Lachlinain and Cary off from the magic of most of Faery—at least long enough for Cary to starve the Lachlinain—the queen had probably been on their side all along.

Maybe.

Anyway, the politics of Faery—and its stability—were no longer her problem. Her problem now was…

"I'm starving. I need pizza." She frowned. "And coffee."

"Those two things sound really bad together," Eriana said.

Cary grinned. "You need more time in the human realm."

Eriana didn't reply, but her gaze jumped to the Nags again.

"And on that note," Danu said, her grin widening, "we shall leave you, Protector. But before I go, I would like to thank you. You have done Faery a great service. And it will not be forgotten."

"No," Tatiana said. "It will not be forgotten."

Cary got the distinct impression Tatiana's comment didn't mean the same thing as Danu's. She made a non-committal grunting noise and nodded her head. All vague ways of accepting the queens' thanks without actually saying anything aloud that might commit her to something.

Dealing with highborn Fae was almost as much of a pain in the ass as dealing with vampires.

"Healer." Danu turned to Eriana. "Will you be coming home?"

Eriana's gaze flicked to the Nags, to Jaxer, and then dropped before reaching Tatiana. Tatiana didn't look at her at all.

"I will remain here a bit longer." She nodded at Cary without looking away from Danu. "I would like to ensure she's fully recovered."

Gee, thanks? Cary was almost positive Eriana's hesitance had absolutely nothing to do with her whatsoever. But she, once again, kept that observation to herself. Wow, she was really working the restraint since she'd died. Hey! Personal growth.

Without another word, the two queens vanished. Though Danu winked at her on the way out.

Cary liked Danu. She didn't trust her any more than she trusted Tatiana. But she liked her. Maybe it was because her first look had been a deer. Cary liked deer.

"We will leave you now, too, Protector," Wisat said.

"Wait." Eriana took a step toward them before stopping herself. She straightened her spine as she faced the Nags. "I would like to discuss... To discuss working with Protectors."

A brief silence filled the room. And Jaxer frowned.

"Once the council has met," Liruk said, "and decided on our level of cooperation with the English and Irish courts—"

Eriana held up a hand. "No. I mean, I would like to work for you. Here in the Americas." She dropped her gaze. "I have no real home anymore. And... I see the use of Protectors now."

Cary pressed her lips together to keep from saying something sarcastic. This particular moment proved a lot more difficult to keep her mouth shut. So much for personal growth.

Liruk and Wisat exchanged another look. They'd been doing a lot of that since arriving.

"We can present your offer to the council," Wisat said. "New mentors are always helpful."

"There will be training," Liruk said, sternly. "And you will be expected to abide by everything we require of you."

Cary almost grinned. Now, that was the Liruk she knew and loved.

"We will let you know if your application is acceptable to the council in a few days," Wisat said in his kinder, gentler tone.

Boy, they played good cop, bad cop well. Cary was a lot more impressed by that when they weren't directing the gambit at her.

"I will await your decision," Eriana said, her chin high.

The Nags vanished in a blink, but before Cary could even begin to start asking questions, they all heard a noise from the front door. "Cary!"

"Marianne!" Cary called back. "I'm in the bedroom."

She fairly bounced up in the bed to give her friend a hug as she swept into the room. Marianne nudged Jaxer to the side with her hip—a move that made him grin—and pulled Cary into a hug that made Cary sigh.

It was good to be home.

"You're back," Cary said, pulling away to take a look at her friend. "You went back to your natural hair."

Marianne touched her short curls. "Yeah, the braids were too much upkeep."

"This looks good too," Cary said. "I've always liked your hair short and natural." Marianne also had good bone structure. "You look good."

There were faint circles under her dark eyes, but otherwise, Marianne did look good—better than she had since breaking up with Gina, actually. She was even back to wearing one of her stunning lipstick colors—a deep plumb shade this time that really worked with her dark brown skin tone.

"We have a *lot* to talk about," Marianne said.

"Are you moving?" Cary winced. She'd meant to ask that later, when they didn't have an audience.

"Girl, I took a three week vacation and you went and got yourself killed. I'm not going anywhere. Yet." She glanced around. "Hey, handsome," she said to Deacon, with a grin.

"It's good to see you, Marianne."

He smiled back and Marianne sighed. "That smile," she said.

He rose from the bed and motioned to Jaxer and Eriana. "We'll give you some time to talk. I'll order pizza." He leaned in and kissed Cary on the head. "And put on a pot of coffee."

She grinned up at him. "I love you."

"I know."

When the room had cleared, Marianne shook her head and fanned her face. "The way you two look at each other." She sighed. "Does my romantic heart good."

"So you're not moving yet?" Cary asked, just to be sure.

"Not yet. I love New York. And the visit was good for me. Seeing old friends again and all. But going in June was a good reminder of how much I hate the humidity there."

"Yeah, humidity sucks," Cary said. Maybe a little too enthusiastically.

Marianne smiled. "I'm not writing it off just yet. But I won't be going anywhere soon."

"I really really want to be supportive, no matter what your decision. And I will be, I promise. But I'm so glad you're not moving yet."

"Me too." She hugged Cary again. "Now, tell me, who was that absolutely stunning woman just in here? The looks she was giving Jaxer were interesting. Lot of lust and anger all at once."

"That's Eriana. And oh boy is there a story there. I don't know it all, but what I do know is juicy."

"Well, don't make me wait."

Deacon knocked on the door before she could start and poked his head in. "Sorry to interrupt. Lucy and Angie are pulling up outside." He hesitated a moment. "And my mother just rang. She and the rest of the family have been in town the last few days. They want to come over and check on you, too. They'll be here in a half hour." He winced. "Actually, most of the local leopards will be here soon. Sorry. I tried to make them wait, but they insisted. Seeing as how you'll be their queen one day and all."

He ducked back out quickly, before she could comment, leaving her to scowl at the door.

His entire family and most of the local leopard shifters were about to descend on her little house. She'd better give them permission to find the place.

All the leopards…

Panic raced through her blood stream.

Yeah, she was definitely not dead anymore.

Oh boy.

THANK YOU

I hope you've enjoyed reading Cary and Deacon's latest adventure! I really had fun writing this one and playing with fairytale tropes in the end. I will admit I even made myself cry while editing the final scenes, and then I felt like Joan Wilder from *Romancing the Stone* LOL. There will be more Cary Redmond adventures to come, and if you'd like a sneak peek, keep reading for an excerpt from The Trouble with Wizards and Old Enemies, the next book in the series.

For readers who enjoy Paranormal Romance or for those or you also reading the Tiger Shifter series, don't miss out on a standalone crossover novel featuring Deacon's younger brother Dylan coming in spring 2021. For updates on that and all of my books, you can join my newsletter [http://eepurl.com/OxQQL], visit my website [https://www.katsimons.com], or follow my author page at your favorite book vendors.

Thanks again for reading!

THE TROUBLE WITH WIZARDS AND OLD ENEMIES

A CARY REDMOND NOVEL BOOK 6

EXCERPT

Cary looked up at the ceiling of the dojo and groaned. She really ought to be used to this view by now. That faint water spot that Lucy had never gotten around to getting painted. The inset lights that felt entirely too bright in her face. The white textured panels that made up the ceiling.

She'd stared up at that ceiling from her back so frequently over the last ten months it was like looking out her living room window into her backyard. Very very familiar.

"You're still overthinking," Lucy said from somewhere off to Cary's right.

She rolled onto her side and looked up at her best friend and current worst enemy.

The petite redhead had her hands on her hips, her mouth turned down in a disapproving scowl. For their training sessions, Lucy wore a simple white gi, the top crossed over her stomach, with an ordinary black belt wrapped around her waist, the uniform flexible and easy for any contingency.

Lucy looked like a cute, harmless woman with her smattering of freckles across her nose, her curly red hair pulled up on top of her head in a loose bun. She even sounded a bit like a child with her high-pitched voice.

But after more than thirty years of training, Lucy was *not* harmless. She had multiple black belts in more than one martial arts discipline, and Cary had personally seen her kick the ass of people twice her size, more than once.

"I don't know how to not think," Cary grumbled as she pushed herself back up to her knees, working at catching her breath.

Lucy kept her dojo spotless, which ensured it almost always smelled like pine cleaner and faintly of incense. Right now, all Cary could smell was her own sweat—which was significantly less pleasant than Lucy's lovely frankincense sticks burning near the front desk by a miniature brass statue of the Buddha.

At least the dark blue mats beneath her hid the blood.

Not that Lucy had made her bleed during this session. In fact, Lucy was a superb teacher and had never once actually hurt Cary in their training sessions. But given how often Cary ended up flat out on her ass, or in some sort of bound position, she kept expecting blood. A nose bleed at the very least.

"You have to let the muscle memory take over if you want to handle shifters who can move significantly faster than you can," Lucy said. "You can't pause and *think* about what you're doing. You just have to do it."

"I did manage to do that once, you know," Cary said defensively.

Okay, it had been while she was protecting and she would have been safe anyway. Still, she'd reacted exactly the way Lucy had trained her and managed to disarm someone with a knife! She'd done it on her own without the magic her bosses had given her. She'd considered it a big deal.

Lucy had congratulated her. And then increased her training sessions by an extra hour a week.

"Besides," Cary said as she climbed to her feet, slowly, trying not to groan aloud, "it's not shifters out to kill me." Right now anyway. "It's a wizard. And he's vanished. Since that vampire incident, he hasn't made another attempt. Maybe the vampires killed him." The previous Master of Portland wouldn't have hesitated if he thought it expedient.

"His protégé who you thought was dead but who isn't is still out there," Lucy reminded her without missing a beat.

Cary scowled. "Yes, but apparently, I drained him of all his magic."

All this mess with the wizard out to kill her—she still didn't know his fucking name—had started with Sheldon, a teenage wizard who'd been killing shifters in an attempt to steal their bodies.

Sheldon—and her former mentor Jaxer—were responsible for Cary meeting her mate, boyfriend, future king of the leopard shifters, Deacon Jones. So she supposed she should thank Sheldon for that. She had grown to love having Deacon in her life. Even if their future was filled with potential…difficulties.

She'd thought Sheldon had died during her confrontation with him, but turned out he hadn't. And thanks to his enraged mentor, she'd discovered she absorbed magic and wasn't the ordinary human woman she'd thought she was before being tricked into becoming a magical Protector.

The last few years had been really complicated.

"Magic or no, he killed shifters and he can kill you," Lucy said. "He knows what you are. His mentor knows what you are. You can't rely on the magic your bosses gave you to protect yourself."

When Cary had become a Protector years ago, she'd been an ordinary human woman rethinking her career goals. Her bosses, the North American Fae who made Protectors—whom she'd dubbed the Nags— and her faery mentor Jaxer had sort of tricked her into the job. The Nags had imbued her with the ability to channel their magic and keep good guys safe from bad guys. And that had been her job ever since. They even paid her for it.

The problem was that when she wasn't channeling that magic, she was still an ordinary woman who could be killed as easily as any other. Unless she was protecting someone, she was vulnerable. All a bad guy had to do to kill her was want to kill her and only her and not be any danger to anyone else.

That last part could be tricky, though. Bad guys by their very definition were usually dangerous to *someone* else besides her. It was all in the intentions of the moment, which made it more difficult to kill her than some bad guys thought because…well, they were bad and intended bad things.

But if a bad guy *knew* how to kill her, knew what she was, they could manage it.

Sheldon's mentor had come close to killing her a couple of times before siccing the vampires on her. He'd figured out that trick. If he could do it, others could as well.

And now that she was in the last part of her seventh year as a Protector—a test year she had to either pass and come into her full powers (whatever that meant), or she'd die and her family would be compensated—she felt even more vulnerable to these issues. Too many people now knew what she was, despite her best efforts. She'd made a lot of enemies in her time as a Protector. Turned out, bad guys hated the person who stopped them doing whatever the hell they wanted.

Who knew?

"You have to learn the stuff I'm teaching you," Lucy continued emphatically. "And you have to have it in your bones. You have to be able to react. *Not* think."

"I swear, this is the first time in my life I've been accused of *thinking* too much."

"Ha! Want me to list the other times."

"No." Cary lowered her chin and gave Lucy a look.

Lucy returned it with a grin. "I have a surprise for you."

Cary groaned. "I'm going to hate it, aren't I?"

"Depends on if you can stop thinking or not."

Cary watched Lucy's back as she disappeared into one of the two back rooms the students used for changing. She came back out followed by a man large enough Cary had to crane her neck back to look up at him.

He was six foot nine if he was an inch, wide and thickly muscled, dark brown complexion, clean shaven, his dark curly hair cut close and tight to his head. He wore a navy blue gi with a black belt circling his waist, the two colors blending together so well it was hard to tell the belts color unless she looked close. His expression when he stepped onto the mat was serious and fierce, and Cary's pulse kicked hard.

"Cary," Lucy said, smiling up at the man who was two and half times her size, "this is Brandon Hawthorne. He's a bear shifter." Lucy met Cary's wide-eyed gaze. "And your new sparring partner."

Brandon grinned.

Oh boy.

ONE HOUR LATER. THE CEILING AGAIN.

That water spot was spreading. She'd better warn Lucy to have the landlord look into it.

"Can you breathe?" Brandon asked, his grinning face coming into Cary's view overhead.

She took a test breath just to make sure. "Give me a minute. Just a minute."

Brandon, as it turned out, was a delightful man. Happy and friendly and easy with a joke.

And he did not pull his punches even a little bit.

"I am never going to keep up with you, you know?" she said, still prone on the ground. It seemed safer down here. The minute she stood up, Brandon and Lucy came at her again.

They'd been tag teaming her for the last hour. And while Cary could *see* Lucy when she moved, she couldn't seem to avoid the hits. Brandon, she couldn't even see most of the time. She'd blink, he'd be in front of her, he'd flip her onto her back. And she'd stare up at the ceiling for a few minutes catching her breath.

"Lucy's right," he said, offering a hand to help her to her feet.

She took the offer gratefully, groaning as he easily lifted her to a standing position—without her having to put much effort into the process. Which was good because she was exhausted and only stubborn will kept her from tumbling onto her face back onto the mat once Brandon released his hold. She straightened her gi top in a bid to delay the inevitable next attack.

"I'm always right," Lucy said, her little girl's voice smug.

Cary snorted.

Brandon's smile widened. To be fair to the bear who kept knocking her on her ass, the man had a really charming smile. Broad and open. He was one of the most laidback shifters Cary had ever met. His movements, when he wasn't knocking her on her ass, were all easygoing grace, almost lazy and slow. And he laughed easily.

He was extremely careful of his strength, too, gentle with her fragile human body, despite throwing her around the place. She knew without having to be told he could break her in half with his pinky finger. Even if he wasn't a bear shifter, he'd likely be able to do that. But he didn't seem inclined to exert any of that power. Given all the shifter power plays Cary had witnessed—and been the focus of—over her years as a Protector, his seeming disinterest in showing off that strength struck her as extremely refreshing.

"Sensei's arrogance aside," Brandon said, winking at Lucy. She rolled her eyes at him. "She is right about you overthinking. You're trying to see me. But you will never see a shifter move. You have to act on instinct and stop relying on your ordinary senses."

Actually, she *could* see shifters move when she was protecting someone. But she took his point. "I don't know how to stop relying on my ordinary senses," she said with a sigh. "I don't know how to stop trying to see you move."

"Instincts take time to develop," Lucy said, rubbing Cary's sore shoulder. "That's why I asked Brandon to help us. You need to get used to acting, just moving, without worrying about everything else. And you need to learn how to do that with someone like Brandon."

"I'm here for you," he said with a friendly nod. "Don't worry, we'll get you there."

Cary finally let out a long sigh and smiled. "Okay. If you're willing to put in the work with me, I'll try my damnedest to stop thinking so much."

"Good girl," Lucy said.

Cary was about to comment on the condescension when a new voice called from the front of the dojo.

"You two done yet?" Marianne said. She stood at the edge of the mat, hands on her hips, shaking her head at them. "Angie's expecting us soon. The restaurant won't hold our reservation all night."

Marianne was a seamstress extraordinaire and a magical weaver. She created most of Cary's clothes now—all with magic pockets that kept Cary from losing her keys and wallet all the time—and she was one of Cary's best friends.

Dressed in a casual, sexy pearl gray pants suit she'd made to fit her curvy form perfectly and complement her dark skin, Marianne looked almost her old self. She'd returned to the short, tight curls she'd kept for most of the years Cary had known her, after a brief stint with long braids. Her makeup was understated except for a bright red lipstick which was a powerful pop of color. She looked both indulgent and annoyed that they weren't ready to go. And her smirk and raised brows said clearly she wasn't waiting long if they didn't move their asses. That was Marianne in every way.

Which made Cary's heart happy to see.

Marianne had gone through a very rough breakup a few months back with her longtime girlfriend, and Cary was still worried about her. Marianne had decided not to move back to New York City, which was frankly a relief, but she hadn't really returned to her pre-breakup self yet. And maybe she never would. But Cary, Lucy, and Angie had been making an effort to keep her busy and distracted so she could at least try to get back to some level of peace.

She waved at them. "Move it, ladies. We don't have all night."

Cary grinned. "You've just saved my poor, sorry self from another ass-kicking and I will be forever in your debt."

"I will take you up on that debt later when you buy the wine."

"Deal."

Marianne's gaze flicked to Brandon and she raised her brows again at Lucy, the question clear.

"Sorry," Lucy said. "Brandon Hawthorne, this is Marianne Johnson. Marianne, Brandon. He's helping me train Cary now."

"Nice to meet you," Marianne said. "Try not to hurt our girl too much."

"It's an absolute pleasure to meet you too, Marianne Johnson," he said.

Cary gave him a look. His voice had dropped at least half an octave, to a pretty sexy base rumble. And he was staring at Marianne with an intensity that could have been intimidating if he weren't offsetting the look with his most charming smile.

Marianne blinked and frowned a little at the bear shifter. But she didn't dismiss him or scowl at his obvious attention.

Which was…good?

Well. Now they had some serious things to discuss over dinner.

"Same time tomorrow?" Lucy asked Brandon, her gaze moving between him and Marianne, too.

"Absolutely." He gave them each a nod of goodbye, his last for Marianne. "See you again soon."

He ambled back to the dressing room, and all three of them watched him go.

"Hm," Lucy said.

"Hm indeed," Cary said.

Marianne did scowl at them and opened her mouth to retort, but Cary shook her head, cutting her gaze to the locker room. She mouthed, "shifter hearing," and tapped her ears.

Marianne nodded in understanding but her scowl didn't drop.

Yeah, they definitely had a conversation ahead of them. Dinner at this new restaurant suddenly seemed the least interesting part of the night.

At least, it did until the Nags materialized at the back of the dojo to give Cary a new job.

~

Don't miss book 6 in the Cary Redmond series
The Trouble with Wizards and Old Enemies
Coming Soon!

BOOKS BY KAT SIMONS

THE CARY REDMOND SERIES

1 – The Trouble Black Cats and Demons

2 – The Trouble with Ghouls and Serial Killers

3 – The Trouble with Leopard Queens and Shifter Wars

4 – The Trouble with Baby Gods and Vampires

5 – The Trouble with Magic and Faery Curses

6 – The Trouble with Wizards and Old Enemies

COMING SOON

CARY REDMOND SHORT STORIES

When Cary Met Jaxer

When Cary Met Pickles

When Cary Met Marianne

When Cary Met Lucy

When Cary Met Angie

Cary and Deacon (Try to) Go on a Date

Date Night Take Two

Third Date's the Charm

Cary vs the Goblin King

Dinner with the Jones

When Cary Met the Good Guys (Collection 1)

Romancing the Leopard: A Tiger Shifters-Cary Redmond Crossover Novel

COMING SOON

ABOUT THE AUTHOR

Kat Simons earned her Ph.D. in animal behavior, working with animals as diverse as dolphins and deer. She brought her experience and knowledge of biology to her paranormal romance and urban fantasy fiction, where she delights in taking nature and turning it on its ear. Her Tiger Shifters series combines romance and the otherworldly with heart-pounding action adventure. Her latest urban fantasy romance series follows the adventures of Protector Cary Redmond as she tries to manage her personal life while saving the world. A lot.

For something a little different, Kat also publishes fantasy romance, science fiction romance, and the occasional hockey romance under the name Isabo Kelly (http://www.isabokelly.com).

After traveling the world, Kat now lives in New York City with her family. She is a stay-at-home mom and a full time writer.

For more on Kat and her future books:
Website: https://www.katsimons.com
Newsletter: http://eepurl.com/OxQQL